PRAISE FOR MARCIA CLARK

Moral Defense

"*Moral Defense* by former Los Angeles prosecutor Marcia Clark has it all: a hard-charging lawyer heroine, tough-as-nails cops, realistic, yet somehow lovable 'bad guys,' as well as fly-by-the-seat-of-your-pants pacing and page-turning twists."

—Associated Press

"In Clark's outstanding sequel to *Blood Defense* . . . [She] deepens her already fascinating lead, while adeptly juggling several subplots."

—*Publishers Weekly*, Starred Review

"This second in the Brinkman series (after *Blood Defense*, 2016) is a nonstop ride marked by legal and moral gray areas, with a cliff-hanger epilogue. Another Clark legal thriller that's hard to put down."

—*Booklist*

"A murdered family leaves only one survivor in this second roller-coaster case for Los Angeles attorney Samantha Brinkman . . . [The case] builds to a rare intensity."

—*Kirkus Reviews*

Blood Defense

"Former LA prosecutor Clark kicks off a promising new series with this top-notch whodunit . . . Clark sprinkles jaw-dropping surprises throughout and impressively pulls off a shocker that lesser writers can only envy."

—*Publishers Weekly*, Starred Review

"On the heels of FX's blockbuster television series, *American Crime Story: The People v. O. J. Simpson* . . . Simpson prosecutor-turned-author Clark . . . launches a new legal thriller series. Unlike in her well-received Rachel Knight books, which featured an LA prosecutor, Clark's latest calls on her earlier career as a criminal defense attorney to fashion protagonist Samantha Brinkman. VERDICT: Clark's deft handling of her characters through a multilevel maze of conflicts delivers an exhilarating read."

—*Library Journal*

"Clark, who served as a prosecutor for the trial of O. J. Simpson, clearly knows this world well. She has the most fun when she's showing readers the world of celebrity trials, from the media circus, the courthouse crowds, the crazies, and the police to the inner workings of the trial itself. You'll push yourself to finish the final pages just to keep pace with the defense team's discoveries."

—Associated Press

"Once again, Marcia Clark has reinvented herself—and the results are stellar. Her knowledge of the criminal justice system is unrivaled, as is her understanding of how the media influences public opinion of high profile trials—and the actions of those involved. But the real magic of Clark's writing is her dynamic, richly textured characters and the visceral, often gritty settings they frequent."

—*Hartford Examiner*

SNAP
JUDGMENT

SNAP
JUDGMENT

A Samantha Brinkman Legal Thriller

MARCIA CLARK

THOMAS & MERCER

Published by Thomas & Mercer, Seattle

www.apub.com

Amazon, the Amazon logo, and Thomas & Mercer are trademarks of Amazon.com, Inc., or its affiliates.

ISBN-13: 9781542045995 (hardcover)
ISBN-10: 1542045991 (hardcover)
ISBN-13: 9781542045551 (paperback)
ISBN-10: 154204555X (paperback)

Cover design by David Drummond

Printed in the United States of America

First edition

SNAP
JUDGMENT

PROLOGUE

November 2nd

Dear Me,

I'm feeling kind of proud of myself.

I did it. I finally told him.

Okay, I did it on voice mail, kind of a weenie move, I know. But there was no way I could've told him in person. He totally loses it when he gets mad. Just leaving him the message made my hands so sweaty I almost dropped the phone. They're still shaking now. It's actually hard to write. I need to take a few minutes.

I'm back. And now I'm kind of mad at myself. What was I so proud of? All I did was tell him we should take a breather for a month or so. I should've just broken it off for good. That's what everyone said I should do. But I thought I should at least give him a chance to change. Nomie said I'd given him too many chances already—her nice way of saying I was just being a coward.

And she was right. Deep down inside, I knew that. I just didn't want to admit it. God, I'm such a loser.

I've been trying to figure out how I wound up in this fucked-up situation. But I do know how it started. It all seemed so romantic at first. The fact that Roan wanted me to call him every night before I went to bed—even though we saw each other every single day—seemed so . . . sweet. Sure, he went ballistic if I forgot to call, but I just thought it showed how much he loved me.

The problem was, he kept wanting more and more. It got to the point where I felt like a prisoner, like I couldn't breathe. Nomie had been saying all along that this wasn't love, that this was some kind of sick obsession. So did Gayle. And Diana and Davey and Phil. But I didn't want to believe them. I kept thinking that if I did everything right, he'd finally be happy—we'd be happy.

But that never happened. If I called three times a day, he wanted four. If I texted every three hours, he wanted every hour. And if I was late or I forgot, he'd totally lose it. He'd scream at me, call me names, and tell me I was a thoughtless, heartless bitch. One day last week, I was in the library studying for midterms, and I missed three of my "appointments" to call him. That night, he came to my apartment, but I wouldn't let him in. I was tired, and I just couldn't deal with his craziness. So he stood out there and yelled at me, then kicked the door so hard he put a hole in it. He probably would've done even more damage if the guys in the apartment across the hall hadn't threatened to call the cops.

It blows my mind that I put up with so much of his insane shit. But I guess I just got so used to it that the crazy seemed normal. It wasn't until just this morning—when I finally read what I'd been writing in this journal for the past month—that I realized how bad, how horrible, it'd gotten. I wish I'd done that sooner! It made everything so clear, the downward spiral, the way he got more and more demanding, the way I kept fighting a losing battle to please him.

And you know what's the worst part? I'd probably still be hooked into that madness if my TA hadn't told me yesterday that I was about to fail calculus. I've never failed anything! And I CANNOT FAIL NOW! If I fail, my parents will make me move back home. That CANNOT HAPPEN.

I finally love my life. No more rules, no more curfews, no more endless lectures about the importance of "success." I love my parents, but I never had a life. It was always run, run, run—from the time I was four—to ballet to gymnastics to drama club to the school newspaper. The one semester I didn't make honor roll, I got grounded for a month. I was so jealous of the kids when they talked about the parties they'd gone to, the shopping trips—even the weekends they spent "just kicking it."

But the day I moved into this apartment—just a couple of blocks from campus!—I thought, Now it's my turn. It was a little scary at first. I'd never been alone before. It was so . . . quiet. But after a few days, I started to like it. I could watch dumb TV shows, wear ratty T-shirts, eat Doritos. It was like every day was a holiday. I was making my own choices, my own decisions . . . living my own life. For the very first time. I felt so light, like a huge weight had been lifted off my chest. I was free; I was . . . happy.

Until I let myself get dragged into Roan's sicko world.

So I am not about to let anything—not Roan or anyone else—make me screw up and have to move back home. If he goes nuts, I'll just have to break up with him for good.

I can't believe it, but the thought of breaking up with him makes me kind of sad. I guess I'm still a little bit hopeful that this wake-up call will get his attention, make him realize he has to change. If he did, we'd be able to get back together. I've got to admit, I'd love that. To go back to the way it was in the very beginning. We had such good times!

November 3rd

How could he do this to me?! How did I not realize what a total monster he was?

I'm so PISSED and so . . . embarrassed, mortified, and . . . I don't even have the words. I can barely breathe. This morning, I was feeling so good, so in control of my life! But when I checked my e-mails, I found seventy-eight—all from strange addresses. I thought it had to be some kind of spam attack. I wasn't sure what to do. I was afraid to open one; I thought it might be some kind of malware attack. But finally, I had to see what was going on, so I clicked on the first one.

Haay, gurl. Some hot photos you took. I hope you're ready for my big, hard dick, cuz I'm soooo ready for you baby. I can tell you're my kind of girl. I like it rough too. Call me. 602-555-0282.

Who was that guy? And why was he writing to me? What the hell was going on?

My heart was pounding so hard I felt like it would break a rib, but I couldn't help myself. I opened the next one.

Foxy Ali. I luv sluts like u. I
can give you what you need. I can
make you scream.

I slammed my laptop closed. I thought I was going to be sick. I dumped the rest of my coffee in the sink and threw my toast in the trash. Were all the rest of the e-mails like this? I didn't want to know. But I had to know. I went through four more e-mails, then the next ten. The same, they were all the same.

What was going on? Why was this happening to me? The room started to spin. I forced a deep breath and tried to think. One word flashed in my mind. Photos. I'd seen it in almost all of the e-mails. And that's when I knew.

I Googled my name. And there they were. The selfies I'd taken for Roan. Because he'd needed to "be with me 24-7." My body, all of me, naked, for the whole world to see. I ached all over as I stared at the photos.

And they were posted on a sleazy porn website called XXXtraSpecial. But that wasn't all. He'd also posted my "invitation": **Cum see me, make my rape fantasies cum true.** And the address to my apartment!

My home!

I ran to the bathroom and threw up until I couldn't breathe. I sank to the floor and sobbed so hard I started to choke. I'd known he'd be mad—I even suspected there might be some kind of payback. But this? I never thought he could do me like this. This was . . . so hideous, so . . . cruel. I couldn't stop thinking, How could he?

And then I thought, what if my friends see it? Or, oh God!—what if somebody showed my parents? I'd just die! Plus, they'd drag me back home! My life would be over!

I closed my eyes, but that didn't block out the memory of my selfies and the disgusting rape "invitation" on that awful website. How many men—STRANGE MEN—had seen my pictures? A horrible image just flashed through my mind of some gross rando guy with a hairy back jerking off to my photos.

The thought made me heave again. I'm so scared. What if one of those perverts actually comes to my apartment? What do I do? I can't call the cops. That'll only make it even more public!

I feel so . . . violated. And . . . dirty. Like an old, over-used dishrag.

All I want to do is go back to bed and hide under the covers. But I have a quiz in calculus, and I can't afford to blow it. Focus, I need to focus. Just get through the exam. Think about what to do later.

I don't know how I made it through that exam. I could barely see; my eyes kept filling up with tears.

I'm trying to think what I should do. I can't tell my parents. They'll just make me move back home. And they'll be worse than ever. They'll probably never let me move back out. I can't bear to even think of that.

I'm going to handle this. I have to handle this! I know what I'll do; I'll install more locks, and I'll use that stick to keep anyone from sliding open my bathroom window, like Nomie told me, and I'll make sure I use that damn peephole before I open the door. There're plenty of things I can do to keep safe.

Nobody who knows me is ever going to see those photos. I'll be okay.

But Roan's got to take them down off that friggin' website. NOW.

ONE

I'd had my usual lousy night's sleep. Woke up at four a.m. and fought to doze off for about an hour before I gave up and shuffled into the shower.

I was groggy, but by the time I'd chugged my third supersize mug of coffee, my head had started to clear, and the world had come into focus—a good news / bad news joke if ever there was one. I opened my laptop and checked the weekly roundup of the latest state and Supreme Court criminal cases, then headed for my office, the criminal defense firm Brinkman & Associates. Right now the only "associates" are Michy—AKA Michelle Fusco, my paralegal / office manager / bookkeeper and best friend since childhood—and my investigator, Alex Medrano, a former client who'd been busted for hacking—a skill that turned out to be just one of the many things that made him the best investigator I'd ever had.

But someday, I'm going to have legions of hungry young lawyers who'll work eighty hours a week, get paid for twenty, but be incredibly grateful for the experience of working for the leading criminal defense lawyer in the country, Samantha Brinkman, i.e., me. That's what I tell myself, anyway.

It wasn't even eight a.m. by the time I got in, but Michy was already at her desk and staring at her computer. I didn't like the expression on her face. "What's wrong?"

She looked up at me. "Have you seen the story about Alicia Hutchins?"

Hutchins. It took me a second. "Graham Hutchins's kid?" Michy nodded. I moved around to look at Michy's computer. "What happened to her?"

Michy clicked on the image of a news anchor and hit the play arrow.

"*In local news, Alicia Hutchins, daughter of famed attorney Graham Hutchins, was found dead in the bathtub of her off-campus apartment. Police have confirmed that her throat was slashed and that the case is being handled as a homicide. Alicia Hutchins was a freshman at the University of Southern California and . . .*"

I reached over Michy's shoulder and hit stop. Murder is a daily fact of life for a criminal defense lawyer. But it was a whole different thing when you knew the victim. I didn't know Alicia, per se, but I did know her father, Graham. And I knew that he'd provided her with a life that was well heeled, well educated, but, above all, sheltered. A gruesome murder like this made about as much sense as a church service for atheists. "I wonder what the cops have."

Michy leaned back and raised an eyebrow. Her tone was sarcastic. "Gee, if only there was a way you could find out."

I shook my head. "I'm not calling him."

"Why not? He always tells you stuff. Besides, he is your da—"

I cut her off. "I told you to never say that word." I refuse to call him Dad. For me, he is—and always will be—Dale Pearson. I met him only a few years ago, when he hired me to defend him in a double homicide. I hadn't known he was my father when I took the case. Imagine my surprise.

It was no surprise, however, that Celeste, my "mother," had lied to me about him. She'd claimed my father was just a one-night stand, when actually, she and Dale had been dating for months. What really happened was she'd found out she was pregnant around the same time she'd found out he had no money—so she dumped him and never told him about me. That's what Celeste does—lies whenever it suits her. It's a life strategy that comes as naturally to her as breathing.

I managed to get the case against Dale dismissed—not just on a technicality but because someone else committed the murders—and he'd recently been promoted to the elite Robbery Homicide Division. RHD picks up all the high-profile cases, and Alicia's murder certainly qualified as that. So it was a fair bet the case would wind up there. At the very least, it was likely that the captain of RHD was getting briefed on it. Which meant Dale probably had the inside skinny.

I dropped my briefcase just inside my office and took off my coat. "I guess it could've just been a random home invasion thing, maybe Alicia forgot to lock the door." For all that USC is a richy-rich-kid school, the campus is in a shitty 'hood where anything can happen. I thought about how her father must be feeling. "Graham must be out of his mind."

Graham Hutchins, a hotshot civil litigator from South Carolina who'd wisely hung on to his southern accent for maximum benefit with juries, was one of my regular sparring partners on the cable show *Crime Time*. Though we weren't what you'd call close, during our time spent together in the green room, I'd heard a lot about his only child, Alicia, who was the light of his life.

Michy had restarted the news footage on her computer, and she sighed as a photo of Alicia in her high school graduation cap and robe came on the screen. She was a beautiful girl by any standard. Long blonde hair that hung straight down her back, wide-set green eyes, and lips that seemed to just naturally curve upward in a semismile. I remembered Graham saying he'd wanted to walk the halls of her high school with a shotgun just to let the boys know "what fate awaited them if they touched a hair on her head."

From what I'd heard about her schedule, I'd wondered *when* he thought any boy would have the chance to get to her. Gymnastics, drama, debate club, the school newspaper—you name it, Alicia not only did it, she stuck the landing. She graduated high school with honors and had her pick of colleges.

I do think kids should have goals and reach for the stars and all that. But they should also get to enjoy some downtime, too—play a few video games, binge something on Netflix once in a while. To me, Alicia's schedule was way over the top. And I was fairly sure the pressure to achieve came from her dad. Graham was one hard-driving, ambitious guy.

And now she was dead. Murdered. Before she ever got the chance to live.

My childhood had been no bed of roses. I'd spent my final year in junior high getting raped every night by Celeste's—AKA Mommy Dearest's—billionaire boyfriend, Sebastian Cromer. And it'd gone on for a full year because she'd refused to believe that her Daddy Warbucks was a raging pedophile. But at least I was still breathing.

Michy pushed back from the computer. "You want me to send Graham some flowers?"

I'd been about to head into my office. Now I stopped. "Can we afford to?"

She sighed. "Of course not. But what's another hundred bucks when we're—as usual—about two thousand bucks in the red?"

A fair point. "Yeah, good idea. Send him one of those orchid pots, something that's actually alive, okay?" I never understand why people send cut flowers to a house in mourning. It seems cruel. Why send something that's basically already dying?

I went to my desk and got to work on my next trial. It was about as dumb as it gets. My guy and his genius buddy had run out of beer, so they decided to go get some more. Without paying. The clerk caught them and called the cops. The other guy fled, but my guy decided to hang around and debate whether it was fair for the clerk to call him a "pussy." They got into a tussle over the issue and were still at it when the cops arrived. Which was lucky for my guy, because he was definitely on the losing end of the minifight. Ordinarily, this was the kind of case I could expect to settle for straight probation. Except the DA had charged my client with robbery for this little escapade, and he had a rap sheet longer than the line for the bathroom at a Bruce Springsteen concert. He was facing twenty-five to life.

An hour later, Alex came in and stopped at my office door. It was still only eight thirty, but for him, that was late. And he was yawning. Very uncharacteristic. "What did you get up to last night?" I took in his clothes—which were the same ones he'd been wearing yesterday. "Or should I say—*down* to last night?"

Alex folded his arms. "For your information, I was up late studying for my license."

He was the best investigator I'd ever had, but he still hadn't gotten his PI license. It wasn't his fault; he was a hard worker—obsessively so—but I kept him plenty busy, too busy to focus on prepping for the PI test. So it was a credible story. But my bullshit-o-meter said it wasn't true. Something about him—and I couldn't say what that was; it was just a gut feeling—told me that this time it was about fun. And that was a credible explanation, too.

Alex is one gorgeous specimen. Dark eyes, with the long, curly lashes we women would kill for but never seem to get, and a mane of thick, shiny black hair. And he was effortlessly charming. All this came in handy when we had to interview female witnesses—who routinely let him know they wouldn't mind an after-hours interview and never had a clue that he was gay.

I stared him down. "No, you weren't."

Alex caved. "No, I wasn't." He paused. "I met someone."

Alex talked about his dates every once in a while, but only when the story ended in a punch line. So the fact that he'd made no effort to joke about this one told me it was different. "No shit?"

He nodded. "No shit. We've only been seeing each other for a couple of weeks, but it feels pretty real."

I waved him over. "Get in here and spill. I want to hear everything. Where does he live? What does he do? How did you meet him?"

Alex came in and sank onto my couch. "His name is Paul Angelo, and he lives in West Hollywood, about five miles from here. I met him in the cold-and-flu aisle of the CVS pharmacy on Santa Monica Boulevard—"

"Doesn't get more romantic than that." I rolled my eyes, then got worried. "You never said you were sick."

An annoyed expression crossed his face. "I wasn't. Michy put a serious dent in my stash of Benadryl with her hay fever spell, so I had to replenish."

Alex is one of those people who needs to be constantly prepared—which is cool. But he takes it to a level that, at best, qualifies as obsessive. He keeps a huge, multitiered and partitioned plastic box in the office that's filled with every cold/flu/allergy remedy I've ever heard of, in addition to Band-Aids, Ace bandages, BENGAY, Tiger Balm, a splint, an EpiPen—you get the picture. He even has an oxygen tank and a defibrillator. "So Paul was sick?"

Alex had a little smile. "No. He was running low on *his* stash of Tamiflu."

My mouth dropped open. "Oh my God. There are two of you nutcases? *And* you found each other? This must be the End of Days."

Alex gave me a mock glare. "Guess I'd better get back to work."

I pulled back. "Pardon me. I meant two of you incredibly helpful, well-prepared gems. So what does he do?"

He flicked a speck off his trousered knee. "He's a pilot for Delta Airlines."

Nice. "So you get to fly free?"

Alex gave me a pointed look. "How would I know? I never have a day off."

I shook my head in sympathy. "Sorry your boss is such an asshole."

He was not amused. "Anyway, we had coffee, and we just talked and talked. It felt like we'd known each other forever. We wound up having dinner the next night, and the night after that, and . . . now we're talking about moving in."

So soon? What, did they turn into lesbians? That kind of fast leap into marriage—and I don't care what they call it; that's what moving in together really is—always worries me. It almost never ends well. Michy says I'm ridiculously pessimistic about relationships. I say I'm just a realist. But Alex looked so happy I didn't want to be a buzzkill. He'd just have to find out the hard way, like the rest of us. "Got any pictures?"

Alex smirked. "We're gay. We *live* on cameras. Of *course* I've got photos."

But as Alex reached for his cell phone, Michy appeared in my doorway, her expression dark. "So you heard about them?"

I was confused. "Heard about . . . ?"

She looked from me to Alex. "Alicia's photos. I thought that's what you were talking about. It just came on the news. They found her nude selfies on a porn website. They went up a couple of days before her murder. And I just heard they got posted to her Facebook page, too."

Alex picked up on Michelle's use of her first name. "You know this girl?"

"Sort of." I brought Alex up to speed on my relationship with her father.

Alex pulled up her photo on his cell. "Pretty girl. There any chance she posted them herself?"

Michelle shook her head. "No way. There was a message under her photos on the porn website inviting guys to come over and play out her rape fantasies—*with* her address and Facebook page link."

I agreed. "I'm with Michy. No way she'd write something like that. This is classic pissed-off ex-boyfriend shit. I'll bet the cops already have him in custody."

"You going to try and get the case?" Alex asked.

Represent that asshole? "Not if we were starving and living in Tent City."

TWO

To no one's surprise, an hour later, it was reported that Roan Sutton, Alicia's boyfriend, had been brought in for questioning as a "person of interest." According to Alicia's friends, she'd broken up with Roan Sutton the day before the nude selfies—and that disgusting, not to mention, life-threatening "invitation"—got posted to the porn website.

I'd gone back to work on my beer burglar's sentencing memo when Michy and Alex came into my office to give me the news that Roan had been taken in. And, to be perfectly honest, to procrastinate. We weren't working on any particularly fascinating cases at the moment.

Michy took a swig from her bottle of water and deadpanned, "Shocking development. Boyfriend gets dumped, boyfriend takes revenge."

Alex's expression radiated disgust. "What a despicable loser."

It really was sickening. I'd heard way too many stories about this kind of thing, and it seemed to be happening more and more frequently. "Will they be able to prove he posted the photos, Alex?"

To say that Alex knew his way around a computer was like saying Stephen Hawking knew a little something about physics. Alex could hack his way into the Pentagon if he wanted to. The only reason the cops had caught him when he'd "transferred" ownership of those two BMW 750Lis to himself was sheer dumb luck. And they knew it. That's why I'd been able to get him a deal for straight probation: the dealership wanted him to show them how he'd done it.

Alex sighed. "I doubt it. If he's even halfway hip, he'd know enough to use a proxy server. In which case, I'd say no, they'll never be able to prove he posted them."

Damn. "What about the Facebook posting? Same thing?"

Alex nodded. "Afraid so."

Bummer. "Well, at least they'll be able to tag him for her murder." It was the most typical, obvious of motives. But clichés are clichés because they're true.

Michy leaned back in her chair. "Not necessarily. It could've been one of the douchebags who answered her so-called rape fantasy 'ad.'"

I made a face. "Rape fantasy. Talk about an oxymoron. I guess that's possible. But for some reason, it feels more personal than that."

"Yeah." Alex grimaced. "Her throat was cut. That seems too grue-some for it to be a stranger. And I heard they found the knife in the tub, under her body."

Which meant it'd been in water for a while by the time they collected it. The odds of finding prints or DNA were infinitesimal. "Did they say where it came from?"

Alex glanced back down at his phone and shook his head. "Says they have no information on whether the knife came from her place or the killer brought it with him."

"Or *her*." Michy screwed the cap on her now-empty water bottle. "If it wasn't Roan, it could've been a girl. Alicia was pretty small, from what I saw. And it happened when she was in the bathtub, probably dozing." Michelle threw the empty bottle into the recycling can. "Oh, and by the way, based on those porn website photos? She had no cellulite whatsoever."

Smart, beautiful, *and* a perfect body? "That alone is reason enough to kill her."

Michy gave me a grim smile. "The list of suspects just quadrupled."

A sick sense of humor is a prerequisite in this business. But she was right: the killer could've been a girl. "I'm surprised they didn't take the photos down from that website already."

"It's not that easy to find these scumbag website owners." Alex stretched and put the back of his hand to his mouth to cover a deep yawn. "Of course, if they'd just ask for my help, I could have him by the balls within the hour."

That might not be a bad idea—offering up Alex's services to the cops. It'd be a favor to Graham for sure, and my relationship with the Five-O could always use a little—or actually, a lot of—burnishing. I've never been a fan of the boys in blue, and the feeling is more than mutual. "Since we're obviously not going to get back to work anytime soon, I may as well call and see if I can squeeze some info out of Dale."

But Dale was in no mood to be squeezed. "It's not my case, and you know I can't tell you anything. Besides, you don't need me to tell you who looks good for this one."

Roan, of course. "Just tell me if the kid has an alibi. And whether you've found anything on the murder weapon."

He huffed. "'Just'? You're asking me to tell you what came out of his interview *and* the crime-scene search."

"No, I'm not. I only asked two short questions, and they can be answered with just two short words. Come on, you know I won't tell."

Dale sighed. "The answer is no and no." He ended the call.

I spoke into the phone. "Great, thanks. Appreciate it. Let's do dinner."

Michy smirked. "Hung up on you again, didn't he?"

Can she *never* miss a thing? "A little." I reported what he'd told me. "He seems pretty sure Roan Sutton's the killer. Then again, cops do rush to judgment."

Alex's lips twitched. "You mean, kind of like *you* just did?"

I folded my arms. "My conclusion was based on solid deductive reasoning—with which both of you happen to agree." I stared them down.

Michy shrugged, as always, impervious to my glare. "Like I said, not necessarily."

Alex set his jaw. "Well, even if he didn't kill her, I hope the little fucker gets nailed for posting those photos. My cousin got revenge porned when she dumped her fiancé. She went anorexic for a year, lost chunks of hair, her skin turned gray. It was horrible."

I stared at Alex. He wasn't the type to turn the other cheek. "And he's not in the hospital?" Alex knew how to fight, and this guy sounded like a perfect candidate for a beat down.

He waved his hand with a look of disgust. "He ran to Mexico."

We all went back to work, but I couldn't stop thinking about what Alex said and what kind of hell Alicia had gone through. I tried to imagine how I'd feel. To know that thousands, maybe millions of strange men were looking at nude photos of me—photos I'd only ever meant my boyfriend to see. I pulled up the website, XXXtraSpecial. Most of the women in the photos looked like pros: heavy makeup, tongue touching open lips painted a deep red, and poses that'd probably be a revelation to some gynecologists. And the quality of those photos was fairly polished.

Alicia's were nothing like that. They were amateurish selfies, and relatively tame. Alicia wore very little makeup, and her smile, meant to be seductive and naughty, looked nervous—and a little bit scared. The poses were as vanilla as they get: one shot was taken from the side as she stood at her desk, bent at the waist; there were a few boob shots and one rather blurry crotch shot—with legs closed. The photos all seemed so innocent, so vulnerable, it was painful to look at them. And the disgusting "invitation" to join in her "rape fantasy" infuriated me.

It deliberately, viciously set her up to be attacked by . . . God knows what kind of filthy pig.

And now she was dead. I didn't care whether Roan was her killer. Just for that alone I hoped they nailed him to the wall. I went to Alex's office. Smaller than mine, but with a window that faced the street, it was a step up from the coffin-size, windowless copy room he'd occupied before we'd moved into our relatively nicer digs here in West Hollywood.

And he'd done a nice job of decorating it. Not. Fighting the gay stereotype, Alex did not do a damn thing with his space. The walls were bare; he didn't even have a small plant. The only item on his desk besides his laptop was a large framed photo of his family. I spoke to him from the doorway. "I know you've got work to do, but would you mind—"

"Already on it." Alex glanced up at me and raised an eyebrow. "You wanted me to find the website owner and call the cops, right?"

I hate when he does that. Reads my mind. "Uh, yeah. But if you find him, let me figure out which cop to give it to." It'd be nice to kill two birds with one stone and give the gift to a cop who was working on the case—and hopefully one I'd pissed off in the past. The group I'd pissed off was fairly large, so the odds that one of them was involved in the case were pretty good.

As I turned to go back to my office, Alex said, "Can they lock this guy up?"

"The website owner?" Alex nodded. "Depends on whether they can prove he had reason to know the photos were posted without Alicia's consent. But Roan should definitely get charged for it. Putting up that bullshit rape fantasy 'ad' shows it was all about revenge."

"How much time will he get? Assuming he doesn't get tagged for murder."

I sighed. "Not much. Six months and a fine."

Alex shook his head. "That's pathetic."

"It really is. If it were up to me, the asshole would get locked up for a few years. Get a chance to explore rape fantasies in prison."

Alex snorted. "Hell, I'd be in favor of waterboarding."

I wholeheartedly agreed.

Just three days later, our wishes came true—and then some. I came in to work Monday morning and found Michy watching the television in my office.

The crawl at the bottom of the screen said, BREAKING NEWS. A reporter who was standing in front of a small house that had a USC banner in the front window said, "Just yesterday, Roan Sutton gave his third interview to the police, and they say there was no indication that his mental or emotional state was deteriorating. But they have no suspects at this time, and it appears—at least at this point—that Roan Sutton has indeed taken his own life."

THREE

Alex came in a few minutes later and said he'd heard about Roan Sutton's death on his way in. "You guys know why they're thinking it might be a suicide?"

I nodded. "Stepped up on a chair and hung himself." Roan lived in one of the old houses that'd been converted for student living. His room had access to the attic—and its exposed beams, the perfect spot for a hanging.

Alex frowned. "And the cops didn't see any signs that he was—"

I cut him off. "Which means nothing to me. They weren't worried about Roan Sutton's emotional landscape. They were trying to solve a murder." I picked up the remote and turned off the television.

Michelle shrugged. "For a change, I don't blame them."

Neither did I. At least not until the next bombshell landed—which happened the very next day. And this time, it landed right in my office.

I'd just finished my fifth cup of coffee of the morning and chewed through about half my onion bagel when Michelle buzzed me. "You available for a consult at eleven? You don't have court."

I checked the calendar on my phone to see if I'd set up any lunch dates. "I'm clear. What's up?" I pulled off another piece of my bagel and popped it into my mouth.

"Graham Hutchins wants a meeting."

I coughed as I nearly choked around the lump of bagel in my throat. "Hello? A little warning would've been nice. Did he say why?"

Michelle chuckled. "I couldn't resist. But no, he didn't. I'd guess he just wants to talk to you about how they'll handle the investigation into Alicia's murder now that Roan's dead. But it's good for you to mingle with people who actually have money. Get to know what that feels like."

It was true. I didn't do much of that—or, to be perfectly honest, any of that. Although I'd left the public defender's office for private practice five years ago, the bulk of my work still came from court-appointed cases. The money was okay, but it'd never do much more than keep the lights on. The big money comes from well-heeled clients, and in the world of criminal law, you get those only by handling high-profile cases. I'd handled a few in the past—Dale's case being one of them—and I'd gained a few paying customers, but I still wasn't doing much more than keeping our noses above water. So it'd be nice if a millionaire corporate lawyer like Graham wanted to hire me—even if it was only for a basic consultation. If all went well, I'd not only make some money, he'd pass my name around to his rich friends.

And even if he didn't want to hire me, even if he just wanted to ask me a few questions, that was fine. He'd been through hell. I'd be glad to help him out, gratis. I swallowed hard to force the rest of the bagel down my throat. "Sure, set it up."

I was curious as all get-out, but I hate wasting time on "What if?" and "I wonder." I spent the remaining time wrapping up a sentencing memo and reviewing a murder case I hoped to plead out—it was a gang-on-gang shooting, the kind of case prosecutors call "NHI." No Human Involved. I thought I had a better than even chance of getting a manslaughter for my guy, because the victim had a longer rap sheet than my client. That's the kind of thing that can really soften up a jury. So my pitch to the DA was going to be that the jury would probably give him manslaughter anyway—why let a trial cut into his drinking time?

I heard Michelle buzz Graham in at eleven o'clock on the dot. I went out to greet him. "Graham, I'm so sorry for your loss. Come on in."

As we headed to my office, he said, "Thanks for squeezing me in on such short notice. I know how busy you are." His smile was forced, and the misery in his eyes was heartrending.

Like so many big-time litigators, Graham had a look that was less classically handsome than it was warm and relatable. Six feet, medium build, his dirty-blond hair short on the sides and in back but dipped low across his forehead, which, combined with the freckles and warm brown eyes, gave him a guileless, country-boy charm. Top it all off with a gentle southern accent, and you have the very picture of juror appeal: nonthreatening to both male and female, the kind of guy you'd want to have a drink with, who'd be there to talk, listen, or, if need be, bail you out—and not judge.

We went into my office, and I closed the door. "Coffee? Water?" I gestured to the coffeemaker and small refrigerator on a table against the wall.

Graham sat down in front of my desk and shook his head. He dropped even the pretense of a smile. His features were slack, shell-shocked.

I decided it might be best for me to take the lead. "I can't begin to imagine what you must be going through. How can I help?"

"I think . . ." He stopped and took a long breath. "I think the police are considering the possibility that I killed Roan."

That made no sense. "But I thought they said it was a suicide."

He stared off, his voice weak. "They said the autopsy hasn't been done yet, so they have to consider all possibilities." He looked back at me. "And they said that means I have to be prepared for all possibilities."

I couldn't blame the cops. He had the best motive imaginable. "Did they ask where you were the night Roan died?" He nodded again. "Where were you?"

His expression turned bleak. "At home with Sandy." I sighed, and he spread his hands. "I know. How convenient—my wife is my alibi. But it's the truth."

It was an entirely plausible alibi—not airtight by any means, but the kind most people, *innocent* people, often have. I frowned. "Does someone say otherwise?"

He nodded. "According to the police, a neighbor saw a man who looked a lot like me knocking on Roan's door that evening."

Graham's perfectly normal alibi suddenly seemed a lot less convincing. "But that couldn't have been you." I leaned back and studied his reaction. It was more to gauge *how* he'd lie rather than *if* he'd lie. I pretty much assume all my clients are guilty. Ninety-nine percent of the time, I'm right. Not that it matters. I'm here to fight for them regardless. But it's good not to have any illusions. I can't do a good job if I go around kidding myself about who I'm representing.

Graham rubbed his cheeks, then dropped his hands into his lap, his expression frazzled. "I . . . Well, it could have been me. I did go to Roan's house that night. I just wanted to get him to take down those goddamn photos." He sighed.

Damn. Just as I'd feared. "What happened?"

Graham stared out the window behind me. "Nothing. I knocked on his door, but he never answered."

"You had no contact with him, then?" Graham shook his head. "And you never got inside his house?"

His gaze stayed fixed on the scene outside my window—which was basically the wall of the building next to us. "No."

I wasn't sure whether I believed him. But if ever a guy needed killing, it was Roan. I'd be happy to do whatever I could to get Graham off. "I expect the autopsy will confirm it was suicide and clear you. But even if it doesn't, even if there's a doubt, the crime-scene evidence should eliminate you—unless you were at his house some other time?" Graham shook his head. "Tell me what you did that day. Did you go to work?"

"Yeah, for a little while. But I went home around four p.m. We were making . . . funeral arrangements for . . ."

For Alicia, his only child. That was one of the saddest lines I'd ever heard. "Did you go out after that?"

This time there was no hesitation. "Once. I went to the CVS to buy Advil for Sandy around nine p.m., but I went straight home."

The fact that Graham didn't hesitate before answering told me the cops had already covered this ground. I got the location of the store from him. Unfortunately, he'd paid in cash. But maybe Alex could find a cashier who'd remember seeing Graham. It wasn't exactly a great alibi—or even a good one—but it was what we had. And it'd give us the kind of mundane detail that would humanize Graham with the jury. Yes, I was already planning for trial. I start the moment a client sits down in my office, and I don't stop until he either walks out of court or gets on the bus to state prison.

I didn't necessarily think Graham's case would ever make it to court. Roan's death looked like a classic suicide to me. And even if they ultimately proved otherwise—which seemed like a long shot—unless the cops came up with something that tied Graham to the crime scene, he was probably in the clear. As for that neighbor, when I got done grilling her, there'd be nothing left of her to bury.

Still, it never hurts to be prepared. So I asked him my stock final question: "Can you think of anything else that might look bad for you?" It's a way of getting a client to come clean without sounding like I'm accusing him of lying.

"Anything else . . . ? No. No, I can't." He blinked away sudden tears. "I just feel like . . . like maybe this is all my fault. When I heard about the photos, I thought, 'Who is she? My Alicia would never take . . . pictures like that.' But then I realized that going away to college was her first real chance at freedom. She probably was going a little crazy." Graham swallowed. "The more I thought about it, the more I finally saw what a tight leash we'd kept her on." His hands were squeezing his knees, and now he stared down at them. "We just wanted the best for her, wanted to make sure she was set up for success and didn't get into trouble like so many kids do. But now, looking back on her life, I wonder if . . . if we pushed her too hard, for too long."

It was one hell of a self-aware—and brave—admission. I had a feeling he was right, but there was no point agreeing with him. "I don't have kids, but I've handled a lot of cases with young adults. From what I've seen, they all go a little crazy at first when they leave the nest. I don't think you should beat yourself up."

When he met my gaze, his eyes were troubled. "What I can't understand is why she sent him those photos. Why didn't she realize he might use them to hurt her?"

I sighed. "Because she was young and naive. She trusted him. Just like all the other girls who learned the hard way that you can trust someone who doesn't deserve to be trusted."

Graham shook his head. He was the picture of despair. "So this kind of thing has happened before?"

I nodded. "Most definitely, and it's getting more and more common."

"I had no idea." Graham's expression was stunned. "What world was I living in?"

I looked at him with sympathy. "Clearly a much nicer one than the rest of us."

FOUR

I convened the troops after Graham left and brought them up to speed. Alex sprawled on the couch. He had the happy-dozy look of someone who was sleep-deprived for all the right reasons. I shook my head. "Seriously, how late was it by the time you guys called it quits for the night?"

Alex shot me an annoyed look. "For your information, we were *talking*. FYI, men *do* like to do that."

Not in my experience, but whatever. "The coroner is probably going to conclude that Roan Sutton was a straight-up suicide. But Graham's paying us to prepare for the worst, so we have to figure out who else might've killed the guy."

Michelle smiled. "And for the record, he's paying us well." She looked around the office. "Might be time to think about . . . I was about to say *re*decorating. But since we never decorated to begin with . . ." She raised an eyebrow at me.

I sat up. "What? The place looks great." At least, it did compared with our old office in the heart of Van Nuys gang territory. The chairs in front of my desk even matched. And most important of all, I had a couch.

Michelle folded her arms. "The place looks like nothing. Nothing on the walls but a law-school diploma, no chairs in the reception area—otherwise known as my office—no plants anywhere, and the carpeting looks like shit. You want to make money, you've got to look like money. We look like a Goodwill store—that's going out of business."

I turned to Alex for support, but he shrugged. "She's right. We definitely could use an upgrade."

I was outvoted. "Fine. As long as you think we can afford it." Michelle handled the business end of things, and letting her do it was one of the smartest moves I'd ever made. Money and I have never kept close company for long. "Back to the case. If it turns out to be murder, Graham's going to be number one on the cops' hit parade of suspects."

Michelle's eyes sparked with anger. "But who could blame him? I mean, the asshole killed his daughter. *And* posted those photos. Fuck Roan Sutton."

No argument there. "Theoretically, the jury will feel the same way. Assuming there's proof Roan killed Alicia. But that gets Graham a manslaughter at best. He'll probably still do prison time and lose his practice. What we need to do is make sure this case never sees the inside of a courtroom."

Alex saw where I was going. "By finding an even better suspect."

"Exactly." And that was the problem. "I never like to assume, but I think in this case it's safe to say Alicia's murder and Roan's death are connected. The cops are going to opt for the easy route and pin Alicia's murder on Roan. Stand by for some really sloppy work on that score."

Michelle sighed. "Well, Roan does seem like the obvious choice."

He definitely was. "But that doesn't take us anywhere good." If Roan killed Alicia, then Graham came out on top as Suspect Number One in Roan's death. "So we need to start by figuring out who else might've killed her. Then we'll have to hope we can find a reason why that person—or someone close to that person—wanted to kill Roan."

Alex stood up and stretched. "Great. For a minute there, I was worried you might be asking a little too much." His tone was sarcastic. "The list of suspects for Alicia's murder has got to be a mile long. I mean, who *wouldn't* want to kill the little girl who'd just started undergrad and never even had a parking ticket?"

Alex can be such a smart-ass. "You checked her out already?"

"Yeah. She didn't even have any asshole comments on her Facebook page."

"It's still up?" That surprised me.

He nodded. "Her friends wanted a place to write to one another about her. Kind of like a memorial."

It was painful to hear, but I thought it was a nice idea—and probably therapeutic for the kids. Not to mention, helpful to us. "Did you get a bead on who her nearest and dearest were?"

"A bunch of kids from high school wrote on her page, but I figured we'd want to focus on the ones she was hanging with at USC, right?"

"For now. But keep everything you've got." Because you never know. Someone in high school might've been holding a grudge. "Is there any way of identifying the pigs who clicked on her photos on that porn website?"

Michelle frowned. "But even if one of them killed her, why would that person kill Roan?"

"I don't know, but we've got to look into it." Anyone who might steer the cops away from Graham would be a welcome addition to the party. "Alex, what do you think? Can you do it?"

He chewed on the inside of his cheek—a habit whenever he was mulling over a problem. "I *think* all those websites have tracking elements that transmit visitors' data to third parties, like Google and Tumblr—"

Michelle looked surprised. "Even if people are browsing in incognito mode?"

Alex gave a mild snort. "Incognito mode doesn't do anything to stop the tracking, which is where I hack in. And I already saw that this porn website shows what people clicked on. So I'm pretty sure I can get the IP addresses of the knuckle draggers who checked out Alicia. The problem's going to be narrowing it down. We could be talking about thousands."

I took a moment to think about that. "Except we're not. We're just looking for the one asshole who actually went to her place. So the computer search is secondary; what we really need are witnesses who can say they saw him hanging around—"

Michy interjected. "Assuming this guy exists."

I gave her an exasperated look. "We're looking for Some Other Dude—so yeah, I'm assuming." SODDI—Some Other Dude Did It—is a timeworn defense. "That means it's going to come down to the usual." In the old days, they called it shoe leather. Door knocking the neighborhood, talking to witnesses. I used to think the Internet would make that obsolete, that it'd open a whole new—and faster—way to find out who, what, and where without leaving my desk. But it hasn't so far, and maybe it never will. I think there's just no substitute for the old-fashioned face-to-face, the *What did you see on the night of . . . ?*

Alex nodded. "I figured. Who do you want to start with? Alicia's friends? Or the neighbors?"

I drummed my fingers on the desk. "Ideally the neighbors, but the cops will have gotten to them already, and I need to know what they said before we hit them up." I thought for a moment. Graham was officially my client, but he wasn't officially a suspect. Yet. So legally speaking, I had no right to get access to the witness statements. But, of course, I knew someone who did. "Let me see if I can snag a copy of the reports."

"I already pulled the list of friends off her Facebook page. Let me get my iPad." Alex—now energized and out of sleep mode—jumped up and headed to his office.

Michelle leaned in after he'd left. "So Alex is in love?"

"Seems so. With a Delta Airlines pilot."

The phone rang, and Michelle stood up. "Duty calls. I assume you guys are heading out?"

I nodded as I powered down my computer. "I'll call you from the road. If we get back in time, want to grab a bite?"

Michy nodded. "Definitely. Barney's?"

"Perf." Barney's Beanery was an old roadside diner on Santa Monica Boulevard, a biker-style bar where Janis Joplin and Jim Morrison used to hang. Great comfort food and a full bar. What more could you want?

Michelle went to answer the phone, and Alex came in with his iPad. "Should be easy to get to all of them today. They live pretty close together."

Which figured, since they were all USC students. I'd asked Graham about Alicia's college friends, but she hadn't told him much—just said that they were "great." Neither he nor his wife, Sandy, had ever gotten the chance to meet them. Alicia had moved out only three months ago. "I assume they all live in dorms?"

Alex shook his head. "Most of them live off campus. Three have a house together on West Thirty-Fifth Place. You want me to call them, set up an interview?"

That'd give them warning we were coming. "I don't know how cooperative they'll be. Let's drop in on them, make it look casual." I wanted to take a temperature check in person. I didn't know how any of them felt about Roan, but if they were fans, they might not love the idea of talking to the lawyer who represented his potential killer—even though the conclusion at this point was that Roan had committed suicide.

Beulah, my not-so-trusty and very ancient Mercedes, was out of gas—as usual, because she guzzles about ten gallons per mile—so Alex drove. He gave me his iPad so I could navigate, and I took the opportunity to check out Alicia's Facebook page to see what I could find out about her friends. But the postings didn't tell me much. They all mourned her loss, talked about how "beautiful she was, both inside and out," and how much they'd "miss her smile" and her "great sense of humor." Sweet, but cookie-cutter stuff.

We made it to the campus in just half an hour—an amazing feat— and Alex navigated toward Thirty-Fifth Place.

The off-campus housing wasn't much to write home about. Rows and rows of dull low-rise apartment buildings and small houses that looked like they'd seen better days half a century ago. But for a student, especially one who was getting her first chance to live out loud, it probably looked like heaven.

I asked Alex to drive us past Alicia's place. She lived close by in a one-bedroom on Thirty-Sixth Place. It was a narrow, two-story beige building. Bicycles were locked into a stand at the side. I saw a maroon-and-gold USC banner in one of the upper windows. I wondered if it was hers.

Alex turned onto Thirty-Fifth Place and parked in front of a small, ramshackle-looking house that was completely festooned in USC colors, from the maroon-and-gold sheets draped around the doorway to the maroon-and-gold curtains hanging in the windows. That kind of rah-rah bullshit always nauseated me. "Looks like the vortex where school spirit smashed into psychosis."

Alex had a sardonic smile. "Or a very cleverly ironic statement."

I glanced at the maroon-and-gold riot and shook my head. "I'll stick with my theory."

"Anyway, that's not the place. We want the one behind it."

Behind it? I couldn't see anything. Alex got out and led the way to a small, fenced-in walkway on the right side of the house. Sure enough, there was another house. It was about the same size as the first, which I estimated to be a two-bedroom at most. It was painted a simple light gray and had a brown roof, brown front door, and brown window trimmings. Not a particularly appealing color scheme, but at least it wasn't a paean to all things USC.

I stopped and studied the place. "Who lives here?"

Alex looked down at his iPad. "Gayle Mortenson, Phil Luros, and Diana Hannigan."

I made a shrewd deduction. "So it's a couple and one girl?"

Alex shook his head. "Not from what I saw on the Facebook page."

Interesting. Coed dorms I was used to. But coed living in tight quarters like these—with no romantic connection—was a new one to me. On the other hand, having a guy around made life safer for the girls. A significant upside—assuming Phil wasn't a total slob.

A voice behind me almost made me jump. "Excuse me, can I help you?"

I plastered a warm smile on my face and turned around to find a voluptuous young woman in jeans and a tight black turtleneck sweater holding a bag of groceries. I recognized the long brown hair and lips—which she pouted Barbie style in just about every one of the photos posted on Alicia's Facebook page. "Hi. You're Diana, aren't you?" I started to put out my hand, then realized hers were wrapped around the bag of groceries. "I'm Samantha Brinkman, a lawyer. And this is my investigator, Alex Medrano."

Her expression darkened. "What do you want?"

Damn, this looked like trouble. I spoke mildly. "Just to talk to you guys about Alicia. I'm looking into her murder."

At that moment, a young man with shaggy, dirty-blond hair, dressed in jeans and sandals—in spite of the fact that it was cloudy and practically cold enough to see your breath—appeared behind her. His voice was harsh and bitter. "There's nothing to look into. That fuckstick Roan killed her. Case closed."

Diana nodded, and I inwardly breathed a sigh of relief. Her chilly reception was about Roan, not Graham. I'd found a sympathetic audience—a very rare experience for me. I've had doors from Bel Air to Boyle Heights slammed in my face. For some reason, most folks don't love the idea of cooperating with the lawyer who's defending a murderer. Go figure.

I introduced myself and Alex again, but now I added, "I'm representing Alicia's father. You're Phil, right?"

He shook my hand, his expression somber. "Yeah. He must be torn up."

"He is. Do you have time to talk?"

"Sure." He fished a key out of his pocket, and we followed him into the house.

FIVE

As I'd surmised, the house was a small two-bedroom, predictably cramped and cheaply furnished, with a battered brown sofa, an ancient Formica dinette table, and old black-and-navy beanbag chairs. But the flat-screen looked relatively new—someone's birthday or Christmas present, I supposed.

And there was no mistaking that this was a students' lair: textbooks on calculus, biology, and psychology were strewn around the living room and on the dinette table. And the contents of the makeshift bookcase—a typical boards-and-bricks styling—ran the gamut, from the *Bhagavad Gita* to Keynesian economics. A filmy, red beaded scarf hung over a lamp on an end table next to the sofa—a nod to "mood lighting" that I remembered from my own undergrad days.

But the place was sparkling clean. A real plus for me, because although I'm not a stickler for decorative touches—empty walls, empty space is just fine by me—I can't stand disorder, dirt, or even dust. Makes me physically queasy. Michy thinks it's a reaction to my chaotic childhood and a mother who never let me so much as choose my own bedspread. I don't particularly care about the reason. I just know that sitting in a dirty, messy room makes me itchy.

Phil gestured for us to have a seat on the living room sofa, and Diana went to the kitchen—just ten steps away—to unpack the groceries. He dropped down into one of the two beanbag chairs across from us. "So is he suing the school or something?"

If only. "Well, she lived off campus so . . . no." But that raised another question I'd had. "By the way, don't freshmen usually stay in the dorms?"

Phil nodded. "Alicia screwed up and applied for the dorms too late. Gayle and I are juniors."

Diana, finished with the groceries, spoke as she came in and flopped down on the beanbag chair next to Phil's. "I'm a freshman, but I couldn't afford the dorm. Gayle's mom met my mom during orientation, and she hooked me up with this place."

I detected a defensive edge in Diana's voice. I guessed that she was the girl from the poor side of town in this crowd. "So how'd you guys meet Alicia?"

Phil flipped his long bangs to the side and pulled a joint out of his jeans pocket. "As neighbors. We all moved in about two weeks before school started, and we kept bumping into each other at the Trader Joe's on Jefferson. We wound up having coffee and found out she lived only a couple of blocks away." Phil lit the joint, took a deep drag, and held it out to me.

I shook my head. "Thanks, but it's just a bad trip for me." Like really bad. Like screaming, rolling-on-the-ground bad. Such a drag.

Phil held it out to Alex, but he declined, too. "I'm a control freak."

Diana smiled and took the joint from Phil. "No shade. More for us."

I turned to Phil. "Would you say you guys were her closest friends?"

Phil sighed. "We were close. But I'd say Nomie was her real BFF."

I remembered seeing a name that seemed close to that on Alicia's Facebook page. "Naomi Dreyfus?"

Diana blew out a stream of smoke and handed the joint back to Phil. "Yeah. They were super tight. Nomie's a freshman, but she lives in the dorm. I think she met Alicia in English."

Alex got her contact information. "Anyone else in your group?"

"Davey," Phil said. "He'll probably show up in a bit. Usually does. He's a junior, lives on Denker." He stood up. "Water? Or I think we might have some beer left."

I thought I might be getting a contact high. I was thirsty as hell. And a little bit hungry. "Water sounds good."

Phil looked at Alex, who nodded. "Water would be great, thanks."

Phil brought back two bottles of Dasani. I took a long pull, then asked, "Did Alicia have any other possible enemies besides Roan?"

Phil answered emphatically. "None."

Diana agreed, though less emphatically. "None that I knew of. She was so . . . sweet, you know? She was smart, really pretty, and she didn't have to worry about money. I could see girls being jealous. But I didn't know anyone who had it in for her. Other than that dick Roan."

This opening was as good as any. "So you knew him?"

Phil put out the joint and snorted. "Unfortunately. He made the big push on Alicia in the first week of classes. Was always hanging around. I thought he was a freak from jump."

"But a hot freak." Diana pulled a cell phone out of her purse that lay on the floor next to her and scrolled, then held it out to us.

A photo showed a slender young man in low-slung jeans and a leather jacket leaning back against a brick wall with one of those sexy James Dean half smiles. He wasn't just hot. He was fire. I saw Alex raise an eyebrow. "I get it."

Diana nodded. "Right? But I smelled something 'off' about him. He was just so . . . intense. And he was all over her from the minute they met. It was way over the top."

Alex looked puzzled. "But obviously, Alicia didn't catch that. Did you guys warn her?"

"I think we all did," Phil said.

Diana was exasperated. "The thing is, she was kind of naive, and she was super ready to cut loose. So I don't think she appreciated anyone telling her what to do, no matter how right we might have been. I also think it was kind of an ego boost to have a guy act that nutso about her."

Naive and ready to party. A very bad combination. And in this case, lethal. "So what happened? How did it all go downhill so fast?"

A flash of anger crossed Phil's face. "He kept getting more and more demanding. He had to see her at least three times a week, then five, then every night—"

"And then he made her call him three times a day," Diana said. "It was crazy. Plus, he was a junior, so he wasn't navigating this place for the first time. It's different when you're a freshman and just figuring out how to deal with a huge campus, harder classes, and . . ." She waved a hand in the air. "A whole new everything."

Phil spoke with sympathy. "And Alicia was really stressed. She had a crazy full schedule, and she said her folks would make her move back home if her GPA fell below a 3.5." He shook his head. "So messed up to put all that on her."

I had to agree. I got that Graham didn't want her to throw keggers, but that really was a lot of pressure—even without a psycho boyfriend in the mix. "So she broke up with him?"

Diana rolled her eyes. "You'd think. But no, not really. She just told him she needed to focus on school for a bit, to take a breather so she could pull it together."

Alex spoke quietly. "So he revenge porned her."

"Yeah," Phil said. "I mean, we didn't know it at the time. I found out only after she . . ." His voice broke, and he paused for a moment. "I figure he had to have posted those photos just before he . . . he killed her."

Diana nodded. "We think she must've confronted him, threatened to report it to the police."

Confronting Roan sounded pretty gutsy—not something I'd have expected based on their descriptions of Alicia so far. "What makes you think Alicia confronted him?"

Diana gave Phil a puzzled look. "Didn't someone say they saw her go to his place the night before she died? I thought I heard that."

Phil nodded. "Me, too. But now I don't know where."

"Anyway," Diana said. "I didn't mean to give you guys the wrong impression. Alicia was naive and a really sweet person, but she was no cream puff. She definitely had the *cojones* to stick up for herself. It wouldn't surprise me a bit if she called Roan out for posting those photos. I know I sure would."

And then he killed her. Because she'd threatened to turn him in? I couldn't believe that was the driving motivation for her murder. Or at least, not the only one. If he'd been that afraid of getting busted for posting those photos, he wouldn't have done it to begin with. My bet was he'd just lost his shit because she finally really dumped him for good after he posted those photos. Alex called himself a control freak, but Roan made Alex look like a jellyfish.

There was a knock on the door, and Phil went to get it. A blast of cold November air blew in. Normally, it would've made me cringe. I'm not good with cold weather. But the pot smoke still hung heavily in the air, and I badly needed to take a full breath. I gulped in the fresh—by downtown LA standards—air and felt my head clear.

A tallish young man in a gray pullover hoodie, jeans, and sandals—what the hell was up with these guys and their sandals in the middle of winter?—walked in. Phil introduced him. "This is Davey Moser."

I introduced myself and Alex again and told him why we were there. Davey had light-brown hair that he wore short and neatly trimmed, and it framed a square-jawed face and brown eyes that tilted down at the corners, reminding me of a young Treat Williams. His initial polite smile dimmed with a look of worry when I explained I was representing Alicia's father.

"What for?" Davey asked. "Is he in trouble?"

I'd given some thought to how I should answer that question. There was probably no point in being coy. When the cops identify a "person of interest"—whether they officially identify the party or not—it always manages to leak out. I'd lose their trust, and more importantly, their cooperation if I didn't level with these kids. And since the universal attitude toward Roan seemed to be "nuke 'im," I thought it was probably safe to tell the truth and hope they'd go the extra mile to help us out.

I shook my head. "Not yet. But the coroner hasn't confirmed that Roan's death was a suicide, so they're not ruling out murder. And Graham has a pretty strong motive for killing him."

Davey set his jaw and spoke with some intensity. "Don't we all?"

That was certainly what I planned to tell the police.

SIX

Davey, who was a junior, said he had transferred to USC from Loyola Marymount because he eventually wanted to get an MBA, and USC had a much better program. "To be honest, it wasn't so much about the education for me. It's that everyone says you can get better business connects here."

That squared with what my stepfather, Jack, had told me about USC. Davey's views of Alicia and Roan pretty much echoed those of Diana and Phil. But he seemed to know Alicia pretty well, so I pressed a little further with him. "Is it possible Alicia also broke up with Roan because she wanted to see other guys?" If so, and Roan knew it, that'd add to his motive to kill Alicia. But another guy in the mix might give me another suspect for Roan's death.

Davey pulled one of the metal chairs from the dinette table next to Phil's beanbag. I couldn't help but think that chair would really hurt on a cold, early morning.

He paused for a moment before answering. "That wouldn't surprise me. Alicia was like a cat that'd been kept in a cage all its life. She wanted to cut loose and do everything, just drink it all in. So, yeah. There might've been someone else. Maybe more than one. She is . . ." His face sagged, then he continued. "I mean she *was* so pretty." He looked at me, his pain sincere. "But it wasn't just that. She was a good person. And for real. Not, you know, syrupy-sweet."

Phil clapped him on the back. "True story. When we first got to be friends, my mom had a heart attack, and my car was in the shop. Alicia not only drove me to the hospital, she stayed with me, held my hand the whole time during my mom's operation."

Diana nodded. "I got the flu over Thanksgiving break, and everyone else was gone. I don't know how she even found out I was sick, but she came over and took care of me. Did my laundry, cleaned up the place, brought me chicken soup and meds."

In memoriam stories always anoint the dead with saintly qualities, so I took these with a grain of salt. But one thing was perfectly clear: Alicia had no enemies here.

In any case, lovely as these stories were, they didn't help me. I needed some specifics about Alicia's actions in the days just before the murder. I threw out a question to the group. "Did any of you see Alicia in the last day or two before her . . . before she died?"

They exchanged bleak looks before Phil finally answered. "No. That's mainly what we've been talking about. How she dropped off the radar completely for a couple of days before . . ."

Diana cleared her throat. "I saw her the night before she left the message for Roan about taking a break." She paused and looked at Davey. "And you, too, Davey, right?" He nodded. "She told me what she really wanted to do was break up, but she felt bad. She thought maybe she should give him a chance to change, and she wanted to run it by me, get my input—"

"And I think to kind of . . . practice what she was going to say," Davey added. "You know, hear how it sounded out loud, make sure it came out right."

Phil's eyes were red. I couldn't tell whether it was the pot or sadness for Alicia. He took another hit and let the smoke drift out as he spoke.

42

"But he posted those photos the next night, so we think she was just too embarrassed to see anyone after that."

Diana nodded and dropped her gaze. "We should've realized something was wrong when we didn't hear from her the next day."

Davey tried to absolve Diana—and the rest of them. "Okay, but in fairness, I remember she said she needed to get ready for a calculus exam. And the whole reason for backing Roan off was to get some space so she could focus on school."

Bottom line: they didn't have any solid information about Alicia's last two days on earth.

I might go back to them later, but for now, it was time to move on. Alex got Nomie's dorm address and asked Phil to call ahead and tell her we were coming. Now that we knew the kids were on our side, we didn't need to go for a surprise attack. We thanked them and took off.

The clouds had cleared while we'd been talking to Alicia's friends, and the sun was poking through the fluffy cotton-ball clouds, clearing out sparkling patches of blue sky. I suggested we walk to the dorm. I wanted to enjoy the clean, fresh, and blissfully pot-free air.

Alex eyed his car, a blue Honda Accord, and glanced up and down the street. "Depends on how long you think this interview's going to go. I'm not thrilled about leaving it here after dark."

I glanced at my watch. It was after three. We had at least two hours of daylight left. "Assuming she's willing to talk, I can't imagine it'll take that long. And if it does, we can always come back another day."

We made it to the campus in five minutes and found Nomie's dorm building—one of several identical four-story brick buildings—at the far end. The students all seemed so mellow. They walked with no particular urgency, lounged on the grassy areas, and chatted in groups on benches and near vending machines. My memory of undergrad at UCLA held no such leisurely pace. I was constantly running, always out of breath, and always late because the powers that be always seemed to love to schedule my classes at opposite ends of the campus, which was the size of a small city.

Nomie had alerted the security guard at her dorm that we were coming, but we still had to present ID and let them take our photos. I noticed that the students had to do a fingerprint scan to get into the building. It was depressing, but it was probably a good thing they were so safety-minded. If Alicia had lived in a place like this, she'd probably still be alive. I wondered why she'd missed the dorm deadline. Had she deliberately dropped the ball so she could live alone? Or had her parents blown the deadline in the hope of persuading her to live at home? It would've been a tough commute from her home in Beverly Hills, but it was certainly doable.

Nomie's room was on the fourth floor at the end of the hall. As we moved toward it, a couple of young males came pounding down the corridor, wide smiles on their faces. As they ran past us, one of them joked, "She's gonna freak when she sees it, dude." The other one laughed and said, "Right?" I knew they were probably just talking about a stupid, innocent, prank. But I didn't like it. I wished I could find that girl and warn her.

Nomie answered the door the moment I knocked. "They told me you guys were coming," she said. She stood back and opened the door wider to let us in. "Just sit anywhere."

There were two twin-size beds, one on either side of the room, and a bookcase between them. Books, a backpack, binders, and spiral notebooks—along with sandals, boots, and fuzzy socks covered most of the available floor space and half the bed on the right. The only "anywhere" I could find that resembled a seat was a chair at a small desk against the wall. An open pizza box on the desk had the remnants of a small, half-eaten sausage and black olive pizza. It looked drier than the cardboard box. All the clutter and mess was making me sweat a little.

Alex wasn't loving it, either. He'd perched on the foot of the bed on the left side of the room, and I saw him wrinkle his nose as he took in the scene. I turned my focus to Nomie. She was biracial, more than average pretty, with big, dark eyes and an oval face that was set off beautifully by her short Afro. She went to the bed on the right side of the room and sat down. When she spoke, her voice was heavy with a sadness that seemed even deeper than that of Alicia's other friends. "I feel like someone cut off my arm. I just don't know how to . . . how to be. The phone will ring, and I'll think, 'Oh, it's probably Alicia.' And then . . ." Nomie wiped away tears with the back of her hand.

I gave her a moment to collect herself. "I assume you knew Alicia was going to break up, or at least ask Roan to give her some breathing room?" Nomie nodded. "By any chance, did you happen to see her after that?"

She picked at a thread on her bedspread and swallowed. "No. But I did see her the night before. Gave her my 'atta girl' pep talk so she wouldn't chicken out. She actually seemed pretty steady on her feet. I was proud of her." A tiny smile briefly lit up her face. "But then I had to go home and help with my grandma. She's got Alzheimer's, and she's staying with my mom until we can find a place for her. So I wasn't even on campus when . . . everything went down."

I could see the guilt written all over her face. "And Alicia never called you during that time?"

Nomie suddenly choked up again. "That's what was so bad. That she didn't feel like she could come to me, tell me about those photos, about what that fucking asshole had done to her. She must've been so humiliated. And maybe she was worried that we'd judge or something." Nomie looked up at me, tears streaming down her face. "I never would have! Why didn't she know that?"

Her pain was heartbreaking, but I had no real answer for her. "Maybe she intended to, Nomie. Maybe she would have if . . ."

Nomie finished my thought. "If she'd had the chance." She paused, a look of resignation settling on her face. "I want to believe that. I want to think she'd feel safe, that she'd know I'd never judge her."

I said I thought she must've known that, then I told her about Graham being a "person of interest" and that I was looking into other possible suspects with regard to Roan's death. "Did you happen to know of any other guys Alicia was seeing?"

Nomie paused. "I don't know about anyone she was seeing. But I do know someone who was coming on to her. Her Italian cinema professor. Barth Foley. Alicia thought he was kind of hot." She sighed. "Then again, from what I heard, most of the girls in his class did." Nomie made a face. "Personally, I thought he was a creep. The kind of guy who uses his position as a pussy magnet. But I don't think Alicia was sleeping with him . . . At least, not from what I could tell."

Nomie paused again, and I could see there was something else on her mind. She seemed to be trying to decide whether to tell me. I reassured her. "If you're worried about violating anyone's privacy, I can promise you I'll never talk. This is strictly confidential, just between you and me."

Unless she had a lead on another suspect. In which case I'd haul her into the police station if I had to tie her to the roof of my car.

Nomie shook her head. "It's not like that. I just . . . This is going to sound a little weird, but about a month before she . . ." Nomie paused and swallowed. "A month before she died, Alicia kept saying she felt like someone was following her, watching her."

Alex took out his notepad. This was just a cover for the mini-recorder in his pocket that ran nonstop with every interview. "Did she ever get a look at the . . . I assume it's a guy?"

Nomie's expression was intense. "Yeah. Around six feet, medium build, a short beard—maybe a soul patch—and a mustache. She said he always seemed to be wherever she was: at Starbucks, at Trader Joe's, at Ralphs."

He scribbled convincingly, then asked, "How about at school? Did she ever see him at the dining hall or the gym?"

She shook her head. "Not that I can remember." Nomie looked from Alex to me, her expression earnest. "I told her to report it to the police, but she didn't feel right about it. What if it was just a coincidence? She didn't want to get him in trouble for no reason. I said I'd stick with her so I could get a look at this guy, see if he seemed creepy."

"Did you spot him?" Alex asked.

Nomie nodded. "And he did seem to pop up almost wherever we went. So I finally just went over and said something to him. I think I asked him what classes he was taking." Nomie paused and furrowed her brow. "Or something like that. Anyway, the guy was perfectly nice. Didn't act hinky or anything. Turned out he was managing a building down the block from Alicia. So we both thought, no big deal, just a coincidence. But now . . ."

I could see she was second-guessing that decision. "He never made a move on Alicia, though."

Nomie shook her head, but she was agitated. "What if I was wrong? What if this guy was a nut, and he got pissed after I confronted him? Flipped out and blamed it on Alicia. Maybe he hacked Alicia's phone, and *he* posted those photos. And . . ."

"Killed her?" Nomie shrugged. It was my job to make the incredible seem perfectly logical, but even I had a hard time buying this one. Still, I gave it a go. "Did you see him around after that?" If he'd suddenly dropped off the radar after she'd confronted him, we might have something here. Nomie paused, her brow furrowed, and I felt a little spark of hope begin to kindle. Could we possibly get lucky so soon?

Nomie sighed. "Actually, yeah. Now that I think about it, I saw him everywhere."

So much for that. Just to be on the safe side, I got the address of the building where he worked so Alex could check him out.

But I should've known better than to hope we'd get a real lead this soon. That would've been too easy.

SEVEN

Alex and I were just about to leave when the last member of Alicia's circle showed up. Gayle Mortenson was a short pixie of a girl, with freckles, green eyes made large by thick tortoise-frame glasses, and curly strawberry-blonde hair. Her biology class had just let out, and she'd come to check on Nomie.

Gayle knew about the problems Alicia had been having with Roan, though Alicia hadn't spoken to her about her plan to back him off. "But I never get to talk to anybody anymore."

Nomie shook her head with sympathy. "She's majoring in cinematic arts—film and TV production—and she scored an internship with Universal."

Gayle held up her hands. "Which sounds great, I know. But it actually means that every waking moment I'm not in class, I'm at the studio, fetching coffee, lunches, snacks, Frisbees, diapers, hairspray—you name it, I've fetched it." She gave a sarcastic smile and thumbs-up. "It's all about learning the craft."

But she was smart enough to know that doing it all well—and with a smile—could be the first rung on her way up the ladder. And she might be small, but there was a toughness about her, a wiry resilience that I had a feeling would serve her well in the trenches of Hollywood. "Then it'd been a while since you had contact with Alicia?"

"About a week." Gayle pressed her lips together. "But the day before she d-died . . . I saw this guy coming out of her building." Gayle frowned. "At the time, I didn't connect it with Alicia, and maybe there is no connection. But it bugged me. He had a weird look on his face, angry, like he'd just been in a fight."

Alex glanced at me. I nodded to give him the go-ahead. "Do you remember what time it was approximately?"

"I remember what time it was *exactly*. I was late getting to the studio, and I'd just looked at the clock. It was three eighteen."

"Can you describe him?" Alex asked.

"Five foot ten, kind of thick—big chest, and he had a gut on him—blondish crew cut." Gayle paused a moment. "I think I remember a burgundy T-shirt, maybe jeans. But the thing that caught my eye—other than his pisstivity—was he lifted his arm and looked at it, like he'd cut it or something."

Alex pretended to scribble. "Did you see a cut? Or any blood?"

Gayle shook her head. "Whatever it was must've been pretty small. I was only about twenty feet away. Then again, I was driving, saw him for only a couple of seconds."

Alex flipped a page in his notebook. "Had you ever seen him before?"

"No, and he didn't look like a student to me. But I guess there's no way to be sure of that."

"And I assume you haven't seen him since?" he asked. Gayle shook her head again. "Have you told the cops about this guy?"

"I did. I thought he might've been the killer. But they said people saw Alicia leave the building later that evening, so unless he came back . . ."

I had to believe the cops had asked the neighbors about this and had come up empty-handed. If so, the burly guy might have nothing to do with the case. I'll take any red herring I can find, but making this burly guy a person of interest in Alicia's murder would help me only if I could gin up some story about how he'd also killed Roan. A tall order. And one I couldn't begin to fill unless I could find him and check out his alibi—which, at this point, seemed pretty unlikely.

So I moved on and asked Gayle whether she thought Alicia might've been seeing the Italian cinema professor but she knew even less about it than Nomie. Assuming anything had been going on between them, they'd either kept it quiet or it was of very short duration. The professor went on my to-do list.

We asked a few more questions, but it was clear we'd gotten all Nomie and Gayle had to give. I exchanged a glance with Alex to let him know it was time to pull the plug, and I stood up. "Thank you, guys. You've been really helpful."

Nomie's expression was earnest. "I hope you can help Mr. Hutchins. I mean, even if the police say it wasn't a suicide, even if he did kill Roan—"

Gayle cut in. "That asshole so deserved it."

I sighed. "I agree."

"But they said it's likely a suicide, right?" Nomie asked. I nodded. "Why would they change their minds?"

A fair question. "If they find other evidence that indicates it was homicide, they'd change the conclusion. They probably won't. But it's best to get out ahead of this as soon as possible." Because I don't trust cops as a general rule. And you just never know.

It was only a little after five o'clock by the time we left, but darkness was already spreading through the sky. I've hated this time of year since I was twelve, when we moved in with Sebastian Cromer. Because the earlier night fell, the earlier Celeste could make me go to bed—which meant that much more time I was alone, isolated in my bedroom—where Sebastian could get to me.

Alex hurried us along and heaved an audible sigh of relief when he saw that his car was still where he'd parked it—with tires and hubcaps intact. As we got in and buckled up, I thought about what we'd come up with so far. "A possible stalker and a bear with a crew cut. What do you think?"

Alex pulled out and headed for the freeway. "I'll check out the stalker, but we both know it's a dead end."

I agreed. "But crew cut guy might give us something to go on." And if I could find a way to tie him to Roan, a possible "other dude" to pin Roan's murder on.

Alex inched up the on-ramp. The freeway ahead was a river of red taillights. Driving during rush hour in LA is like wading through a tar pit. He slowly merged into the right lane. "Of course, we're assuming he was there to see Alicia, which might not be the case. She's not the only tenant in that building."

"True, but we won't know unless we try." I pulled out my phone. "Let's see what our friends on the Thin Blue Line have on him." Alex looked perplexed. "The Thin Blue Line? Refers to cops? Comes from an eighties documentary?" Alex shrugged. I shook my head. I'd only been a kid myself back then, but at times like this, Alex really made me feel old. I hit Dale's private cell number.

Dale answered with an exasperated sigh. "I can't give you anything, Sam."

"Really? Even if I'm representing your number-one person of interest?"

Dale sighed again. "I'm not really on the case."

"Yet." It'd taken Dale a while to climb back into the chief's good graces after having been charged with the double homicide, but he'd finally found his way back into RHD, and I knew Dale was overdue for his next case. It'd be great for me if he got this one. And the fact that he'd hedged his answer with "really" told me the captain might already have talked to him about it.

Now he read me the party line. "No case has been filed. You're not entitled to—"

I cut him off. "I see, then you don't want Alex's help? Because from what I hear, there's a bunch of computer work in this case, and we both know you don't have anyone on the job who can touch him." I let that sink in, then added, "I'm giving you a chance to look like a genius." There was a long pause. "So let's share. Luckily, we're in the neighborhood."

He finally capitulated. "Do me a favor and give it a half hour. The fewer people see you here, the better."

Since we weren't really in the neighborhood—in fact at this point we were about forty minutes away from the downtown area where Dale worked—I didn't mind doing him that favor. I looked at the clock. It was a quarter to six. "See you at a quarter after."

The detectives in RHD work long hours when they have an active case going. But when they don't, they generally clear out by five. Alex pulled into the parking lot at ten after six, and we headed into the building. A police officer escorted us up to Dale's floor, where I saw that the place was virtually empty except for the cleaning crew.

Dale seemed to be aging backward since the murder charges got dismissed two years ago. It even looked like there was more pepper than salt in his regulation cop haircut. He was smiling into his cell phone when we walked up to his cubicle and perched on a table across from his desk. Dale looked up, then sighed as he said, "I've gotta go. Eight o'clock still good?" He listened for a moment, then said, "Great, I'll pick you up," and ended the call.

I folded my arms and smirked. "The crime-scene tech again? What was her name, Susan?" Every time I checked, Dale seemed to have a new babe.

Dale gave me a deadpan look. "Not that it's any of your business, but no. It's a woman I met at the fund-raiser for the children's hospital." He sat back. "And the crime-scene tech was Janet, not Susan." He nodded to Alex. "How you doing?" They'd bonded over the dirty-cop case we'd been involved in last year.

"Good." Alex tilted his head at the phone. "Sounds like you are, too."

Dale smiled. "Not bad for an old man." He hit a key on his computer. "So your client . . . Graham Hutchins. If all goes well, he should be fine. But even if it turns out to be a homicide, for a change, I don't mind helping you. If I was in his shoes, I'd shoot the bastard and burn his house down."

Alex and I both knew that wasn't just hyperbole. He'd actually killed a prostitute who'd threatened my younger half sister, Lisa. He'd gotten away with it so far, but there was a very dicey junkie out there who could nail him to the wall if he ever sobered up and realized what he'd seen.

I told Dale what we'd learned about the crew cut guy but played it close to the vest about the stalker story. We didn't know yet whether we could even link him to Alicia's murder, let alone Roan's death. But my job was to keep all options open. And I didn't want the cops to dig into my potential fall guy and muck things up. So the less they knew about him, the better. "I need the witness statements from the people who lived in Alicia's building."

Dale pulled up a folder on his computer and scrolled for a moment. "We did work that up." He turned around and leaned back in his chair. "Okay, I know what I can do for you. What can you do for me?"

This was Alex's bailiwick. He said, "I assume you've seized Alicia's and Roan's phones and computers?" Dale nodded. "I can tell you whether someone besides Roan could have posted the photos on that porn website."

Dale drummed his fingers on the arm of his chair for a moment, then he turned back to the computer and hit a key. The printer whirred to life. "I don't have to tell you to keep this quiet, do I?"

I pulled the pages of the police reports from the printer. "We were never here."

EIGHT

As I scanned the witness statements, Dale said, "The detective in charge had a couple of unis talk to the neighbors about the guy Gayle described."

"Unis? Why?" Don't get me wrong—some unis are great, but since they're usually newbies, they don't have a lot of interviewing experience, and the first crack at a witness can be a make-or-break situation. Ask the right questions and a memory is sparked; ask the wrong ones—or fail to ask the right follow-ups—and a memory is buried or, worse, distorted. Bottom line: no decent detective delegates the door knocking on a tip as important as Gayle's. "Who's the detective?"

Dale's expression was cynical. "Rusty Templeton."

Of course, who else? "Pure genius putting him on the case." I'd locked horns with Rusty last year when I'd handled the Cassie Sonnenberg case. He was the stereotypical burnout case riding out his last few years until retirement. "Is he still on it?"

Dale made a face and nodded. "For now."

I scanned the reports. At first glance it looked like only one of the neighbors corroborated Gayle's sighting of Mr. Crew Cut, and that neighbor didn't know whether the guy had made contact with Alicia. "Any chance you might wind up with the case?"

"No clue. As of now, I'm just helping out." He turned to Alex. "You can check out Alicia's phone and laptop. But I'm afraid Roan's were wiped clean."

Alex looked skeptical. "I'll need to see that for myself. It might seem like everything's been erased when it's really only 'lost.' You just have to know where to look, and your guy probably doesn't. No offense, but he's a cop, right?"

Dale shot him a look. "Right." His tone was sarcastic. "And cops can't possibly know anything about tech."

Alex shrugged. "Not saying he doesn't know *anything*. It's just unlikely he knows as much as I do."

Dale glanced at me, and I gave him a little smile. "You know he's right. No offense."

Dale stood up. "It'll take some doing to get you access to Roan's phone and laptop. I can't promise anything. But I can bring you Alicia's. Wait here."

When Dale left, I spoke to Alex in a low voice. The news that Roan's laptop and phone were wiped worried me. "Why does someone who's about to commit suicide scrub his shit like that?" Even if Alex managed to figure out that it was only "lost" and not permanently erased, the fact that the effort was made worried me.

Alex shook his head. "It is weird. But . . . the whole theory about his suicide was that he felt guilty about killing Alicia. Maybe that's why he tried to wipe everything, too?"

That actually made sense. And then another reason occurred to me. "Remember, he'd been dragged in for questioning more than once before he died."

Alex tapped his forehead. "Of course. Duh. He was probably afraid of getting busted for posting Alicia's selfies."

And rightly so. That didn't necessarily prove he'd posted Alicia's selfies. He might've had other things on his computer to worry about, like bootlegged T-Pain albums. But the wiped computer certainly added to the likelihood that Roan was the one who'd posted her photos.

A few minutes later, Dale returned with Alicia's cell phone and laptop. He handed the phone to Alex and set the laptop on the table across from his desk. "I'm trusting you not to alter anything." He gave Alex a stern look.

Alex returned his gaze. "I would never do a thing like that." His tone sounded a little offended.

Dale raised an eyebrow. "No, but she would." He tilted his head toward me.

Alex thought about that for a moment, then nodded. "That's fair."

I looked from one to the other and folded my arms. "Would you both like to kiss my ass now? Or later?"

Alex sat down at the table and turned on the power for Alicia's laptop. While he waited for it to boot up, he turned on Alicia's phone. Within minutes, he began to shake his head. "First of all, this is an iPhone, and it's not jailbroken—so it wouldn't have been so easy to hack."

I'm a tech Luddite, so that meant nothing to me. "What's jailbroken mean? And why does someone do that?"

"People hack their phones to get rid of built-in restrictions that limit the software they can download." Alex saw my confused expression. "For example, if an iPhone is jailbroken, the user isn't limited to downloading apps from the Apple store. But the point is, it's easier to hack into a jailbroken phone. Since Alicia's isn't jailbroken, it's a little less likely that a third party could've hacked into her phone to get the photos and post them to the porn website."

It would've been nice to have a reason to point to a mysterious third party who could've posted Alicia's photos. I didn't know how I'd link that person to Roan's murder, but still. It's always good to have another theory—or more accurately, a red herring or two . . . or three. "You said it's unlikely, but it's not impossible for someone else to have hacked into her phone, right?"

Alex pulled out his iPad. "No, it's definitely not impossible. There's spyware you can load into a phone that isn't jailbroken. And Alicia didn't delete the photos from her phone." He held up the phone. Sure enough, there they were—all her nude photos. "I can definitely confirm that she sent them to Roan. But she didn't send them to anyone else. So unless someone besides Roan had managed to load spyware on her phone and knew about the photos—which seems pretty unlikely, since there's no spyware on her phone now—I'd say Roan had to have posted the photos to that website."

Not great news, but I'd take "unlikely" over "impossible" any day. It meant I got to keep my third-party mystery guy. Or girl. I didn't want to limit my options. "What else could someone find out by hacking her phone?"

He scrolled through the phone. "A shit ton. If someone installed spyware on it, he or she could've monitored every phone call, text, and e-mail *and* tracked her movements."

I was loving this. The beauty of being a defense lawyer is that I don't have to prove anything. All I have to do is poke enough holes in the People's case to give the jury reasonable doubt. This new information presented exactly the kind of juicy scenario likely to distract and confuse a jury.

Dale was less enthused. "But who else besides Roan would want to hack her phone?"

Of course, there was that. The question hung in the air, along with its corollary: Who else had motive to kill Alicia besides Roan? The answer to both was "no one." And that led to the obvious conclusion: if Roan hadn't committed suicide, the best—and only logical—suspect for his murder was Graham.

Dale gave me a meaningful look but spared me the verbal "told you so" as Alex moved to Alicia's laptop.

I wasn't ready to let it go. "Alex, you said there's no spyware on her phone right now?"

"No, right. I checked. But that doesn't mean it was never there."

Dale saw where I was going. "Is there a way to find out whether it had been there before?"

Alex nodded. "There might be. I'd need more time to do that."

A few minutes later, Alex turned his chair around to face us. "She never stored the photos on her laptop, so the phone is the only way someone besides Roan could've gotten them. Someone also posted her selfies to her Facebook page after they were posted to the porn website, so I was trying to see if I could trace that person, but the link is broken. I might be able to find a back door, but that would take a lot more time than we have right now, and it might not be worth it. Once those photos, with her Facebook link and physical address, hit the porn website, anyone with a little hacking experience could've posted those photos to her Facebook page."

So the person who'd posted her photos to the porn website wasn't necessarily the person who'd posted them to her Facebook page. Meaning someone who'd never even met Alicia could've posted the photos to her Facebook page. "Why would someone do that? Just for the lulz?"

"Yeah, just a prank—a sick joke." Alex closed Alicia's laptop, his mouth twisted with disdain. "It's pathetic."

I asked Dale when they expected to get the official coroner's report on Roan, but he didn't know. He did, however, have some new information for me. "I just wanted to give you a heads up: Roan's parents are insisting there's no way he committed suicide."

This did not surprise me. "Because there's no way he killed Alicia."

He stood up. "Right. And they're putting pressure on everyone to hold the coroner's feet to the fire. The captain said they've contacted the city councilman and the county Board of Supervisors."

I guess it made sense. If Roan were my kid, I'd probably go apeshit, too. "So this is going to get hot."

Dale gave me a grim smile. "Familiar territory for you. But I thought you should know, just to be prepared."

I'd been right in the center of a searingly hot bull's-eye in Dale's case. I thanked him for the warning. "Guess we'll take it as it comes. We'd better get back to the office."

As we turned to go, Dale said, "I trust you'll keep me up to speed if you find anything."

I stopped and smiled. "Of course. Goes without saying. And you'll do likewise, right?"

He gave me a flat smile. "Like you said, goes without saying."

Alex and I headed for the elevator. As we stepped inside, he gave me a sidelong glance. "No way we're telling him diddly, right?"

"Of course not." And Dale didn't plan on giving us diddly, either. I knew that smile.

It was after seven o'clock when we got back to the office. Just in time to make my seven thirty dinner date at Barney's Beanery with Michy. She asked Alex if he'd like to join us.

He rolled his eyes. "So you two can grill me about Paul all night long? No, *gracias*."

I *tsk*ed him. "Don't be such a Debbie Downer. If I had a new bae, I'd spill."

Michelle threw a glance over her shoulder as she pulled on her coat. "You sure you want to go down that road?"

I spread my hands. "What? I told you guys about Niko." The superhot Krav Maga teacher I'd met when I enrolled—then bailed—out of his class. I just couldn't make the weekly afternoon commitment. The nights were a different matter.

Alex flashed his eyes at me. "Last I heard, you two had dinner at the Tower Bar. That was six months ago. Either he was a one and done, or you somehow forgot to give us any updates."

I wasn't the best sharer in the world. "Fine, I'll catch you up over dinner."

Which would be easy, since Niko had been on tour giving master classes for the past six months.

NINE

It was a fun dinner—once they got over the fact that my "share" about Niko amounted to about three calls, none of which involved hot phone sex. And after what I'd just learned about the nonexistent nature of cell phone privacy, there'd be no "hot" anything on my calls. From now on, I planned to keep my cell phone conversations limited to the basics of where to meet and when.

The next morning, I was listening to the news, standing in front of my closet and trying to decide what to wear, when I heard a raw-sounding female voice say, "My name is Audrey Sutton."

I turned to the television and saw a rail-thin woman in her fifties with short, windblown hair and red-rimmed eyes holding a small sheet of paper in shaking hands. She continued. "My son, Roan Sutton, was found dead in his house last week. The coroner has issued a preliminary finding that he committed suicide. I am here to tell you that is not true. I know my son. He was not depressed; he was not suicidal. He was *murdered*. And he did not kill Alicia Hutchins!" Her voice broke, and she paused for a moment before continuing. "I'm calling on our city councilman, Lonnie Forrester, and our county supervisor, Shirley

Carmichael, to make the medical examiner do his job. And then make sure the police do theirs and catch the animal who killed my son!"

My first thought was, *Dale wasn't kidding*. My second thought was, *Get moving on Roan. Fast.* I had to find witnesses who'd say Roan was acting dicey after Alicia's death—like someone who'd commit suicide. Because if the autopsy left room for doubt, Audrey Sutton's plea might tip the scale in favor of homicide. I had to do whatever I could to keep that from happening.

I wasn't worried so much about Audrey's opinion. She wouldn't be the first mother to be in denial about a child's mental state or what he was capable of doing. But I was plenty worried about the statements Roan had given to the cops. Since they'd surely targeted Roan as the one who'd posted the revenge porn and killed Alicia, they weren't about to help set him up with a mental defense. As far as they were concerned, the saner he came off, the better. So I was betting those statements would only give Audrey Sutton more proof that he was sane and balanced, not the least bit suicidal.

The decision to find out what I could about Roan made my wardrobe choice easy. I'd be spending the day at USC, hunting down every source I could find that would paint a picture of Roan's behavior and state of mind—both before and after Alicia's death. And that meant the dress code of the day was jeans and a sweater. I need people to relax and spill their guts, and they tend to get nervous when they know they're talking to a lawyer. So I do my best to help them forget what I am. I dress down and try to fit in with the crowd.

While I put on my makeup, I called Alex and told him what our plans were for the day. "So you need to wear student-y clothes."

He has no problem with casual, but he does it with taste, and he hates it when we really have to go down-market.

He huffed. "I'm fine with jeans. And I'll even wear a hoodie. But I absolutely refuse to do those tacky friggin' sandals."

"I'd refuse to be seen with you if you did. Especially in November."

"Not in June, July, or August, either. I'm not kidding, those fugly, clunky things should be illegal. Unless you're a monk."

I had to laugh. "I'll pick you up at the office."

He paused. "Ah, how about I pick you up at your place, give you a break from driving?"

It sounded generous and thoughtful. It wasn't. "Your mistrust of Beulah is hurtful . . . and unfair."

Alex sighed. "Hurtful, maybe. Unfair? Girl, be serious. I want to make it to the campus sometime today. God forbid this case winds up in trial, but if it does, you'll have the money to buy a real car. And you'd better, because if you don't, I'll have someone torch it. I swear."

Since I couldn't deny that Beulah had crapped out on me repeatedly, and I hate being on the losing end of an argument, I capitulated. "Fine, be here in fifteen."

I finished my makeup, pounded three cups of coffee, and threw on a sweatshirt. Twenty minutes later, Alex and I were rolling toward the freeway. We talked about Audrey Sutton's television appearance, and I told him what I wanted to do. "We need to find out everything we can about Roan's state of mind. So we need to dig into his history as much as possible. In particular, I'd like to know whether he'd ever revenge porned any other girls before Alicia."

Alex glanced at me. "To see if she made him more nutso than usual?"

"Yeah. But even if he has done it before, I think we can argue that shows some mental issues, too."

Alex headed south on the 101 Freeway, which was packed. "It definitely shows he was a vindictive asshole. But I'm not sure it shows that he was as shaky as we'd like."

That was true. "No one thing will do that. It's going to be cumulative. He did revenge porn, *and* he wasn't sleeping well, *and* he was into Kurt Cobain—"

Alex shot me a look. "Hey, *I* like Nirvana."

"You know what I mean." I told him my worries about Roan's police statements.

He looked grim. "That's a bitch, all right. I don't suppose you'd be able to get the cops to admit they weren't looking for signs of mental problems?"

I stared out the window. "Oh, I'm sure they'll admit that. The problem is, it's not enough. It'll just seem like Roan was only as messed up as you'd expect any guy to be in his situation. They'll never admit that Roan looked seriously unhinged."

Alex turned to look at me. "Assuming he did."

I stared back at him. "Don't get all objective on me. We need him to be unhinged. Think positive." Making sure Roan's death stayed a suicide was our first—and best—line of defense.

I'd called Nomie before we left, but I got her voice mail, so I left a message asking her to let me know if she had time for a quick visit. Gayle answered at the house and said she'd be in class all day but that Davey and Phil should be there. Sure enough, Davey answered the door when we got there. I saw an open laptop on the dinette table. "I hate to break into your study time." Not enough to not do it, obviously.

Davey waved me off. "Gayle told me you were coming." He called out to Phil. "Hey, they're here."

A few seconds later, Phil came shuffling out in bare feet, his hair mussed up and scratching his stomach. Elegance and beauty personified. He headed into the kitchen and opened the refrigerator. "Get you guys anything? We've got beer."

I watched, amused, as he hung over the open refrigerator door. "No, we're good. Thanks."

Phil settled into the beanbag chair with his cup of blueberry yogurt, and Davey plopped down in the beanbag chair next to him. I asked whether either of them had seen Roan after Alicia died. As I'd expected, neither of them had. "What about before that—when was the last time you saw him?"

Phil stared into his yogurt cup. "I think maybe a week before Alicia said she wanted to take a break."

Davey said, "Probably around that same time."

I knew what they were going to say, but I had to ask. "Was he acting weird in any way? Depressed?"

Phil shrugged. "Not really." He looked at Davey. "You?"

Davey shook his head. "I didn't notice anything."

As I'd expected. I tried another tack. "Did Roan ever tell you about revenge porning any other girls before Alicia?"

Phil said no, but Davey did remember him mentioning it. "He didn't tell me her name, but yeah. I remember him saying some girl really had it coming, so he fucked her up."

YES. Progress. I leaned in. "Did he elaborate?"

Davey frowned, then shook his head. "Just said he'd posted her selfies on a website."

Alex had taken out his notebook and pen. He asked, "Did Roan mention which one?"

"No. At least, not that I remember." Davey paused. "But none of us was tight with Roan, so he really didn't talk to us much." He added, his tone sarcastic, "I'm sure you couldn't tell. I was actually pretty surprised when he told me about that other girl."

I wondered if Roan had done it deliberately, hoping Davey would carry the message back to Alicia—an implied threat about what would happen to her if she stepped out of line. "Did you tell Alicia about that?"

Davey reddened. "No. I wanted to, but . . ." He hung his head. "The thing is, we all knew he was bad news right from the start, so we tried to get her to drop him, but it just pissed her off. I figured if I told her, she'd just defend him—like she always did."

I nodded. "You're probably right."

Phil finished his yogurt and set the cup on the floor. "You should talk to his buddy Miguel."

Alex's lips twitched as he suppressed a smile. "You know a friend of Roan's?" I could hear the note of incredulity in his voice. We'd been asking for information on Roan since we sat down. It'd taken Phil this long to wake up and join the party.

Phil pulled a joint out of his pants pocket. "Yeah. Miguel. We were roomies our freshman year. I didn't know he was tight with Roan until Roan told me his bro Miguel had scored tickets to a Lakers game."

Alex wrote down the name. "Do you know Miguel's last name?"

Phil lit the joint and took a drag. "Miguel . . . ah . . . Lorenzo?" He blew out a long stream of smoke. "Yeah. Lorenzo. He lives about a block away from Roan, on Hoover."

It might be too much to hope for, but I asked anyway. "Do you happen to have a phone number for Miguel?"

Phil held the joint out to all of us—ever the polite host. Alex and I declined; Davey accepted. "Maybe. It's old, though." He took his phone out of his other pants pocket and scrolled. "Here you go." He read it off to Alex.

Alex wrote it down. But I knew that a friend of Roan's was unlikely to be a friend of ours. "Could you maybe check to see if he's around—without telling him about us?"

Phil studied me, then nodded. "Sure." He pressed a key on his phone, and after a few seconds, I heard a man's voice answer. Phil, wisely using Roan's death as cover for the call, offered his condolences. It was a brief conversation and when it ended, Phil told us Miguel was on his way home. "Told me to call him back in ten." He gave us the address. "If you head over there now, you'll catch him."

I wanted to get the lay of the land before we jumped off the cliff. "Did he seem pretty broken up?"

Phil stubbed out the joint in the ashtray on the coffee table. "Hard to tell. He was in the car. Said a cop was close by, so he couldn't stay on the phone. Guess you'll find out."

Davey gave us a sympathetic look. "Good luck."

I knew what he meant. A shitbird like Roan was unlikely to have a prince of a guy for a friend. Who says practicing law isn't fun?

TEN

The nice thing about our witnesses being USC students was that they all lived within a few miles of one another. It took Alex less than five minutes to find Miguel's place: an upstairs apartment accessed via an open staircase in a small four-unit building. It was a little farther from campus, which meant it had less of the student-poor vibe and more of the working-poor vibe—dying postage-stamp-size lawns sporting empty beer cans, bottles, and broken toys; old couches parked on curbs; and grimier, more run-down-looking houses.

As we moved toward the building, the smell of bacon grease wafted out through the window of the downstairs apartment, and a baby's wail, thin and insistent, mixed with the sound of a vacuum cleaner. But as we mounted the stairs, those sounds began to be drowned out by a heavy bass. By the time we got to the door of Miguel's apartment, the thumping bass was so loud it made the metal handrail vibrate. The music sounded like Hispanic hip-hop. I didn't recognize the artist.

I looked at Alex. "Ready?" He reached into his pocket, flipped on the mini-recorder, and nodded. I knocked on the door. No answer. I knocked harder. Still no answer. I knocked as hard as I could and called out, "Miguel?" The volume on the music was abruptly turned down. The door swung open, and the odors of pot and French fries floated out, making me simultaneously nauseous and hungry. A slender young man with shoulder-length black hair, dressed in baggy jeans and a plaid shirt over a white T-shirt, stood scowling at us. "Who are you?"

On the way over, Alex and I had worked out a lie about being affiliated with a watchdog group monitoring the LA coroner's office. But we obviously hadn't had time to dummy up business cards or pick up official-looking forms to put on clipboards. And this guy seemed too smart to game without the suitable accoutrements, so I made the snap decision to go with the truth. "I'm a lawyer, Samantha Brinkman, and this is my investigator, Alex Medrano. I assume you're Miguel Lorenzo?"

He passed a suspicious gaze between Alex and me. "What do you want?"

I knew we were about ten seconds away from a slamming door, so I went straight at it. "To ask you about Roan Sutton. I represent Alicia's father, Graham Hutchins—"

His expression darkened. "Roan didn't kill her. That's all I've got to say." He started to close the door.

Alex stepped in closer. "Was that Big Pun you were playing?" Miguel gave him a piercing look, then nodded. "Sounded like 'It's So Hard.'" Alex had a nostalgic look. "A classic. Too bad he checked out so young."

Miguel's expression softened a little. "Yeah. Heart attack. But the dude weighed, like, seven hundred pounds, so . . ." He threw me a flinty look, then gave Alex a chin bob. "I guess you can come in. But I got class at four thirty, so you'd better make it quick."

I glanced at my watch. That gave us only about a half hour. We'd need to loosen him up fast, and I had a feeling that wouldn't happen if I did the questioning. As we followed Miguel inside, I motioned to Alex to take the lead on this one.

The apartment just barely qualified as a one bedroom, with a small living room / dining room that was minimally separated from the tiny kitchen with a pass-through counter. The brown tweed sofa looked like it'd been "rescued" from the curb ten years ago. Looking at it, I had a feeling we weren't the only living things in that room. In front of it was a banged-up low-slung coffee table stacked with comic books, textbooks on graphic design, and artist sketch pads. Three plastic white lawn chairs faced the sofa on the other side of the coffee table. I sat in the one closest to the door for a fast escape in case whatever was living in the sofa made an appearance. Alex sat next to me.

Alex spoke in a soft, low voice. "How'd you and Roan meet up?"

Miguel sat on the sofa and spread his arms across the back. "I've actually known him since junior year in high school. Used to hang out, play video games, talk about designing our own."

Then he'd known Roan for quite a while. This was a lot better than I'd expected. I had to force myself to keep quiet. Alex continued. "Then I guess you'd say you guys were pretty tight."

Miguel stared at the coffee table. "In high school, yeah. A little less so once we got here, but we'd hang every so often."

Alex made a move to reach into his pocket. I knew he was about to take out his notebook, but I had a feeling Miguel would clam up if this started to look too official. Fortunately—maybe because he'd realized the same thing—Alex checked himself and dropped his hand back to his knee. "Did Roan talk to you about his girlfriends?"

Miguel gave a *humph* and a twist of a smile. "Of course. What else would we talk about?"

Alex—who'd probably never found girls to be a topic of choice—wisely opted not to answer that. "You remember anyone in particular?"

Miguel gave him a hard look. "No one he killed, if that's where you're heading."

Alex shook his head. "It wasn't. We're looking into the revenge-porn side of things. We think maybe one of the guys who saw her photos killed her."

Of course, we didn't think that. And even if it were true, it wouldn't do Graham any good. He'd still have a strong motive to kill Roan, since he'd believed—like everyone else—that Roan had killed Alicia. But the lie worked. Miguel relaxed. "Yeah, I remember him complaining about this girl named Laurie during our freshman year here. Said she was a drama queen, and her bullshit was driving him crazy. I know he broke up with her, but I don't remember him ever saying he posted her selfies on a porn website." Alex got Laurie's last name—Schoenberg—and the name of her dorm, Cardinal Gardens. Whether she was still there, Miguel didn't know. Alex moved on. "What do you think about the possibility that Roan committed suicide?"

Miguel set his jaw. "I don't believe it. That wasn't him. At all."

Alex didn't argue. His voice was mild as he asked, "He didn't get depressed or anything, then?"

Miguel looked out the window that faced the side of the next building. "I mean, yeah, sometimes. He had it kind of rough when he was a kid. His folks divorced when he was twelve. His dad kind of faded from the scene, and his mom just completely checked out. Some days she couldn't even get out of bed." He shook his head. "Lucky for him, he had a couple of older brothers who could at least put dinner on the table."

Alex spoke softly. "Seems to me like Roan had plenty of reasons to be depressed."

Miguel blew out a breath. "He never seemed depressed—at least not to me. But he could get kind of . . . intense, wound up." Miguel made a circle in the air with his finger. "Like his thoughts were racing, and he couldn't get out of a loop in his own mind."

Alex tilted his head and frowned. "Like, obsessive?"

Miguel pointed at him. "Exactly." He dropped his hands into his lap. "I don't want to believe he was feeling bad enough to kill himself without at least trying to talk to me. But . . ." Miguel sighed, his expression bleak. "I guess anything's possible. I mean, how well do we really know anyone?"

No argument there, but we needed some solid support for Roan's suicide, and this existential conundrum just wasn't going to cut it. Alex probed Miguel with a few more questions about Roan's state of mind—back then and more recently—but Miguel didn't have anything of substance to add.

We thanked him, and I gave him my card in case he thought of anything else we hadn't covered. I had not one shred of hope that I'd ever hear from Miguel, but he did put my card in his pocket. At least he didn't throw it in the garbage while I was standing there. I take my wins where I can find them.

When we got back to Alex's car, I asked if he knew of a way to find out whether Laurie Schoenberg was still at Cardinal Gardens. He gave me an icy look. "I'm going to pretend you didn't ask me whether I could do something that ridiculously easy." Alex pulled his iPad out from under the driver's seat and began tapping keys. "First bit of good news, Cardinal Gardens houses upperclassmen as well as freshmen. So she could totally still be there."

While Alex continued to type, I saw Miguel trot down the stairs and head toward campus, his backpack bouncing behind him. A few minutes later, Alex gave me a triumphant look. "I want you to repeat after me: I will never doubt you again, Alex."

I held up a middle finger. "Repeat this. What've you got?"

He gave me a flat look. "Witty." He read from his iPad. "Laurie's got a biology class until five o'clock. She's still in Cardinal Gardens. Her room number is—"

I held up a hand. "I don't care. I'm starving, and we have just enough time to hit McDonald's before we try to ambush her."

Alex made a face. "McDonald's? Seriously?"

The smell of fries at Miguel's apartment had been driving me crazy. I had to have some. I gave Alex a warning look. "Just give me some damn fries and no one gets hurt."

Alex smiled. "Yeah, the smell got to me, too."

Alex found a McDonald's, we got our fries, and by ten after five, we were standing in front of Laurie's building at the Cardinal Gardens dorm complex, hoping to snag Laurie on her way in.

Alex had pulled up a photo of Laurie Schoenberg, who was a serious-looking girl with lots of wavy black hair, wide-set brown eyes, and high cheekbones. She couldn't have looked more different from Alicia if she'd tried. My guess was that Roan's "type" had more to do with an emotional landscape than a physical one.

But as we watched the students stream past us, I started to lose hope. It'd be just dumb luck to find her this way—like trying to find a Democrat at the Country Music Awards. Plus, I was freezing. It was too cold to stand around like this. "What if she decided to go out to dinner? Or do some errands? Or go bang her boyfriend?"

Alex rolled his eyes. "Poetically put. Let's give it until five thirty. If we don't find her, I'm sure I'll be able to track her down tomorrow. I've got her class list."

By five thirty, I declared Laurie a no-show. "Come on, this one can wait until tomorrow." I turned and headed for the car. After a few seconds, Alex followed.

Back in the car, I checked my e-mail on Alex's iPad and found a Google Alert for Graham Hutchins. I'd learned to tag my high-profile clients so I could monitor what was being written about them. Also because they don't necessarily realize the importance of letting me know when the press hits them up. In Graham's case, it was much less of a worry. He was an experienced talking head on the cable circuit, and he knew how to handle himself. But I opened the link anyway, just out of curiosity. And . . . Shit. I leaned back and closed my eyes. This could not be happening.

Alex had just merged onto the northbound 101 Freeway. "What?"

I hadn't realized I'd said that out loud. "Graham just started a war."

ELEVEN

Alex threw me an alarmed look. "What do you mean?"

"Graham's still handling that basketball player's libel suit against the *Daily Sun* for their reporting on that rape charge. *TMZ* caught him on his way to court and asked him what he thought of Audrey Sutton's press statement saying the coroner got it wrong."

Alex was perplexed. "And he answered them?"

"I guess you could say that." I refreshed Graham's quote on my phone. "He said: 'Someone who could raise a murderer—and a lowlife who posted revenge porn—cannot be trusted to tell the truth. I'm sure she was just trying to pressure the coroner into calling it a homicide so she can squeeze money out of me with a wrongful-death suit.' End quote."

He echoed my sentiment. "Oh shit."

"Exactly." I punched in Graham's cell phone number and got his voice mail. I was just about to leave a message when a call came in on my phone. It was Graham. He'd undoubtedly checked to see the phone number of his caller before answering. I took the call and said, "Yeah, I'll bet you're screening."

Graham's voice was agitated. "Reporters have been blowing up my phone for the past two hours. They fucking chased me all the way to my car when I left court."

All his experience with high-profile cases, and this shocks him? "Look, I get it. You've been through hell this past week or so. But you can't do this." Ordinarily, I could trust Graham to figure out the likely consequences of what he'd done and know how to handle this fallout. But clearly, not now. "The reporters are probably parked on Audrey Sutton's doorstep as we speak. You should expect a reaction from her, and it won't be pretty. Whatever she says, do not respond in any way, shape, or form until you talk to me. Okay?"

He gave a heavy sigh. "Yeah, of course. I knew the minute I opened my mouth it was a mistake. What's going on with the investigation on Alicia's . . . case?"

I told him they were working on it, that even though it seemed obvious Roan was guilty, they still had to put together the evidence to prove it. Then I told him not to beat himself up about losing it with the reporter, that anyone with half a brain would understand he was in bad shape. "Just go home, pour yourself a drink, and let your partners handle your appearances for a few days. As long as you don't respond, the whole thing will blow over."

When I ended the call, Alex asked, "Is that true? Will it all blow over?"

"In theory." But I could already tell this case was going to bring me a whole new kind of crazy. The family on my side of the case usually kept a low profile. They knew better than to expect any public sympathy for their son/daughter/grandchild/niece/nephew—who'd *allegedly* killed/beaten/threatened the victim. Publicly grieving parents were usually the prosecutor's bailiwick. But if this case went to trial, I'd be walking about a hundred miles in their shoes.

Alex exited the freeway and headed south on Highland Avenue. "Are we going after Laurie tomorrow?" I nodded. "Then I might as well drop you home and pick you up in the morning. Her first class gets out at nine a.m. We'll have to leave by seven thirty if we want to make sure we catch her."

Which meant I had to be up by six thirty. Ugh. It's not that I'm one of those people who have to get at least eight hours a night. It's that I wake up screaming most nights by three or four a.m. and usually can't get back to sleep. It's the gift from my childhood—when I was tortured by the nightly visits of that ooze-sucking pond scum Sebastian Cromer—that keeps on giving. So just in case I do manage to nod off again, I try to keep early-morning business to a minimum. "Okay, but that little bitch had better not skip class tomorrow."

Alex raised an eyebrow. "Too bad that lucky, lucky girl doesn't realize how much she has to look forward to."

It was after seven p.m. by the time I got home. I was tired, cranky, and stressed. I poured myself a triple shot of Patrón Silver on the rocks, took it into the living room, and gazed out at the city. The one perk of my tiny apartment was its view. The building was at the top of a hill above Sunset Boulevard, and at night, the city lights sparkled from Santa Monica to downtown LA. Even the inching crawl of traffic looked beautiful, like a slow-moving river of lights.

I stretched out on the sofa and turned on the TV. I didn't want to see a replay of Graham's star turn on *TMZ*, but I did want to see if the Suttons had fired back at him yet. I flipped through all the news programs I could find. Nothing. So far, so good.

I hadn't spelled it out to Graham—I didn't think I needed to—but if this feud continued, it was more likely to hurt Graham than the Suttons. The Suttons weren't in danger of being charged with anything. But Graham was. And the safest move for the coroner's office would be to call Roan's death a "possible homicide." That way, the cops would have to do an investigation. Even if they didn't solve it, the coroner would be off the hook.

But if the conclusion was suicide, the cops would have no reason to investigate. In fact, if the cops did do an investigation, the police chief would probably take heat for wasting resources. He'd probably also get accused of pursuing a case that would ordinarily be dropped, just because it involved rich white kids. In that scenario, the coroner would be left holding the body bag with never-ending criticism—from Audrey Sutton and every parent who identified with her—that he'd let a murderer walk. The hotter the case got, the more likely it was that the coroner's office would decide to call it a "possible homicide" and drop it on the cops' doorstep.

So what we needed most was for the case to cool down and let people move on to the next tragedy. The last thing we needed was for Graham and Audrey Sutton to keep fighting.

But I couldn't lock Graham in a cage—much as I wanted to. All I could do was hope he'd learned his lesson. I poured myself another drink and rewatched the season finale of *Game of Thrones*. At one a.m., I crawled into bed and prayed I'd be too tired to dream.

It almost worked. The nightmare—in which I'm repeatedly stabbing Sebastian, who not only doesn't die but also grows into a twenty-foot monster that pins me to the wall, and ends as he opens a giant maw of a mouth to devour me—woke me up at five thirty. For me, that wasn't half-bad. I wanted to lie in bed for a little longer, but my throat was scraped raw from screaming and I'd forgotten to bring a bottle of water to bed with me. I got up and headed for the bathroom.

Alex showed up at seven thirty sharp with coffee and bagels—the true way to my heart. We're comfortable enough not to need to make small talk—not that either of us was the type to try—and we said little as Alex wove his way through the morning rush-hour traffic. It was heavier than usual, so much so that when we finally made it to the campus, we had to break into a run to get to Laurie's class in time.

I was still panting—and trying not to show it—as the students began to trickle out. Laurie was among the last, bringing up the rear in a crowd that encircled the professor—a young Ryan Gosling look-alike. I'm sure that had nothing to do with the size—or the overwhelmingly female percentage—of the entourage that followed him out. Seeing Laurie's shining eyes as she looked at him made me decide to deploy Alex. "Go get 'er, cowboy."

Alex glared at me, but he moved toward her quickly. I lagged behind to give him time to work his magic. And even from ten feet away, I could see it in action. When he said, "Ms. Schoenberg?" Laurie at first turned toward him with an irritated look. But that irritation turned to sunshine as she registered Alex's gorgeousness. It never fails.

I caught up with them as Alex was introducing himself. When I joined them, he included me in the introduction as well. She gave me a shrewd look. "This is about Roan, isn't it?"

Thanks, *TMZ*. I admitted it was. "I hate to bother you at a time like this. I know you and Roan had a relationship and that he broke up with you—"

Laurie's eyes widened. "What?"

The word had a few extra *T*s the way she said it. "No? That's wrong?"

She gave an angry head toss, her tone sarcastic. "Uh, yeah. Totally wrong. That friggin' dickhead—" She paused. "Sorry, I know I shouldn't speak ill of the dead and all that. But I didn't exactly sit shivah when I heard Roan committed suicide. And where on earth did you get the idea that *he'd* broken up with *me*?"

I was glad she wasn't mourning and even gladder she was pissed off at him. "His friend Miguel."

Laurie's expression turned cynical. "That figures."

There must have been about twenty classes in the same building because students kept jostling us as they moved in and out. "Want to go sit somewhere a little more comfortable?"

Laurie pointed to a patio to the left of the building, where there were tables, chairs, and vending machines. "I'd take us to the dining hall, but I've got another class in fifteen minutes."

I held up a hand. "Not a problem. I appreciate this."

We sat down at a table in the far corner of the patio, and I bought myself a cup of coffee. I'd worked up a sweat when we ran across the campus, and now the cold air was turning that sweat to ice. I offered to buy Laurie a cup of coffee or snack, but she declined and patted her stomach. "I'm still trying to get rid of the 'freshman fifteen.'"

Alex smiled his sparkling smile. "You look great to me."

Laurie blushed a little. "That's really nice of you."

I gave Alex a hard look, signaling him to knock it off. I had a lot of ground to cover, and we couldn't waste any of it while he flexed his sexy-guy muscles. "Did you know Miguel?"

Laurie took a second to refocus, then shook her head. "No. I just meant it figured that's what Roan would've told his friend."

It did figure. "Then I take it the truth is that you broke up with him." Laurie nodded. "When was that? And can you tell me why?"

Laurie raked a hand through her hair. "Last year. He was my first boyfriend in college. Lucky friggin' me. Things were cool at first. He seemed super into me, great for the ego, you know?" I nodded. "But then he started to get more and more possessive. He wouldn't let me do anything by myself. Got totally PO'd when I went to a movie with my roomies."

There was an obvious pattern here. "Did he make you call him a lot?"

Laurie looked momentarily surprised, then nodded. "He did it to Alicia, too?"

I said, "He made her call him three times a day. Did he do the same with you?"

Laurie's expression turned glum. "Yeah, and it drove me crazy. I let it go on for way too long, but I finally broke up with him."

I wrapped my hands around the cup of coffee for warmth. "How did he take it?"

Laurie suddenly bit her lip, and I saw her eyes fill. "He . . ." She blinked back the tears. "You know what he did to Alicia?" I nodded. "He did that to me, too."

I gritted my teeth and tried to control the anger in my voice. "You mean revenge porn?" Laurie nodded. "Did he post it on a website called XXXtraSpecial?"

Laurie shook her head. "No, it was a different one." Her cheeks reddened, and she dipped her head for a moment, then said, "I heard he included her address and an invitation to rape her; is that true?" I told her it was. "He didn't do that to me." She swallowed hard. "Just posted my self—ah, my photos."

"Just." Welcome to college. I guess it could've been worse. She could've been roofied and gang-raped while a group of their friends watched and filmed it on their phones. But I kept my bitter thoughts to myself. "Can you tell me what website Roan posted them on?"

She gave a half glance at Alex, then dropped her head.

Alex, his expression grim, asked, "They're still up, aren't they?" She nodded, her expression miserable. "I won't look, I promise."

A tear, resisting her best efforts to stop it, rolled down her cheek. "I tried to get them taken down, but I couldn't find the website owner."

I put a hand on her shoulder. "If you give us the name of the website, Alex might be able to help you."

Alex gave her a Kleenex. His look of sympathy even melted *my* heart. "I'll try and get them taken down," he said.

Laurie's face cleared, and her voice had a thin ray of hope. "Do you think you can?" Alex said he'd give it his best. She pulled out her cell phone, typed, and then scrolled. She handed it to me.

The website was HOT GRLZ XXX. As she'd said, it wasn't the same website where Alicia's photos had been posted. But like Alicia's selfies, Laurie's poses were relatively tame, her makeup minimal and natural. And though she'd tried to put on a sexy smile, she, too, had that same vulnerable, semiscared look. I wrote down the website and gave the phone back to her. Alex asked her a few more questions about her efforts to get the photos taken down, and then I moved on to the final piece of business.

I didn't expect—and didn't want—to hit pay dirt with this one. "Do you remember where you were when you heard about Roan's death?"

Laurie blinked a couple of times. "No, not really."

I pushed a little harder. "It happened ten days ago. On November eighth. Can you tell me where you were that night?"

Laurie paused, then gave me an incredulous look. "You're checking my alibi?"

I didn't bother to deny it. "I have to ask."

A little smile lifted the corners of her mouth. "I guess I can't blame you; I did fantasize about killing the asshole. But I do have an alibi. I was in Dayton, Ohio, for my grandfather's funeral. You can check airline records, class records, dorm records, whatever."

I answered her smile with a conciliatory one of my own. "Sorry."

Laurie waved off the apology. "It's cool. If he didn't kill himself, I'd like to hang a medal on whoever killed him."

I suspected she was about to have a lot of company, and I needed to warn her about that. "This case has been in the news, and if it keeps heating up, you'll probably hear from the press."

I could see her blanch as she processed the fact that that would mean thousands more eyes on her photos. She gave Alex a pleading look. "Can you . . . ?"

His gaze was serious. "I'll do everything I can."

Hopefully he'd get her photos down by the time reporters found her. But her story would do Graham a lot of good.

The more people who thought Roan needed killing, the better.

TWELVE

Alex and I headed back to his car. As we buckled up, he asked, "Alicia's building?"

"Yep." It was time to talk to neighbors and find out what the cops had missed. According to their reports, no one had seen or heard anything amiss on the night of Alicia's murder. One neighbor corroborated Gayle's sighting of the crew-cut guy earlier that day, but that same neighbor—plus one other—had seen Alicia leave the building after he was gone. I was sure we could get more out of them than that. But even as I mentally prepared for our next interviews, I couldn't stop thinking about Laurie's predicament. "How're you going to get those photos taken down?"

Alex pulled out and edged into traffic. "I'm going to try and track down the website owners and . . . figure out a way to persuade them."

"Let me know when you get to the persuading part." I could help him with that. But as to the former, he was on his own.

It took just five minutes to get to Alicia's apartment. The small beige stucco building was sandwiched between houses clearly occupied by students—maroon-and-gold Trojan banners in windows, sheets dyed with peace symbols for curtains, multiple bicycles and mopeds, etc. And it had only eight units: four upstairs, four downstairs. I expected the manager's apartment to be on the downstairs level. Upper-level floors are more coveted—mostly by women, for security reasons. But I didn't see a manager's sign on any of the doors. Then I remembered the police reports hadn't mentioned any contact with a manager. Maybe he or she didn't live on the premises.

We started with the downstairs level and knocked on the first door on the left. It was the apartment directly below Alicia's. An elderly man with flyaway white hair that swirled around his head like a baby bird, dressed in worn-shiny slacks with suspenders, a T-shirt with yellowed stains on the armpits, and house slippers, answered the door. He peered at us through thick wire-frame glasses. "You back again?" He bored in on Alex. "I told you guys I'm not talking to any reporters. Go away." He started to close the door.

Alex held up a hand and talked fast. "Wait! I'm not a reporter. We've never been here before." He pointed to me. "She's a lawyer; I'm her investigator. We're working for Alicia's father."

The old man—listed on the police report as Oliver Chalmers—shot Alex a sideways glance, then gave me the once-over. "What do you want from me? I didn't see anything."

According to the police report, though, he had seen a man leaving the building who fit the description Gayle had given—whom I'd taken to calling Crew Cut. And Chalmers had seen Alicia leave the building after he'd gone. I asked him about Crew Cut. "Had you ever seen him here before?"

He stuck out his lower lip. "No. Never seen him since, either. And I know Alicia was still alive when he left, so I don't know what he has to do with anything."

Whatever the condition of his eyesight, old Oliver's mental faculties and hearing seemed to be just fine. "Did you hear any unusual sounds coming from Alicia's apartment?"

He gave me an irritable frown. "I told all this to the police already."

There was no mention of his hearing anything in the reports. Either the unis hadn't written it down, or Dale had held out on me. I told Oliver that it wasn't in the police reports. "Can you tell me what you heard?"

He gave a grunt. "Some bumping around, like maybe she was moving some furniture or something."

I looked over his shoulder at the walls in his apartment. They didn't look all that thick, and sound can really travel between floors. "Did you hear any voices?"

Oliver screwed up his face, making his features bunch together. "Thought I heard hers. Maybe that guy's, too. Sounded like a higher voice and then a lower voice. Wasn't much, maybe went on for a minute or so. That's it."

I glanced at Alex to make sure he was getting all this. He had his notepad out, but he wasn't even pretending to be writing it down. That told me his recorder was definitely on. "By 'that guy,' do you mean the one with the crew cut?"

He nodded. "Kinda heavyset. Too old to be a student. Looked like a construction worker. Walked back and forth in front of the building a couple of times, like he wasn't sure he was in the right place. That's what caught my eye."

This was more detail than I'd seen in the report. More reason to think there was a follow-up report I didn't get. "Did you see him go up to Alicia's apartment?"

He pointed to the stairs behind us. "Saw him go up, but I didn't see what apartment he went to."

"But you did hear voices," I said.

Oliver paused and sucked in his lips. "About ten, fifteen minutes later."

A weird time gap. "Was Alicia home when you first saw him in front of the building?"

He pushed his glasses farther up his nose and stared off for a moment. "Hadn't thought of that before, but now that you mention it, no. She wasn't. I saw him go upstairs, and then five or ten minutes later, I saw her head toward the stairs."

So Crew Cut might've been waiting for her. "Do you remember what time that was?"

Oliver shrugged. "I don't know exactly. Kinda late in the afternoon. Maybe around four or so."

Alex asked, "Did you see him leave?"

He shook his head. "But I heard him. Wasn't that long after Alicia got home—maybe a few minutes after—he went clomping back down the stairs." He saw me about to ask the next question and cut me off. "Not saying it was him a hundred percent. But I know who lives upstairs, and no one walks that heavy."

I pushed to see if he'd hold firm. "Could've been someone else's boyfriend."

He shrugged. "Could be. Just don't think so."

Oliver Chalmers was going to make a great witness if things got that far. "Did you see Alicia again that day?"

His expression saddened. "I got tired, took a nap, but I know she went out after that guy left, 'cause I heard her come home later that night. I recognized her step."

It occurred to me that Oliver might be helpful on another tack. The "he needed killing" tack. "Was there a guy who visited Alicia during the past month or so?"

He squinted at me again. "You mean that skinny one with the big mouth?"

I pressed my lips together to keep from smiling. "I think so." I pulled up Roan's photo on my phone and showed it to him. "Does that look like the guy?"

Oliver made a stink face. "Yep. That's the one."

I liked where this was going. "Did you have a run-in with him?"

He stuck out his chin. "I sure did. He was standing outside her door and yelling and screaming. Using all kinds of rough language. I wouldn't have it. I came out and told him to stop. He yelled at me, called me names, then he kicked a hole in the door." Oliver snorted. "A bully and a punk, if you ask me."

"Was that the only time you heard him yelling at Alicia?"

"I heard him hollering at her a few other times, but those times he was inside her apartment."

This was perfect. I went back to Crew Cut. "You said you heard the burly guy leave the building. But you didn't notice how long after that Alicia left?"

He sighed. "I didn't see her go. Only reason I know she did leave was because I saw her come home later that night." Oliver paused and dropped his gaze. "Never did see her again, though. Terrible what happened to her. Just don't see why anyone would do a thing like that— least not to someone like her."

I had no answer for him. And after a few more minutes, it was clear Oliver was out of answers, too.

We thanked him and moved on to other neighbors. The two downstairs apartments at the back of the building were occupied by male students, all of whom knew Alicia, all of whom were clearly upset by her death, but none of them had seen or heard Crew Cut or Alicia that day. Not surprising given the fact that they were behind the stairway and had no view of the front of the building. And the cops had checked their alibis and cleared all of them as potential suspects.

A young Mexican couple occupied the apartment at the front, across from Oliver Chalmers. Oliver had said they pretty much kept to themselves and were almost never around. "Those guys work all day and all night."

When we went to their door, Alex sniffed. "Someone's home. I smell cooking, might be mole sauce."

I knocked, and a young woman in her twenties with long black hair pulled into a high ponytail answered the door. I introduced Alex and myself and began to ask her if she'd seen Crew Cut, but her expression told me she was having a hard time understanding me. I let Alex take over. He asked her in Spanish if she'd been home on the day in question. She said she and her husband had been at work and didn't get home until after nine. They'd never seen Crew Cut, and they hadn't seen anything suspicious on the night Alicia got killed. The woman made the sign of the cross and said it was a tragedy what had happened.

We headed upstairs. Alicia's apartment was on the left, at the end of a short, open hallway, and it faced the front of the building. Crime-scene tape still crisscrossed the front door. That surprised me. It'd been a good ten days since her death. Usually, the cops release a scene within a week. I wondered whether that meant anything or whether there was just no push from the property owner to release the crime scene. The latter seemed likely. I doubted there'd be any big demand for the apartment where a young student had just been murdered.

A Vietnamese family lived in one of the rear-facing apartments. The father was at work, and the mother spoke no English, but her twelve-year-old daughter did, and she agreed to translate. I asked whether anyone in the apartment had seen Alicia the day she died.

Chinh, the little girl, said she had not; she had been at a friend's house that day. But when she posed the question to her mother, the older woman gave a long answer. Chinh translated. "My mother says that she saw Alicia leave the building that night, after the bad man came. She says Alicia looked very upset."

The bad man—another sighting of Crew Cut? Or someone else? "Can she describe the man? And tell us what he did that made her think he was bad?"

Chinh posed the questions, and her mother gave another lengthy answer. "The man was big"—she held her hands about two feet apart to show he was wide—"and he had very short hair. My mother says he didn't really do anything bad. She just didn't like his . . . his vibe."

That was Crew Cut. It had to be. I looked from the very traditional mother to the daughter. "She said 'vibe'?"

Chinh sighed. "No. But that's what she meant. Some words just don't translate."

Point taken. "Was the bad man gone by the time Alicia left?"

Chinh translated my question again, and her mother responded. Chinh asked her what I assumed were a few clarifying questions, then turned back to me. "She doesn't know, but she heard the door open and close, and then about an hour later, she saw Alicia leave. So she thinks probably he was gone."

That meant Crew Cut might actually have gotten inside Alicia's apartment. "Would your mother recognize him if she saw him again?"

Chinh posed the question. This time, I didn't need Chinh to translate the answer. The mother nodded emphatically. This mother would come in handy if we could find him.

I bumped around with a few more questions, hoping for more details on the comings and goings around Alicia's apartment, but the mother had gone to bed shortly after Alicia left.

Chinh confirmed it. "We all get up real early and go to bed early. Even me." She looked a little embarrassed. "I think it must be genetic or something."

We talked for a few more minutes, then thanked Chinh and her mother and headed to the other rear-facing apartment upstairs, where four more male students lived.

I started to knock, but Alex held up a hand as he looked at his phone. "These guys were all down in Palm Springs at the time of the murder."

I'd seen that in the police report. "Since when do we take the cops' word for it?"

He gave me an impatient look. "Since *I* checked their alibis. They weren't here."

Oh. "Then maybe you can save us some more time. Anything you want to share about our next and last stop?" The last of the units was the other front-facing apartment across the stairway from Alicia's apartment. Four female students shared the two-bedroom space.

Alex scrolled through his phone again. "Three of them were down in Palm Springs."

I sighed. "Let me guess: they were with the guys in 2C."

Alex smirked. "I'm sure they were studying for midterms. The only one home was Bethany." He glanced at his phone again. "Bethany Archer."

It turned out Bethany, a tall, model-thin African American student, was the one I'd heard about on the news, the one who'd also seen Crew Cut—and saw Alicia leave the apartment later that evening. Bethany was sure Alicia left "two or three hours" after she noticed Crew Cut on the landing near Alicia's apartment.

But that's all she could tell us. She couldn't say whether he got inside Alicia's apartment or, if he did, when he finally left. Nor could she say when Alicia came home.

Bethany looked apologetic. "I was on the phone having a major fight with my boyfriend—he was being such a dick. So I decided to hell with it, I'm outta here, and I went down to Palm Springs. All I know is, I saw Alicia leaving as I was locking up, and I didn't see the guy anywhere around."

We chatted with Bethany about what she knew of Alicia—which wasn't much beyond the fact that she'd thought Alicia's boyfriend was "fire"—until she learned he'd probably killed her.

After a few minutes, I had to call it quits. As we left the building, I called Michelle. "We're on our way back. How's it going? Any new clients? Preferably rich ones who insist on paying cash?"

Michelle sounded upset. "I was just about to call you. The rich one you already have is going to have a fit when he sees this. I'm sending you the link right now."

I looked at the link. "Oh hell."

"Exactly."

THIRTEEN

As soon as we got into the car, I played the link. As I'd feared, Audrey Sutton had fired back. And no more impromptu appearances on the front lawn for Audrey. This time she was in a studio, with full makeup, and seated across from a fawning reporter I didn't recognize. I noticed a piece of paper was in her lap. A speech? If so, she wasn't reading from it now.

Audrey spoke straight to the reporter, and, curried and coiffed though she was, her anger came off her in waves. "Money has *nothing* to do with it! But it figures that a man who raised the kind of daughter who sends nude selfies would think that."

The reporter baited her. "But didn't your son post those photos on the porn website?"

Audrey almost came out of her seat. "He most certainly did not! Roan would never have done such a thing. That girl was obviously nothing but a little slut. Who knows how many boys she was seeing? Or how many she sent dirty photos to? That's who killed her, one of those guys. Not Roan! Not my son!" She paused to take a breath, then spoke with a bloody intensity. "That monster, Graham Hutchins, came to a snap judgment based on no evidence whatsoever and killed him!"

The reporter's voice oozed feigned sympathy. "Audrey, do you have something you want to say to the city officials and coroner's office?"

She tried to rein it in, but her hands were shaking. She folded them in her lap. "Roan did *not* commit suicide. But since the county coroner is too incompetent to figure that out, I've hired a private pathologist to examine my . . . my . . . son's body." Audrey's voice caught, and she had to stop to collect herself. Then she picked up the piece of paper that was in her lap and began to read.

"I have stood by and watched as the coroner and the police drag their feet and refuse to do their jobs, just because the killer is a wealthy, influential lawyer. I know my son did not kill Alicia. And Roan would never have committed suicide. Graham Hutchins is a murderer, and I will not rest until I see him behind bars. That is why I have hired Dr. Cecil Mortimer, a nationally renowned private pathologist. I have every faith that Dr. Mortimer will arrive at the truth, and that the truth will finally bring Graham Hutchins to justice. I want to thank the kind and generous people who have sent in the donations that made this possible." She put down the paper and looked at the reporter. Her cheeks were flushed, and her voice shook as she said, "I know Dr. Mortimer is going to find that Roan was murdered, and when he does, I want the police to finally do their job and arrest Graham Hutchins!"

The link ended on the image of Audrey's furious face. I'd thought she might retaliate, but this was even worse than I'd expected. I'd been looking for alternative suspects to prepare for the remote possibility that Roan's death might get classified as a homicide. But deep down, I'd been fairly confident that wouldn't happen, that the coroner would ultimately reach the conclusion that it was a suicide.

Now, all bets were off. I didn't know anything about Dr. Cecil Mortimer, but I did know something about privately retained experts.

They tended to lick the hand that fed them. A private pathologist would do backflips to find a way to claim Roan was murdered just so he could grab his big media moment—and probably make some pretty nice dough.

And that would put added pressure on the county coroner. If there was any gray area in his findings, an outside expert's contrary opinion might just be the extra nudge that would push him into changing his opinion and declaring Roan's death a homicide. I slumped down in my seat. "This could be a real disaster."

Alex looked perplexed. "I know Audrey's paying him and all. But couldn't this Dr. Mortimer wind up agreeing that it was a suicide?"

"In a perfect world, where all private experts are ethical—and clouds rain M&M's and Colin Farrell's begging me for a date."

Alex sighed and nodded. "I'll check him out."

We headed back to the office. When we got in, the phone was ringing, and Michelle looked harried. "Reporters have been calling nonstop. They want a comment on Audrey Sutton's interview and her hiring that private pathologist."

I wanted to punch the wall and scream. "Okay, here's my friggin' comment: I think it's amazing that the woman who called an innocent murder victim a slut just publicly announced that she'd hired herself a real, pay-for-play whore. And by the way, if Alicia was such a slut, then what does that make her son?"

Michelle sighed. "I think we'll just go with a 'Could not be reached for comment' for now." She hit a key on her computer. "But Graham's going crazy. He's been calling every ten minutes. You need to talk him down."

I could well imagine he was losing it. I would be, too. Even without knowing what Dr. Mortimer would find, just hearing that a private pathologist was coming into the case would make the public, AKA our jury pool, more suspicious of Graham. I went into my office and called him. He was both scared and fuming. "Who is this whore pathologist Mortimer? And how dare that woman talk about my daughter that way? I'm going to sue her for libel and take every last penny she's got!"

I spoke as calmly as I could. "Which will probably amount to twelve dollars and fifty-two cents." Alex had hacked into Roan's school records. He was getting by on a combination of student loans and a partial scholarship. "And all you'll do is keep this fight going. That's the last thing we need right now. As for Mortimer, I've got Alex checking into him. But I think we should consider getting our own pathologist, see if we can get some more support for the suicide finding." I knew Graham understood the value of battling experts. If we got someone good—and Graham could certainly afford to hire the best—it'd help to cast doubt on Mortimer's conclusion if he concluded that Roan's death was a homicide. "But we don't have to do it right now. I doubt Mortimer's going to move that fast." Especially if he billed by the hour.

Graham's anger had ebbed, and now his voice sounded ragged, worn. "That's probably a good idea. But if we've got time, then let's hold off for now. I know it's crazy to think this guy will be honest . . ."

"It is, but there's no harm in waiting to see what he says." I needed to get back to our more immediate problem. "Look, Graham, about Audrey Sutton. I know it's awful to have to hear what she's saying. But we need to stay above it, let it die down. So turn off your TV, stay off your computer, and—"

He interrupted me. "Bella Hanberry wants us to do an interview."

Bella was a local morning-show anchor who liked to do human-interest pieces. Ordinarily, I'd be fine with it. She was pretty low-key. But I couldn't be sure that she wouldn't try to goad Graham into a slugfest over Audrey Sutton's remarks.

I had to be careful how I handled this. Given the mood Graham was in, if I pushed back too hard, he might tell me to shove it. "I like

Bella. That's a great way to tell people who Alicia really was. But let's give it a little bit of time, okay? You want people to focus on Alicia, not on what Audrey Sutton said."

Graham took a little convincing. In true trial-lawyer fashion, he wanted to fire back right away, drown out what she'd said, and get in the last word. But I explained that it wouldn't work that way. He'd just provoke an even bigger war—one that would do neither Alicia nor Graham any good. By the time we were done, he seemed to have accepted the wisdom of laying low. For now, at least.

It was six o'clock by the time we finished the call, and I had other cases to attend to. I finished my sentencing memo and did some more research on my motion to suppress a client's confession.

The latter had looked promising at first: the cop had glossed over his right to have a lawyer appointed for him. But my client was a chatterbox who seemed to think the cop really meant it when he said my client was "basically a good guy." He'd taken the bait and told the cop he was a good guy, too, and that's why he'd agreed to talk to him—even though *he knew his rights* and *knew* he didn't have to talk to the cop *without a lawyer*. The motion was basically DOA. I was performing triage on a corpse.

Michelle came in as I was trying to find some case authority to resurrect it. "It's almost eight. You staying?"

I leaned back in my chair and stretched. I definitely didn't want to. "I'd better. I need to do some catching up."

She put a hand on her hip. "Speaking of catching up, you need to get busy with your time sheets."

I groaned. "I'll do it tomorrow." I have to submit time sheets to the county in order to bill for my court-appointed cases. But filling them out makes watching paint dry seem like a white knuckler.

Michelle folded her arms. "No, you won't."

She was right. I wouldn't. "Okay, fine. I'll do it now." My motion to suppress that confession was a waste of time anyway. My time would be better spent trying to beat the DA into submission to give my client a deal.

Michelle put on her coat and wrapped a burgundy-fringed scarf around her neck. "Want me to have a pizza sent up?"

That sounded perfect. "Sure. Thanks."

One minute later, Alex came in and told me that he'd checked out the guy Alicia had thought was stalking her. "We can cross him off the list. He was in San Diego that whole week."

I hadn't held out any real hope that the apartment manager would pan out anyway. But it was one more setback at the end of a day that had already delivered some major blows. "Great. Perfect. Any more leads you'd like to shred while you're at it?"

He raised an eyebrow. "Not tonight." He pointed a finger at the paperwork on my desk. "Whatever you're doing, you should wrap it up and go home. You're in a mood."

I didn't argue. Mainly because he was right. I gave him a bitchy smile and waggled my fingers at him. "Bye, see ya."

He rolled his eyes and went out to pick up Michy.

They left the office, and I pulled out my time sheets and dived into the drudgery of adding numbers with decimal points. Half an hour later, the buzzer sounded at the outer door. It startled me at first, then I remembered Michelle had said she'd ordered pizza for me.

My stomach grumbling in anticipation, I went out to Michelle's desk and hit the button to unlock the door.

And let in two of the biggest men I'd ever seen. The one on the left was white, bald, and had a multicolored tattoo of an eagle on his head. The one on the right looked Hispanic and had slicked-back black hair. Both had the kind of thick, hard muscle that bulges through even an extra-large shirt.

I swallowed the bile that was rising in my throat and tried to act calm. "Can I help you?"

The bald guy let his gaze travel casually around the office before returning to me. His voice was deep. "You need to come with us. Now." His tone said no one had ever refused.

I pictured my Smith & Wesson .38 in the drawer of my desk. If I ran, I could probably get to it before they got to me.

But then the Hispanic guy spoke. "Javier Cabazon wants to see you."

I stopped breathing. Any thought of resistance came to a screeching halt. I might be able to temporarily scare off these gorillas, but I'd never be able to outrun Cabazon. "I'll get my coat."

FOURTEEN

Their car—a blacked-out Range Rover—was parked on the street. I felt like I was moving between two buildings that'd come to life as we headed to the car. The Hispanic guy sat in the back with me. The white guy drove. He headed west on Sunset for about twenty minutes, then turned right. I saw that we were on Stone Canyon Road. Bel Air. It figured Cabazon would live there. Last I checked, so did Sebastian, the billionaire child raper.

But unlike Sebastian, my trouble with Cabazon was largely of my own making. It was a perfect example of how one stupid, impulsive act can snowball into an avalanche that buries you alive.

It all started with a court-appointed case, the type no one wanted. Which was why Judge Crowder had let me know he'd owe me big time if I took this one off his hands. "This one" was Ricardo Orozco, a shot caller for the Grape Street Boyz, and a more foul, despicable piece of human excrement would have been hard to find. He'd led the attack on the house of a shot caller from the rival gang, the Southside Creepers. He and a couple of his gang homies fired more than a hundred rounds into the place—only to discover that they had the wrong house. And managed in the process to kill a six-month-old baby and maim a twelve-year-old girl for life. Even his own gang members had posted and tweeted their shame about what had happened. Not Ricardo. He'd laughed about how the girl was a *puta* and how "now she was never gonna get laid with that gimp leg," and said the baby was "pra'ly just gonna grow up to be a fuckin' Southside Creeper piece of shit" and was "better off dead."

It was one of the few times in my life I would've been okay with losing a case. Unfortunately, the case against Ricardo hinged on a single eyewitness. When that witness went belly-up (thanks to the usual—though unprovable—gang persuasion), the only charge left standing was illegal possession of a firearm by an ex-con. The cops had found a gun in Ricardo's bedroom—not the murder weapon—when they'd served a search warrant on his place. I'd squeezed the prosecutor for a deal—the low term of sixteen months in state prison—in return for his guilty plea. It was a deal Ricardo was happy to take because, with credits for good time and work time, it was just an eight-month vacay with his homies.

He'd given me a sneering grin of triumph as the bailiff led him away. That finally pushed me over the edge. I lost my shit. And did something really stupid. I sidled over to the bailiff's desk, flipped through the custody sheet that shows who's supposed to go where, and changed Ricardo's prison cell assignment. To the Southside Creeper tank. The guards ushered him into the wing at 1:04 p.m. By 1:05, he was dead.

The sheriff's office launched an investigation, of course. But the sheriff's investigation was the least of my worries. Ricardo's father, Ernesto, and his maniacal brother, Arturo, didn't trust the deputies to do an honest job. And because I'd gotten such a great deal for the dearly departed Ricardo, they wanted to hire me to find out what had really happened. I had no choice; I had to take the case so I could control what they learned and buy time to figure a way out of that mess.

Over the next few months, I sweated out visits with them that grew increasingly ugly as, week after week, I failed to serve up the guilty party. Ultimately, it was Dale who helped me set up an already dead sheriff's deputy as the fall guy by cobbling together counterfeit Facebook postings that supposedly showed the deputy was affiliated with the Southside Creepers and had deliberately put Ricardo in the wrong tank as payback for the shooting.

The Orozcos had grudgingly accepted the explanation when I presented them with that "proof," but I could tell they weren't happy. It left them with no one to punish. The deputy was already dead. But as days went by without any further contact, I'd thought I was in the clear.

Until I came home one night to find Javier Cabazon in my living room. Ernesto and Arturo Orozco, two of the many gang leaders who worked for Cabazon, had told him they didn't buy my story. Based on information they'd gotten from a friend of the court clerk—who'd seen me near the bailiff's desk—they believed I'd been the one who altered the custody list. Since I was a dangerous target, i.e., someone whose death would get some attention, they had to get his permission to kill me.

Senor Cabazon told them he would have his people check out my story. A few days later, he gave the Orozcos the result of his investigation: I had not done it. I'd told them the truth; it was the sheriff's deputy, who was indeed an affiliate of the Southside Creepers. The Orozcos accepted the verdict. Not that they had a choice. They might run the Grape Street Boyz, but Cabazon ran an international operation. Cabazon was a fleet of tanks. The Orozcos were the back wheel of a bicycle.

When Cabazon told me that he'd backed my story, I thanked him for confirming to the Orozcos that I had told the truth. He was not amused. In a voice as sharp and cold as a surgical knife, he told me that he had connections everywhere—including in the Southside Creepers—and he knew the deputy had nothing to do with Ricardo's prison placement or the Creepers. He knew I had done it. And he had no objection. He thought Ricardo was an "embarrassment."

But then he uttered the words that'd filled me with dread: he was sure a lawyer and her detective father would prove to be useful to him one day.

And now, that day had come.

We pulled up to a massive set of gates. The driver reached out and pressed his thumb to a glass pad set into a brick column. The gates slowly opened. As he pulled into the driveway, I noticed surveillance cameras mounted on the pillars on either side. The driveway became a winding road that wove through a forest of trees. There were men in camouflage fatigues who were armed with assault rifles at various points. From what I could see, they encircled the property. It felt like we'd been driving for an hour by the time we emerged from the forest, though realistically, it couldn't have been more than a couple of minutes.

To call the building that loomed above the trees a house would be like calling Fort Knox a safe-deposit box. It was at least three stories high, the width of three city streets, had at least four medieval-looking turrets—probably more behind the building—and each of them had two armed guards.

As we parked at the foot of the dark-green stone steps, I noticed that the builder had used that same stone on the residence. The color was likely an effort to make the place blend in with the surroundings—but the choice of stone was likely an effort to make the place bulletproof, a feature that was obviously a high priority. Neither of my two escorts held onto me as we moved up the steps toward a massive set of doors. Why bother? Even if I managed to outrun them, there was an army in the trees behind me. I wouldn't make it ten steps.

For all its massive size, the exterior of the Cabazon *casa* was fairly plain and austere. No fancy architectural details. So I expected the interior to be more of the same. But as I entered the house, I saw that it was tastefully—even artistically—decorated, in a modern Spanish style. As we moved through the foyer, a great room, and then a long hallway, I couldn't help but admire the handmade inlays in the stone floors, the exposed wood-beam ceilings, and antique-looking brass light fixtures that gave off a soft, golden light. The intermittent Gabbeh rugs, wall tapestries, and dwarf palms in one-of-a-kind oversize pottery added nice touches of color.

The den—my ultimate destination—was more of the same: a huge, rough-hewn wooden desk with black iron moldings that looked like it'd been found in a medieval palace in Barcelona; burgundy and deep-blue Gabbeh rugs; and rich, soft-looking leather chairs and couches. And a perfect fire burned in the brick fireplace to my left. It was big enough that I could feel the heat even from where I stood almost fifteen feet away. To be honest, some of that heat probably didn't come from the fire. I'd been sweating like a squirrel at a dog show ever since Cabazon's death squad had walked into my office.

Cabazon sat behind the desk. As the two goons deposited me in a huge brown leather chair that made me feel like Alice in Wonderland, he relit his pipe. The familiar smell of cherry tobacco filled the room. He waved off my escorts. "You can leave us."

They grunted and left. I fleetingly wondered what I should say. *Nice to see you?* It wasn't. *I've been thinking of you?* I'd been trying not to.

Fortunately, Herr Cabazon took the question off the table. "I have a . . . situation that I believe you can help me with. I have a nephew, Jorge Maldonado, who is in a bit of trouble."

"What kind of trouble?" I suspected it was deportation trouble.

I was about to tell him that I didn't practice immigration law when he continued. "He's been arrested for murder."

If murder charges qualified as "a bit" of trouble, I wondered what Cabazon would call "a lot" of trouble. I took a wild guess. "Gang related?"

He frowned as he took a pull on his pipe. "I doubt it. Though my sources tell me the victim belonged to the Playboy Rollin' 60s, my nephew is not a gang member."

I wondered who his sources were and whether any of them were cops. Probably. "Did you talk to your nephew about it?"

He looked at me like I'd just asked whether he wore Spanx under his Hugo Boss slacks. "Of course not. He is in custody."

I tried to keep the impatient look off my face. Of course, I knew Cabazon wouldn't want to risk showing his face at a prison, and he couldn't talk on the phone: every word would be monitored. "I meant before he got arrested."

Cabazon's expression darkened. "I never had the chance. He got arrested at the scene of the crime." His features softened. "Jorge is like a son to me. My wife and I took him in when he was only six, when his father—my brother—was deported back to Honduras." Cabazon opened a manila folder on his desk and slid a photo over to me.

I picked it up. It showed a young girl—late teens, maybe early twenties—medium pretty with a round face; narrow blue eyes; and chin-length, shaggy, blonde, overprocessed hair with black roots. She wore heavy black eyeliner and pale-pink lip gloss. Her rosebud lips were curved up in a smile that revealed a gap between her two front teeth. "Who is this?"

Cabazon slid the folder over to me. "According to the police reports, she is Tracy Gopeck. The state's primary eyewitness and the only one who identified Jorge as the shooter."

I flipped open the manila folder. Sure enough, there was a police report. How Cabazon had managed to get it was a worrisome question. But it paled in comparison with what I knew he was about to ask me to do.

"My people have tried to find her on the Internet, but she does not seem to exist. And I cannot send them out to look for her, because she might be in protective custody." His people couldn't afford to poke around where cops were involved. "I need you to find her and tell me where she is located." He tapped his pipe on a small gold-rimmed dish and gave me an icy smile. "I do not believe that should be too difficult for a lawyer and her detective father."

I wanted to tell him to shove that folder up his ass. I wanted to tell him I didn't care that he'd unleash the Orozcos on me. But even if I was willing to risk it, that didn't mean the carnage would stop with me. What would he do to Dale? And why should this velociraptor stop at Dale? There was no reason to think he wouldn't go after Michy—and Alex. I was boxed in. Just as he'd intended. My only move for now was to go along with it. "I'll do what I can."

Cabazon's look said he didn't like that answer. "You have two weeks to get me that address."

Shit! Two weeks? To find someone who'd managed to fly under the Internet radar? Who might be in protective custody?

And even if I could, I knew what would happen next.

Tracy Gopeck would be dead.

FIFTEEN

It was past ten o'clock by the time Cabazon's baboons dropped me back at the office. I needed to tell Dale what we were facing, but I was so drained after the constant ebb and flow of adrenaline that I couldn't muster the strength to call him. I drove home, got into the shower, and scrubbed my skin till it burned to get the stink of Cabazon's evil off me. Then I fell into bed and passed out.

By the time I woke up it was almost seven a.m. For a change, I'd had a dreamless sleep. I guessed the antidote for nightmares about one monster was the waking reality of another one.

I flipped through the calendar on my phone to see what I had planned for the day. I had an appearance downtown on a burglary case at nine a.m. Jail overcrowding had persuaded the judge to release my client, Earl Haggar, on his own recognizance. This naturally meant that Earl, a major-league doper, was in no big hurry to resolve his case. So when the DA offered a midterm sentence of four years—not bad considering Earl had been caught inside the victim's house holding a fistful of watches (not even Rolexes or Piagets, just a couple of Invictas and Timexes)—he'd said he wanted to "ponder" the deal. I'd gotten him a continuance until today's date. But I'd warned him that if he blew his appearance, the deal would be gone, and we'd have to go to trial, which would very likely mean he'd wind up with six years.

This appearance was perfect timing. Dale worked just a few blocks away in the Police Administration Building, AKA the PAB (a name so banal it bordered on the ironic), and I needed to talk to him in person about our Cabazon problem. I might be paranoid, but I didn't want to risk texting, e-mailing, or talking about this on the phone. Better paranoid than arrested.

I drove to court, inwardly chanting for Earl to: (a) show up on time, (b) be sober, and (c) take the deal. Of course (a) was a nonstarter. Nine a.m. was the equivalent of four a.m. for Earl. He didn't show up until almost ten thirty. At which time his red eyes, cotton mouth, and sloppy smile told me that (b) was also a nonstarter. Could my wish for (c) possibly, against all odds, come true?

Before I could ask him, the judge called our case and asked whether "Mr. Haggar is planning to accept the prosecutor's most generous offer?"

I was about to ask for more time to discuss the matter with my client, but Earl had other ideas. He spoke in a slow, sleepy rumble. "I been thinking about it, Your Honor, and I just . . . I don't think the offer's all that generous. 'Specially since the guy ripped me off for an ounce of Kush."

The victim was a customer? That was news to me, but the DA didn't look surprised, and he wasn't jumping up to claim it was a lie. Time to capitalize. "Your Honor, we believe we have an argument that this was a claim of right. The so-called victim owed my client money. He didn't have it, so he said he'd pay in property like . . . watches."

The DA, a young one, looked perplexed. "I . . . uh, I don't think that qualifies as a claim of right defense, Your Honor."

He was right. It didn't. But the judge looked a little confused, too. This was delightful. Full speed ahead. "Actually, it does. And in any case, I certainly intend to extensively cross-examine the victim about his dealings with my client." The judge was nodding. Excellent. I decided to go for broke. "So in good conscience, I can't urge my client to take the deal, because I don't think this is a winnable case for the People. But I might be able to recommend my client take a deal for straight probation." I glanced at the prosecutor to see if I'd pushed too far.

He still looked confused, but the confusion seemed to be giving way to resignation. The judge looked at the daunting stack of files on the bench that showed he still had a full calendar to get through. "Mr. Prosecutor, what's your position? I don't see this as a crime of the century if what I'm hearing is true."

The DA snuck a look at me, then turned to the judge. He nervously licked his lips. After a moment, he said, "I guess I'm okay with probation."

See, this is what I love about my job. You just never know what's going to happen next. We took the deal, and Earl entered his plea on the spot. The judge set the case for sentencing to give the probation department time to investigate and make sure Earl wasn't a serial killer masquerading as a marijuana dealer / burglar. The judge called the next case, and I walked Earl out to the elevators. "How come you didn't tell me the guy was buying from you?"

I half expected him to say it was all bullshit. But I should've known better. Earl didn't have the brainpower to come up with a lie that good on the spot. He shrugged. "Just didn't want to burn a good customer. But it wasn't worth prison." The elevator dinged its arrival, and Earl started to get in, then turned back to me. "Hey, maybe you can send me some business?"

I looked at him and sighed. "Earl, I'm a lawyer, not a pot broker. Try and stay out of trouble, okay?"

He grinned at me as the doors closed and gave me a thumbs-up. I was not optimistic. I got a large coffee from the snack bar and called

Dale. Luck was with me; he was in the office. I told him we needed to talk—privately. He paused for a moment, then suggested we meet at Badmaash, an Indian gastropub across the street from the PAB. I could tell by his clipped tone that he knew this couldn't be good.

I got there before him and was glad to see that we'd beaten the lunch rush. I picked a table in the back corner and took a seat facing the door. I hadn't thought I'd be able to eat, and I'm not usually a fan of curry, but the smells coming from the kitchen were making my mouth water.

A few minutes later, the restaurant started to fill up. Dale entered just ahead of a group of women I recognized as prosecutors. They were all checking him out and enjoying the view from behind. One of them even moved past him to get a look at the grill. Her smile said she liked what she saw. He spotted me, and as he headed toward my table, the woman gave him a sparkling grin. He gave her a little nod and kept moving. I wondered if he'd have given her more than that if I wasn't here—and about to discuss serious business. The thought kind of grossed me out. I never called him "Dad," but still . . . yuck.

The moment he sat down across from me, the waiter appeared and asked for our orders. Dale apparently came here a lot because the waiter asked if he wanted "the usual," a samosa with masala potatoes and peas. Dale said that sounded good. I ordered the hot, spicy Indian sausage but passed on the waiter's offer of beer. "Just water, please."

Dale said he'd have the same, then leaned in. "What's up?"

Out of the corner of my eye, I saw a couple of the women who'd been ogling Dale take note of our seeming tête-à-tête. "I had a visit from Javier Cabazon."

Dale's expression hardened. The waiter brought a platter of pickles and preserves. Dale waited for him to leave, then leaned in again. "What kind of visit?"

I described the encounter with Cabazon's flying monkeys and the medieval castle they took me to. Then I told him what I'd read in the police report. It looked like an early report, and it was fairly sparse. It seemed Jorge Maldonado had gotten into a fight with the victim, Victor Mendes. A neighbor called the police. Just seconds before they arrived on the scene, Maldonado shot him. Tracy Gopeck had been standing there, and she'd seen the whole thing, up close and personal. Maldonado had been arrested on the spot. Clearly, Tracy's ID of Maldonado was going to be rock solid from a legal standpoint. She definitely was Cabazon's big problem.

I told Dale what Cabazon wanted us to do—and how we needed to find a way to save Tracy. "The problem is, I'm not sure why Tracy was there—or whether she'd been with either Maldonado or the victim."

Dale nodded, his knee bouncing under the table. "If she was hanging with the victim, she won't trust us. She'll want to see Maldonado go down."

I didn't think she'd trust us even if she was just a bystander. We'd have to tell her that her life was in danger. The only way we'd know that was if we were aligned with Cabazon. In which case, why should she believe that we were trying to save her? If I was her, I'd just think we were trying to help Cabazon "disappear" her.

I continued. "The thing is, I can't put Alex on this, and I have a feeling he wouldn't be able to track her down via computer anyway." Cabazon surely had some pretty talented hackers of his own. Cyberspace was the new criminal frontier. No respectable crime boss would try to do business in today's world without at least one decent hacker. And, of course, asking for Alex's help with Cabazon would force me to tell him how I got into this mess to begin with, i.e., by setting up Ricardo Orozco to get killed in prison. I needed to give Alex plausible deniability in case I eventually got caught.

But more importantly, getting either Alex or Michy involved in this would only put them more squarely in Cabazon's crosshairs. It was bad enough that they were associated with me; the last thing they needed was for him to find out they were working on this with me. The more Cabazon thought they knew, the more likely he was to see them as a threat. Especially if I failed to deliver on Tracy Gopeck. The only thing I could do to protect them was keep them as far away from his business as possible. I figured—or maybe just hoped—that as long as they weren't involved in what I was doing, Cabazon wouldn't have any reason to think they knew about his business or posed any kind of threat to him.

Dale sat back. "Then we have to do it the old-fashioned way."

I nodded. Bribery, shoe leather, and luck. "Unless she is in protective custody, in which case none of that shit's going to help. Is there any chance you can find out whether the cops have her?"

He straightened his silverware and spread his napkin on his lap. "Maybe, if she's in state custody. But if the feds have her, maybe not."

Dale couldn't go around asking questions about a federal case without raising suspicion. This was shaping up to be a nightmare already. "Anyway, I brought you the police report." I pulled the manila envelope out of my briefcase and handed it to him.

He opened the flap and looked inside. "Jesus H. Christ. How in the hell did he get this?"

The waiter arrived with our food, which smelled fantastic. I waited for him to leave before answering. "My guess? Even if the feds have it now, this probably started out as a local case. Either nephew Jorge Maldonado has lawyered up, and Cabazon owns that lawyer, or Cabazon's got connects in the department. Now it's your turn to guess who that might be."

Dale picked up his fork. "I don't have a clue." He took a bite and chewed, but his expression showed his mind wasn't on the food. "Whoever it is, I'd love to find out. And bust his ass—"

I raised an eyebrow. "Or her ass. Check your gender bias. But we don't have that luxury right now. Cabazon gave us two weeks. It's Wednesday. Assuming you need a couple of days to clear the decks, that means we've got about ten days."

He ran a finger between his collar and his neck. "This is really bad timing. I'll squeeze in whatever I can between now and Saturday, but I've got meetings and reports that have to go in by Friday. I don't have an excuse to be in the field." He stared at his food. "But as of Friday afternoon, I'll see if there's a case I can jump on to give me a reason to be out of the office. And I'll take vacation time if I have to."

I was in a bind, too. I had court appearances, motions, and jail visits with clients stacked up. But I had a little more freedom than Dale—the upside of being my own boss. Of course, the downside was that I had no insurance, no retirement, and no steady paycheck. "I can do some of the legwork. We just need to decide what that is."

Dale looked down at the envelope and nodded. "I'll get back to you after I've had a chance to read this. But what do you propose we do if we find her?"

How do we win her trust? How are we going to save her? Good questions, all. I'd been wondering the same things. "I don't know. I'll have to figure something out."

Dale didn't look comforted. But there was no reason why he should. We finished our meal in silence. I guess I'd expected some fin-ger-pointing. After all, the predicament we were in was pretty much—well, actually totally—my fault. But Dale never even hinted at it. I probably would've indulged in at least a small dig. On the other hand, Dale looked like he was still a little bit in shock. When he recovered, I'd probably be in for months of blame gaming.

After lunch, I headed back to the office. When I got in, the TV in my office was on, and Michy and Alex were watching it, their expres-sions somber. I dropped my briefcase on the floor next to the sofa. "Who got shot?"

Michy pressed a button on the remote, and the footage began to rewind. "Your client's chances . . . with the jury." She stopped the rewind and hit play.

And there was Graham and his wife, Sandy, sitting with Dr. Bob—a shrink with questionable credentials but a made-for-daytime-TV earnest expression. A lead weight dropped into the pit of my stomach.

Dr. Bob reminded the audience of what Audrey Sutton had said about their daughter, Alicia, then asked if they wanted to respond. Boy, oh boy, did they.

Sandy led off. "Well, it's very clear that the Suttons raised a controlling misogynist of a son. You can ask any of Alicia's friends; he was absolutely crazy. Called her day and night, demanded that she call him multiple times a day."

Dr. Bob said, "That is indeed very controlling behavior—something I've talked about a good deal on this show. Is that why she broke up with Roan?"

Graham looked straight into the camera. "Yes. And we believe he posted her photos on that website to punish her for it."

Dr. Bob nodded, wearing his usual fake-concerned expression. "And, of course, posting that so-called invitation to fulfill Alicia's rape fantasy along with those photos was a very dangerous thing to do. But what do you say to those who blame your daughter for sending him those photos in the first place?"

Sandy took over. "That she was a young, naive girl who trusted a very sick, unhinged man who took advantage of her trust. A man who was obviously so deranged, he decided that if he couldn't have her, no one could."

Dr. Bob gave Sandy his "kindly dad" look. "Then would you say Roan Sutton was also the kind of person who'd take his own life?"

Sandy set her jaw. "I'd like to think he had enough of a conscience to kill himself after what he did. But I can't speak to his obvious mental illness." And then, in an obviously scripted moment, she added, "You're the doctor. What do you think, Dr. Bob?"

Dr. Bob gave a sagely nod. "I think he's a prime candidate for suicide." He turned to the camera. "This case is a hot potato, and I'm sure we'll be talking about it again in future episodes, so be sure to follow us on DrBob.com for updates. We'll be back to wrap this up in just a few. Stay tuned, folks."

Shit. Shit. Shit.

SIXTEEN

Michy clicked the remote to pause the footage and looked at me. "I thought you told him to lay low."

I was still staring at the screen, wondering what had gotten into Graham. "I did. He's just . . . losing it."

She turned off the TV and put the remote back on my desk. "Look, I get that he's in a lot of pain. He just lost his only child, and Roan is Suspect Number One. But he's going to talk his way into a murder case if he doesn't pull it together."

And Graham knew that. "I have a feeling that's what he wants— subconsciously speaking. He's got all kinds of guilt about the way they pressured Alicia to perform all her life."

Michy sighed. "It'd be such a shame if he winds up putting his own head in the noose." She put a hand to her mouth. "Sorry, that just slipped out."

"I'm sure Roan forgives you." And I couldn't have agreed more. "The thing is, I don't know what I can do, short of locking Graham in his basement."

Alex said, "I might be able to help."

I sat down on the couch. "Fire away. I'm all ears."

He gave me a searching look. "It's not legal."

I stared back at him. "Like I said, I'm all ears."

He leaned against my desk and folded his arms. "I can plant spyware on his phone."

I asked, "Don't you need to get ahold of the phone to do that? How do I pry it out of his hot little hands?"

Alex smiled. "You don't. Remember I told you and Dale about spyware that can be loaded onto an iPhone?" I nodded. "What I didn't want to say in front of him is that you can do it remotely. You don't need to have physical access to the phone."

I loved the idea of being able to get to Graham in time to stop him from doing any more damage. But the notion of going all NSA on my own client made me more than a little squeamish. Apart from my ethical discomfort—a rare occurrence for me—if I got caught, I'd lose my bar card and face a whopper of a claim for invasion of privacy, just for starters. But as they say, desperate times call for desperate measures, and I didn't know how bad things might get, so I decided not to rule it out just yet. "Let's keep that in our back pockets for now. In the meantime, I'll have another talk with him."

Alex pushed off my desk. "Suit yourself." He headed for the door, then stopped and turned back. "By the way, on the sort of good news front, I checked out that private pathologist, Dr. Mortimer." He passed me his iPad. "Here's what I got on him. Seems like he does a lot of work for the defense."

I scanned his CV. Alex was right. "Matter of fact, he's never been hired by the prosecution."

Michy frowned. "Is that bad?"

"Kind of. It means his opinion's for sale. Basically, he's a whore; he'll say whatever he's paid to say." Of course, if I'd hired him, I'd call him a leading authority with an impeccable reputation—because then he'd be *my* whore.

Alex said, "But won't the cops know that, too? So even if he does claim Roan was murdered, they won't necessarily go with that, right?"

I handed his iPad back to him. "That's the hope." And I'd start my campaign right now by putting the bug in Dale's ear. Cops talk—a lot. By tomorrow morning, every cop in RHD would know that Mortimer was a hooker.

Alex nodded and went back to his office.

Michy started to follow him out, then stopped. "About keeping Graham off the airwaves, you might want to talk to the wife, too. Maybe if you explain what kind of disaster they're courting, she can cool his jets."

But even though I wasn't happy that Graham had decided to do Dr. Bob's show—especially after all my warnings against media appearances—I was irritated by the finger-pointing. "The thing is, they're grieving parents, too. You'd think the public would remember that."

Michy threw up her hands. "You're right. You would think. But . . ."

She was right. It was hard to predict how viewers might react, what might cause them to turn on someone. I took my phone out of my briefcase and moved to my desk.

But we were both wrong, it wasn't Graham's idea—as I learned when I called Graham and started to kindly and gently tear him a new one.

He was breathing hard. It sounded like he was jogging. "They contacted Sandy without my knowing it. I only went along to try and keep a lid on things."

To say that his plan hadn't worked would be like Snow White saying that apple might not have been her best choice of dessert. "Okay, I get it. But no more guest appearances. If you need me to, I'll explain it to Sandy myself."

Graham's voice was heavy. "She knows. She just . . . reacted in the moment. But I think she . . . we'll . . . be flying under the radar from here on out. A friend of ours recorded the show. Neither one of us liked what we saw, so . . . don't worry."

But, of course, that was crazy talk. I was going to worry until the coroner came out with a final decision that Roan's death was a suicide. And probably keep on worrying long after that. Because there is no statute of limitations on murder.

Alex came back in to give me a report on my latest request. I'd asked him to confirm that it was Roan who'd posted Alicia's photos. "I've been trying to break through the proxy server that was used to post the photos to the porn site, but no dice." His tone was aggravated.

Damn. "Can you figure out who posted them on her Facebook page?"

Alex waved a hand. "Not so far. Best I can tell, her Facebook page was hacked, because it looks like she posted the photos herself—"

I cut him off. "No way she'd do that."

He nodded. "I agree. But the hacker could be anyone. Her Facebook address was posted on the porn website. My only other hope is Roan's hard drive. Dale said I could come by tonight, and he'd get me to a room where I could check it out."

The mention of Dale reminded me of Cabazon. My heart jumped into my throat. We had so little time to find this Tracy person. And then we'd need to figure out how to keep her from getting "microwave ovened"—Brazilian slang for killing someone by putting tires around the victim's neck and setting him on fire.

Alex's voice broke into my miserable reverie. "Want to come?"

I stared at him, unsure what he meant at first. "Oh, to the station. No, that's okay. You go. I'll get some work done. Report back when you have something."

Alex started to leave, but he stopped at the doorway. "Do you want me to keep digging on Roan's family?"

I'd asked Alex to get what he could on Roan's background. I was primarily looking for evidence of mental instability, and hopefully for some earlier suicidal behavior. "You come up with anything yet?"

He sighed. "Not as much as I expected. His parents got divorced when he was twelve, so I've been trying to get the paperwork on that."

A divorce can generate a treasure trove of dirt. It reminded me of the saying that in criminal court, the worst people are on their best behavior, and in civil court, the best people are on their worst behavior. "That should give us something—unless they had their records sealed."

Alex sighed and nodded. "Which they might have because so far, nothing."

I told him to carry on and not worry about it. Ultimately, I knew we'd have to try and find people on Roan's side of the fence who were willing to talk to us about him. His mother was obviously out of reach. I'd bet his father was, too. But I might get some cooperation from his brothers. Siblings can be one another's best friend—or worst enemy. "When do you plan to leave?" I looked at the digital clock on my desk. It was six already.

Alex looked at his watch. "How did it get that late? I'm outta here."

He left, and just to make Michelle happy, I got to work on my time sheets. I'd barely made a dent in them when she came in to tell me she was heading home, coat on and scarf wrapped around her neck. "It's almost seven thirty. Go home. Whatever you're working on can wait, I'm sure."

I sat back. "I'm working on my time sheets."

Her look of concern turned off faster than a guy listening to his girlfriend talk about her exes. "Stay as long as you like. Got a blanket? You can crash on the couch. I put toothpaste and a toothbrush in your desk drawer."

I raised an eyebrow. "You're all heart."

She softened—but didn't let me off the hook. "Seriously, want me to order you a pizza?"

Remembering how that offer worked out the last time, I shook my head. "No, thanks. I'm good."

Michelle left, and I put my head down and kept grinding. I must've nodded off at my desk, because when I heard the outer office door open, my head was laying on the last of my files, and there was a little spot of drool on the time sheet. I jerked up, my heart pounding.

But it was just Alex. He called out, "Sam? You still here?"

I rubbed my face and tried to wake up. "Yeah. What're you doing here?"

He came into my office and sat down on the couch. "You told me to report back. And Michelle called me and said you'd be working late." He gave me a little smile. "You been sleeping?"

I wanted to deny it, but honestly, it was a waste of time. "Yeah. Damn time sheets. What'd you get?"

Alex leaned forward, his forearms on his knees. "Nothing. *Nada.* Zip. Roan's hard drive wasn't totally wiped clean. Like I said, that's really hard to do. So I did find the photos on it. But there's no evidence he posted them from that computer. In fact, there's no evidence he sent them anywhere at all."

This had the beginnings of a nicely confusing, jury-tantalizing distraction. "So are you saying Roan didn't post the photos?"

Alex gave an impatient sigh. "No. I'm saying he didn't post them from his computer. He could easily have posted them from his phone. But his phone truly is wiped clean, and he didn't have an iCloud account."

Not as good as I'd hoped, but not horrible. "Then Roan could've posted the photos, but so could someone else if they'd hacked Alicia's phone—or Roan's for that matter, right?"

Alex shrugged. "Yeah. I did confirm that Alicia sent them to his phone, so he did have them on there at some point." He slapped his knees. "Okay, ready to hit it?"

I was.

But by the time I got home, I was wide-awake. My little nap had screwed up my rhythm. I took a hot shower, poured myself a drink, and put my feet up on the coffee table. I turned on the TV and was flipping through the channels and looking for something to watch when the eleven o'clock news came on.

A young reporter with hair so perfect he looked like a Ken doll was standing in front of a bar. " . . . and this was where our reporter, Jack Chen, just happened to be when Audrey Sutton and her friend left the bar. Ms. Sutton was very inebriated, and when Jack took out his phone and snapped a photo, she became irate and knocked the phone from his hand. A—I don't want to say a fight, exactly—but an altercation ensued, and the police were called."

The anchor asked, "Is Jack going to press charges?"

The reporter gave a half smile. "No, he said he wasn't really hurt, and his phone is still working, so . . ." The reporter shrugged. "That seems to be the end of it."

Not if I had anything to say about it.

SEVENTEEN

It was after one a.m. by the time I got into bed. Not good. I had an eight thirty appearance in Van Nuys the next morning. That meant I had to be up by six and out the door by seven a.m. I tossed and turned for at least an hour before finally falling asleep. Six a.m. came way too soon. I smacked my phone to stop the alarm, stumbled out of bed, and slogged into the shower. Although I pounded three travel mugs of coffee before I left, I was still feeling fuzzy and slow, and I headed to my car like a bird dragging its feathers. As I headed over Laurel Canyon, I tuned in to a political podcast I knew I could count on to piss me off and jack my brain into gear.

Today was the status conference on my vehicular manslaughter case, and I was hoping to talk the prosecutor into reducing it to a DUI with injury. But the prosecutor, Art Sawgus, was tough on plea bargains, so I really needed to be on top of my game.

I made it to the courtroom just as the bailiff was unlocking the door. Excellent timing that I hoped was a good omen. A flood of lawyers and their clients and families rolled in behind me, but Art was a no-show. An older guy, who didn't even bother to tell me his name, was standing in for him. He said he couldn't deal out Art's cases, but I made my pitch anyway. Maybe this guy would be a weaker link. It was worth a shot.

I pointed out all the weaknesses in his case—among them the fact that my guy, who had no record, would make a sympathetic witness on the stand—and finished with the ultimate threat. "The case is very losable for the prosecution, and I'm sure Art knows that. So it's a fair bet he'll hand this dog off to someone else. And that someone just might be you. I'm offering you a chance to make sure it isn't."

Divide and conquer. Pit the deputy DAs against each other by framing one up as the dump*er* and the other as the dump*ee*. It was one of my favorite strategies. I gave him my confident but nonchalant smile and waited to see if it would work.

Behind him, I saw that the sheriff's deputy was leading the custodies into the courtroom. My client, Jonathan Keller, looked like the classic new kid who always got knocked around by the class bully—wire-frame glasses and all. I nodded to him. As he nodded back, I told the prosecutor to take a look at him. "Think the jury's going to have a hard time believing him when he swears he wasn't high, and it was too dark for anyone to see your victim—who, by the way, *was* high and darted into traffic?"

For a change, I wasn't exaggerating. I'd gone out to the intersection in question and seen for myself how dark it was at night. But the cops had written my guy up as being stoned out of his mind, and if the jury bought that, they'd nail him for gross negligence manslaughter. The judge would probably max him out and give him ten years. I didn't think my guy would survive a stint that long.

The prosecutor turned around and glanced at Jonathan, who was looking particularly frail and vulnerable between two beefy, tatted-out gangbangers.

He turned back to me and was about to answer when the judge took the bench. All I could do now was hope I'd planted the fear of failure deeply enough to scare him into a deal.

As I moved over to my side of the courtroom, the judge called our case. "People versus Keller. I see it's on for a status conference." The judge looked from the prosecutor to me. "Counsel, what's your pleasure? Are we setting it for trial or can we all get along and plead this case out?"

I tried to look casual as I held my breath and waited for the prosecutor to answer. He was staring down at his file and frowning. He was thinking. That was good. He threw a quick glance at Jonathan again, then cleared his throat. "I believe we have a deal. We'll let Mr. Keller plead guilty to a DUI with injury." The prosecutor turned to face me as he continued. "But it'll have to be an open plea. No promises on the sentence."

That could mean as much as a three-year sentence. But I had a good feeling about this judge. I'd already talked to my client about this possibility, but I made eye contact with him now just to make sure he was still on board. He nodded to me. I faced the judge. "That's acceptable. But I'm putting the DA on notice that I will be calling witnesses at the sentencing hearing." I planned to pull on every heartstring I could find to get the minimum ninety-day sentence. I'd call Jonathan's ailing mother, his autistic brother, his girlfriend. Hell, I'd even bring in pictures of his dog, Max, and hire an actor to pose as Jonathan's veterinarian so he could speak movingly of the love Jonathan had showered on Max—a lovable beagle who would surely die of a broken heart if Jonathan were gone too long.

We took the plea, and I went over to Jonathan and quietly gave him a thumbs-up. "I'll tell your peeps."

He had tears in his eyes. "Thank you, Ms. Brinkman."

I stared at him and whispered, "Do not . . . do that." His buddies on either side were looking jealous, and if they saw him cry, it'd be the perfect excuse to beat the crap out of him for acting like a pussy.

He nodded and blinked hard. "See you."

I headed back to the office, feeling victorious and praying Jonathan could stay out of harm's way. With a little luck, I might get the judge to let him serve the rest of his sentence at a small, local jail where he wouldn't have to navigate bangers, murderers, and rapists.

And Michelle was smiling when I got in, a sign there was more good news. She got up and motioned for me to follow her into my office. "I caught this online first, and then I saw that Sheri was going to run with it. They're promo-ing the heck out of it."

I'd called Sheri, the host of *Crime Time*, to offer a suggestion for her show—and a quote she could use if she did the story. "Then it worked?"

"To be fair, she might've done it even if you hadn't called her. I didn't get the whole thing, but I think I got most of it." Michelle picked up the remote and turned on my TV.

A young Asian man was sitting across from Sheri. The chyron said his name was Jack Chen.

Jack said, "According to Audrey Sutton's estranged husband, that's why they got divorced. The court refused to give him sole custody, but the kids wound up bouncing between their houses because she kept falling off the wagon."

The image froze, and Michelle clicked the remote to turn off the TV. I smiled. "So the show's airing tonight?"

Michelle nodded. "I've set it to record. You really think it'll help?"

"Hell yeah." Not only would it take some of the heat off Graham, it would also—hopefully—dent Audrey's credibility. Plus, an unstable home life made it more likely that Roan would have the kind of emotional problems that might lead to suicide. "I need to try and talk to that father—and Roan's brothers. Is Alex in?"

Michelle rolled her eyes. "He's been working nonstop to find the owner of that porn website. And bitching up a storm because apparently, the guy's much better at hiding than most of the other website owners. Feel free to ask him all about it."

I hoped that wasn't all he was working on. I went to his office and knocked on the door. "It's the NSA. We want to know what you're doing with that unicorn costume."

Alex opened the door and gave me a tired look. "Really? Must you?"

"Clearly, the answer is yes." I asked whether he'd seen the footage about Roan's father.

"Yeah. I don't know whether that means he'll talk to us, though."

I didn't, either, but it was worth a try. "Have you located him? Or any of Roan's family?"

He *tsk*ed with annoyance. "Of course. Ages ago. You ready to hit them up?"

"I think so. Where are they?"

Alex went back to his desk and picked up his iPad. "The oldest brother, Scott, lives in Venice. He's a music producer."

"Does he work there, too?" Venice was very doable, and it'd be nice to get out to the beach—even if it was cold as hell this time of year.

Alex looked down at his iPad. "Yes. The second brother lives in the Bay area, and the father lives in Tucson."

They'd be more of a hassle. But it was just a one-hour plane ride to either locale, and Graham would foot the bill. "Let's see what we get out of Scott. We can hold off on the others for now."

Alex took his jacket off the back of his chair. "I assume we're going now?"

I nodded. "I'm hoping Scott saw the promo for the piece about his dad."

Alex asked, "Because it might loosen him up?"

"Exactly." We went out to Michy's desk, and I told her where we were going. "I don't know how long this'll take."

"No problem. I'll lock up around six-ish. Call me if you get anything delicious."

The odds of that were very slim, but I promised I would, and we headed out into the hazy winter day to go find a dead boy's brother.

EIGHTEEN

This time, I drove. Venice—a beach town that used to be fairly down-market, especially when Jim Morrison lived there—had gentrified over the years. Now, even the tiny, cottage-style houses cost a fortune. And the ones on the canal? Forget it. You're talking about high seven figures.

But there are neighborhoods that aren't so great. And there are gangs. Scott's music studio was between the great and not-so-great areas, a dicey proposition, and Alex wasn't keen on putting his ride in jeopardy again. So Beulah was the perfect solution. Because no one in his right mind would steal her.

I could smell the ocean for miles before we got to Venice, and when I turned left onto Ocean Boulevard, the sea came into view. It was a blustery day, and the water was choppy, but the wind had blown away the haze, and the waves sparkled like topaz under the bright sun.

Alex used his phone to navigate, and we wound up at the east edge of Venice on a seedy street in front of a trashed-out warehouse. "Seriously? This is it?" I'd hoped we could at least see the ocean from Scott's studio. Crazy dreamer that I am.

"This is the place." Alex opened the passenger door and wrinkled his nose. "Try not to breathe. It's Urine City out here."

Even with the warning, the smell hit me like a fist when I got out. I covered my nose and mouth with my wool scarf and followed Alex, who was speed walking toward a grease-covered metal door to our right. We'd tossed around some ideas for cover stories, but in the end, it seemed best to just tell the truth. If I did wind up needing Scott's testimony, it'd only piss him off to find out I'd lied to him. And a pissed-off witness is generally a very unhelpful witness.

Alex pulled the handle on the metal door, but it didn't budge, so he knocked. It made a hollow clang. A few seconds later, a voice crackled through an ancient-looking speaker in the wall next to the door. "Who's there?" I announced Alex and myself and said we were there to talk to Scott. I waited to hear the voice again, but instead, there was a loud buzzing sound. Alex pulled on the door again. This time, it opened.

We walked into a narrow, dark corridor with a cement floor. When we got to the end of the hall, a door opened on our right, and a young woman in overalls wearing Snoop Dogg braids that started high up on the sides of her head and draped her face like—well, like dog ears, stepped out and eyed us suspiciously. "What do you want with Scott?"

I noticed her eyes lingered a bit longer on Alex as she spoke. So did Alex. We had our game down to a science now. I let Alex do the talking. To my relief, the smell had faded to a mere noxious echo.

Alex flashed her a warm—but not too warm—smile. "I promise this won't take much time. We just need to ask him a few questions about Roan." She hesitated, and Alex shifted into second gear. He held out his hand. "I'm sorry, I didn't catch your name."

She just barely touched his fingers before withdrawing her hand. "I'm Zandra."

Alex gave her hand a slight squeeze along with a wider smile. "Zandra, what a cool name. I'm Alex." He gestured to me. "And this is Sam."

She didn't extend her hand to me, so I gave her a little wave. "Hi."

Zandra glanced in my direction, then looked back at Alex. "Let me see if he'll—"

At that moment, a tall, muscular man with curly dark hair and a long, scraggly beard and mustache came out. It was Scott, no doubt about it. I could see the resemblance to Roan in his strong jaw and high cheekbones, but Scott definitely wasn't the looker his brother had been. He was dressed in a pullover hoodie, jeans, and . . . sandals. Damn, sandals again. He looked from Alex to me. The flicker in his eyes when he looked my way said it was my turn to take the hit for the team. I put out my hand. "Hi, I'm Sam." As he shook my hand, I introduced Alex and told him why we were there.

Scott put his hands into the front pouch of his sweatshirt and leaned back against the doorway as he studied me. "You reporters?"

I shook my head. "No, I'm a lawyer, and he's my investigator." I tilted my head toward Alex.

Scott didn't seem entirely sold on the idea of talking to us. "What do you want to know?"

If I asked a gentle, open-ended question like, *What was Roan like as a kid?* he might decide this was going to be too much trouble and shut me down. I needed to make him feel like he had to answer, and the only way to do that was to provoke him. "Did you know he posted Alicia's selfies on that porn website?"

Scott's eyes narrowed. "No. And I can tell you right now, he'd never do a thing like that."

Except he had definitely done it to Laurie. But there was no need to contradict him. He'd taken the bait; he wouldn't back out now. "Then I'm guessing you don't believe he could've killed Alicia, either?"

He shifted his weight onto his left hip in a move that was faintly menacing. "There's no fucking way he killed her."

If I'd been alone, I'm not sure I would've continued to press him. That's how hostile his vibe was. But Alex knew how to fight—probably a lot better than Scott. I wasn't worried. Still, I tried to soften up the tone a little. "Roan seemed to be very . . . demanding with Alicia. From what I hear, that's why she broke up with him. Did you ever see him act that way with girls?"

Scott's gaze drifted over my left shoulder. When he spoke, his voice was pained. "Roan . . . It was weird. I didn't get it. He was the best-looking of all of us, but he could be really needy and insecure around girls." He quickly added, "But he never hurt anyone, never hit a girl or anything."

That we knew of. I wondered if girls would eventually come forward to say otherwise. But this was a good segue for my last question. "He did hurt himself, though, didn't he? Did he ever talk to you about having suicidal thoughts?"

Scott's lips quivered, but he clenched his jaw. "No, he never did. But I was always so damn busy. Maybe if I'd been around more . . ." He swallowed, then cleared his throat. "He must've been in a lot of pain to—to do something like that."

What struck me was the fact that Scott didn't reject the notion of Roan committing suicide the way his mother had. It clearly didn't seem that unbelievable to him. "Your mother doesn't believe it. She's saying someone had to have killed him."

Scott nodded, his expression weary. "Yeah, I heard she blames the girl's father. Mom is . . . Mom. She's got her issues, and I'm sure she doesn't want to believe she screwed up that badly."

I chose not to tell him that I was representing the girl's father. "Then you think she won't accept Roan's suicide because she feels guilty?"

Scott shrugged. "It's just a guess. She's got a lot to feel guilty about."

I treaded lightly with my next question. "Because she was an alcoholic?"

Scott sighed, but his tone was agitated. "Yeah." He turned to look behind him for a brief moment, then asked, "Anything else? I've got to get back to work."

I could've thought of a few more questions, but I suspected we'd gotten all we were going to get out of him. "Not a problem. Thanks for your time, Scott."

He turned and walked back into his studio without a word. Zandra, who'd taken it all in, slipped inside and closed the door.

I stared at the door. "Don't trouble yourselves. We'll just see ourselves out, thanks."

Alex shook his head. "Some people's children."

I followed him out, and we headed back to Beulah. As I drove us out of that stink pit, we compared notes. I led off. "I thought you said he was a music producer. I didn't hear any music."

Alex shrugged. "Me, either. What a weird place." He pointed to the intersection just ahead. "If you turn left, we'll be on Ocean Boulevard."

Where we could get another eyeful of that gorgeous view. The wind was still blowing, and the palm trees that lined the boulevard were bending and swaying to and fro, reminding me of willowy dancers in Carmen Miranda–style hats. I rolled down my window a little to get the full blast of the sea air—and wipe the stench of Scott's place out of my nose. "I didn't expect him to say he thought Roan killed her. But he seemed to believe it was very possible that Roan committed suicide."

Alex had rolled down his window, too, and he was leaning out with his head tilted back to get the full blast of clean air. "Yeah, that was good. And he confirms Roan's bizarre attitude toward women. Not that we needed it."

We definitely didn't. Everyone and his dog seemed to know that Roan was an obsessive, controlling freak. I doubted we'd get much more from his father or other brother. "We can revisit if we get desperate, but for now, I think we let the rest of the family go."

The interview hadn't taken long, so we got back to the office by five thirty. Michy was just ending a call when we walked in. "Good timing. That was Dale."

My heart froze. Had Cabazon made contact with him? I tried to keep my tone light as I asked, "What did he say?"

"Just that you should call him on his cell. Is something wrong?"

Damn Michelle. I can never keep anything from her. "No, not at all. Just kind of tired."

I went into my office and closed the door. I had no doubt Michy and Alex were exchanging *what's going on with her?* looks. I punched in Dale's number. The moment he answered I asked, "Are you all right?"

He gave a quiet, mirthless laugh. "Yeah. I may have a lead on our, ah . . . JC matter. But that's not what I'm calling about."

JC. Javier Cabazon. Nice touch. "Then what are you calling about?" The tension of worry made the words come out a little sharper than I'd intended.

Dale's tone was sarcastic. "Pardon me. I thought you might like to hear some inside news on Graham's case. But no sweat if you don't. I can get back to—"

I stopped him. "Sorry, sorry, sorry. I've been a little on edge. I'm sure you can figure out why. What've you got?"

"The hairs found on the shirt Roan was wearing when he died came from Alicia. It's a microscopic match and a DNA match."

Hairs could cling to clothing for months, so this was no game ender. But it was another piece of the puzzle. "So it's looking a little more solid that Roan killed her."

"Definitely getting there."

I ended the call thinking this was not such great news for me. The clearer it became that Roan killed Alicia, the more people would believe that Graham had killed Roan. It just fit.

A little too well.

NINETEEN

For no particular reason, I decided we deserved to knock off early and go have dinner. I went out to Michelle's desk and saw that Alex's door was open. "How about The Hudson, guys? My treat." It was a casual place on Crescent Heights Boulevard, and I loved the huge tree in the middle—also the great comfort food: outrageous mac and cheese, crispy chicken sliders, and great short-rib tacos.

Michy, who'd been yawning—no doubt because she was working on our quarterly tax forms—immediately perked up. "I'm so in, I'm almost out."

But Alex didn't answer. I went to his doorway. He was staring intently at his computer. "I can't believe you didn't hear that."

He jerked up and blinked. "Hear what?" I repeated my generous offer. Alex shifted his gaze back to the computer screen as he said, "No, thanks. I'm in the middle of something."

I hate it when people act cryptic. "Of what?"

Alex spoke without looking up. "I don't want to jinx myself. I should know by tomorrow whether this works."

Being weirdly superstitious myself, I couldn't knock him for not telling me. "Okay, good luck. But do me a favor and throw the dead bolt when we split." Alex frowned at me. "I've seen some weird characters in the 'hood lately." He raised an eyebrow. "Just humor me, okay?" I couldn't tell him about the Cabazon duo. Not that I really thought they'd be back so soon. Senor Cabazon wouldn't send his minions back out until he had a reason to think I wasn't going to deliver. But a little extra precaution couldn't hurt. Besides, I really had seen some weird characters around here lately.

He sighed. "Fine."

As Michy and I left, I heard him typing. I called him from the car just to make sure he'd set the dead bolt.

Michy and I caught up over mac and cheese and chicken sandwiches. Michy's on-again, off-again romance with Brad, a hard charger who was slaving away at a white-shoe law firm downtown, was off-again at the moment.

She speared another forkful of mac and cheese. "He's great, and he's sweet, and he really treats me well."

I took a swig of my Corona. "What an asshole. You should dump him immediately."

She shot me a mock glare. "But he's so boring. His cases are all—"

I filled in. "About how many zeroes you can add after the three. I know." Corporate law truly was deadly. "Working with me spoiled you."

Michelle raised an eyebrow. "If by spoiling me you mean working me fifty hours a week for a paycheck that may or may not appear, I guess you're right."

"Exactly. It's the thrill of the unknown. Keeps the blood flowing—really fast." I took a bite of the mac and cheese. "Doesn't he have anything else going on in his life?"

Michy rolled her eyes. "When would he have time? He works fifteen hours a day." She took a sip of her beer. "What's up with you and Niko?"

I shrugged. "Nothing at the moment. He's in New York teaching a master class. But that's a good thing. I don't have time for him."

Michy lifted her bottle of Corona. "I'll drink to that. What did Dale have to say?"

I told her what he'd said about finding Alicia's hairs on Roan's shirt. "I know it's kind of a foregone conclusion that he killed her. But the more that kind of stuff comes out . . ."

Michy nodded. "I know." She took another sip of her beer, then traced the label with her finger as she spoke. "I just keep thinking about those websites. What it must be like to be . . . violated that way. It's got to be so humiliating. I'd be devastated."

I'd been thinking about that, too. Alicia's and Laurie's photos were still posted on those hideous websites. Just the thought of it made me queasy. I pushed my plate away.

Michy looked at me with sympathy. She didn't know the details of my childhood, but she knew enough of the broad outlines to understand how a loss of control of this kind hit close to home for me. She gave me a reassuring smile. "Well, just to focus on the bright side for a moment, if you do wind up going to trial on Graham's case, you know who you'll want on your jury."

My smile was grim. "Women. All women. But preferably young ones." Who wouldn't judge Alicia for taking the nude selfies to please her boyfriend. And who'd be outraged at Roan just for posting those photos, let alone killing her.

We didn't order dessert. I think the talk about revenge porn killed both our appetites. But we'd taken an Uber, so we did indulge in another beer.

It'd been a long week, so we called it a night by nine thirty, and when I got home, I tried to call Dale, but it went straight to voice mail. I called Alex. That went to voice mail, too. I was thinking about going back to the office to make sure he was okay, but two seconds later, he texted me: Leave me alone.

So he was okay. Annoyed at me, but okay. Annoying Alex was a satisfying way to end the day, so I put myself to bed by eleven o'clock.

And woke up choking on my own screams at four thirty. Thankfully, I was able to put myself back to sleep until seven. For me, that counted as a good night.

I was dressed, coffeed, and nearly out the door when Dale called.

He spoke hurriedly and in a low voice. "What are you doing tomorrow?"

Tomorrow was Saturday. He must have a lead. "Hanging with you, I guess. What's up?"

"Tell you when we meet up. Be ready to go by seven a.m."

"Can we make it—" I would've asked him to make it eight o'clock, but he'd already ended the call.

Between Alex and Dale, I wasn't getting a lot of respect.

I headed for the office and stopped on the way to pick up bagels and coffee. And when I got in, I was glad I had. I found Alex sitting on a cot in his office, bleary-eyed, with his shirt twisted. But when he saw me in the doorway, he smiled. "I smell coffee. And are those bagels?" He glanced at the bag in my hand.

I held it up. "And cream cheese. Come eat. Then tell me what on earth you're up to—and when you snagged that cot." This was the first time I'd seen it.

Alex went to the men's room to "freshen up," and I set out our morning fix.

Michy came in and made a beeline for the coffee. "Just what I needed. I overslept. And man, it's cold out there." Southern California cold. But still. I told her Alex had spent the night in the office. She shivered as she held the cup of coffee close to her chest. "What the hell is up with him?"

Alex walked in at that moment. He took half a bagel and spread it with cream cheese as he said, "Ask me nicely and I'll tell you."

I handed him a cup of coffee. "This is me asking you nicely. What the hell is up with you?"

He took a leisurely bite of the bagel, washed it down with a long sip of coffee. Then he dabbed at his mouth with a napkin.

I put a hand on my hip. "If you don't start talking in the next ten seconds, I will take a hit out on you, I swear."

Alex grinned. "I found him."

It took me a second to process that. Then it hit me. "The guy who owns the website where Alicia's photos were posted?"

He nodded. "Yep. Name and address."

Michy set down her coffee and took half an onion bagel. "What are you going to do?" She had a worried look on her face.

Alex finished another sip of coffee. "I'm going to ask him to take down that whole damn website. I'm going to be nice until he shows me it's time not to be nice. And if he argues, I'll ask him again. A little less nicely." He looked at us. "Get it? That was my version of Patrick Swayze—in *Road House*. 'Be nice until it's time to not be nice.'"

I had no idea what he was talking about. I turned to Michy, but she shook her head. We had nothing.

This wasn't the most detailed plan I'd ever heard. "Do you know how big this guy is? Whether he has guns? Or friends who live with him?" Alex definitely hadn't thought this through. Alex looked down at his coffee and frowned. "I could ask my uncle for backup."

His uncle, Tomas Medrano, was a bail bondsman, and as most bail bondsman are, he was one tough dude. And so were his employees. They'd backed us up before, when I was representing Dale. "I'd say to get Tomas at the very least. But before you do that, why don't we see where he lives, check him out, get some idea of what we're up against? I assume he's somewhere fairly close." Or Alex wouldn't have said he intended to go see him.

Alex rubbed his eyes. "Yeah, you're right. I'm not thinking too clearly. I just can't wait to get my hands around that asshole's neck."

Michy and I exchanged a smile. This was one of the many reasons we loved Alex. "Did you get any sleep?" I asked.

He gave a huge yawn. "Couple of hours." He threw his empty coffee cup in the trash and stretched. "I'll go back to my crib and crash for a bit. We're more likely to catch him at home if we go later anyway."

We made him take an Uber home. He didn't live far—like Michy and me, he lived in West Hollywood, close to the office—so it wouldn't cost much, and I didn't trust him to drive in his condition.

With Alex gone and no client meetings, Michy had the chance to crack the whip and make me finish my time sheets. The hours dragged by as I went through one case after another. I prayed for some distraction—any distraction. And Michy brought in salads, so I didn't even get to break for lunch. When I finally finished the damn things, it was three thirty. I took them out to Michy. "I'm done. I think this might actually be worse than waterboarding."

Michy rolled her eyes. "Stop whining. It's how we get paid."

I huffed and stomped back into my office.

Ten minutes later, Alex showed up, bright-eyed and raring to go. "He lives in Culver City."

I groaned. "Traffic's going to be a bitch." Crosstown traffic was always bad, but it really sucked at this time of day.

Alex wagged a finger at me. "No woman, no cry. I'll drive."

I picked up my coat and purse and gave a despairing look to Michy. "Wish us luck."

Michy held up crossed fingers. "Luck."

As we inched southbound on La Cienega Boulevard, Alex used the opportunity to explain to me in excruciating detail how he'd managed to crack through the website owner's firewall. I understood not one word of it. When he finally pulled up to a nondescript pale-yellow apartment building on Motor Avenue, I said, "Um, that's amazing. But could you maybe tell me the guy's name?"

Alex's lips twitched. "Sorry. I've just been working on this for so long. His name's Devon Shackley. I Googled it and got four photos."

Alex pulled a sheet of paper out of his file folder and gave it to me. One had short dark hair and a mustache. A second had shoulder-length blond hair and a nose ring. A third was bald. The fourth had short blond hair and a soul patch. "So I guess we wait and see if anyone who matches one of these guys comes out or goes in?"

Alex looked at me like I'd suggested we use a divining rod. "No, we wait until someone opens the door, then follow them in and go up to his apartment."

That would be easier. And it took only fifteen minutes before a very helpful young woman held the door open for us as we hurried toward it, looking harried and grateful. I smiled at her. "Thanks."

She smiled back. "No problem."

As she headed down the hall, I whispered to Alex, "And that's how us nice women get killed."

Alex lifted a sardonic eyebrow. "'Us . . . nice'? I don't think you and she have that in common."

I gave him an indignant sniff, which he ignored as he led the way to the elevator. Our quarry lived on the fourth floor in apartment 4F: 4F—unfit for military service. How apt. We'd decided to play it simple and pretend to have accidentally knocked on the wrong door. Not exactly elegant, but it didn't need to be. We were just trying to get a sense of who we were dealing with.

Alex knocked, and a burly man in his thirties with heavy eyebrows answered the door. He looked like the guy in the fourth photo—but the soul patch was gone now, and his jowls looked heavier. His appearance was almost as hostile as his tone as he said, "What can I do for you?"

Alex put on a charming smile. "I'm sorry to bother you. I'm looking for Felicia Underwood."

Devon Shackley gave an irritable grunt. "No one here but me. And I don't know anyone named Felicia . . . whatever."

I suddenly had an idea. I quickly raised my phone and took his picture.

He shot me an angry look. "Hey, what the fuck do you think you're doing?"

I gave him an innocent look. "Nothing! Just checking Felicia's text." I turned to Alex, who looked a little startled, and showed him the phone. "She's in 2C, goofball. Come on." As I pulled Alex toward the elevator, I smiled and waved to Devon. "Sorry!"

I heard the door slam behind us. When we got back to the car, I told Alex to head for USC. Then I made a call.

TWENTY

Gayle was in class until five o'clock, so we decided to hit up Alicia's neighbors first. I showed Oliver Chalmers the photo of Devon Shackley. I'd taken a photo of him because I was worried the photo Alex had was too old. "Does he look like the guy with the crew cut who might have visited Alicia the day she died?"

He squinted at my phone screen and scratched the top of his head. "Don't know. Might be. But I wouldn't swear to it."

Which, of course, would be what I'd need him to do in court. I'd been so hopeful when Shackley had opened the door. He seemed to fit everyone's description of Crew Cut. On the other hand, Oliver hadn't ruled him out. Maybe Chinh's mother would come through. This time, Chinh wasn't there, but I managed to make myself understood to the mother and showed her the photo. She seemed nervous as she peered at it, then shook her head. I couldn't tell whether she meant "no" or that she didn't know. I asked her again, "Was this the man?"

She shook her head harder this time, then backed away and closed the door. Damn. Alex and I exchanged glum looks. I glanced at the photo on my phone screen. It was a little blurry but not bad. If Devon

Shackley was Crew Cut, they should be able to identify him. "Maybe this isn't our guy."

Alex was disappointed, too. "Maybe not. It did seem like a bit of a coincidence."

It did. But in a way, it didn't. "Since Shackley operated the website, he'd get first dibs on Alicia's address. How long had her photo been up when Crew Cut got here?"

Alex rubbed his chin. "I don't remember exactly. Not long. Maybe a couple of hours? Anyway, I see your point. And it's not over yet. We've still got Bethany and Gayle."

But Bethany wasn't home. I checked my phone and saw that it was almost five thirty, so we headed over to Gayle's house. Davey answered the door. He said Gayle was there, but Diana and Phil weren't. "There's a jazz concert at Thornton."

I could tell Phil had only just left. The cloying, sweet smell of pot still lingered in the air. Everyone in that house must live in a constant state of contact high, at the very least. "Not a problem. We just need to see Gayle this time."

Davey called out to her. A minute later, she emerged from her room. She looked exhausted, and her smile was forced, as though it took all she had to make it happen. "Hey. What's up? Anything new?" She sank down on one of the beanbag chairs and stretched out her legs.

We remained standing. One way or another, this wouldn't take long. I reminded her of the guy with the crew cut she'd seen leaving Alicia's apartment. "You remember him, right?" Gayle nodded. I held out my phone with his photo. "Might this be him?"

Gayle peered at the screen, then reached for the phone. I gave it to her and tried not to hope as I watched her study the photo. She began to nod. "Yeah, sure looks like him." She handed the phone back to me.

Finally, some good news. Though I wasn't sure how good. "Are you sure?"

"Pretty sure. Did you take that photo?" I nodded. "Is he kind of thick? Big arms, chest?" I nodded again. "Gotta be him. So you think he killed Alicia?"

What did I think? I still wasn't sure. "Maybe. He might've gone back to her apartment later. But I'm also thinking that if Roan didn't commit suicide, maybe this guy killed him."

Gayle looked confused. "Why? Did he know Roan?"

An excellent question. Just because Roan posted on his website—which we assumed but still hadn't proven—that didn't mean the guy knew Roan. "We're trying to figure that out." I glanced at Alex to see if he had any more questions for Gayle. Alex was texting on his cell phone. He never checked out on a witness interview like that. I wondered what he was doing. "Alex? Anything you want to ask?"

He looked up, his expression only mildly guilty. "Sorry. I just had some business to take care of. No, that'll do it. Thank you, Gayle. You were incredibly helpful." He edged toward the door.

I gave her a look of concern. "Try and get some rest, okay? I know they squeeze interns like a sponge mop."

She gave me a weary smile. "But at least the pay's great."

The studios paid their interns bupkes. I told her we'd keep in touch, and we headed back to Beulah. As soon as we got into the car, I turned to face Alex. "What the hell was up with all the texting?"

Alex looked wholly unrepentant. "You wanted me to wait and check out Devon Shackley before I made a plan. So I did. And now I'm making a plan."

I wasn't sure I liked the sound of that. "To do what?"

Alex gave an impatient sigh. "To spend some quality time with my new best friend, Devon. Whatever he was up to at Alicia's place, it couldn't have been good. I'm betting it had something to do with extortion."

I'd been thinking about that, too. Shackley might have visited Alicia so he could demand money to take down her photos. "So what's your plan?"

Alex told me he'd come up with the plan after I'd sent him home to get some sleep, and he'd already set it up from his home computer. "But you're not going to like it."

It was risky, to say the least. But he was wrong. I did like it. "I want in."

Alex leaned back against the headrest and groaned. "You can't be there. What if something goes wrong?"

"All the more reason why I *should* be there." I started the car. "You can waste time arguing or get on board now. Either way, we'll wind up in the same place."

"Mierda." He threw up his hands. "Fine."

I called Michy from the road and told her we wouldn't be coming back to the office tonight. "There's no point. We're just leaving USC, and it's already six o'clock."

"Great. I'll pack up and head out."

Nightfall came early this time of year, and by six o'clock, it was pitch-black outside. We drove back to Devon Shackley's apartment.

Alex's plan was simple—but multifaceted. That morning, after I'd sent him home, he'd Photoshopped a nude photo of a girl that looked like a selfie, added her name and address and a milder version of the invitation posted with Alicia's photo to "come over and play," and posted it on Shackley's website.

I parked near the entrance to Shackley's parking garage. According to Alex's research, Shackley drove a red Mustang. Of course he did. "So now we wait for him to take the bait."

Alex folded his arms and stared at the building. "Yep."

"And if he doesn't?" Alex was banking on this guy being consistent, but who knew with a freak like this? To put it mildly, the plan was far from foolproof.

"I have a plan B."

I sank down in my seat, thinking this could be a very long night.

I listened to a podcast by Malcolm Gladwell, then watched the news on my phone. "We should've picked up some food. I'm starving."

Alex barely took his eyes off the building as he pulled a small bag out of his pocket. "Here, this should help."

He handed the little bag to me. It was a pack of raw almonds. Not even the tasty smoked kind. "Must you always be so healthy? It's disgusting."

But I ate them anyway, which tells you how hungry I was. By eight thirty I was ready to call it quits, but Alex refused. "Just give it another half hour, okay?"

We'd been there for almost two hours, so I wasn't keen on making it three. But in for a penny . . . "We pull the plug at nine. No matter what."

We didn't. Alex talked me into giving it another half an hour.

At twenty minutes after nine, Shackley's red Mustang pulled out of the garage. Alex said, "Showtime."

I gave him a few seconds' lead, then pulled out and followed. I made sure to keep two car lengths back, but we weren't worried about losing him. If Alex's plan had worked, we knew where he was headed.

I felt my palms get sweaty on the steering wheel as I pictured all the ways this plan could go very, very wrong. I tried to put those thoughts out of my mind and focus on a more positive scenario, but my brain kept throwing up images of a bloody ending that left both Alex and me in jail, or the hospital, or both.

I lost Shackley a couple of times but then picked him up again as he drove south to Culver Boulevard, then turned right onto La Salle Avenue. That's when I knew we were in business. "Looks like he's taking the bait."

But no sooner had I said that than Shackley pulled over and parked the car. This was not the address he should have been aiming for. Alex, who'd been sitting low in his seat, jerked up. "What's he doing?"

I had to keep rolling, but as I drove by, I saw Shackley get out of his Mustang and move toward the back of the car. I tried to slow down without being obvious. "Can you see what he's doing?"

Alex swore under his breath. "He's getting something out of his trunk."

My heart gave a sharp thud. "What? Is he getting a gun?"

"I don't think so. It looks like . . . a towel? I can't tell."

I pulled over at the end of the block. "A gun can be wrapped in a towel. Alex, we need to let this go."

He shook his head as he stared into the rearview mirror. "I can't. I'll drop you off. You can Uber home."

Damn it. I couldn't let him do this alone. "You're not dropping me anywhere."

I looked in the rearview and saw that Shackley had gotten back into his car and was pulling out into traffic.

I let him have a five-second lead, then pulled out and followed him. Nothing about this felt good.

TWENTY-ONE

I stayed a couple of car lengths behind Shackley. The address Alex had posted was just one block away, on Braddock Drive. But when he reached it, he didn't stop; he kept on driving. I nodded toward Shackley's car. "Hey, I think we're toast." A part of me was glad. I parked just short of the address on Braddock Drive and watched as Shackley slowly pulled away.

Alex swore under his breath. *"Pendejo."*

But one block later, Shackley pulled over and parked. He got out and began to walk back toward the address. It was on.

Alex reached for the door handle. "You don't have to come in. I've got this."

I looked pointedly at his windbreaker. "You're not even carrying, are you?" He shook his head. As I'd thought. I opened my purse and took out my .38. "Well, I am." I put it in my jacket pocket and nodded toward Shackley. "And I'm betting he is, too."

Alex blew out a long breath. "Okay. Just stay back. You can't make money if you're in jail."

Actually, you can make money. Not much, it's true. But I didn't think the point was worth arguing at the moment. We watched as

Shackley went to the door of the house and knocked. It opened, and the moment he stepped inside, we got out and ran around to the back door.

As expected, it was unlocked. It opened onto the kitchen. We quietly tiptoed in and ducked down behind the stove. One second later, I saw Shackley stride through the living room and approach a woman with long black hair whose back was to us. I turned a furious look on Alex and mouthed, "WTF?" A man—a big, strong one who knew how to fight—was supposed to be there. Not a woman. I started to stand up, but Alex put a finger to his lips and pulled me back down.

Shackley was growling, "I know what you want, bitch—and I'm gonna give it to you." She protested and backed away, but he pushed her down on the couch and shoved a hand under her sweater. She lifted a knee to kick him, but Shackley seized her thigh and yanked her legs open.

That was it. Screw Alex and his bullshit plan. I reached for the gun in my pocket and prepared to run to her, but suddenly, Shackley went flying backward.

He landed flat on his back, winded. The woman jumped up and went after him. And now I could see that the woman was Louisa, an employee of Alex's bail bondsman uncle, Tomas. Louisa was smaller than Shackley, but she was throwing punches with the powerful yet surgical blows of a pro. As she turned Shackley's face into a smashed pumpkin, Tomas came rushing out of another room. He threw a few good kicks at Shackley's gut, then flipped him over and zip-tied his hands and feet.

Louisa was more than okay, but I was still pissed off at Alex. "You are such a dick sometimes."

Alex was completely unperturbed. "I knew you'd never go along with having a woman involved, and if I told you, we'd get in an argument, and I'd do it anyway. So why waste time arguing?"

I was uncomfortably familiar with this logic. Because it was mine. "You don't think we could've found out what Shackley was up to without using Louisa? What if he'd gotten the jump on her?"

He looked at me like I'd said the Easter Bunny might take out The Hulk. "In case you didn't just see her in action, there was no way that was going to happen. Besides, she had me and Tomas here for backup. And I had to know what his game was. The only way to be sure was to set up the bait and see what he did."

I wasn't in the mood to concede anything, but it was entirely possible that Alex was right. This had been the only way to know what Shackley was really up to. And in point of fact, it wasn't what we'd thought. We'd both believed his game was blackmail. But it was much, much worse. I still wasn't happy, but we had an asshole waiting in the next room. "Let's go ask some questions."

Shackley was on his stomach with Tomas's foot on his neck. I didn't particularly want to see his face—especially now—but I needed to be able to hear what he had to say, and that'd be difficult with his face smashed into the floor. "Can we turn him over?"

"Sure." Tomas grabbed him by the arm and yanked it—a little harder than necessary. Shackley let out a yelp as he landed on his back.

I could feel the anger rising in my chest as I looked at this puke and wondered how many women he'd assaulted. "So this is why you have that fucked-up website? So you can get first dibs on the women who've already been screwed over by their boyfriends?"

Shackley sputtered and gurgled for a few seconds. When he spoke, his voice was thick and wet. "You're full of shit. I just give them what they want."

I wanted to kick him in the crotch so badly it made my leg shake. "You lying sack. Tell the truth. Is this what you did to Alicia?"

He spit out a tooth. "Who the hell's Alicia?"

The gun felt heavy in my pocket. I had to force myself not to reach for it. "The one you killed, asshole."

Shackley's eyes got wild as they bounced among the four of us. "What are you talking about? I didn't kill no one!"

I stared down at him. "I've got witnesses who saw you at her apartment the day she was killed."

After a moment, recognition spread across his face. "You're talking about that chick on the news? Yeah. I did go see her. But I didn't kill her. I didn't do nuthin' to her!"

I spoke with harsh sarcasm. "Right. The same nuthin' you just did to her." I pointed to Louisa. Shackley was silent for a long moment. "I've got witnesses in that building who heard what you did to Alicia." I didn't, of course. But he didn't know that.

His eyes made another trip around the four faces hovering over him and landed on me. "I-I thought she'd be into it. That's what her post said!"

I couldn't help myself. "You lying sack. You knew she didn't post that."

He bent his knees and tried to wriggle away from me. "All I did was try to get with her, but she was a total bi . . . I mean, she said no. So I left! I swear! Nothing happened!"

That was at least partially true. The coroner hadn't issued a report yet, but Dale told me they'd done a rape kit and found no evidence of sexual activity. I couldn't bear to look at this piece of shit any longer. I glanced at Alex, who nodded and took over.

He asked, "How does it work? Do you filter the photos people send you?" Shackley nodded. "Did you post Alicia's photos before or after you went to her apartment?"

Shackley tried to lick his bloodied lips. "After."

It was even more obvious than I'd thought. Shackley didn't even post the photos until he'd had a chance to go after the girl.

Alex's nostrils flared. "So you use your website to get first dibs."

Shackley's fear shone in his eyes. "I only go after them if they ask for it." His voice got higher. "It's not my fault if they're cockteases!"

Alex glared at him; his voice was harsh and cold. "You trying to tell me you think they really have a rape fantasy?" Shackley didn't answer. "You sick puke. You're nobody's idea of a fantasy anything!" He drew back his foot and kicked Shackley in the side so hard he screamed.

I don't think I'd ever seen Alex that angry. I would gladly have let him go on kicking Shackley until he passed out, but we had one more piece of business. I stepped in and asked, "Where did you go after you attacked Alicia?"

Shackley was trying to catch his breath. "Work. Night manager at Wendy's. On Venice."

That sounded a lot like a real alibi. Damn. "What are your hours?"

He grimaced as he spoke. "Six thirty to midnight."

So much for Alicia's murder. I asked whether he'd been working on the night of Roan's murder. He was. "Where'd you go after work?"

Shackley was taking shallow breaths. It was a few seconds before he could answer. "Met friends at . . . Backstage Bar."

I'd check all this out, of course. But from the sounds of it, this was probably the last we'd see of this miserable dung heap—unless he decided to call the cops on us. I rated the likelihood of that at something below zero.

But Alex wasn't done with him yet. "I'll tell you what's going to happen now. We're going to take you home. And you're going to shut down that pile of sewage you call a website. From now on, I'll be watching you, and if you ever operate another one, it'll be the last thing you ever do. *M'entiende, cabròn?*"

Shackley nodded as best he could given the sorry state of his head.

I thanked Tomas and Louisa. Especially Louisa. "Where'd you learn to fight like that?" Now that I had a better chance to look at her, I could see the serious shoulders and biceps under her long-sleeve T-shirt.

She wore a proud smile. "My dad taught me when I was a kid. Said he wanted me to be able to take care of myself."

A pang unexpectedly hit me in the gut. I would've loved to have a father who taught me things like that when I was a kid. I forced a smile. "Your dad's a great guy."

Tomas nodded. "He's my cousin, and he is one helluva guy."

Tomas and Louisa carried Shackley out to Tomas's car. Alex said Tomas and Louisa would take Shackley home, and Alex would drive Shackley's car back to his place. "Then we'll all 'help' Shackley take down that disgusting website."

After they'd loaded Shackley into Tomas's car, Alex walked me back to Beulah. I hit the remote to unlock the door and turned to him. "I can't even imagine how many girls will have you to thank for putting this asshole out of business."

Alex stared at Shackley's car. "I'm not done. I'm gonna get that dick who owns the website where Laurie's photos were posted, too."

I smiled at him. "You're on a mission."

He nodded, his expression serious. "I guess I am."

I got into my car. "Just make sure you don't get caught." I closed my door and rolled down the window. "But, of course, if you do . . ."

Alex leaned down and finally smiled. "You'll be there."

"Right."

He patted the roof, and as I drove off, I pushed the button on my phone to turn the ringer on. I didn't think he'd run into any trouble tonight.

But you never know.

TWENTY-TWO

It'd been a long day—and night—and I was bone-tired.

I took a quick shower to get rid of the dried-up adrenaline sweat, put on my flannel PJ pants and T-shirt, and poured myself a shot of Patrón Silver. I'd more than earned it. I lay down on the couch and took a sip of my drink as I gave myself a moment to stare out at the clear night sky and decompress. Alex had shut down that hideous website—and its even uglier operator. But I'd just lost a straw man. It would've been nice if I could've thrown Devon Shackley at the cops to pull them off Graham's trail. But to be honest, I'd never held out much hope for that angle anyway.

I noticed the message light on my landline was blinking. Only one person ever called me on that phone. Dale. He didn't leave a message, just told me to call him. Maybe he had more news on Tracy Gopeck. As I picked up the phone and pressed his number, I hoped he'd at least tell me we could get a later start. I really needed to sleep in.

Dale squashed that hope. "I called you because I decided we should get on the road a little earlier, by six thirty a.m. We're going to see Tracy Gopeck's mother, and she lives in Riverside."

Damn. That'd be at least a two-hour ride. I promised to be ready when he came to pick me up. "But would you mind bringing coffee?"

Dale sighed. "Fine."

"And bagels?"

"Seriously? Why don't you just eat breakfast?"

Because the contents of my refrigerator consisted of lime wedges, lemon wedges, olives, and half a stick of butter. But if I told him that, he'd lecture me about healthy eating and go all "Dad" on me—which I cannot, and will *never* be able to, bear. "I can't eat anything else that early."

He gave another sigh and agreed to bring the bagels, then ended the call.

I looked at my phone. It was almost one a.m. I finished my drink, then put myself to bed, thinking I might get lucky; my brain might not have enough time or energy to crank up the nightmare.

In fact, not only did I *not* wake up screaming, I overslept. Pressed for time but triumphant—every time I managed to sleep through the night I felt like I'd handed Sebastian another defeat—I raced into the shower. At six thirty on the dot, I ran down the stairs to find Dale already waiting.

He was driving the usual unmarked car that screamed "cop"—or more accurately "detective." I saw two Venti hot Starbucks coffees in the cup holders and a brown bag that smelled like onions and garlic on the passenger seat. I got in, put the bag on my lap, and pointed to the two coffees. "What are you gonna drink?"

Dale stared at me. "You're kidding, right?"

I waved him off. "Never mind. We'll need a pit stop anyway. I'll refuel then."

He shook his head. "That's an awful lot of caffeine."

See what I mean? I held up a hand. "Uh-uh. No. You do not get to do that."

Dale rolled his eyes as he pulled into the street. "I printed out the information I got on Tracy's mom—Shelly Connor—and the family. It's in the pocket of your door."

I sipped my coffee as I read the printout. Shelly was forty-five. She had three daughters and two sons of her own, ranging between the ages of twenty-one and twelve. Tracy, at nineteen, was the second eldest of the crew. Shelly's eldest daughter, Tiffany—a name that guarantees there'll be a stripper pole in her future—had moved out when she was seventeen and was living with her boyfriend. The younger kids—Tammy, Tony, and Tommy (why do parents do this to their children?)—ages sixteen, fourteen, and twelve respectively, all lived at home. Tammy had been busted in her freshman year for drinking on school grounds—a violation I could relate to, having been busted for stashing a bottle of Jack Daniel's in my locker—and got detention for a week. Her bust immediately made me wonder whether she had the same reasons for drinking that I'd had—a pedophile in the house.

Shelly was currently living with Benjamin Posner, who added three boys of his own—ages twenty-one, sixteen, and fourteen—to the clan. They all lived at home.

Benjamin had been laid off from his job at the Acorn Furniture manufacturing plant six months earlier, and they were on welfare. Shelly had no criminal history, but Benjamin had a couple of busts for possession of powder cocaine. He'd pled guilty and been placed on probation in both cases. Benjamin had managed to successfully complete probation the first time but violated probation in his second case when he got busted for driving under the influence of alcohol—coincidentally, the day he got laid off. He'd done four days in jail and pled guilty for time served. His oldest son, Ronnie, had been suspended for fighting in school once during his sophomore year and twice in his junior year. He didn't get in trouble in his senior year, because by then he'd dropped out. He worked off and on for a small house-painting company. The middle son, Chuck, had been to juvenile hall for stealing from a couple of liquor stores. But Luke, the youngest son, was clean—so far.

Not exactly *The Brady Bunch*. I grabbed an onion bagel out of the bag and opened the small container of cream cheese. "How come there's nothing on Tracy?" I spread the cream cheese on my bagel and took a bite.

Dale glanced at me. "Because I couldn't find anything on her. As in, *nothing*."

I swallowed the bite of bagel. I could think of only one reason for that. "She's in protective custody."

Dale reached into the bag, pulled out an everything bagel, and handed it to me to do the honors. "That's my first guess. My distant second is that she hooked up with someone like Alex, and he hacked into the system and deleted her records."

I spread cream cheese on the bagel and handed it back to Dale. Not that I doubted Alex could do anything he wanted, but even he had never mentioned being able to hack the police department's databases. "Can someone even do that? I thought your databases were pretty secure."

Dale sighed and shook his head. "Nothing's that secure anymore. Last year, some hackers broke into a police database in Massachusetts and encrypted the files so no one could access them. Not even the cops. The hackers demanded twenty thousand bucks to break the encryption. The department couldn't find anyone else who could do it, so they had to pay up."

This was excellent news for me. If those idiots could find a way to break into a police database, Alex could certainly hack in and do more useful things—like make criminal histories disappear. But we'd have to reserve that superpower for the very rare, deserving cases, because if Alex got caught . . . I didn't even want to think about it. I turned my thoughts back to Tracy. "The fact that you came up with nothing must mean there's really something to find."

Dale took a sip of coffee. "Maybe. But maybe not. If she's in protective custody, they might have decided it was better to just do a complete blackout, even if there isn't much there. Why take chances?"

I took another bite of bagel and washed it down with the last of my coffee. "But if she is in protective custody, the cops must think Jorge Maldonado's involved in something big." I took Dale's coffee out of the holder.

Dale raised an eyebrow. "Can't imagine what that might be."

"Right." If the cops thought Jorge had dirt on Javier Cabazon, that would definitely qualify as "something big." I took a sip of Dale's coffee. "So the cops are using the murder rap to squeeze information out of Jorge?"

Dale eyed the cup of coffee in my hand. "Seems likely."

I snorted. "Huh. Seems impossible. No one screws Cabazon over and lives to talk about it. Especially not a grateful nephew."

"I'm not saying their play will work. But I can see why they'd give it a try."

"We're assuming Tracy didn't just ghost on the cops and decide to hide out until the case blows over." That wasn't the greatest likelihood, but it wasn't impossible, either. "If she is hiding out, they'll need to let Jorge go at some point—unless they have some other evidence."

Dale reached out and took his coffee from me. "That'd be best for everyone, as long as Cabazon never finds Tracy. But we can't count on getting that lucky. And if she is in protective custody, I don't know how we persuade her to trust us."

True. Tracy was undoubtedly looking forward to getting her testimony over with and going into witness protection. They'd give her a new identity and monthly checks—for a while, and maybe for life. Why on earth *would* she cooperate with us? "We just have to hope we can get her to see that we're telling the truth, that there's no such thing as witness protection when it comes to Cabazon."

"Assuming we get her to believe us, then what? Do you have a plan? 'Cause I sure don't."

Actually, I did have the broad outline of a plan in mind. But I needed more information before I could fill in the specifics. "I'm working on it." I leaned back and looked out the window at the rusting train tracks, burned-out buildings, and ugly procession of strip malls. We rode in silence until Dale pulled off the freeway and navigated to a neighborhood that looked like it belonged in a third-world country.

The shell of a car with no wheels or license plate sat on the front lawn of one house—if you could call a weed-infested patch littered with old beer cans and cheap liquor bottles a lawn. A dog whose ribs were showing slunk down the street in search of food. A young girl who looked no more than fourteen years old held a diapered baby on her hip and the hand of a toddler wearing a stained onesie who stumbled drunkenly next to her.

The broken windows and eviction notices on the house farther down the street said the owners had abandoned it, but the needles that littered what used to be flower beds said others had taken their place. A heavy fog of despair hung over the whole neighborhood. Dale turned right at the corner and pulled up in front of a small house with an old-fashioned front porch. The steps that led up to the porch sagged, and the paint was peeling everywhere. Tattered blue-checkered curtains hung in the front windows. But the tiny postage stamp of a lawn had some patches of grass and even a couple of white rose bushes on either side of the walkway—no small feat given Southern California's years of drought.

I saw that there was an old black Ford pickup truck in the driveway, but I couldn't tell whether anyone was home. "What's our cover story?" To put it mildly, there was nothing official about this visit—no one could ever know who we really were.

Dale pointed to the glove box. "I found some pamphlets for a counseling center for juvies at the station. I figured with all those kids, Shelly might like a little help—especially since she qualifies for six months free."

I gave a short chuckle. "We're quite the bargain." But it was a smart play. It gave us a believable reason to ask about Tracy. I looked at the little house and tried to imagine how so many people could live there. From what I could see, there were, at most, three bedrooms. Just thinking about the cramped quarters made it hard to breathe. I reminded myself that it was just a visit; I didn't have to live there. I opened the glove box and took out the pamphlets.

Dale scanned the house with that cop gaze, always in search of danger signals—and points of escape. "Ready?" I nodded. "Let's do this."

We got out and headed up the walk.

TWENTY-THREE

Shelly answered Dale's knock on the door. I knew it had to be her, because Tiffany, the only other adult female in the family, didn't live there anymore. Otherwise, I'm not sure I would've tagged her as the mother. She was slender and vaguely pretty the way people with no outstanding features can be. Her light-brown wavy-frizzy hair flowed down to the middle of her back. The colorful peasant blouse, blue pull-on pants, and short sheepskin boots completed an overall bohemian impression. Dale introduced us as John Lefcourt and Elizabeth Murdock, the people from the Peace at Home counseling center.

Shelly smiled and swept a stray hair out of her eyes. "Yes, come on in. I'm so happy to see you."

The sweetness of her welcome made me feel guilty—until I remembered that Dale and I were on a mission to save her daughter's life. We moved into a cluttered living room where every piece of furniture looked like it'd been thrashed beyond repair years ago. The Poly-Fiber stuffing was seeping out of an aging blue sofa, the formerly beige carpet was now covered with stains and riddled with rips and holes, and the cable-spool coffee table had been the site of some serious mishaps—both food- and non-food-related. It was banged up as though someone had tried to kill it. Next to the sofa was a fake leather recliner with a broken footstool, and on the other side of the coffee table was a barrel chair, its original color no longer discernible after multiple repairs with a variety of different-colored patches.

I perched on the edge of the barrel chair—which looked like the safest bet, insect-wise—and Dale braved a place on the sofa. The smells of old bacon grease and dirty socks permeated the air. As I suspected, the house had just three bedrooms, and I could see them all down the short hall that led out of the living room. The doors were closed, but rap music thumped behind at least two of them.

Shelly sat down next to Dale and gestured toward the bedrooms. "As you can tell, it's a full house. Lots of teenagers"—she paused, then smiled—"and lots of drama."

Dale gave her a sympathetic smile. "Almost ninety percent of our work is devoted to families with teenagers because . . . well, they generally do pose some of the most challenging problems. Our records show that your eldest, Tiffany, is living with her boyfriend, is that correct?"

Shelly nodded, her expression bland. "They were so in love. It just seemed right to let them start their lives together."

Letting a seventeen-year-old girl move in with her boyfriend struck me as anything but "right." But what did I know? I didn't have kids. I asked, "Does she live nearby?"

Shelly frowned. "In Redlands, down by San Bernardino. Is there some reason why you'd need to talk to her, too?"

Yes, because I wanted another source of information on Tracy. This obviously was not the explanation that suited. "I only wondered because if she was close by, she might've been taking care of the other kids—in which case, we'd need to talk to her, get her input on them."

It sounded lame to me, but Shelly bought it. "I don't see too much of Tiffany these days. She just had her second baby, so as you can imagine, she's pretty busy."

Her *second* baby? Jeez.

Dale took over. "Just for our records, can you give us Tiffany's last name and address?"

"They didn't get married, so she still has her maiden name, Gopeck," Shelly said. "They live at 1313 Calhoun Street."

"Do your other three children go by the name Gopeck also?" Dale asked.

Shelly shook her head. "Their father's name was Traffort."

Shelly's current last name was Connor, so that meant there had been another husband after him. And now there was Benjamin Posner. I'm not one to judge, but our Shelly was one busy mama. I decided to get to the point. "Does Tracy still live here?"

Shelly's bland smile fell away. "No, Tracy hasn't lived here for a long time." A look of bewildered sadness spread across her features. "She was such a good girl, a smart girl. But she started running away, and . . . I just couldn't seem to keep her home."

Her reaction—confused but not really concerned—struck me as bizarre. No kid repeatedly runs away just for shits and giggles. But Shelly seemed to be fine living in the mystery. "When was the first time she ran away?"

Shelly stared off in the distance. "I believe it was right after Benjamin moved in. When she was twelve."

Warning bells went off in my head. I was about that same age when Celeste moved us in with Sebastian. I forced myself not to jump to conclusions. Not every preteen girl was victimized by a pedophile. "Did she have problems with Benjamin? Or his sons?"

Shelly gave me an earnest look. "No, not at all. Everyone got along great."

I wasn't buying it. "Are you sure? You didn't see any kind of . . . tension? Or fights between them?"

This time Shelly was adamant. "Absolutely not."

I gave up and moved on. "Do you know where she went when she ran away?"

Shelly shook her head. "I never knew. She'd be gone for a few days, maybe a week—sometimes two weeks. Once in a while she'd come home on her own, but mostly the police would bring her back. I always asked her where she'd been, but she'd never say."

Dale glanced at me—a signal that he wanted to jump in. "Did she get any counseling in juvenile hall?"

He'd taken a shot in the dark—but it was a safe bet Tracy had been to juvenile hall, and probably more than once. Sure enough, Shelly replied, "They said she did, but it definitely didn't help." She gave Dale a weak smile. "That's why I'm so hopeful that we can qualify for help from your center."

This time, I didn't feel guilty about giving her our fake story about the counseling center. I was pissed. Shelly's uselessness in the face of Tracy's obvious anguish proved yet again that neglect—no matter how benign—could be just as devastating as active abuse. "Are you still in touch with Tracy?"

Shelly had a weary look. "I haven't spoken to her in months. I called her a few times, but she never returned my calls. Eventually, I gave up."

I wondered how long "eventually" was. A month? A week? "Do you know where she lives?"

"I know where she lived when she first moved out," Shelly said. "But that was almost two years ago, and I found out she doesn't live there anymore because I went there when she stopped returning my calls."

Dale cleared his throat. "Did you report her missing?"

Shelly looked down at her hands, which were folded in her lap. "No, I . . . I guess I should have. But she disappears so much, I was sure she'd turn up again." She gazed over Dale's shoulder. "She always does."

I'd noticed a few family photographs in cheap metal frames on a side table. One showed Shelly with a man—her current amour, Benjamin, I surmised. The second was a photo of her two boys, and the third showed a dark-haired girl with a hand on the shoulder of a shorter blonde girl. Both the photo Cabazon had given me and the DMV photo Dale had pulled up showed Tracy to be blonde. I pointed to the photo. "Is the little one Tracy?"

Shelly glanced at it. "No. That's Tammy. My youngest."

I didn't see any other photos that seemed to be of Tracy on the table. "Do you have any photographs of Tracy?"

"I suppose I must have a few somewhere. I can't recall where at the moment." Shelly looked perplexed. "I don't understand why that's important."

And I didn't understand why a mother would have photos on display that showed all but one of her children. I was trying to come up with a reason to ask that question when footsteps on the flimsy wooden porch announced the arrival of another member of the tribe. A man in his forties, with longish, stringy brown hair; big, round blue eyes; and the ruddy complexion of a drinker came in and slammed the front door behind him. He stopped at the entry to the living room and glared at Dale and me, then at Shelly. "Who are these people?"

Shelly made the introductions. Not surprisingly, this phenomenal catch of a man was Benjamin Posner. She gave him a shaky smile. "They're going to try and get us into the counseling program."

Benjamin snorted. "Counseling. What a crock." He nodded toward the kitchen. "We got any of that pot roast left?"

He was the prototypical angry white male, and I just couldn't help but bait him. "Don't you think Tracy might've been better off if she'd had counseling?"

His face darkened. "That girl was nothing but trouble from jump. Counseling wouldn't have done dick for a piece of work like her."

Shelley recoiled as though she'd been slapped. "Ben, please don't talk about her like that. Tracy had her problems but—"

"But nothing." He sneered at her. "Face it. The girl was a friggin' whore." Benjamin shot a heated look at Dale and me. "She didn't tell you about that, did she? About how every time she ran off, the cops caught her tricking?"

Shelly looked miserable, and even though I still thought she was a piss-poor excuse for a mother, I wanted to slap this asshat across the face. Fortunately for both of us, Dale saw the danger signs in my eyes and stepped in. "Mr. Posner, the program will want to know a little more about what was going on with Tracy. Do you happen to know who any of Tracy's boyfriends were?"

He spoke with bitter sarcasm. "Anyone who had ten bucks to spare."

His words were calculated to wound Shelly, and I could see that they did. But I needed a real answer. "When she left for the last time, did she move in with anyone?"

Shelly grasped her knees and tried to recover, but her voice shook as she spoke. "I think she was seeing a boy named, ah . . . Corey?" She nodded to herself. "Yes, Corey Washington. He came by one day not long before Tracy left for the last time. But we only spoke for a few minutes, and she didn't say she planned to move in with him. So . . . I don't know if she's with him now."

Shelly was pathetic. Benjamin was a pig. I'd had enough. I'd considered asking how the youngest daughter, Tammy, was doing. After what I'd seen in that house, I was more certain than ever that her bust for possession of alcohol was a symptom of some kind of abuse. But I didn't think I could stand to hear the clueless lies I knew I'd get from Shelly and her amour, Benjamin. I caught Dale's eye. He nodded and stood up. "Thank you very much for taking the time, Ms. Connor. We'll be in touch." He looked at Benjamin but didn't offer to shake. "Mr. Posner."

I thanked Shelly, gave her asshole boyfriend a curt nod, and followed Dale outside. The moment we got into the car, Dale said, "Don't start yelling till we get out of range, okay?"

We buckled up, and Dale pulled away. I managed to hold off for two blocks, but then . . . "Fuck those two! Both of them! What on earth is that idiot mother doing shitting out a million babies when she can't be bothered to even figure out where the hell they are? And that crap excuse for a human Posner. I bet he beats the shit out of her on a daily basis. Not that I mind!" Dale wore a little smile. "What? Don't tell me I'm wrong!"

Dale shook his head. "You're not wrong. I agree with everything you said." He steered onto the freeway. "Tell me, did you get a molest-y vibe off him?"

I'm usually a little too good at spotting the pedophiles. "Honestly, I was so pissed off by the time he walked in—and he was such an obvious asshole—I don't know. I could go either way."

Dale looked troubled. "Well, something went on in that house." He drummed his fingers on the steering wheel for a moment. When he spoke, his tone was soft, tentative. "How come you never ran away?"

My stomach tightened. Dale was the only one I'd ever told about exactly what I'd gone through during the year I'd spent living in hell, AKA Sebastian Cromer's mansion. He'd wondered why I hated Celeste, so I'd had to tell him what Sebastian had been doing and how she'd accused me of lying and turned a blind eye to it all. Even when I'd shown her the photo I'd managed to take of Sebastian reaching for me as I lay in my bed, she'd simply claimed I'd "set him up." But I'd never spoken to Dale about it since. And until now, he'd never brought it up. I knew it wasn't just because he wanted to save me the pain. It was also because it made him lose his shit. Dale had been in custody during his murder case when I told him what Sebastian had done to me, and Dale had gone so crazy they had to carry him out of the visitors' room.

I gave him a sidelong glance. I wasn't sure he'd want to hear about my runaway days, but since he asked . . . "Who says I didn't?"

He almost did a double take, then asked, "What made you go back?"

I couldn't keep the bitterness out of my voice, and I didn't try. "He did. He couldn't risk letting me out of his sight. Couldn't risk my telling people what he'd done to me. He knew that at some point I might find someone he couldn't buy off. And he had the money to pay for the best to track me down." Not that it took investigative genius to track down a thirteen-year-old with no money and few friends.

Dale gripped the steering wheel so hard I heard it squeak. "Where did you go?"

"The street, the park, my English teacher's house." I couldn't go to Michy's place. That was the first place they'd look.

Dale glanced at me. "Your English teacher? Why didn't she call the police?"

I stared at him. "That was the last thing *he* wanted to do." Mr. Pruitt—"call me Bobby"—was just a kinder, gentler version of Sebastian. But anything was better than that sadistic monster. Just thinking about that time made me feel like I was drowning in the darkness again. I didn't want to talk about it anymore. "Do you think Tracy really was hooking? Or was the jackass just trying to piss Shelly off?"

Dale glanced at me again, saw that the subject was closed. He swallowed, then set his jaw, his expression grim. "I don't know. And since I can't access her information in the database, the only way to find out would be to find people who knew her back then. But—and I don't want to sound like a callous jerk here—we've got a much more immediate problem to solve."

True. We had a life-or-death problem, and limited time to solve it. Just because Cabazon had deputized us to find her, that didn't mean he wasn't deploying his own resources as well.

And if they found Tracy before we did, she'd be dead. I'd been committed to saving her before, but I was twice as determined now.

Tracy deserved to have someone in her life care whether she lived or died.

TWENTY-FOUR

We'd stopped for lunch on the way back and wound up hitting the usual Saturday evening traffic, so it was almost six thirty p.m. when Dale dropped me back home.

He was going to track down the reports on the murder, but he didn't want to be seen at the department on a Saturday. It'd raise too many questions, since he wasn't working an active case.

But we couldn't afford to lose a whole weekend, so Dale was going to try and get in touch with Tiffany, the eldest sister, who lived in Redlands. We were hoping she was in contact with Tracy—and that she'd be willing to cooperate. If not, I'd have the rest of the weekend off.

I needed it. It'd been a tough week and an even tougher day for me. I went through my e-mails for a couple of hours, scanned the news programs I'd recorded to see if there was any mention of Graham—and only finally exhaled when I saw that no more bombs had exploded. After a shower and a double shot of Patrón Silver, I got into bed and checked my e-mail on my phone. Niko was supposed to be back from New York tomorrow, and we'd planned to have dinner. But he'd written to tell me that he couldn't make it; they'd asked to extend the master classes he was teaching for another week. I was relieved. After my visit with Tracy's mother and her cretin of a boyfriend, I had no appetite for sex or romance.

I went to bed feeling drained and wound up having a horrible night. Not surprising given the visit with Tracy's mother.

On Sunday morning, Dale called to tell me he hadn't reached Tiffany, so I could stand down for now. I dragged myself through the usual chores on Sunday: laundry, the dry cleaners, some minimal grocery shopping, and all the dusting, scrubbing, and vacuuming—the latter of which I always found soothing. The rest, I just held my nose and powered through.

Sunday night, I celebrated by getting together with Michy and Hank, AKA Harriet—a great cop who'd turned into a great friend, an irony Michy never failed to mention—for some Christmas shopping at the adult Disneyland known as The Grove. We capped it off with dinner at The Whisper, a casual speakeasy-style lounge with live piano music. It was icy-cold outside, but the patio was enclosed and had good heaters. And we all had shots of Glenlivet—the best heater of all.

We'd just ordered dinner when Michy's phone dinged. She frowned as she reached into her purse. "That's the Google Alert for Graham's case." She looked at me as she fished out her phone. "How come your phone didn't ding?"

I sighed. "'Cause I put it on silent." I'd just wanted one quiet day. Was that too much to ask? Apparently so.

Michy scrolled for a second, then put a hand to her forehead. "Oh my God."

Hank and I exchanged looks. As I pulled my purse onto my lap and dug around for my phone, Hank asked, "What?"

Michy stared at the screen. "Audrey Sutton must be paying off someone at TMZ."

I fished out my phone and found the story. "Graham got fired for sexually harassing his paralegal when he was a first-year associate."

Hank rolled her eyes. "Well, that sucks. Did he respond?"

I nodded as I read. "He swears it was just a misunderstanding. He thought she was interested, so he made a pass at her at an office Christmas party—"

"How timely," Hank interjected sarcastically as she glanced at the red-and-green lights strung around the restaurant. The whole Grove had been decked out for the holidays, which were fast approaching.

Michelle added, "He says he apologized to her at the time and that it all would've blown over if the managing partner's son hadn't wanted him out."

Hank folded her arms and sat back. "So it was just office politics, not the fact that he couldn't keep it in his pants? I'm not buying it."

But Hank was a cop. There wasn't much she did buy. Not that I blamed her. "And I'm sure you're not alone." Some might believe Graham, but I'd bet most wouldn't.

In the battle for the hearts and minds of potential jurors, my side had just taken another body blow.

Not the best way to end the weekend.

When I got in to the office Monday morning, Alex came out to tell me that he'd made some progress in my absence. "Remember that Italian cinema teacher Nomie mentioned?"

The "hottie" professor. How could I forget? Every school had at least one. And I was sure that a film- and TV-oriented school like USC had many more than that. "You talked to him?"

"Just briefly on the phone. I said we were looking into Alicia's murder, and he seemed willing to talk, but I think we should see him in person."

Using Alicia's murder—not Roan's death—as our entrée was a deliberate choice. It immediately made us more sympathetic—translation: encouraged more cooperation. No one wanted to look like they were stonewalling an investigation into the murder of an innocent, and well-liked, young woman. "Nice job, Alex. Did you set up a time?" Intuitive instincts like his were what set the talent apart from the hacks.

Alex glanced at his watch. "I made an appointment for ten thirty. He said he could give us half an hour."

I noticed that his watch looked new—and suspiciously like a Baume & Mercier. "Nice watch. Is it real?"

His smile, part proud, part embarrassed, said it all. "Yeah. It's a gift from Paul. He gets great deals on duty-free."

Yet another perk of dating an airline pilot. "Sweet." I hoped this worked out. Because if Paul hurt Alex, I'd hunt him down and wear his skin as a cape.

I checked in with Michy. "Any *more* news from *TMZ*?"

Michy held up her hands and raised her eyes to the ceiling. "Thank God, not so far. But the day is young."

I thought about calling Graham to get the full story but decided against it for now. The full story didn't matter, and the last thing I wanted to do was give him the impression that it did. It'd only encourage him to talk to yet another reporter. I'd warned him repeatedly not to do it, and he'd repeatedly ignored me. My only hope was that the story would play itself out. It really was the very definition of old news.

I looked up Jorge Maldonado's case on the court website and found the name of his attorney—Diego Ferrara. I'd never heard of him. I didn't know the prosecutor, Rick Moringlane, either. He must be new to the downtown courthouse. I'd have to find a nonsuspicious way to get his take on Ferrara and on the murder case. That was all the progress I had time to make on Tracy's case for now, so I spent the rest of the next hour working on some of my other cases.

At nine thirty, Alex came to my office and knocked on the doorframe. "Ready?"

I picked up my purse and glanced out the window. The view it gave of the side of a brick building wasn't inspiring, but it did give me a sliver of sky that let me check on the weather. The leather jacket

I'd brought, because the sun had been shining when I left that morning, might not cut it now. Clouds had moved in, and the sky had darkened. It looked like it might rain. I kept a black wool scarf and spare raincoat—one that had wool lining—in the bottom drawer of my desk for emergencies like this. I shook out my coat, put it on, and wrapped the scarf around my neck.

Alex smirked. "Nice look, Nanook."

Alex was one of those people who never got cold. I glared at him. "Shut up."

I told Michy we'd be back after lunch, and we headed down to the garage. Since we expected to be done with the interview way before dark, Alex said he'd drive. "The less you drive that clunker, the better."

We were just ten feet away from Beulah. "You may not insult my ride. She's a classic."

Alex hit the remote to unlock his car and opened the driver's door. "No, she's a relic. There's a difference."

I held up a hand as I opened the passenger side door. "I am not even listening."

We got in, and as Alex pulled out of the garage, he said, "She can't hear you, you know."

I gave an exasperated sigh. "I know that." But Alex raised an eyebrow. I didn't bother to argue, because it was true. I did have a weirdly superstitious, overpersonalized attitude about Beulah. It wasn't healthy.

I spent most of the ride privately obsessing about whether Dale had learned anything new since Saturday. I'd expected to hear from him first thing this morning, but he hadn't called, and when I'd called him, it'd gone straight to voice mail. I couldn't stop worrying that Cabazon had decided to contact Dale personally to put more pressure on—and what form that pressure might take. Guys like Cabazon weren't long on patience. They solved problems with bullets, not brains. I had to make sure Dale and I didn't become two more problems he needed to solve.

I decided that if I hadn't heard from Dale by the time we finished with the professor, I'd tell Alex to stop at the PAB and go see Dale in person.

We managed to get to the professor's office a few minutes early. I knocked on the door, and a deep voice inside told us to come in. Professor Barth Foley wasn't exactly who I'd pictured him to be—but he was close. Thick brown hair long enough to curl down his neck in the back, a sexy smile, and brown eyes that crinkled at the corners under bushy eyebrows. I'd expected a pierced ear, a leather bracelet, and maybe a tasteful tattoo, but no. He did, however, wear a chain bracelet, visible because his shirtsleeves were rolled up to reveal tanned and somewhat muscled forearms. A young woman sat in the chair in front of his desk. As she turned to give us an annoyed look, I saw that she was pretty—of course she was.

For some reason, her annoyance amused me. I gave Professor Barth an extra-warm smile. "Sorry, I know we're early. Want us to wait outside?"

He returned my smile, and I enjoyed the likelihood that that probably irritated her even more. "No, no. We were just wrapping up." He told her, "I think you can take it from there, Meredith. If you have any other questions, you know where to find me."

She said she did, thanked him, then left—but not before throwing a bitchy look at Alex and me. I gave her a saccharine-sweet smile, and we moved to the chairs in front of his desk.

He called out to her, "Would you close the door, please?"

I couldn't resist. I turned around and smiled. "Thanks."

Meredith shot me a death glare as she closed the door.

TWENTY-FIVE

He offered us coffee from the pot on the table behind him, but we declined. And when I called him Professor Foley, he flashed me a smile with a little extra wattage and said, "Call me Barth."

I'd give him this much, he was true to type. I didn't need to give Alex a sign for him to know that this witness was mine. "I hear Alicia was in your class."

The smile faded. "She was." His eyes strayed off. "I can't believe she's . . . gone."

I told him no one could. "And there doesn't seem to be anyone besides Roan who had an ax to grind with her."

Barth looked sad and . . . what else? He seemed troubled. "No, that's true. Everyone liked Alicia." He met my gaze. "Roan was in my class, too."

I hadn't known that. "What did you think of him?"

Barth's mouth twisted. "Honestly? He was a bright kid, but there was something . . . odd about him. It seemed to me that he was a little tightly corked, like 'contents under pressure.' I didn't really see what he and Alicia had in common."

There was a little twinge in his voice. I thought I knew why. "What did you think of her?"

His face brightened. "She was like a little diamond, beautiful in every way. And she was smart, had a deep understanding of the filmic arts."

And of Professor Barth, I suspected. "When was the last time you saw her?"

Barth knitted his brows. "I guess it was a couple of days before she . . . died."

"Was that in class? Or after?"

"Both. She stayed after class to talk about the film we were studying, *Bicycle Thieves*."

I wondered whether she'd told him about her plan to break up with Roan. "How was she? Did anything seem to be bothering her?"

Barth stared off to my left again. "I didn't notice anything in particular at the time, just that she seemed a little . . . anxious. But now, in hindsight, I'd say it was more than just anxious. She seemed . . . agitated."

I decided to push a little harder. "Did you know if there was some problem between her and Roan?"

He rubbed the arms of his chair. "I . . . Uh, no."

He was clearly uncomfortable. I sat in silence for a beat to let his discomfort grow. "Where did you see her after class? Was it here? Or did you go somewhere?"

Barth took a deep breath, then met my gaze. "Is this confidential?"

He'd broken down more easily than I'd expected. I did the usual lawyer thing to put him at ease. "Give me a dollar." He fished his wallet out of his back pocket and handed me the money. "Consider me retained. You're covered." I tilted my head toward Alex. "And he's my investigator, so he's covered by the privilege, too."

Barth expelled a long breath. "We were kind of dating. It hadn't been long. Just a couple of lunches, plus one dinner—after I'd given a special night lecture for a seminar series on Depression Era films in Europe."

I was about to ask whether they'd slept together, but then I realized it didn't matter. What mattered was what people knew. "Did Roan know you were seeing her?"

Barth clasped his hands together, his forearms still on the chair. "I d-don't think so. I certainly never told him."

But he looked awfully edgy. Something else was bothering him. "What would've happened to you if the dean had found out you were dating a student?"

Barth sighed heavily. "I would've been fired." A look of alarm crossed his face. "You said this was privileged."

I held up my hands. "It is. You have nothing to worry about." At least not from me. If someone else found out, Barth was on his own. "Did Alicia tell you about the nude selfies she'd sent to Roan?"

His eyes bounced away, and he shifted in his seat. "No. I only found out about that after she . . . died." He shook his head. "I can't believe he did that to her. I didn't have a great feeling about Roan, but I never would've thought he'd do something as ugly as that."

He seemed genuinely upset, but there was something off here. "Can you tell me where you were the night Alicia died?"

Barth looked distracted. He ran a hand through his hair. "Uh, yeah. I was at a writer's roundtable here at the university. Didn't hear about her . . . her death until the next morning."

Alex's phone dinged. I turned to look at him, startled. We always turn off our phones during interviews. He lifted his hands and shrugged. "Sorry! I need to go take this. Meet you at the car?"

I nodded and waved him off. "Go. I can wrap up." I saw by Alex's expression that he was purposely giving me some "alone time" with the professor. A very good move.

Barth seemed to visibly relax the moment the door closed behind Alex. "I don't want you to hear this from someone else. I'm not proud of it, but the night Alicia died, I was with a . . . a colleague."

I put it bluntly. "You mean you were having sex with a woman." He nodded. This man was a total hound. He seemed to feel a little guilty about it, but I didn't think that's what was bothering him. I took a shot at another possibility. "Did you know that Roan had posted revenge porn before?"

Barth's face reddened, then he nodded. "I was talking to a group of students after class about *Juliet of the Spirits*, a Fellini film—"

"I'm familiar with it."

He nodded. "And about how after her husband cheated on her, Juliet engaged in a number of . . . ah, unusual sexual activities. I called it a journey of self-discovery, but one of the girls said it sounded more like payback. After the group broke up, Roan bragged to me privately about how he'd given his girlfriend the ultimate payback after she broke up with him."

The reason for his edginess—or at least a part of the reason—became clear. "So he told you he'd revenge porned a girlfriend in the past, but you never told Alicia."

Barth shook his head, his expression guilty. "I should have told her. But I was afraid she'd think I was just being jealous, trying to break them up." After a moment he added, "And I worried that maybe Roan had found out about us, and that's why he posted Alicia's photos."

I thought that last part was strange. "Why? According to Alicia's friends, he posted the photos right after she broke up with him. Seems like that would be the more obvious motive." I peered at Barth. "Unless you have reason to believe Roan did find out about you and Alicia."

He stared down at his desk. "No, as far as I knew, Roan never found out."

Then why did Barth seem so frazzled? "Did you see Roan after Alicia died?" He shook his head. "Did you see him shortly before her death?"

"I saw him in class a day or so before."

"Did he seem depressed? Distracted?"

Barth frowned. "Not that I remember. But I didn't have any personal contact with him outside of class in the last few days." He spread his hands. "Like I said, Roan had his issues. At times it seemed like a cloud of anger swirled around him for no discernible reason. At least none that I could see. But those last few days I don't remember seeing anything particularly unusual about him."

I still got the feeling there was something else going on with the professor, but I couldn't seem to get at what it was. So I asked my last question. "Did you have a class on November seventh?"

Barth's brows furrowed. "The seventh? Was that Friday?" I nodded. "Just in the afternoon."

"What about that night? Did you have any meetings or a date?"

Recognition made his face sag. That was the night of Roan's death. "No. I stayed home. Alone. But why are you asking about him? I thought he committed suicide."

I looked into his eyes. "Some questions have been raised. I'd advise you to stick around if you don't want to raise any more of them."

I reassured Barth that his affair with Alicia would remain a secret between us and told him that there was nothing else for him to worry about. His failure to tell Alicia that Roan had revenge porned another girl didn't make him liable for anything. "And your reasons for not telling her make sense. Don't worry about it."

For now. I knew he was holding out on me about something. Whether it had to do with Roan's death was another matter. But I was going to find out. One way or another.

I met Alex at the car, and as he drove us back to the office, I filled him in on my interview with Professor Barth—and my sense that he was holding out on us.

Alex got that determined look I knew so well. "I'll check him out. If there's something there, I'll find it."

I almost felt sorry for poor old Barth.

We were just ten minutes away from the office when Michy called to tell me I had a visitor. I stopped breathing for a second—was it one of Cabazon's men?—and then she told me it was Dale. When we got in, I let Dale and Alex chat for a few minutes, then tapped my wrist. "Ticktock, boys. I've got prosecutors to shred." Dale and Alex exchanged an amused look. I waved a finger between the two of them. "And don't do that 'isn't she cute' thing. It's nauseating."

Michy smiled and gave me a thumbs-up.

Dale held up his hands in mock surrender, but Alex gave a disapproving *tsk* as he headed for his office. As I led the way into my office, I said loudly, "So what popped you out of your cage?"

Dale gestured to the door, and I nodded. He closed it and sat down in one of the chairs in front of my desk. I took the chair next to him and spoke in a low voice. "What do you have?"

Dale kept his voice low, too. "Actually, I have two things. First, the coroner put out a tox report on Alicia Hutchins. They found low levels of Oxy in her blood."

"Not enough to kill her." He shook his head. I thought, *But probably enough to party on.*

Dale sighed. "I don't think it means much. Just more proof that she was really enjoying her freedom—as kids do."

In and of itself, Dale was right: this news wasn't shocking; a lot of kids did oxy—and much more—just for fun. But it was a step further than I'd thought she'd gone, a small fissure in the persona I'd come to know as Alicia. I filed it away for future consideration. "Thanks for that." But he could've told me that on the phone. "I'm guessing the second thing has to do with Tracy Gopeck."

He nodded. "I checked out the reports on the Maldonado murder. The victim was a shot caller for the Playboy Rollin' 60s."

"That's what Cabazon said. But he didn't think this was a gang thing. You disagree?"

Dale shrugged. "Not necessarily. Maldonado got stopped with some members of the Guttah Gunz gang when he was seventeen, and they used to be rivals of the Playboys. But I hear they haven't been beefing for a while now."

"As far as you know." These gangs changed direction when the wind blew. "It's not like we're talking about ExxonMobil and Goldman Sachs." I hadn't considered the gang angle, since Cabazon seemed so sure it wasn't about that. But now, I put that possibility back in play. "Does Tracy show up in any gang files?"

"No," Dale said. "But remember, nothing shows up on her at all. So it's a toss-up whether the murder is gang-related. Here's the main thing I came to tell you: the first crime-scene report—not the one Cabazon had, which, by the way, was prepared by a couple of unis in Rampart Division—mentions one civilian witness. It had to be Tracy, but her name was blacked out. That tells me she's most likely in protective custody. But LAPD must've handed it off, because the reports don't show that any of our detectives were assigned to it. The problem is, I couldn't find any information on who they handed off the case to, and I can't dig around too much without someone noticing."

"How come they blacked out her name in that first report but not the one Cabazon gave me?"

Dale said, "Because I'm guessing the one Cabazon gave you came from Jorge Maldonado's lawyer."

Diego Ferrara. "If so, then Cabazon must've hired him."

Dale nodded. "So we'd better find out fast whether that's true, because if so, we've got competition."

Meaning, Cabazon would've ordered Diego Ferrara to look for Tracy, too. More pressure. Just what we needed.

I wondered why there was no record that showed who'd taken over the case. "This seems awfully hush-hush—don't you think?"

"It does," Dale said. "But I can't say whether it's really so hush-hush or I just didn't know where to look to find the paperwork."

And he couldn't bounce around too much or someone would notice. Finding this girl was going to be even harder than I'd thought. "I'll talk to the lawyer, find out if Cabazon hired him, and see if I can get him to tell me who's handling the case."

Dale looked pessimistic. "Assuming he knows."

True. If it really was a big secret, Diego might not know who got the case after LAPD handed it off, either. "Then let's assume he doesn't. If he only knows about the LAPD officers, will you be able to ask them who they handed off the case to?"

Dale's expression was strained. "It'd be risky. But if there's no other way . . . I guess so. I just hate to create a trail."

One that would lead to us getting busted by the cops *and* killed by Cabazon.

Perfect.

TWENTY-SIX

After Dale left, I did some research on Maldonado's lawyer. If Diego Ferrara had been privately retained, odds were that Cabazon had hired him, because Maldonado didn't have much money. My quick Internet search showed that Maldonado was just twenty-six years old, had no college degree, and worked as a bouncer at Sound Nightclub. That didn't add up to someone who could afford to pay even a low-rent lawyer for a murder case. So either Cabazon was footing the bill or the court had appointed Ferrara.

I accessed the state bar website and saw that Ferrara was thirty-seven years old and a sole practitioner. And according to his website, he did more immigration and low-level civil law—like landlord-tenant, divorce, and workman's comp—than criminal law. That was not someone who had the chops to handle a murder trial. Or, for that matter, someone who could afford the fairly ritzy office suite he occupied in Century City. So either Diego had another source of income, or someone else, like Cabazon, was bankrolling him. The fact that he did immigration law tipped the balance in favor of Cabazon.

But I couldn't afford to guess wrong on this one. I had to know for sure, which meant I'd need to meet him face-to-face. And that meant

I'd need a good cover story—one that would make him comfortable enough to talk about the case but not raise any suspicions about my motives. Because if he was on Cabazon's payroll and he got suspicious, the first person he'd tell would be Cabazon. I had to tread lightly.

As I gazed at his website photo—he was handsome in a semisleazy, low-class lawyer-y way, with slicked-back hair, a big oily smile, and a trim mustache—I had the beginnings of an idea. But it wouldn't work if I went straight at him. I pulled up his Facebook page and asked to be his "friend" using the dummy account (that showed it belonged to a hot blonde) Alex had set up for me. An hour later, I was in. I scrolled through his postings and saw that he was planning to attend an office holiday party being thrown tomorrow night by Westerly, Farrel, and Goring—a huge civil litigation firm in his building. It'd be perfect if I could "bump into" Diego there. The only problem was, I didn't have an invitation.

If I could find one on the web, I could probably make a good-enough copy to slide by. But after an hour of scouring the Internet, I had to give up. I cast around in my memory for someone who might have an "in" at the firm, but I'd never had the slightest interest in civil litigation—or the lawyers who practiced it. I was hosed.

But wait. I sat up in my seat as I realized I did have an "in." Michy's boyfriend, Brad, was a slave at a huge corporate firm. I couldn't tell Michy the truth about why I needed the invite, and I hated the idea of scamming her, but for her sake, I couldn't let her near anything related to Cabazon. And this was a life-or-death situation. I apologized to her in my head even as I dreamed up the lie I was going to tell her.

I went out and sat on the edge of her desk. She was cleaning up one of my motions. Without even a pause to look up, she asked, "What's going on?"

"I want to see if I can cozy up to a civil litigation firm and get some white-collar work."

Michy stopped typing and stared at me. "That is the best business idea you've ever had." She gave me a suspicious look. "So I have a hard time believing it."

With good reason. I hate paper cases. They can pay great money because defendants who're charged with fraud are sometimes bank presidents and CEOs. But they are booorrrrinnng. I mean truly deadly. I smiled and shrugged. "Not saying it'll work, but it's worth looking into." I told her I needed Brad to wrangle me an invitation to the Westerly office party.

Her tone was sarcastic, but it had a touch of admiration. "Well, look at that. Our little girl is all grown up." She picked up her cell phone and typed in a text. "If Brad's not buried or getting reamed by a partner, he'll get back to me fast."

I thanked her and went to Alex's office. His door was closed. "It's the TSA. Your Precheck status has been revoked for stealing that box of Thin Mints back in 2010. Open up."

His voice came through the door. "I'm not here. Try back later."

I opened the door. Alex glared at me over the top of his monitor. I waved. "Just trying to inject a little humor into your day."

He rolled his eyes. "Emphasis on *little*. They just keep getting worse."

"I feel bad for you that you don't appreciate my whimsical stylings." I told him what Dale had said about the coroner's finding of OxyContin in Alicia's blood sample. "It's been ruled out as the cause of death, but we should follow up and see where it takes us. See if you can set us up to talk to Nomie today."

Alex picked up his cell phone. "What about the others?"

The way they'd talked about Alicia gave me the impression they didn't know. I hadn't necessarily gotten the impression that Nomie did, either, but if anyone knew, it'd be her. "Let's stick with Nomie for now. We can branch out later depending on what she says."

On my way back to my office, Michy held up a victory sign. "Brad says no problem, he knows a paralegal at Westerly who owes him a favor. I'll get it from him when I see him tonight."

I went over and gave her a fist bump. "You're the best, Michy."

"True. So score us some clients with actual bank accounts."

I smiled to hide the wave of guilt. "Will do. And congratulations on getting back together with Brad."

Michy sighed. "Yeah, whatever."

But as I sat down at my desk, I thought, *Why* not *offer up my services while I'm at it?* There was no reason I couldn't use the party to get close to Diego *and* try to score a source for some white-collar work. It didn't have to be a complete lie. Feeling better, I went back to my sentencing memo.

Half an hour later, Alex came in. "Nomie can meet us at Lemonade in an hour."

I looked at my skull clock—a gift from Michy for my last birthday. The little hand was on the upper edge of the rictus smile. It was almost four o'clock. Traffic was going to be awful. "We'd better get going."

I packed up, threw on my coat and scarf, and stopped at Michy's desk. "We probably won't be back, so have fun with Brad tonight." I let Alex move past me toward the door and whispered, "Feel free to give him a little something extra for his help."

Alex turned back and sighed. "I totally heard that, and you are a pig."

I rolled my eyes. "Oh please, Mary Poppins."

We headed out, and Alex let me drive Beulah because it was getting dark and we were headed back to USC. Alex had his head buried in his iPad, so I tuned the radio to a jazz station to keep myself awake as I navigated the freeway.

At three minutes to five, I pulled into a parking space near Trousdale Parkway. Lemonade is a California cuisine cafeteria-style place. I hadn't known that Nomie worked there, but as we entered, I saw that she was behind the counter and in the process of taking off her apron. I waved to her and pointed to a table next to the window. She nodded to me then spoke to the man next to her.

We sat down at the table. I asked, "You hungry?"

Alex looked at the counter where the dishes were laid out. "Kind of, yeah. I think I'll have the vegetarian chili."

I'd been eyeing the mashed potatoes, but I knew I should probably do something equally as healthy. "Me, too."

Nomie came over, and I offered to buy her dinner, but she declined. "I've been serving the stuff for the past three hours. I can't even look at it. But I'll take a Coke."

Alex stood up. "I'll go. Coke for you, too?" I nodded, and he went over to the counter.

I leaned in. "I have something to tell you about Alicia. If you don't already know, it might be upsetting, so I want you to be prepared."

She gave me a sad look. "Someone slashed her throat. I think I can probably handle anything you're going to tell me."

That was fair. I told Nomie about the coroner's finding of OxyContin in Alicia's blood. "Did you ever know she did drugs?"

Alex returned with our food and drink. The chili smelled delicious.

Nomie put a straw into her Coke and sighed. "I saw her doing cocaine a couple of times. But both times were at a party, and people were passing it around." She shrugged. "As far as I knew, she never had her own." Nomie paused. "But about a month ago, I went with her to get mani-pedis—I only did the pedi—and she asked me to get her wallet out because her nails were still wet. I found some pills."

I guessed. "Oxy?"

Nomie nodded. "That did worry me. I told her it was dangerous, but she said she only did it for fun once in a while. She wasn't addicted or anything."

I took a sip of Coke. "Did you believe her?"

She stared down at her drink for a moment before answering. "Yeah. Look, from what I heard, she had no peace her whole life. It was all about performing, winning, being the best, and that left almost no time for friends or boyfriends or anything normal. She had to be Ms. Perfect. So I guess what I'm saying is, I get it."

There'd been a lot of heat in those words. Something else was going on here. "Are you saying she was just a trophy for her parents?"

Nomie played with the straw wrapper. "I'm not saying they didn't love her. I'm just saying they didn't realize what they were doing to her."

This was sounding awfully one-sided. Alicia was a part of the equation, too. Everyone seemed to be forgetting that. "Alicia could've told them they were being too hard on her, don't you think?"

She twisted the wrapper around her finger and gave a little shrug. "Maybe that was her problem. She didn't want to disappoint them." Nomie met my gaze. "Did her parents tell you she was a cutter?"

I had to take a moment to absorb that. "No. Are you sure they knew?"

She dropped her gaze to the table. "I thought they must have, but maybe not. Alicia said she was careful."

If this were true, there would be some mention of old scars in the coroner's report, but since it wasn't finalized yet, I hadn't seen it. "Does anyone else know about it?" Nomie shook her head and pulled the straw wrapper off her finger. "Would you say you're her closest friend?"

"Probably. Whoever her friends were in high school, she didn't seem to be missing them. Barely ever mentioned them."

But then again, she probably never had time for them. I had a hunch about Nomie, and I decided to play it. "You trusted her, too, didn't you? With quite a bit, I'm guessing."

She glanced up at me, then her gaze slid over to Alex. After a beat she said, "Alicia was only the second person I'd ever come out to in my life. I was raised in a strict Baptist household in Fayetteville, Georgia. I knew if I told my folks, they'd make me come home and put me in some messed-up conversion therapy program." She paused and bit her bottom lip. "But Alicia was totally cool. I could talk to her about it—about anything, really." Nomie gazed out the window. "I know this is going to sound weird, but I think part of the reason she understood me so well was because she was always afraid of disappointing her parents, too."

That made perfect sense to me. "Did you come out to the others after you told Alicia?"

Nomie's gaze drifted off to the right, and a little smile played on her lips. Her smile seemed to echo a memory. "Alicia told me not to worry, that they wouldn't care—and they'd keep it on the down low. So I told them. And she was right." She looked at me. "Coming from where I did, it took me a little while to believe that people really might be able to accept me for who I am."

Alex gave her a look of sympathy. "I'm here to tell you, they will. Trust me."

Nomie looked at him with surprise, then back at me. I nodded. "Yeah, he really does know. And you seem to have landed in a good group."

"Totally. They're pretty dope." But she wasn't smiling anymore.

I followed up on that sign. "Is there someone in the group who isn't so dope?"

"No, no. It's just . . . I got the feeling Alicia was hiding something. I wondered if maybe that Italian cinema professor wasn't the only other guy Alicia was seeing."

Another interesting wrinkle. But unlike the Oxy, this one might be helpful. "Are you thinking she might've been seeing Phil or Davey?"

Nomie pushed her glass away. "No . . . I mean, she could've been. And maybe it wasn't a guy. I just know she seemed to be going out at night when I knew she wasn't with Roan or that professor."

I asked her to take a guess at who Alicia might've been seeing—or what she might've been doing, but Nomie couldn't come up with anything. We'd have to find another way to check that out. After chatting for a few more minutes, we called it a day and walked Nomie out. "Want a ride back?"

Nomie looked out the window at the darkening sky. "No, thanks. I need to walk."

I put a hand on her shoulder. "I'm truly sorry for your loss, Nomie. I can't imagine how hard this must be for you."

Her eyes filled, and she blinked back the tears. "Thanks."

I watched her walk away, thinking about how much she'd lost when Alicia died.

But at least she was living in a place that gave her a solid chance of finding a new family—one of her own choosing, that wouldn't consider her flawed just because she was born different.

TWENTY-SEVEN

As we got back in the car, Alex said, "Don't worry, even if her family doesn't get on board, she really will be okay. I meant what I told her. She'll find a lot of acceptance out here."

He should know. Alex, having been raised in a Hispanic family that was devoutly Catholic, didn't dare come out to his family while he was living at home. He'd kept his sexuality a secret until he moved out and got a job. And even so, he'd only told his brother and sister. His mother still didn't know. "You're right. It's just a bitch that she had to lose Alicia so soon. She's a freshman. She's only been here since August."

Alex shook his head. "It really is a bad break."

But nowhere near as bad as Alicia's. We were silent for a few moments, and I mentally replayed our conversation with Nomie. She'd given us some new insights into Alicia. "Funny, I was—and wasn't—surprised to hear she was a cutter."

He pulled out his cell phone. "Me, too. In a sad way, it really fits. I was just going to text Dale and ask when he thinks we'll get the coroner's report."

"Great idea." I wasn't sure what this new information would buy us, but I believe in turning over every stone. You never know when a juicy red herring will pop out from under one of them. "And we need to set up interviews with Phil and Davey. Separate ones."

Alex was typing on his phone. "On it. Tomorrow?"

I remembered I had a party to go to that night. "Only if it can be early in the day. I've got a place to be later on."

Alex chuckled. "Yeah, I heard you setting it up with Michy. I thought you hated paper cases."

He knew from personal experience because I hadn't wanted to take his case. The only thing more painful than a fraud case was a computer fraud case. "I do. But I figure I can have you do most of the legwork." I glanced at him. He wasn't laughing anymore. "Not so funny now, is it?" He loved searching for witnesses, digging up information, and being out in the field, but working a fraud case offered none of that kind of intrigue.

Alex folded his arms and shot me a mock glare. "I—unlike some people I know—am able to put personal predilections aside in favor of expedience. In this case, money."

I glanced at him. "Yeah? Well, I guess we're about to put that to the test." Assuming I actually managed to dig up any clients.

I dropped Alex off at his car and got home by eight o'clock. For some reason, I was super tired. And it was only Monday. I got into bed by nine thirty, knowing I was tempting fate. The earlier I went to bed, the more likely I was to have the nightmare. But I just couldn't keep my eyes open.

I couldn't believe it when I woke up and saw that it was morning. Seven thirty in the morning to be precise, according to the clock on my nightstand. A major win. Winning is such a great way to start the day.

I checked my phone for messages. Alex had texted me at ten o'clock last night. He'd set up a meeting for us with Phil at noon. Fantastic. Now if we could just catch him sober. Or maybe not. He might be more willing to spill if he'd had a little lubricant. Maybe I should score some weed to give him as a host gift.

I texted the idea to Alex. He said he could handle it. Someone—maybe Paul?—must have access. I knew it wasn't Alex. He hated the stuff even more than I did.

I didn't have any court appearances, and we wouldn't leave for our meeting until eleven, so I'd planned to roll in by nine. But Beulah had other plans. She sputtered to a stop at the intersection of Sunset and Crescent Heights and refused to start again. Her favorite doctor—i.e., my mechanic—was just two miles away, but it took half an hour for AAA to get to me and another half hour to get Beulah into the station. By the time I got to the office, it was a quarter to eleven.

Michy gave me a sad smile. I'd texted her about Beulah. "Sorry, Sam. That truly sucks. Don't bite my head off, but it might be time . . ."

I couldn't even muster the juice to argue. "I know. I think I'm finally ready to cut the cord." This time felt like the last straw. What if I'd had a court appearance? Or been in trial? I needed something reliable, and Beulah did not do "reliable."

"But I happen to have a bit of good news." Michy held up a square piece of cream-colored cardboard. "Your invitation to the Westerly party."

"Excellent. Thanks so much, Michy." I dropped my purse on her desk and took it. It was one of those expensive invitations, with a dark-green border and pretty cursive writing. I fanned myself with it. "Fancy. I hope you thanked Brad for me."

Michy smiled. "Oh, I did. Most definitely."

I gave her a thumbs-up. "Any wardrobe ideas for this shindig?"

She leaned back in her chair and stared off. I knew she was picturing my closet. "That little black dress with the square neckline, and that imitation-diamond collar necklace."

I grimaced and shook my head. "The dress *she* gave me so I wouldn't embarrass her in front of her country club ladies? Not only no, but hell no." Celeste liked to throw parties and invite five hundred of her closest friends. On occasion—the occasion being when she needed me to entertain her buddies with the lurid details of my cases—she'd asked me to come. I don't know why, but for years, I actually went to them. Then I got wise and started turning her down. Eventually, she stopped inviting me. And then, I stopped taking her calls. Michy cheered when I told her not to put Celeste's calls through. She'd been telling me to cut Celeste off for years. And she was right. It's been two years since we've spoken, and it feels great. I honestly don't know why it took me so long. But I guess you get there when you get there.

But Michy wasn't having it. She folded her arms and gave me a stern look. "Screw her. It's an original Diane von Furstenberg. Suck it up and wear it. It'll give you class, and you need all the help you can get."

She was right. But damn. Alex emerged from his office and saved me from having to admit it out loud. "You ready to hit the road?" he asked.

I took my purse off Michy's desk and put the invitation inside. "We should be back here by five."

She frowned. "The party starts at six thirty, and you'll have to go home and change after you drop Alex off."

I waved her away. "Piece of cake; I'll make it."

Michy gave me a skeptical look. "Just in case, I'll stop by your place at lunch and pick up your outfit so you can change here."

"Okay, thanks." There was no point in arguing. She wasn't really concerned about my getting to the party on time. A six-thirty invitation meant most people wouldn't get there until seven thirty. This was just her way of making sure I wore what she'd picked out for me.

Alex and I headed out, and he spent most of the ride giving me an earful about the dangers of driving a "useless hunk of metal" like Beulah. When he finally finished his rant, he waited for me to fire back. For a change, I said nothing. I was actually thinking Beulah might have pissed me off for the last time.

I'd suggested meeting Phil at one of the cafés on campus so he'd be alone, but Alex thought he'd speak more freely at home. If he wasn't alone, we could always offer to buy him lunch. Knowing him, he was bound to have the munchies. And in case he didn't, Alex could stoke his fire with the great Chronic he'd scored. *Then* he'd have the munchies.

I'd thought about whether we really needed to dig deeper into Alicia's life. But ultimately, I'd decided I had no choice. Roan's death had to be linked to Alicia's murder somehow. And the only way to find a link, other than Graham, was to find someone who might have it in for both Alicia and Roan.

From what I'd learned about Roan, the list of people who might want to kill him was probably lengthy. If he was still alive, Alex and I would probably be on it. There was no point in going to the trouble of sifting through that huge haystack when I could get the same answer by exploring the much narrower question of who might've wanted to kill Alicia. Once we identified her enemies, we could focus in on which one also had a motive to kill Roan.

We made it to Phil's house in record time and got there fifteen minutes early. Ordinarily, I'd wait outside for at least ten minutes to be polite. But in this case, I thought it might be wise to get the lay of the land as soon as possible. If we had to waste time getting him stoned, we may as well start sooner rather than later. I sniffed at the door as I knocked to get a sense of what condition Phil would be in, but I couldn't smell anything. I glanced at Alex. "You?" Alex shook his head.

Phil answered the door with a hazy smile. A cloud of pot smoke flowed out to greet us. We were in luck. Or rather, we were in "business as usual." "Hey, Phil. Thanks for seeing us."

He bobbed his head. "Not a problem. Come on in."

I asked if anyone else was around. More luck. Phil was alone. He offered us water. I accepted, but Alex cast a nervous glance at the sink full of dirty dishes and empty bottles and wrappers on the counter, and he declined. Phil brought me the water, then flopped down in one of the beanbag chairs. Alex and I settled in on the sofa.

We made small talk for a few minutes, asked how classes were going, whether he'd seen the latest Marvel Comics superhero movie and how everyone was dealing with Alicia's death. He told us it was tough on all of them. That gave me a natural segue to ask whether he thought any other guys were into Alicia, besides Roan.

Phil burped a little inside his mouth and patted his chest. "'Scuse me. You mean during the time she was hooking up with him?"

I tried to ignore his bodily functions. "Or before she started seeing him."

He stretched and folded his arms behind his head. "I know I was crushing on her. But a lot of guys were. Davey, too."

We'd thought that might be the case, and we'd decided that if we were right, Alex should do the questioning. This was guy territory. Alex took the lead. "So did you and Alicia ever hook up?"

Phil half closed his eyes, his head still resting on his arms. "Nah. We made out at a party once, but that was it."

Alex sat back and crossed his legs boy style, with his left foot on his right knee. "Was that before or after she met Roan?"

Phil sniffed. "Before. And she was drunk. Barely remembered it the next day. I kind of dropped a few hints that I wouldn't mind if we did that again, but she wasn't interested."

Phil took a bathroom break, and when he sank back down on the beanbag chair, he asked, "I tell you about her and Diana?"

This was new. "No, what about them?" I asked.

Phil took a pipe out of his back pocket. "Diana's here on scholarship. Her folks are broke. They've got three kids still at home, and her dad's on disability." He paused to light the pipe and took a deep drag. Smoke drifted out through his next words. "When she first moved in, she said she was going to have to get a job because her scholarship wasn't a full ride. I figured she'd get a waitressing gig or something. But she didn't. And she didn't seem to be hurting for money. I finally found out she was stripping." He blew out the rest of the smoke, and I held my breath. "No, not stripping. What's that thing . . ." Phil made a gesture with his free hand to indicate something long and vertical.

"Pole dancing?" I asked.

Phil pointed at me. "That's it. I found out totally by accident. Went to a bar out in Pasadena with some old buddies from high school, and there she was. The minute I recognized her, I got out of there."

I felt sorry for her. "Did anyone else know?"

He took another hit and held in the smoke as he shook his head. "I got the feeling she didn't want anyone else to know, so I kept it to myself."

I didn't know what this had to do with Alicia. "Did Alicia find out?"

Phil blew out the smoke in a rush. "I'm not sure, but I think so, because I saw her leaving with Diana one night, and they were both all done up. Like the way Diana was when I saw her dancing. Alicia was acting weird, all nervous and excited, and when I asked where they were going, she got super cagey, wouldn't tell me."

His deduction seemed reasonable. Especially since Alicia was a real dancer. And it was such a great "fuck you" to use all those childhood dance lessons to wind her mostly naked body around a pole. But it also brought up some new investigative possibilities. One in particular was foremost on my mind. "Can you remember the name of the place?"

Phil stared off for a long moment—for so long I was about to repeat the question when he finally said, "I think it was The Pink Palace." He shook his head with a look of disdain. "Genius name."

It was pretty lame. I saw that Alex had typed it into his iPad. I turned back to Phil. "Did you ever go and see whether Alicia was dancing there?"

Phil made a face. "I really don't dig those places. I only went there that night because my buddies wanted to go. If Alicia was dancing there, too, I didn't want to know." He yawned without covering his mouth. "It's kind of a sad thing to do."

Sad for Diana, who did it out of necessity. But not so for Alicia, who did it by choice, probably to exact revenge and get her rebel on. I wondered how Diana felt about that. We talked for a while longer, but Phil was starting to nod. If we wanted to get more out of him, we'd have to come back. He was tapped out for now. We thanked him and left.

When Alex drove up the on-ramp to the freeway, I shared the idea Phil had given me. "Remember Nomie said Alicia thought someone was stalking her?"

Alex nodded. "But I didn't think there was anything to it."

I had pretty much dismissed the idea, too. But I was ready to reconsider it now. "If she really was dancing at that place, it might turn out to be true after all."

What better place to pick up a creep like that? And what better suspect to pin Roan's possible murder on than a crazed, jealous stalker?

Finally, I'd landed on a theory that might give me some traction.

TWENTY-EIGHT

We'd left Phil's place in plenty of time for me to drop Alex at the office and go home to change for the party. But, of course, traffic being what it was—seriously, who *are* these people who get off work by three in the afternoon?—we didn't get back until four thirty.

Michelle was on the phone. She waved me over as she said, "She just walked in, Mr. Hutchins. Hold on and I'll put you through." Michelle pushed the hold button. "He wants an update. I suggest you ask him for one, too, find out if he's been yakking to reporters again."

A good idea. "Got it." I headed into my office and thought about what I should say. It was too soon to tell him about my stalker theory, and I was 100 percent sure Alicia wouldn't have confided her fear about that to him, because Graham would surely have made her move back home. So I told him we were still gathering information, but we thought we'd have some new leads soon. In essence, nothing. But I used the opportunity to ask him the question Nomie's latest revelations had raised. "Did Alicia ever see a therapist?"

Graham's tone was shocked—and a little miffed. "No, of course not. Why would she? And why are you asking?"

Just the fact that he reacted that way told me so much. Everyone has problems, and if they're lucky, they get to talk to a therapist about them. Graham's attitude struck me as not only backward but also a symptom of someone who'd engage in willful denial to avoid admitting that he, or anyone close to him, was less than perfect. I never would've suspected someone who was otherwise as sophisticated and intelligent as Graham would react that way. "I only ask because a lot of people do see therapists nowadays. And a therapist can have useful information."

That mollified him. "Oh. Well, no, she didn't." He cleared his throat. "I, ah, I also called because I was wondering if you might be able to find out whether Audrey Sutton has hired a private investigator to go after me?"

Fingers of dread crawled up my spine. "I can certainly try. Tell me why you think she did."

There was a beat of silence. "Maybe I'm just being paranoid, and it might just be *TMZ*, but a guy I used to work with at my old law firm—"

"The one who fired you for harassing—"

He cut me off. "No, the one after that. Some man who claimed to be working for a company that was putting together a lawyer's 'Who's Who' asked my friend—Martin Beamon—a bunch of questions about me."

That might—or might not—be fishy. "Well, you have been in the news lately, so that could put you on the radar of a company like that. Did Martin get the name of the company?"

Graham's tone was frustrated. "No, he didn't think anything of it until later, and by then he'd forgotten whatever name the guy gave."

I dealt with the most immediate problem first. "Did he tell you what he said to the guy?"

"He said he only gave the guy good stuff about how everyone liked me, how I got great results for my clients, that kind of thing."

I guess we'd find out soon enough if that was all Martin had said. "How good a friend is this Martin Beamon?"

There was another long pause. "We used to be buddies back in the day, kept in touch for a little while after I joined Hocheiser, Leslie & Friedman, but we haven't seen a whole lot of each other since."

It might be nothing, but still . . . I didn't like the sound of this. "Would you mind if we got in touch with Martin?" I wanted to judge for myself whether he'd caused any damage—witting or unwitting.

Graham coughed. "Excuse me." He held the phone away and coughed again. "Sorry. Just a little water went down the wrong way. I'd appreciate it if you didn't contact him just yet. I don't want him to get the idea I don't trust him."

A decent point. No matter how respectful it was, my follow-up would likely come across as Graham's vote of "no confidence." We didn't need to turn a friend into an enemy. "Fair point. But we may have to revisit this decision depending on what happens next."

I told Graham to try not to worry—he had enough on his plate. He thanked me and added, "I'm sorry, Sam. Didn't mean for this whole thing to turn into a *National Enquirer* story."

The sorrow in his voice was painful to hear. Whatever his flaws as a father, he'd truly loved Alicia. Having to deal with all this media insanity while he was grieving for her death was more than anyone should have to bear. "No apology necessary, Graham. I'm happy to help."

We ended the call with my promise to look into the private investigator issue and his promise to let me know if there were any further developments on the tabloid front.

I picked up my purse and briefcase, intending to head home, but I got two phone calls from clients, back-to-back. By the time I finished the last call it was after six. As usual, Michy was right. And I was stuck with her choice: the damn black dress Celeste had bought for me once upon a time.

I changed in my office, pulled out my portable makeup mirror and did a fast touch-up, then combed my hair and slipped on the black suede platform heels Michy had picked out. I walked out and did the model turn for her.

She gave me an approving nod. "And I brought your beaded black clutch."

I hate changing purses. "No one's going to care what kind of purse I carry."

"You are so ridiculous." Michy went into my office and dumped my purse out onto the couch. She took the credit cards, driver's license, and money out of my wallet and stuffed them into the clutch, along with my lip gloss and keys. "There." She looked at her watch. "That took all of thirty-seven seconds." She handed me the clutch and my cell phone. "Now call an Uber." She gestured to the mess on the couch. "I'll drop all this and your briefcase at your place on my way home." Michy went back to her desk.

Having no other choice, I did as I was told. Five minutes later, my phone said my driver, Hamid, had arrived. I walked out. "Okay, *adios*, I'm a ghost. Wish me luck."

Michy stood up and hugged me. "Go get us some rich clients."

Alex came out of his office and looked me over. "Nice. You should dress like that more often."

I glared at him. "I'd rather chew ground glass."

Alex turned to Michy, his expression puzzled. "What'd I say?"

Michy tried to suppress a laugh. "Celeste bought it."

Alex shrugged as he gave my dress an appraising look. "Just because she's a narcissist doesn't mean she can't have good taste." When I turned to glare at him again, he waved. "Have a great time."

I huffed and walked out.

I almost never find myself in Century City. It's all massive office buildings and hotels—very high-end but totally charm-free. Westerly, the firm that was throwing the party, was in a high-rise building that was all chrome and glass. But the law offices were opulent old school: thick burgundy rugs, expensive leather sofas and chairs, lots of cherry-wood and mahogany furniture and brass accent pieces. Westerly commanded two entire floors, but the party was on the main floor where the imposing reception area was located. Two beefy, muscled men wearing earpieces and dark suits that were two sizes too small for them stood at the door to keep out the crashers. I wondered who'd bother to crash a boring lawyer party—then remembered that's what I was doing.

As a general rule, I hate parties. Actually, *hate* isn't a strong enough word. I detest them. I suck at small talk, and I'm not a "people person." But since I was here on a mission of my own choosing—as opposed to having been roped into a social obligation—for a change, I wasn't resentful.

I scanned the crowd. It was largely an older and very well-heeled bunch, and I noticed lots of big, flashy diamond rings and pricey necklaces. There was a tiny smattering of millennials—mostly female—in short skirts and cropped slacks, and all in four-inch stiletto heels. Probably a mix of young associates, mistresses, and wannabe one or the other. A string quartet in the corner played tasteful classical music. I went over to the bar, ordered a shot of Patrón Silver on the rocks, and moved around the room, looking for Diego Ferrara. A hunky waiter in a short white jacket and pleasingly tight pants walked by with a tray of mini broccoli-and-cheese quiches, and I snagged a couple to soften the blow of booze on my empty stomach.

It took a while to make the full circuit of the rooms—they'd included two conference rooms as well as the oversize reception area to hold the crowd—but I eventually found my quarry. Diego, dressed in a black suit with white pinstripes—laughably mobster style—was chatting up an older couple, whose clothing and jewelry screamed MONEY. I saw the woman glance around the room with an expression of mild desperation.

Sam to the rescue. I sailed over and introduced myself, then made the woman a friend for life by turning to Diego and saying, "I've heard good things about you."

A flicker of surprise crossed his face. He quickly covered with a wide smile. "Thanks. I've heard great things about you, too. You do criminal, right?"

As I nodded, the older couple murmured something about it being nice to have met us and moved off. "And I hear you do immigration and civil. So how'd you wrangle an invite to this hootenanny?"

He smirked. "Perk of being friendly with the receptionist. My office is in the building."

I returned his smirk. "Nice. You know, I've been thinking about expanding my practice." I could see his eyes light up. Since I was the more famous one, and his law practice was about as low-rent as you can get, our joining forces would be a much bigger benefit to him than it would to me.

He grinned and clinked his glass against mine. "I'd definitely drink to that. Where's your office?"

We talked about office space, our respective staffs, and other painfully boring subjects. Finally, I managed to steer the conversation to our respective caseloads. On the way over, I'd thought up a few smooth segues that would get him to talk about Jorge Maldonado's case without making him suspicious, but now that I'd met him, I knew I could let go of that particular worry. This shitkicker would be happy to brag about his only big murder case.

Sure enough, after a one-minute summary of his civil cases, he told me he was handling a "heavy-duty" murder case. He tried to sound nonchalant, like it was just one of the many big trials he had pending, but his fatuous smile totally blew the effect.

I, of course, pretended to be wowed. "Sounds great. How'd you score that one? Court appoint you?"

He gave me a sly look. "No, that's the best part. It's privately retained and all in cash. My client's uncle does business with a cousin of mine."

Maldonado's uncle . . . was Cabazon. And Cabazon did "business" with Diego's cousin. That answered one question: Cabazon had hired Diego. I decided to see if I could bait him for more information—but carefully. "Should be great money. It's a gang case, isn't it? If so, it'll probably go to trial." Prosecutors weren't dealing a lot of gang cases, and if a client has deep pockets, a trial can mean a nice stack of cash.

"It's not really a gang case. Kinda weird. No one really knows why Jorge killed that guy." He leaned in with a conspiratorial wink. "I mean *allegedly* killed that guy."

I tried not to grimace. "Who's your IO?" The investigating officer is the detective in charge of the case.

Diego frowned. "I forget." He shrugged. "It's not really a cop case, anyway. The whole thing hangs on an eyewitness."

That'd be Tracy Gopeck. I'd hoped to get the name of the cop handling the case, but I couldn't press him for it without sounding suspicious. So I opted to try to get a sense of our deadline. "When do you start trial?"

"We're supposed to start picking a jury in ten days." Diego polished off his glass of champagne. "But it's not gonna happen unless the DA stops stalling and lets me talk to his star witness."

Witnesses don't have to talk to defense lawyers, but the defense is entitled to have a chance to at least ask if they'll give an interview. I suspected the DA was holding back on that meeting until he could find a more secure place for Tracy. Which was precisely why Cabazon was in such a big hurry. I wanted to see if Diego knew that. "Why do you think he's stalling?"

Diego made a dismissive wave. "The DA's scared. He knows I'm going to put so many holes in that eyewitness, the jury'll wonder what they're doing there."

The false bravado didn't fool me. The truth was, the DA had an airtight case if Tracy didn't go sideways. And no one would be afraid to go to trial against Diego Ferrara. He knew it, and I knew it. And that told me he also knew exactly why the DA was stalling.

I had no doubt whatsoever that Diego's retainer would be doubled if he managed to find out where Tracy was before she got to court. And he wouldn't give a damn what happened to her when he did.

Dale and I definitely had competition.

TWENTY-NINE

I told Diego I'd call him next week to arrange a meeting and talk further about merging our practices. He gave me a smile that said he liked the idea of merging in general. I tried not to roll my eyes and excused myself to go to the ladies' room.

I'd intended to make good on my lie to Michy and really try to make some connections that might scare up some business, but after talking to Diego, all I could think of was Tracy Gopeck getting microwave ovened. I took the stack of business cards out of my clutch and left them on the receptionist's desk.

I Ubered home and called Dale on my landline. I didn't bother with "hello." "We've got to move faster." I told him about my chat with Diego.

Dale swore under his breath. "But I can't say it's a surprise. And being Maldonado's lawyer, he's got an inside track on what's happening with the case."

That was true. Since Diego was representing Maldonado, he was entitled to get discovery on an ongoing basis. That meant he had all the police reports. So we were running a lot blinder than he was. "Our only hope is that he doesn't know what to do with what they're giving him.

But it's sounding more and more like Tracy's in protective custody." I told him about Diego's remark that the DA was stalling on giving him access to her.

I could hear Dale breathing. "It does. But I can't get into the witness protection angle without getting noticed."

That was going to have to be my move. "I'll see what I can get from the prosecutor." I paused. "Be nice if I could find a way to get him to give me access to her."

Dale snorted. "How the hell do you think you're going to do that?"

"I don't know." It was just wishful thinking. But you've gotta dream, right?

I heard the vacuum cleaner start up on Dale's end. Our mutual go-to when we needed to solve a problem. "I'll try and come up with something."

"Me, too."

We agreed to get together and brainstorm by Thursday if neither of us had any genius ideas before then. I spent what was left of the evening trying to come up with a brilliant lie that would persuade the prosecutor to take me to Tracy. The best I could come up with was to claim I'd been hired to deliver a hundred-thousand-dollar bequest from the deceased uncle Tracy never knew—and it *had* to be delivered to her in person. Pathetic. I looked at the clock. It was past midnight. I gave up and went to bed.

I'd hoped my brain would cough up a solution while I slept, but when I woke up the next morning, I still had nothing. My other hope was that Dale could line up someone for us to talk to, someone who could give us some daylight that'd help with our quest to get to Tracy, but I had no messages from him on my phone or in my inbox. I dragged into the office at nine o'clock, feeling like my legs weighed a hundred pounds each.

The minute I opened the door, I knew another bomb had dropped. The phones were ringing, and Michy was a ball of tension as she picked up one line and put the other one on hold. I waited for her to end the call she was on, then asked, "What the hell?"

"Did you listen to the news this morning?" I shook my head. "Dr. Cecil Mortimer came out with his report. He said Roan was murdered. His suicide was a setup. Mortimer claims he sat down with the county coroner to share his findings, and he's sure that now the county coroner's final conclusion will be that it was a homicide, not a suicide."

"Exactly what I expected from that hack." But I could feel my temples begin to throb. "Did the coroner respond? Or is it just Mortimer's spin?"

Michy shook her head. "So far, it's just Mortimer's spin."

That was good, but still. Hack or no, the media would definitely run with Mortimer's report. And it was bound to ratchet up public opinion against Graham. I made a mental note to have Alex dig deeper into Mortimer and find something specific we could use to shred his credibility as I went to my office and turned on the television. The local Channel Four news was playing a clip that showed Audrey Sutton standing outside a house—hers, most likely—and talking to a group of reporters. She was full of righteous indignation. ". . . I said all along that Roan would never kill himself. And I was right! Now it's time for the police to do their job and arrest Graham Hutchins!"

I changed the channel to see if I could find any clips of Dr. Mortimer or the county pathologist, but there weren't any. They'd both probably just issued statements.

If the coroner did wind up agreeing with Mortimer, the cops would be on Graham's doorstep in a heartbeat—at the very least to ask for another voluntary interview. I didn't think they'd have enough to get a warrant—yet. But Mortimer's challenge might provoke the coroner into working overtime to see if he'd missed anything. If he came up with something new and compelling enough, Graham could wind up in handcuffs. I needed to think of some moves, and fast. But first I had to call Graham and tell him about this, on the off chance he hadn't already heard.

He had heard, and he was scared. "Can they arrest me now?"

"No. Mortimer's just a hired hand. The cops aren't going to do anything based on what he says."

"But what if the coroner agrees with him?"

I could hear the panic rising in his voice. I made mine doubly calm even though that was my worry, too. "Even if he does, they don't have enough to make an arrest. All they've got is that witness who claims she saw you knocking on the door earlier in the evening. And she wasn't that solid." I paused. "Unless there's something you're not telling me. If so, now's the time to come clean."

He cleared his throat. "N-no. There's nothing. I swear."

They always swear. And then I get blindsided. But Graham wasn't my usual gangbanger / drug dealer / burglar. He was a lawyer, and he knew the importance of being honest with me. There was no point wasting my breath on a lecture he'd probably given to clients himself. "Okay, it shouldn't happen, but if the cops ask you to come in for questioning, you refuse. You remind them that I'm your lawyer and that they need to go through me. Since they don't have probable cause to arrest you, they can't make you go anywhere. And you aren't giving them any more statements."

"But won't that make me look guilty?"

"You let that be my problem." He was right. Some people would definitely think so, no matter what I did. But I'd weed them out during jury selection. "And now more than ever, you need to watch out for reporters. Stay close to home and don't go out unless you have to. And I don't need to tell you to stay off the airwaves, do I?"

Graham sighed. "No. Maybe I should leave town."

For a lawyer, he had alarmingly bad judgment about how to handle PR. But I guess corporate lawyers don't usually have to worry about this kind of bad press. "No. Do not leave town. The press will have a field day. Just sit tight and let me do my job."

When I ended the call, I went out and told Michy to give the press our usual party line: my client is innocent, and we intend to prove that he had nothing to do with . . . in this case, Roan's death. "Is Alex in?"

The phones had finally slowed down. Michy sighed. "So in. He was already here when I got in at eight. Not that he doesn't always work hard, but what is up with him?"

I'd noticed it, too. "I know he was working on tracking down the owner of the website where Laurie's photos were posted, but that wouldn't have taken him this long." I shook my head. "He must be up to something." I just hoped that if it was illegal, he wouldn't get caught. He'd only just completed probation. "But whatever he's doing, he'll have to stop. We need to move a lot faster now. Graham might be just inches away from getting arrested."

Michy was alarmed. "But I thought I heard you tell him the police didn't have enough on him?"

"They don't. But that could change any minute. And who knows what the coroner's going to say?" Or what Graham might be hiding from me?

I went to Alex's office and knocked. This time I didn't even try to joke around. He called out for me to come in. When I opened the door, his grim expression told me he'd heard the latest news.

Alex said, "The only thing I can think of to do right now is to go see that strip-club owner." He looked at his watch. "But it's only nine thirty. I doubt he'll be in before three or four."

I paced in front of his desk. I didn't want to wait. I needed to do something . . . anything. Now. But Alex was right. A club owner wouldn't be in until the afternoon. "Is there anything on the Internet about Mortimer's statement?"

Alex shook his head. "Nothing beyond what they've been reading on the news."

I told him to go granular on Mortimer's past. "I need something simple and graphic that'll make him look like the clown he is." I paced some more as I tried to come up with some other ideas. Much as I hated it, the only other thing I could think of to do right now was call Dale. "I'm going to see if I can squeeze any more information out of Dale. Speaking of which, what have you been working on night and day?"

He shrugged. "Just following up on some ideas."

I should've known better. Alex didn't like to let anyone see his work in progress. He'd let me know when he'd finished whatever it was, and it was polished, shining, and perfect. Until then, I could ask till I was blue in the face, and he'd just stonewall. "Okay, pick me up around two thirty and we'll head out to The . . ." I made a face. "Pink Palace."

Alex rolled his eyes with disgust. "I mean seriously. Why such a tacky name?"

I sighed. "Because they can."

I went back to my office and called Dale. He answered on the first ring, his voice tight. Now, because of Cabazon, whenever we called each other, we both got edgy. I told him I was just calling to ask whether he had any skinny on Graham's case.

He spoke in a low voice. "You can't know this." I promised I'd keep it to myself. "They've got touch DNA on the rope and on Roan's body."

Oh shit. Touch DNA—it comes from the skin cells people shed whenever they touch anything—could really ratchet up the pressure for us. The cops would be banging on Graham's door to get a DNA swab any minute. "Where on his body?"

He whispered, "I don't know. I just overheard Rusty telling the captain about it."

I started to whisper, too. "Is the coroner going to cave and say it was a homicide?"

His voice got even lower. "I haven't heard anything about that."

This was bad. Really bad. "Are they talking about making an arrest?"

His voice suddenly returned to normal. "Not yet. So anyway, thanks for the call. I'll be in touch." He hung up.

Someone must've just walked into his cubicle.

I paced around my office as I thought about this new intel. Foreign DNA on the rope—especially since it was touch DNA, as opposed to DNA from a bloodstain—didn't necessarily mean anything. It could've come from anyone who'd used it in the past. Possibly even the person who'd sold it. Same thing with the DNA on Roan's body. No matter where on his body they'd found it—even if it were on his neck—it could've come from anywhere. A scarf he'd worn after someone else borrowed it, a razor he'd shared with someone else—even his own hand: all he'd have to do is touch someone else's skin, then touch his own neck.

But if any of that touch DNA wound up matching Graham . . . no question about it, he'd be toast. He wasn't a friend of Roan's. They didn't hang out, share scarves, or share razors. It'd be hard to come up with an innocent explanation for finding his DNA anywhere on Roan's body. So I had to make sure the cops never got the chance to take a DNA swab from Graham.

The possibility that a DNA comparison might get Graham off the hook was a nonstarter. Sure, he could be telling me the truth—he might really be innocent. But I didn't win cases by assuming my clients were innocent.

No, the safest thing to do right now was to keep Graham quiet and out of harm's way. And hope that either I could come up with a viable suspect or the cops would tag someone else for Roan's murder. If they did come for him with an arrest warrant, I'd have to hope for the best.

But I needed to face facts. I was running out of time. If the coroner did change his preliminary findings and conclude this was a homicide, he'd probably take a little while to make it look good—but not long. I'd guess not more than a week. And the minute he made his change of heart official, the cops would be running hard to dig up probable cause to arrest Graham so they could get his DNA sample.

I was anxious to get moving. I looked at my skull clock. The little hand was hovering over its left eye socket. It was only ten thirty. But there was nothing else I could do on Graham's case until it was late enough to go to that strip club, and pacing around my office wasn't helping anything. For the time being, the best thing I could do was clear the decks and finish the most pressing work on my other cases. I had a sentencing memo and a trial brief on a ten-count burglary case that didn't seem likely to settle.

I worked straight through the next four and a half hours and took only a brief break for lunch when Michy brought in Cobb salads for everyone. I was just putting the finishing touches on my trial brief when Alex came to get me at four o'clock. I'd thought we were going to leave earlier.

I picked up my coat. "Kind of late, don't you think?"

"Actually, no. I doubt he'll be there much before five, and I didn't want to waste time waiting for him to show up."

I told him Beulah was still in the shop, and he said he was very happy to drive. I ignored his insultingly eager tone. As we headed out, I told Michy we probably wouldn't be back till six-ish and not to stay past five thirty. She promised she wouldn't stay a minute later.

It was one of those pale-gray days, when the sky feels like an old, threadbare blanket and the sun never really appears. I hate days like that. I like the weather to make up its mind. Give us either bright sun or pouring rain—the in-between stuff depresses me. I brought Alex up to speed on what Dale had told me about the DNA—and the coroner's likely decision to call Roan's death a homicide.

He gripped the steering wheel and hit the gas a little harder. "Then we've got to come up with something pretty soon if we're going to keep Graham out of jail."

"Right." Just hearing him say that made my stomach clench. I channeled my anxiety into the mission at hand. "What do you think about Alicia pole dancing? Assuming Phil's right about that."

214

Alex looked perplexed. "I get the whole 'good girls gone bad' thing and how she was spreading her wings or whatever. But it seems kind of over the top if you ask me. I mean, that can really be dangerous. What do you think?"

I was a little less skeptical about that than Alex. "I think Alicia was up for anything, the more risqué the better—to a point. So taking a pole-dancing gig for a little while does kind of make sense to me. Especially if she was only going on the nights when Diana was dancing, too. That'd make her feel safer. It's like the Oxy. She had some pills, but she wasn't addicted or even doing it very much. So, yeah. To me it all fits. It's just another—more fun—way of cutting."

Alex tapped the steering wheel. "That's right. I'd forgotten about that."

Twenty minutes later, he pulled into the parking lot of a run-down-looking building at the edge of the industrial section of Glendale. It used to be bright pink with a black door. Now, both colors had faded, and it was a very pale pink with a grayish door. The *I* in PINK had succumbed to time and weather, and the blank space made it look like "The Punk Palace." I liked that name better.

It was five thirty, and the place was open, but no one was there. A jukebox was playing "Last Child" by Aerosmith. Great song. We found the owner behind the bar, getting the cash register ready for business. As we took in the cheap wooden tables and chairs, and the obligatory stage and pole, he called out to us in a thick Armenian accent. "Can I help you?" We walked over and introduced ourselves. He was a stout five foot eight, with a wispy comb-over, a black collared shirt that was open almost to his hairy Pooh Bear belly, a gold cross on a long necklace, and heavy gold rings on seven of his fingers. He said his name was Armand Bedigian. I told him we were there to talk to him about Alicia.

He reared back with a frown. "I can't tell you anything about that poor girl's death—may she rest in peace." Armand set his jaw. "I run a clean shop, and I keep my girls safe."

So she had been dancing here. Score one for the home team. I assured him we weren't interested in making any complaints. "We just wondered if anyone here gave her a hard time."

Armand counted out a fistful of five-dollar bills. I marveled at his confidence. We could've come here to rob him for all he knew, and we outnumbered him. Then I saw the shotgun next to the register. He finished counting, made a note, then put the money into a drop bag. His tone was less confrontational now that I'd assured him we weren't here to blame him for anything. "She never told me anyone was bothering her."

Alex sat down and leaned forward, his forearms on the bar. "But I bet you watch your girls pretty carefully. Did anyone catch your eye?"

Nice job, Alex. Way to feather in a compliment to grease the man's memory.

Armand leaned back against the register and thought for a moment. "You know, there was a guy who only seemed to come on the nights Alicia was dancing."

I felt a little spark of hope. "Did she have a regular schedule?"

He raised his hand palm down and tilted it from side to side. "More or less. She usually danced on Tuesdays. But the girls like to trade nights with one another, and I have no problem with it."

That would definitely make someone who showed up only on Alicia's nights stand out. "Was the guy there when she danced on other nights?"

Armand stared off for a moment. "That I can't say for sure."

Damn. It would've been nice to know. If he showed up only on Alicia's nights, that would mean he knew her schedule—and, more importantly, knew her. "Did he ever approach her? Talk to her?"

Armand shook his head. "This is why I noticed him. He would stand over there." He pointed to the wall next to the entrance. "Never came closer, always left after Alicia was done."

Very weird. "And she never told you that anyone came up to her when she left for the night?"

His headshake was vehement. "Never. I would have told her to point him out and gotten rid of him immediately. I don't want trouble for my girls."

It sounded like the mystery fan was a stalker, and yet . . . "Has he been back since she died?"

Armand made the sign of the cross. "Rest her soul. No. He has not."

That gave me a whole different idea. I pulled out my cell phone and showed him a photo of Roan. "Is that him?"

He took a good long look. "No. The guy had long hair, down to here." He pointed to his shoulder. "Black or brown. And a mustache. Also, I believe he wore glasses." Armand paused for a moment, then nodded. "Yes. Glasses with a black frame."

I asked for his height and weight, though I knew those kinds of estimates were notoriously unreliable. But it might give us a general idea. Armand asked Alex to stand. "He was your height, maybe a little taller. But he was bigger than you." Armand gestured to his chest and spread his hands to indicate more width.

Alex was five feet ten, so this guy was between that and six feet tall. And Alex was slender, so the guy was medium build. That definitely ruled out Roan. I didn't have a photo of Professor Barth, but he was shorter than Alex and had short hair and didn't wear glasses. So that ruled him out, too.

Armand's description had really narrowed it down.

To about three million men in just the Los Angeles area alone.

We were on fire.

THIRTY

When we got back to the car, Alex asked, "We hit up Diana?"

I nodded as I snapped in my seat belt. "And we'll have to make sure we do it alone." Diana's—and Alicia's—side gig as a pole dancer appeared to be a secret, and I didn't see any reason why that should change. Yet. Of course, if this stalker theory panned out, I'd make sure it was headline news.

Since it was past six o'clock, and Armand had said she wasn't working tonight, I was hopeful Diana would be at home. But it was dinnertime, so I doubted we'd find her alone. "How about I text her and invite her to grab a bite with us?"

Alex took out his cell phone. "Good idea." He tapped a few keys, then scrolled. "I think Ebaes will fit our budget. It's an Asian fusion pub, and it's close, on Union."

"Sold." I texted Diana and hoped she hadn't made plans for the night. It was a Wednesday, so I was betting our chances were good. A minute later, my bet paid off. She agreed to meet us there in half an hour. I told Alex.

He smiled as he pulled into traffic. "Never underestimate a student's appetite for a free meal."

We got there early and grabbed a table next to the wall that offered the most privacy. It was a casual, cheery place, with white Christmas lights strung around the room and a blackboard that announced events, happy hours, and specialty menu items.

Diana arrived ten minutes later, and I watched the male heads turn as she walked by. Her tight burgundy turtleneck sweater and skinny jeans left no mysteries to be explored, and her shiny black hair made a sultry dip over one eye. It was a markedly sexier look than I'd seen in most of the other girls on campus, who largely eschewed makeup and dressed in slouchy sweats and hoodies. I wondered whether this had always been Diana's style or whether it'd morphed since she'd gotten into pole dancing.

She greeted us as she slung her purse over the back of her chair and sat down. "Thanks for inviting me out. I was thinking I'd be stuck with a two-day-old pizza night."

I told her it was our pleasure. The waiter—who'd already tried to get us to order before she got there—appeared at our table as though he'd been shot out of a cannon. We ordered chashu pork and spicy garlic edamame as appetizers and an assortment of rolls—shrimp, tuna, and, for Alex, a USC Trojan roll. I had a feeling he did that to annoy me, the only UCLA Bruin at the table.

We caught up on innocuous topics like classes and grades and the world in general until we were halfway through our meal. I hadn't been able to think of a delicate way to bring up her employment at The Pink Palace, so I finally decided to just go for it. After all, it wasn't as though she could deny it. I told her we'd learned that she worked there and that Alicia had been dancing there, too.

Diana put down her chopsticks, her expression cold. "And now I guess that means everyone will know."

It might. But for now, I could assure her, the secret was safe with us. "We have no interest in causing you any grief, and I'll bet it's good money. I'm only asking because we heard Alicia might've had a stalker."

Diana blew out a breath and sat back in her chair. Her tone was dismissive. "Oh, that. Yeah, she did tell me she felt like someone was following her at one point." She gave a sarcastic half laugh. "I figured it was probably just some PI her parents had hired to check up on her. Anyway, she let it go, said she was just tripping."

The note of envy in her voice when she mentioned Alicia's parents was impossible to miss. "Did you guys ever dance on the same night?"

Diana took a bite of edamame. Her tone was a little derisive. "Always. She never wanted to go alone."

That's what I'd figured. "Did you go in on nights when Alicia didn't?"

Diana's expression turned slightly bitter. "Of course. I couldn't afford to only do one night a week."

How far did this animus take her? I didn't know what to make of it, but I intended to find out. "Did you ever notice a guy with long hair and glasses at the club on the nights she danced? Always stood near the door?"

She frowned and shook her head. "But I wouldn't have had the chance. I was always backstage when she was dancing." I asked her whether she'd ever seen a guy like that when she was dancing. She paused. "Long hair and glasses?" She stared out the window for a moment. "I don't remember seeing anyone like that. Did Armand tell you about this guy?"

I nodded. "Said he only seemed to show up when Alicia was dancing. But from what he knew, the guy never made contact with her. Did Alicia mention anyone like that to you?"

Diana slowly shook her head. "Then it's true? Someone really was stalking her?"

There was concern in her voice, and it felt genuine. Interesting. So the animosity toward Alicia's privileged life didn't go *that* far. "We think it's possible."

I poked around for a little while longer in the hope of sparking a memory that might give us a new lead, but Diana didn't seem to know anything else. We got the check, and she said she had to get back to study for her psych midterm.

After she'd left, I asked Alex what he thought of her attitude toward Alicia. He folded his napkin and put it on the table, his expression contemplative. "I'm not sure. She obviously resented Alicia to some extent. But she did confide in Alicia about the pole dancing. Doesn't seem like Diana told anyone else about that."

A great point. "But maybe Alicia figured it out on her own? Stumbled on it by accident—like Phil."

Alex had a little smile. "Probably not exactly the way Phil did, but sure, it's possible she saw or heard something that tipped her off to it."

And then confronted Diana about it. "In which case, when she asked Diana to get her a gig there, Diana might not have felt like she could refuse."

Alex looked pained. "Because if she did, Alicia might not keep her secret?"

I shrugged. "Just throwing it out there. And I'm not even saying Alicia threatened to do that—at all. I'm just saying Diana might've been afraid of that."

He still looked pained. "I hope we're wrong about all this."

I sighed. "Yeah, I do, too."

Unless the potentially fraught relationship between the girls led to something good for us. That seemed unlikely, though, at this point.

I paid the check, and we headed back. Alex dropped me at home at a little after eight. I slogged up the steps to my apartment, more dispirited than tired, and very ready for a drink and some mindless TV.

But as I unlocked the door, I smelled smoke. Without thinking, I stepped inside to find out what was burning—and recognized the smell of cherry tobacco.

Javier Cabazon sat in the chair next to the sliding-glass door. The apartment was dark, the only illumination the city lights in the night sky that spread out behind him. "Good evening, Ms. Brinkman. Have a seat."

Anger overrode my fear. "No, thanks. I'm good." For the hundredth time, I regretted not carrying my .38 in my purse.

He dusted off a pants leg and nodded. "As you wish. I would like a progress report."

I could barely hear him over the pounding of my heart. Had Diego told him about our meeting at the party? I'd worried he might do that. I knew it'd take Cabazon about two seconds to realize that I'd deliberately engineered the meeting and that it had nothing to do with merging my law practice with Diego's. I had my story ready, but I sure as hell wasn't about to use it unless I had to. I told Cabazon that we'd been talking to members of Tracy's family. "But they don't seem to have been in contact with her for some time."

He made a face. "I am not surprised the family does not wish to have contact with a daughter who has become a *puta*."

Again with the whore accusation. But that told me Cabazon knew a little more about Tracy than he'd let on. "What makes you so sure she's a prostitute?"

Cabazon looked at me with disdain. "I have my sources. Unlike you, I choose to believe them. If you spoke to her family, you must already have heard this."

I felt my whole body break out in a sweat. For a brief moment, I wondered if he was having me followed. But Dale knew how to shake a tail. No, Cabazon was merely telling me that we had to have heard it because it was common knowledge. "Maybe I just don't like to assume anything."

He raised an eyebrow and stood up. "You will need to move more quickly. I expect to hear back from you within the next seven days."

"I'm doing all I can. But I'm a lawyer not a magician—and neither is Dale. And we can't afford to raise any suspicion." My words were brave, and I'd managed to keep my voice steady, but I moved off to the side as he drew near. I quickly scanned his jacket for a pistol-size bulge as he approached the door, but it was too dark to see.

He noticed the direction of my gaze and smiled as he reached for the doorknob. "I do not need to carry a gun. Go check your balcony."

Cabazon walked out. I locked the door behind him with shaking hands even as I acknowledged how useless that was. I went to the sliding-glass door and saw that a slender man had just lowered himself to the balcony below mine. I watched as he swung a leg over the rail and dropped down to the driveway below. He ran over to a blacked-out Range Rover that was idling there and opened the door for Cabazon, who emerged from the stairway and got inside. After the Range Rover backed out, I turned to go inside and noticed a stray bullet on the floor of my balcony, just outside the spot where Cabazon had been sitting.

If I'd tried anything, that guy would've dropped me where I stood.

I used my landline to call Dale and unblocked my number so he'd know it was me. When he picked up, I heard smooth jazz playing in the background and a woman's voice asking where he kept the vodka. Dear Old Dad was on a date. "Sorry to interrupt," I said. I told him about my visit from our buddy Cabazon.

Dale kept his voice low. "Hang on—I'm taking this into the bedroom." He called out to his date that he'd be right back. He swore under his breath as he moved and asked when I was finally going to get a police lock put on my door.

I'd nixed the idea before, and I nixed it again now. "He'd just catch me somewhere else. At least here, there are people around. Do you have anything else?"

A few seconds later, his voice still low, he said, "We can hit up the older sister, see what she has to say. I called her this morning, and she seemed cooperative."

Dale didn't sound particularly amped for this interview. "Then she didn't have any info on where Tracy might be?"

He sighed. "No. But she might know more than she thinks she does. You meet with that prosecutor yet?"

I knew he'd ask that. "No, but I'm still working on some ideas." I needed to figure out how to persuade the prosecutor to put me in touch with Tracy. So far, I hadn't come up with anything viable. "I'll reach out to him on Friday." Most courts don't hold trials on Fridays, which means it's the best day to find prosecutors in their offices.

Dale's date asked if he wanted pimento or blue-cheese-stuffed olives. Dale opted for regular. "I've got a meeting in the morning that I can't get out of. I'll try and set us up with Tiffany for tomorrow afternoon."

The adrenaline that'd flooded my body during Cabazon's visit had finally ebbed, and I was feeling a little queasy. "Sounds good. And by the way, I prefer pimento olives, too."

Dale's voice relaxed. "Seriously, it's not even close. I only keep the blue cheese around for those who don't know better."

He promised to call me as soon as he heard from Tiffany, and we ended the call.

As I headed to the kitchen and poured myself a shot of Patrón Silver, I thought, *At least one of us is having a fun night.*

THIRTY-ONE

I woke up Thursday morning with a slight hangover. I'd needed a little more—well, actually a lot more—than a single shot of tequila to take the edge off after my encounter with Cabazon. But at least I slept through the night. The triumph of that was worth the buzzing in my head.

Beulah had made a full recovery—or as full as any car with more than 200,000 miles could make—so I Ubered to the station and picked her up. The mechanic and I had become like family. We even exchanged Christmas cards. That's how often I'd had to take her in.

Gavril Derderyan, a short, slender man in his fifties with a thick head of hair and startlingly pale-blue eyes, wiped his hands on an oil-stained rag and shook his head. His Armenian accent sounded almost Russian to me. "When you are going to let this old lady retire, Sam?"

"Depends on how much she's going to cost me this time," I said as I braced myself for his answer.

He looked over at Beulah and sighed. "Anyone else, it costs seven hundred and fifty. For you—good customer, like family—I make it five hundred and fifty."

Ouch. "Make it five hundred even, and I'll pay cash." We did this dance every time, so I'd stopped at the ATM on the way over.

Gavril squinted at me. "You always have to squeeze my balls?"

I squinted back. "Yes."

He gave another sigh. "Fine. Five hundred." He wagged a finger. "But next time, I don't let you squeeze."

The fact that he said "next time" without even a second's hesitation told me I really should let the old lady retire. I gave him the stack of twenties and tried to breathe my way through the pain.

I headed to the office, and when I parked and got out, I patted Beulah's roof. "Get ready, old girl. I think we've reached the end of the road."

I almost felt sad as I headed upstairs. Until I remembered all those twenties.

I found Alex sitting on the extra secretary's chair we'd found abandoned in the hallway. He'd rolled over to Michy's desk, where they were having coffee and Krispy Kreme doughnuts.

My stomach rumbled at the sight. My hangover had made the idea of food unappealing, so I hadn't had any breakfast, but now, the smell of those little circles of delight made my stomach rumble. "Got enough for one more?"

Michy held up the box. I saw two glazed doughnuts—my favorite. She smiled. "Always. Dig in."

I was surprised to see that Alex had finally emerged from his cave. He'd been locking himself in his office every spare waking moment for the past week. As I dropped my purse and briefcase next to Michy's desk, I asked him, "What brings you out into the world? Are we due for another month of winter?"

Alex licked some stray jelly off his thumb. "I found the jerkoff who owns the website where Laurie's photos were posted."

I took a glazed doughnut out of the box and started to take a bite, then realized that my stomach still felt a little funny. I set it down on one of the paper towels Michy had put out. "How come it took so much longer to find him than the other guy?"

"It didn't. I just had to figure out what to do with him."

I couldn't resist the siren song of the doughnut. I took a bite and willed my stomach to be okay with it. "No more takedowns WWE-style, then?" I was relieved.

He shook his head. "Not that I'd have minded, but I wanted to do something a little more painful."

Uh-oh. "Such as?"

"Take his money." Alex smirked. "I hacked into his website account and diverted all the money he makes on clicks to a battered women's shelter and Covenant House."

Covenant House. "That place for runaway teens?" He nodded. "Nice." So smart.

He grinned. In an infomercial hawker's voice, he said, "But wait, there's more!"

His expression told me I was going to like this. "How're you going to top that?"

"I'm not. But I am giving him a dose of his own medicine. I Photoshopped his fugly face onto a great body—nude, of course—and posted the pics plus all his addresses on a bondage-and-discipline porn website with an invitation to bring whips and chains."

Michy and I laughed. I had to admit, it was poetic justice. "You plan to tell him you'll take it down at some point?"

Alex nodded. "As soon as he takes down his website. I have a feeling once he sees he's not making any money, he won't mind. But I'm going to make sure he understands that I'll be tracking him for the rest of his life—just in case he thinks he can start up again under another name."

I gave him a fist bump. "I friggin' love it."

Michy gave him a high five. "Laurie's going to be so happy. You'll have a fan for life."

Alex's smile softened. "I'm planning to tell her the minute his website goes down." He looked at his fancy-shmancy watch. "We should get going. I told Davey we'd meet him at The Good Karma at ten thirty."

I risked another bite of my doughnut. So far, my stomach seemed to be on board. "How come I didn't know about this? And what's The Good Karma?"

Alex looked confused. "I left you a message at home. It's a café on West Thirty-Fourth, right by the school. Is something wrong with your phone?"

Damn. "No, just my head." I remembered that I'd noticed the yellow message light blinking that morning, but in my post-adrenaline, fuzz-brained state, I'd forgotten to check. I tossed the remains of my doughnut—no sense pushing it—into the trash. "I'm ready."

Michy put the cover on my cup of coffee and handed it to me. "For the road. What time do you think you'll be back?"

I looked at Alex. "Around one?"

Alex nodded. "Maybe earlier."

It had to be. Dale and I were supposed to see Tiffany later today, and I didn't want to postpone the meeting. We couldn't afford any more delays.

Alex grabbed a jacket, and we headed out. Alex drove, and we talked over our strategy for the interview. I told him I thought he should ask the "boy questions," i.e., how Davey felt about Alicia.

Alex wasn't so sure. "I'll start. But I have a feeling he'll be more open with you."

Interesting. Alex was pretty good at reading people. "What makes you say that?"

Alex paused for a moment. "You know, I'm not sure. Just one of those vibe-y things."

It was cloudy and windy, and although we only had to walk a couple of blocks, by the time we got to the restaurant, I was frozen to the bone. Davey was already there. He'd tucked into a lemon meringue pie. I was still hungry after having bailed on my doughnut, and the sight of it made my mouth water. I waved to him as I walked over. Alex stopped at the counter to get iced tea for himself and a hot tea for me.

I sat down. "Hey Davey, thanks for making the time."

He pointed to the pie. "Thank *you* for a great breakfast—or actually, brunch, I guess."

Alex came over with our drinks and asked Davey how his life was going. We chatted about that for a few minutes, then got down to business.

Alex told him that we'd heard Alicia played the field before hooking up with Roan. "We were wondering whether you ever went out with her?" Davey looked a little taken aback. Alex added, "I'm only asking because we're looking for more insight, trying to figure out what was going on in her life apart from Roan."

That seemed to satisfy him. "I never went out with Alicia. I mean, she was pretty and all, but I loved her like a friend. I felt kind of . . . protective of her."

Alex gave a little nod. "Like a big brother."

Davey's tone was earnest. "Exactly. Alicia always knew she could come to me with any problems, and I'd always be there for her."

Alex probed a little further. "What kinds of problems did she have?"

Davey's mouth opened, then closed. He seemed flummoxed. "Oh, ahh . . . well, she sometimes partied a little too hard, and she'd get into sort of dangerous situations." He shook his head. "Frat boys. I had to carry her out a couple of times."

Alex told him we'd heard a few people say Alicia was a bit off the chain. "Would you agree?"

Davey gave a little shrug. "I guess. But a lot of kids go kind of nuts in the beginning of their freshman year."

It was the most generous—and perhaps the most realistic— observation I'd heard yet. I wanted to nail down a suspicion I'd had.

"Davey, do you think people are exaggerating the wild-child bit because of how she died?"

Davey paused for a moment. "You mean, like that might explain her . . . her murder?" I said yes. He nodded. "Very possible."

The more we heard her friends spin tales of Alicia's exploits, the more I'd begun to think that we might be getting an exaggerated account—and that there could be an aspect of self-preservation to it. It'd be reassuring to the others if they could point to something she did that might've led to her murder. That's not to say she didn't do a little swinging from the chandeliers. But I'd detected a tinge of melodrama in some of the descriptions. I'd wondered whether it was the somewhat typical adolescent tendency to romanticize the death of a peer—a kind of James Dean-ization that turned a mildly reckless, but largely just unlucky, friend into a larger-than-life rebel and glamorously edgy renegade. But as I'd mentally replayed our interviews with Alicia's friends, it'd occurred to me that the answer might be much simpler and more elemental: her friends might've just needed an explanation for her murder that would make them feel safer.

I had another question. "Did Alicia ever tell you she thought someone might be stalking her?"

Davey looked upset. He pushed away his pie, unfinished. "She did."

"Do you think it was true? I heard she pretty much dusted it off after a while."

Davey frowned. "I totally thought it was true. From what she said, the guy showed up everywhere—too much to be a coincidence in my opinion. I think the only reason she eventually shrugged it off was because he never approached her or did anything bad. And she knew if her folks found out, they'd make her move back home. That was a very big deal for her."

Davey seemed to be the only one who'd taken her fear seriously at the time. "Did you tell her to go to the police?"

He sighed. "I talked to her about it, but there wasn't much to report. He never spoke to her, never threatened her, and she didn't get any weird notes or anything. Like she said, it's not a crime to follow someone."

"Did you ever see him?"

Davey shook his head. "I never did." He squinted at a point over my right shoulder. "I think she said he was medium height and he had . . . short hair?" He gave a frustrated sigh. "I can't remember. Her description was so generic." Davey's expression was bereft. "He could've been anyone."

I turned the questioning over to Alex, and he asked Davey whether he'd seen Alicia with any other guys or knew about any other men she might've dated, but Davey had no clue. He didn't even mention Barth, the Italian cinema professor. That didn't surprise me.

He may have been a big brother to Alicia, but there are some things a girl will only tell another girl.

As Alex was wrapping up, I got a text from Dale: We're on to see our friend at 5:00 p.m. Meet me at my place.

A tiny sprig of hope grew in my heart. If Tiffany could give us a line on her sister, I wouldn't have to go to the DA. That'd be great.

Because the move I'd finally come up with to pry information out of the prosecutor was risky as hell.

THIRTY-TWO

Dale lived in Porter Ranch. If I wanted to get there in time to make it to Redlands by five, I'd have to leave the office the minute we got back.

But I couldn't tell Alex or Michy what I was really doing, so when we were about ten minutes away from home, I pretended to get an e-mail from the prosecutor on a robbery case in the San Fernando branch court. I waited until Alex pulled into the garage, then said, "I've got to go back out. Looks like the DA might be willing to cut me a deal on the Dobov case. Traffic to and from's going to be a bitch, so tell Michy I'll probably go home after that."

Alex steered into his parking space. "Got it." But he paused, one hand on the driver's side door handle. "Say, what'd we decide to do about Professor Barth?"

I'd sort of tabled that angle. The fact that he had no alibi for the night of Roan's death was intriguing, but I had no real reason to think he had a motive to kill Roan. His feelings for Alicia didn't seem to run that deep. Still, we were under the gun, and nothing else seemed to be panning out. "Get what you can on him, see if you can find any threads to pull."

He opened his door. "Will do. Oh, and I might have something for us on Dr. Mortimer."

"Great." I wanted to hear about that, but I had no time. I told him I'd call and check in when I was done, then I got into Beulah and headed for Porter Ranch.

Dale's place was a charming Spanish-style house—three bedrooms, two bathrooms, and it had an enclosed courtyard in front. He'd echoed the Spanish theme with ochre-colored tiles around the entrance on the outside, and on the inside he'd replaced the carpeted floors with matching ochre-colored tiles, thick throw rugs, and a chunky wood coffee table and end tables with black iron frames. The high ceilings, skylight in the living room, and the sliding-glass doors that led out to the small patio let in plenty of sunlight, so the overall feeling was airy and spacious.

And he kept it sparkling clean. Not just well dusted and dirt-free. I'm talking neat freak, perfectionist, T-squared positioning of the coffee table books, clean. Me, I'm into clean. I scrub floors and counters and all that jazz once a week. But I don't mind leaving the occasional books, papers, or files lying around. On the rare occasion Dale visited me at my place, it made him nuts. So I made it a point to never straighten up before he came. It was my selfless contribution to helping him overcome his obsessive-compulsive issues.

Dale came out the moment I pulled into the driveway. He'd dressed down for the occasion and wore jeans and a long-sleeve black Henley. I'd be willing to bet he had the same philosophy I did: dress for your audience. Dale had said Tiffany was on welfare and had two small children. It'd be off-putting to wear a suit or a sports jacket, like he was some government worker looking for a reason to cut her benefits. That's why I was similarly dressed in jeans and a blue pullover sweater.

Dale pointed to the garage, which was open and empty. "Go ahead and park there. We'll take my car."

He drove a white Lexus. It was, of course, sparkling clean. As I belted up, I asked, "You just buy this?" It still had remnants of that new-car smell.

Dale backed out of the driveway and headed for the freeway. "About two years ago. Why?"

This kind of neat-freak-itis just had to be a sign of some kind of personality disorder. "No reason."

As he steered onto the 101 Freeway, we talked a little about what tack we should take with Tiffany and what we hoped to get from her. Then I filled Dale in on Graham's case. "Any word on when we'll get Roan's official autopsy report?"

Dale moved into the diamond lane and pushed us up to more than eighty miles an hour. Cops are some of the most insane drivers simply because they can be. They know they'll never get a ticket. "I'd say within a week or so."

Just as I'd thought. I hoped Alex was coming up with something good on Dr. Mortimer. Or something bad on Professor Barth. I was anxious about Graham's case, but at least—unlike the search for Tracy Gopeck—it didn't pose the threat of death. I could tell Dale and I were both tense about our upcoming meeting with Tiffany, so I decided to lighten the mood. "How'd your date go the other night? You still trolling for talent among your crime victims?"

Dale had met—and begun dating—one of the two women he'd later been accused of murdering after he'd responded to her burglary call. I'd thought it was a bad idea to date crime victims, and I told him so at the time. And now I never miss a chance to slip in a dig about it.

Dale threw me a sidelong glare. "I know you think that never gets old. But it did. About two years ago. And I'd say you're on pretty shaky ground here. Tell me, how's your love life going?"

I was busted. I supposed I could brag about Niko, but two dates—actually more like one and a half—were nothing to brag about. "It's going great. Never been better."

Dale's voice was sarcastic. "I'm very happy for you."

It was a little past five when we got to Tiffany's house, and the sun was almost gone. The neighborhood looked a lot like her mother's—sadly. The tiny tract homes were run-down, the small patch of land in front of them that passed for a lawn was dirt, weeds, and random garbage—one old baby shoe, a shredded bicycle tire, an empty milk carton.

But unlike her mother's 'hood, the cars parked in the driveways and on the street—though all compacts and subcompacts—were, for the most part, well tended. It was a common phenomenon in Southern California, where people are judged by the cars they drive.

The car parked in Tiffany's driveway—a green Toyota Tercel—was no exception. It gleamed in the fading sunlight. Her house, on the other hand, looked like it hadn't been painted in decades; sheets were tacked up in the front windows; and a rusty tricycle, a broken Hula-Hoop, and fast-food wrappers littered the weed-choked front lawn.

When Dale knocked on the door, I heard a baby squall. A woman called out in an irritable voice, "Just a minute!"

It took about that long for her to come to the door. The woman, whom I assumed was Tiffany, looked at us with weary eyes, the squalling baby on her hip now subdued by a pacifier. She blew a wisp of ink-black hair off her face and looked us over. Her eyes landed on Dale. "You the guy who called the other day about that program?"

Dale nodded and introduced me. We'd decided to use the same cover story we'd given Shelly, this time saying that we needed to talk to as much of the family as possible to determine whether Shelly qualified for our counseling services.

Tiffany invited us in and led us to the living room couch, which was just ten feet from the front door and covered in baby clothes, bottles, and pacifiers. The small, cluttered room smelled like burned SPAM and old milk. Bags of pretzels, Doritos, and an impressive array of empty beer bottles filled the small coffee table. "Excuse the mess," Tiffany said over her shoulder, her tone casual. She cleared enough space for us to sit down on the couch and took a seat across from us in an armchair that was stained and worn.

She wore a bland expression that reminded me of her mother's, but where Shelly's seemed soft and hazy, Tiffany's just seemed numb. She rocked the baby absentmindedly, as though she was on autopilot. Evidence of a hard life was etched on her weary face. She looked a lot older than any twenty-one-year-old I'd ever known.

I was surprised to see very little resemblance between Tiffany and what I'd seen of Tracy in the photos. Where Tracy had a soft, round baby face and straight blonde hair, Tiffany had high cheekbones, a strong chin, and wavy black hair. I noticed a slight resemblance in the almond shape of their eyes, which looked like Shelly's. But whereas Shelly's and Tracy's eyes were hazel, Tiffany's were brown. I looked around to see if there were any photographs of Tracy. The only ones I saw were of Tiffany with a toddler—who didn't seem to be home right now—and Tiffany with a Hispanic man I assumed was her boyfriend.

I let Dale handle the preliminary routine questions about her family that went with our cover story. So we found out that her boyfriend, Jesus Jimenez, was a truck driver who was currently between jobs. He'd just taken their older daughter, Erin, out to the park. And we learned that Tiffany had moved out to live with him *before* she got pregnant.

That got my attention. I'd assumed the pregnancy was what made her move out. I saw Dale's antennae go up, too. I stepped in. "Then you were about sixteen when you moved in with Jesus?"

Tiffany looked at me, then let her eyes slide past me. "Yeah."

"How'd your mother feel about that?"

The bland look subtly hardened. "She didn't have a say in the matter."

I got the feeling that Tiffany and I had a lot in common. The question was, would she be willing to talk about it? I moved in slowly. "Had Benjamin moved in with you guys by then?" Tiffany nodded, and I could see she knew where I was going. I had to be careful not to push too hard or too fast. "I guess it got pretty crowded."

The baby began to cry again. This time, Tiffany draped a small blanket over her shoulder, opened her blouse, and lifted a breast into the baby's mouth. "Yeah, I guess that's one way of putting it."

I again offered her an opening. "What's another way of putting it?"

She narrowed her eyes at me. "That my home turned into fucking hell."

I nodded. "Was it Benjamin?"

Tiffany took a deep breath and looked from me to Dale. "I'm only telling you this so the other kids can get some help."

I had to squash the pang of guilt as I nodded again. "I understand, and I appreciate that."

Tiffany exhaled and closed her eyes for a brief moment. "Benjamin was an asshole, but he didn't try anything. At least not with me. It was his douche-bag son Ronnie. From the time they moved in, I never had one night of peace."

My hands had curled into fists, and I was squeezing them so tightly my knuckles hurt. "I assume you didn't feel like you could call the police."

Tiffany's voice was bitter. "You assume right. When I told my mother, she got into it with Benjamin, said Ronnie had to move out. But Benjamin took Ronnie's side, of course. He said I was the one who came on to Ronnie. That I was just pissed because Ronnie turned me down."

Such a familiar lie. Molesters—and their apologists—always put the blame on the victim. "What happened?" I asked. "Did your mother back down?"

Her eyes softened. "No, Mom stood by me. She knew I didn't lie. But for some reason, she couldn't kick Benjamin out. I have no idea what she sees in that piece of shit. Anyway, that's why she let me move in with Jesus."

At least her mother had believed her. That was a lot better than I'd gotten from Celeste. But the fact that Shelly couldn't bring herself to dump that loser Benjamin was unfathomable to me. There was nowhere else to go with Tiffany's story, but it was a perfect segue into our real reason for being there. "Do you think Ronnie went after Tracy, too?"

Tiffany's expression was sad. "I can't say for sure. She never told me. But I do know they fought like crazy, and she'd always leave the room when he came in, so . . . let me put it this way: it wouldn't surprise me."

I wanted to probe further, but it wasn't as though we could do anything about it now, and I doubted Tiffany knew any more than that. I moved on. "Are you in touch with Tracy?"

Tiffany slipped the baby off her breast and held it to her shoulder as she patted the baby's back. "I haven't heard from her in at least a year. She's never been real good about keeping in touch." She paused. "Not that I blame her. Tracy had it tougher than any of us."

I noticed my fists were still clenched. I forced my hands to relax. "Why do you say that?"

Tiffany pointed to a red LeSportsac knockoff on the floor near my end of the couch. "Could you hand me that?"

I gave it to her, and she removed a red wallet, took out a small photograph, and passed it to me. I saw three girls who looked to be between the ages of eight and twelve. The eldest appeared to be Tiffany. The youngest had her same black hair and high cheekbones. I pointed to the blonde girl in the middle. "Tracy?" Tiffany nodded. I said, "She had a different father?"

Her voice was bitter. "You could say that. Tracy's father was my uncle. Good old Uncle Pete raped my mother."

The revelation hit me like a sledgehammer. For a moment, we all sat in silence. It was so quiet, I could hear the baby breathing. That explained so much about Shelly's attitude toward Tracy. And yet . . . it wasn't Tracy's fault that she was the product of a rape. I handed the photo back to her. "What did your father do about it?"

Tiffany put the photo back into her wallet and dropped it into her purse. "He didn't call the cops, if that's what you're asking. In fact, he talked Mom out of it." Her features twisted with disgust. "Of *course*. But he never spoke to his brother again."

"And he and your mom eventually got divorced?"

Tiffany looked down at the baby in her arms. Her voice was sad. "No, Dad died. Drunk driving accident." After a moment, she added in a sarcastic tone, "But I'm sure his brother's still around."

I couldn't help myself. Though it had nothing to do with our mission, I asked, "How do you know? Are you in touch with him?"

She gave me an incredulous look. "You nuts? Of course not. But isn't that the way life works?"

I nodded. "Kind of." But it didn't always have to. "Can you give us some information on him?"

Dale raised an eyebrow. But he wrote it all down.

THIRTY-THREE

We left shortly thereafter, and as we got into the car, I asked, "What are you going to do about that scumbag Uncle Pete Gopeck? And that asshole Ronnie?"

Dale's expression was grim. "I'm going to run Gopeck through the system and see what kind of sheet he's got—and where he lives. If he's in LA, I might be able to do something. Especially if he's on parole."

Because an asshole like that was probably in violation of one condition or another every single day. "What about Ronnie? Do you have any connects in Riverside?"

Dale shook his head. "No. That one's tougher." He stole a sidelong glance at me. "Sam." He waited for me to turn toward him. "Whatever you're thinking of doing . . . don't. At least, not till you run it by me."

As if. I didn't want my options limited to legal measures—like getting him on some wimpy probation violation. Because I had no doubt he was on probation for something. But I had no intention of giving Dale a reason to check up on me. "Sure."

He set his jaw, but he wisely let it go. "I guess you're going to have to hope your gambit works on the prosecutor."

Just the thought of it gave me a sinking feeling. "Yeah, I'll go see him tomorrow."

When we pulled up to Dale's house, he offered to throw something together for dinner, but I was too depressed by all we'd heard today, not to mention mega nervous about gaming the DA. "Thanks, but I'll pass this time." I got out and headed toward Beulah.

Dale parked the car at the curb and followed me into the garage. "Sam, I meant what I said. Don't move on those jerks without telling me. You can't afford to get caught. Especially now."

I hit the remote and unlocked the car. "What makes you think I'll do something illegal?"

He put his hands on his hips and stared at me. "Can we stop playing games?"

I opened the door. "I'm not. Those shitbirds have to be into something they can get busted for. I'll just bring it to the attention of the proper authorities."

His tone was sarcastic. "Right, you're going to call the cops. Sounds just like you." Dale sighed. "Please let me handle this. Okay?"

I gave him a flat look. "Sure, no problem." I got into my car.

He had a wary look on his face as I pulled out of the driveway. And as I drove off, I looked in my rearview mirror and saw that he was still standing in the driveway, watching me.

Dale didn't *know* so much as guessed at some of the things I'd done. He knew I'd set up Ricardo Orozco to get killed in prison. And I'm sure he guessed that I'd used the Orozcos to get rid of a murdering cop—though I'd never openly admitted it.

But there was a lot more he didn't know and would never know. As I thought about it now, I imagined he suspected that was the case. But suspecting isn't knowing, and I'm a solo player by nature. Unless I absolutely had to have his help with Ronnie and Uncle Pete, I'd take care of them myself. Maybe not right away—all the stars would have to line up. But I'd keep them in the back of my mind, and when the opportunity came along, I'd be ready.

It was almost ten o'clock when I pulled into the driveway of my building. Since Cabazon's last visit, I'd made it a habit to stop and scope out my balcony before pulling into my parking space. The lighting wasn't great, but it looked like I wouldn't have the pleasure of his company tonight.

I headed up to my apartment, my only thought the size of the drink I was going to pour. I dropped my purse and briefcase in the living room and decided to take a shower. I was feeling the familiar swirling anger in my gut that I used to have all the time when I was a kid. Hearing Tiffany's stories had kicked the too-thin covers off my past. I needed to calm down. I stood under the hot water until it ran cold, then bundled up in sweats and went out to the kitchen and poured myself a triple shot of Patrón Silver on the rocks.

I'd taken a big, long swig before I saw that I had a message on my landline. It was from Alex. Someone named Greg Engler, who was a student at USC, needed to see me ASAP. He claimed he had some information for me on Roan's death. Alex said he thought the guy sounded legit, so he'd set up a meeting with Greg at the office tomorrow morning, nine a.m.

Good. I'd be squeezed for time—I had to go downtown and see the prosecutor, Rick Moringlane, tomorrow, too—but I needed to make faster progress on Graham's case. And besides, the prosecutor wouldn't be available until the afternoon anyway. I'd already put in a call to his secretary to set up an appointment, and she'd told me he'd be available any time after one thirty. And besides, if I didn't keep busy, I'd just get more worked up about the meeting.

I opened my laptop to review what I'd found on the Internet about the prosecutor. Rick Moringlane had the look of a true believer, the kind who was sure he was doing the Lord's work. Short brown hair, wide smile, open face, nothing to hide. He wasn't a baby DA, but I wouldn't expect a baby DA to be handling a case like this. He'd been a prosecutor for nine years, had a decent win-loss record and no personal dings on him from anyone—at least not on Facebook or Twitter.

I'd say the fact that he didn't have any negatives on Twitter was meaningful, but he hardly ever posted. I'd made a few calls to try and get some intel on him, but he'd just been transferred from the Long Beach office a couple of months ago, so he hadn't developed a reputation downtown yet.

True believer could work for me. He didn't have to be persuaded that there was any foul play by prosecutors or cops to buy my story. I sighed as I closed my laptop. Ordinarily, I wouldn't waste ten seconds worrying about being able to sell a prosecutor on anything. But the looming threat of death—Tracy's, mine, Dale's—changed everything. There was no room for failure. This had to work.

And it could. Though, given the way my luck was going, I had no reason to be optimistic. But I had to do my best to stay positive, to have a little hope. This could all go swimmingly. It *should* go swimmingly. Or so I told myself.

As for my chances of a nightmare-free night, I had zero hope. Hearing about Ronnie and Uncle Pete had ruined any shot I had at getting a decent night's sleep. And I couldn't afford to try and drown my demons in tequila. I needed a clear head for tomorrow's events.

I took a couple of Advil as I got into bed, thinking that might help. It didn't. I woke up thrashing and sweaty at three a.m. Desperate to get some rest, I got up and made myself a cup of warm milk—kept at the ready for just this purpose. I managed to doze off at five thirty and sleep until the alarm woke me at seven—tired but clearheaded. I got into the shower and practiced what I'd say to Deputy DA Rick Moringlane.

Fear and anxiety made me move faster than usual. I got out the door by a quarter to eight. So I stopped to pick up coffee and some Egg McMuffins for the troops.

Alex was already in his office when I got in. I put the bag of food and tray of coffees on the table behind Michy's desk and called out to him that breakfast was served. Michy—who was working on our books—kept typing but grinned. "Breakfast of champions."

"More accurately, I decided we deserved a break today." I dropped my purse and briefcase on the couch in my office, and when I went back out to get my coffee and Egg McMuffin, Alex was already biting into one.

He looked up. "Thanks for this. I love this junk, though I guess we should try and find some healthier options."

I sat on the edge of Michy's desk and unwrapped an Egg McMuffin. "Healthy food is for pussies. So what've you got on my good buddy Dr. Mortimer?"

Alex had a grim smile. "You'll love this. It looks like our good buddy has screwed up on the cause of death before. The victim was a little girl, four years old. Her parents were in the process of getting divorced when she died. The coroner found wounds on the body that indicated a sharp force injury, but she stopped short of calling it a homicide, said they needed to do more testing. The father wanted a better answer, so he hired Mortimer. It took Mortimer less than a week to come out with his finding that the cause of death was multiple stab wounds."

I swallowed my mega-bite of the sandwich. "I assume the child lived with the mother, and the father blamed her?"

Alex nodded. "Right. He went balls to the wall to get her arrested."

Michy folded her arms and leaned back. "And did the cops bust her?"

Alex took a sip of his coffee. "They sure did. The mother sat in jail for a few weeks—until the coroner came out with the test results. The child had died of dog bites—not stab wounds. The neighbors in the house behind theirs had been taking care of a relative's German shepherd. A very big German shepherd."

This was fantastic. "So the mom got released, case closed, no murder?" Alex nodded. "How come the press didn't pick up on this?"

He gave me a superior look. "Maybe because they're nowhere near as good as me?"

I nodded. "That's a given. But seriously, it must've been reported somewhere."

Alex caved in. "It was. In McCall, Idaho. Population twenty-nine hundred. I'm sure the press would've gotten there eventually, but . . ."

There was no big emergency to investigate Mortimer's past at this point, when the coroner might wind up agreeing with him. "Michy, get this over to—"

But Michy was already typing. "I'm on it. I'm sending to our connect at Associated Press and the *LA Times*. And then I'll call it in to Sheri and KNX Newsradio."

Print, television, and radio. That should do it. I smiled. "Perfect." I liked the way this day was starting. "Nice job, Alex." I looked at my watch. Our new witness was due in soon. "Moving on, did you actually talk to this guy Greg Engler?"

Alex pulled over the spare secretary's chair and sat down. "Yeah. Not for long. He wouldn't tell me much. He only wanted to talk to you. But I got the feeling he really does know something."

I'd looked over the police reports while I wasn't sleeping last night. "I didn't see his name listed anywhere in the witness statements."

He nodded. "Correct, he's not there. Which either means he's bullshitting us or he ducked the cops. Obviously, I'm betting on the latter."

Michy had just bitten into her Egg McMuffin when the buzzer sounded at the outer door. She put down her sandwich. "Shit. He's early."

I stood up. "Finish your breakfast. I'll take him in." I handed her a napkin and pointed to the corner of her mouth. "You just might want to . . ."

Michy wiped off the crumbs and hit the buzzer. I turned to see a husky young guy with shaggy shoulder-length brown hair and big brown puppy-dog eyes. He wore a gray muffler, navy-blue pullover hoodie, and jeans. I was relieved to see he was wearing sneakers—not sandals. I walked over to him and introduced everyone as I shook his hand. It was clammy and cold. He gave each of us a nervous nod, and I led him into my office.

When Alex followed him in, Greg glanced at me with alarm. I motioned for Alex to close the door, then told Greg, "Don't worry, he's my investigator." I gestured to the chairs in front of my desk. "Have a seat."

Greg sat on the edge of the chair and fiddled with the fringe on his scarf. "The thing is, this has to be confidential." He stole a glance at Alex. "Sorry, man. No offense."

Alex had a little smile. "None taken."

It was good to start the day with a bit of a laugh—though I was careful to keep it inside. "No, Greg. What I meant was, it's okay. He's part of the team, so he has to keep everything you say secret, too."

His eyebrows lifted as he looked from me to Alex and back. "You sure?"

I couldn't help but smile now. He was kind of adorable. "Very sure. Tell me why I don't see your name in the police reports."

He laced his fingers together in his lap. "Because I told the cops I didn't know anything."

I studied him for a moment. "But that wasn't true, and you want to tell me and not them because . . . Feel free to fill in the blank."

Greg stole another glance at Alex, then stared at his lap as he answered. "Because I'm a premed student, and I think I might need a lawyer at some point." He looked at me, his expression anxious. "My dad's a doctor, and I . . . uh . . . I stole his prescription pad and . . ." He swallowed, and his last words came out in a rush. "I wrote scrips for Oxy."

My brain made the connection before I was even aware of it. "And you sold it to . . . Alicia?"

Greg shook his head. "No, to Roan."

Then Roan must've been Alicia's source for the Oxy Nomie had seen in her purse. Why did this not surprise me? "How did you know Roan?"

Greg took a deep breath. "He was a friend of a friend. We didn't hang out that much. It was mainly business. That's why I was at his place the night before Alicia died, when they had a huge fight."

I was confused. "They had a fight . . . in front of you?"

His brow knitted. "Not exactly. I was doing a deal with Roan, and Alicia knocked on the door, so he told me to go wait in the bedroom. They had a huge fight. I heard the whole thing. Alicia was screaming and crying."

Alex turned to face him. "What was she saying?"

Greg stared straight ahead. "She kept begging him to take down photos." He looked at Alex. "I didn't know what she was talking about at the time, but from the news, I figure she must've meant the nude selfies, right?"

Alex nodded. "Did you hear what Roan said?"

Greg let out a long breath. "He said he didn't post them. But . . ."

I took a guess. "You didn't believe him?"

Greg shrugged. "It's just that he didn't try real hard to convince her. He just said it real casually, like he didn't care. Like maybe he wanted her to know but didn't want to get in trouble by admitting it. Because Alicia kept saying it had to be him, that he was the only one who had the photos."

I finished the thought. "So who else could've done it?" Greg lifted his hands and shrugged. I agreed with him. It had to be Roan. "What did Roan say to that?"

Greg furrowed his brow again. "That Alicia had the photos, too, and he was sure she'd passed them around. And he called her a bitch and a slut and . . . a bunch of other things." He rolled his shoulders back and blew out a breath. "It got real ugly, man."

Slut. The use of that word told me so much. "Did Roan mention any other guy by name?" Greg shook his head. "What did Alicia say?"

He stared at a point on my desk as he spoke. "That at least she hadn't slept with anyone else, which was a lot more than he could say."

Whoa. Roan, the possessive, obsessive maniac, cheated on Alicia? I did not see that coming. "So she was accusing him of cheating on her?"

"That's the way I took it."

"Did she mention any names?"

Greg gave me a sheepish look. "No, but she didn't have to. I was at Roan's apartment the week before, and I saw him with her."

I raised an eyebrow. Our little Oxy dealer was a fount of information. "Did you know the girl?" Greg nodded. "Who was it?"

He inhaled. "Diana."

THIRTY-FOUR

"Diana? What the fuck?" I said to Alex after Greg had left, clutching my business card in his cold, clammy hand.

He'd given me his statement in exchange for my promise to represent him if he got busted for selling Oxy. I considered it a bargain. Since he had no record, it'd only take me one appearance to knock out a deal for straight probation. The statement he'd given us was more than worth the effort.

Alex wrinkled his nose. "It's pretty tacky. But you could feel the envy when we talked to her."

I agreed, but that was the least of it. I looked at my skull clock. It was only ten. If she was in pocket, we could brace her up right now. That'd put me just minutes away from the downtown courthouse—where I had to go that afternoon anyway when I met with the prosecutor on Tracy's case. "See if you can get Diana to meet with us by eleven or so." I didn't think the interview would take long. "But keep it light; don't tip her."

Alex shot me a look. "Gee, ya think?"

I sighed and shook my head. "Yeah, sorry."

Five minutes later, he was back—and wearing his coat, a cool double-breasted peacoat. "Let's hit it."

I stood up and put on my very uncool—but warmly lined—raincoat. "We should take two cars. I've got a court appearance downtown afterward."

Alex followed me out to Michy's desk. "I don't mind waiting."

It was tempting to have him nearby. Just for moral support. But I might be acting weird, because, you know . . . life or death, and I didn't want him to get suspicious when he saw me sweat. "Thanks, but it might be a while."

I told Michy where we were going—and that I had to make a pit stop downtown after that. "I should be back this afternoon. But it's Friday." When traffic would be at its worst. In LA there was no such thing as "life in the fast lane."

She shook her head. "So I'll see you sometime tomorrow. Anything going on downtown I should know about? As in, something involving billable hours?"

I had my lie ready. I knew better than to try and pull it off on the fly with Michy. "Unfortunately, no. I'm just standing in for Norman on that burglary case." It'd been my case, too, but my client had taken the county lid deal I'd gotten for him. Norman's client was proving to be a little less realistic. We headed to the door. "Call me if anything good happens. Otherwise . . ."

Michy nodded. "It can wait."

Alex had arranged for us to meet Diana at Bacaro L.A.—a relatively nice but cheap restaurant on Union Avenue—where we could find some privacy. The promise of a free meal was turning out to be a real boon for inspiring cooperation. Viva la poor student.

It started to rain on the way over—nothing heavy, just drizzle, but the greasy road made traffic slow down to a crawl. It was a quarter after eleven by the time I got there. Fortunately, Alex had already arrived. He'd snagged a table in a quiet corner, and I saw that Diana was already hunched over a bowl of soup. As I sat down, I said, "Smells good. What is it?"

She paused to come up for air. "Chicken vegetable."

I let her engage in chitchat with Alex while she finished her soup. But the moment she put down her spoon, I let her have it. My voice was low but firm. "We found out you were hooking up with Roan behind Alicia's back. I'm not here to judge. If that's the way you roll with your friends, that's your business. But your holding out on me is my business. What else aren't you telling me? People's lives are on the line here, Diana. You need to get a grip on what's important."

If I thought she'd be cowed by my confrontation, I was very much mistaken. She sat up and locked eyes with me, her gaze defiant. "Everyone knew Alicia was hooking up with that professor. So why shouldn't I hook up with Roan?"

I held her gaze. "You don't really need me to answer that." She deflated a little and looked down at the table. "When you say 'everyone knew,' I assume that means you think Roan might've known about it, too?"

A little defiance came back into her eyes. "He definitely knew."

There was only one way she could be so sure. "Because you told him."

She didn't deny it. "He had a right to know what was going on. And besides, I was sick of the way they all stepped on their tongues around her."

Jeez, jealous much? But maybe she had specifics. "Including Davey and Phil?"

She waved a dismissive hand. "All of them."

I knew about Phil; he'd admitted it. "What makes you think Davey was such a fan? He told me they were just friends."

But Diana had spent all her hostility. She slumped a little and shook her head. "Maybe so. I don't know." She played with the empty packet of sweetener near her coffee cup. "I actually did like her. She was . . .

sweet. I guess I just couldn't deal with how she seemed to have it all. A rich family, perfect grades, a bunch of guys who were hot for her . . . She didn't have to sweat for any of it."

Or do pole dancing to buy groceries. "How did Roan react when you told him about Alicia and that professor?"

She set her jaw. "Pissed as fuck. And betrayed. They all used to hang out, go to the professor's place for wine and pizza and all."

I hadn't known they'd been such a chummy group. "You mean Roan and Alicia and some others from the class used to hang out together?"

She nodded. "He couldn't believe Alicia—or that prof—would do him like that. Said he was going to screw them both over."

Alex and I exchanged a look. He leaned toward her. "Did he say how?"

Diana shook her head. "But I actually didn't take him all that seriously. Roan popped off a lot, and it never amounted to anything."

Except for this last time. "Is there anything else you're holding back?" I added with mild sarcasm. "Because now would be a good time to unburden yourself."

She stared down at her empty bowl and frowned. "No, there's nothing else." Diana looked up at me, contrite. "Sorry about going off on you like that. I do feel bad about hooking up with Roan. I shouldn't have done it." She sighed. "It's just . . . I liked her, but I also resented her." She shook her head sadly. "I'd always thought Alicia was so lucky."

The irony required no comment. I glanced at my phone and saw that it was almost one o'clock. I needed to get over to the courthouse. When we wrapped up, a much more subdued Diana thanked us for lunch and promised to let us know if she remembered anything else. I offered her a lift back to campus, but she'd ridden her bike over, so she declined.

After she left, Alex and I walked to our cars. I was glad we were driving separately. I had some work for him to do. "I know you've been checking into Professor Barth, but we need to step it up a notch." Now it wasn't just that I could tell he was hiding something or that he had no alibi for Roan's murder. I sensed there was a lot more to Barth's story, and that might mean he also had a real motive to kill Roan—though I wasn't sure what it might be.

We got to my car first. The rain clouds had cleared, but the air had gotten downright frosty. Alex put his hands in his pockets. "You think he'd kill Roan to keep him from telling the dean about the affair? 'Cause I'm not sure I buy that."

"No, I agree. And it didn't even sound like they dated that much. But there's more to this, and we need to find out what it is."

Alex said he was on it, and I headed to the courthouse. I deliberately parked in the farthest lot. The walk would calm my nerves.

The wind kicked up as I made my way toward Temple Street. I bent my head to keep my hair out of my eyes—and to keep my face from freezing. I was glad when I got inside the lobby. The walk had helped to burn off a little nervous energy. But as I rode the elevator to the eighteenth floor, my stomach began to churn again. I gave the receptionist my card and told her to tell Rick that I was here to talk to him about the Maldonado case. She told me to take a seat and picked up the phone. I forced myself to take deep breaths as I sat down and rehearsed my lines for the thirtieth time.

Ten minutes later, he walked into the reception area, a wide smile on his face. Rick Moringlane was a little shorter than I'd expected. But he totally looked like the Boy Scout type I'd seen in the photo. He came over and extended a hand. "Ms. Brinkman, I've heard of you. Nice to meet in person."

He'd heard of me, but that didn't seem to be a bad thing. So far, so good. I shook his hand and said, "Likewise."

He gestured to the door. "Come on back."

I followed him out into the hallway and up to the security door. He punched in a number on the keypad and held the door open for me. I walked in, and he led the way to a tiny office on the right side of the building. Tiny, but it had a window—a major perk, I knew, from my days as a public defender one floor above.

It was a typical county lawyer's office: regulation wood laminate desk, standing metal file cabinets, and files stacked on a table against the wall. There was a family photo on a short bookcase behind his chair that showed Rick, his lovely bride, and a smiling toddler in a pink dress with pink bows in her hair, but unlike most county lawyer offices, there were no posters on the wall, no knickknacks on the desk. He sat down behind it, and I took one of the metal-framed county-issue chairs across from him.

He leaned back in his executive chair and smiled again. "I heard about you defending your father on that double. I can't imagine what that must've been like."

It was a fairly common question—one I absolutely hated answering. But I needed to get on his good side, so I gave over to it with good humor this time. "Yeah, it was crazy." We chatted about the case for longer than I'd have liked. Then I turned the tables and asked how he liked working downtown—and barely listened to his answer.

Finally, he let us get down to brass tacks. "So what's your interest in the Maldonado case?"

I exhaled slowly and gave him a look that I hoped was a lot calmer than I felt. "I may have a client who witnessed the murder."

THIRTY-FIVE

Rick had been leaning back and rocking in his chair. Now, he stopped rocking. "You want to give me his name?"

I shook my head. "Not yet. Obviously, he's going to want a little consideration on his own case, and I want to make sure there's an opportunity here before I give you specifics."

He studied me for a moment. "Well, you're going to have to give me something to go on, even if it's just a general overview of what he'll say. And what kind of charges is he facing? Is it a strike case?"

I gave him my fictional client's history. "No, no. Just a commercial burglary. And he's got a minimal rap sheet, just a couple of juvie busts. We're looking for probation." Rick tilted his head to one side, then nodded. So far, so good. "As for what he can do for you, I believe he can corroborate your key eyewitness's testimony."

That got him—as I'd known it would. He leaned forward. "Corroborate how? Did he see it go down, too?"

I shook my head and gave him a little smile. "Let's just say he saw enough to cure your eyewitness's credibility problems."

Rick frowned at me. "Exactly what credibility problems do you think I have?"

I held up a hand. "My bad. Maybe the fact that your witness has a rap sheet a mile long isn't a problem for you."

He blanched a little. "How do you—who told you that?"

I had him. Time to play my trump card. "I know your main witness is Tracy Gopeck." Her name wasn't supposed to be public knowledge yet. If that didn't convince him that my client really did have the goods, I was toast.

Rick took a moment to absorb that. "Does he know her?"

That'd be too easy for him to check out. "No. But he was in the background when she was talking to the cops at the crime scene. He caught her name. I used my . . . sources to look into her background."

He gave me a suspicious look. "What sources?"

"Not the kind you have to worry about." I waited for him to put it together: my father was a detective with LAPD, therefore . . .

And he got it. He nodded. "I definitely could use some help with her credibility."

Here came the hard part. "The thing is, I'll need to talk to Tracy myself. I won't know if my client's information really is corroborating until I hear what she has to say."

He shook his head. "No way."

I had to get him to tell me where she was. I pretended to be puzzled. "I'll be happy to do it with you there, Rick. I just can't expose my client until I know that there's something in it for him. Plus, there's a gang connection to this case. If his name gets spread around, it could be big trouble for him."

He rocked in his chair for a moment. "I can't bring anyone to her right now. It's not secure enough yet."

I played my answer with mild exasperation. "Look, I know you've got her in protective custody. You want to blindfold me or whatever, that's fine."

Rick gave a little smile, but he shook his head. "I'd be okay with that, but it's not up to me."

I wasn't going to get access to Tracy from him—that much was clear. But that wasn't my only objective. I made my last move. "How about if my father talks to your cops? Would that help?"

He looked contrite. "Sorry, but no. It wouldn't. It's not even up to them."

And bingo. I had my answer.

I held up my hands. "Then I guess we're at a stalemate." I picked up my purse. "I'd really like to help you out, Rick. Here's what I suggest: try and talk to the powers that be, see if you can get them to bend a little. If anything changes, let me know." I stood up and held out my hand.

As he stood and shook my hand, he looked so disappointed I almost felt bad for him. "Okay. And if your client changes his mind about fronting his information, let me know. Please tell him he can trust me. Even if I can't make him a deal, I'll make sure his name doesn't get out."

I shrugged. "I'll try. But you know he's right to be nervous. There's a reason you've got Tracy in protective custody."

Rick walked me out.

As I left the building and headed for the PAB to talk to Dale, I thought I'd done a pretty good job for my client.

Too bad he'd never get the chance to thank me for it.

By prearrangement, I texted Dale to say I was on my way. He met me outside, and we headed to the nearby Panorama Café on Hill Street. I ordered hot tea, and he ordered coffee. After the waiter brought our drinks, I leaned in and kept my voice low. "The feds have her."

Dale wrapped his hands around his cup. He hadn't bothered to wear a jacket, and the cold wind blowing outside was a bit much even for him. "That jibes with what I found out. She's nowhere in state custody. She had to either be out on her own or with the feds."

Which begged the ultimate question: Where was she? "But if she's with the feds, she could be anywhere in the country."

Dale's expression was bleak. "For what it's worth, my guess is they're keeping her local for the sake of convenience."

That was cold comfort. "Which just means it's easier for Cabazon—or Diego—to find her, too." For all that people yap about the safety of protective custody, it can be porous as hell.

We mulled over our options. Given what DA Rick Moringlane had said, we could now be fairly sure Tracy was in federal protective custody and not just hiding out on her own. The problem was, that meant Dale would have to be deployed—something we'd hoped to avoid. "I'm afraid you'll have to get this ball rolling. Based on what Moringlane said, I think it's pretty clear that LAPD cops caught the case first." And between the two of us, Dale was the only one who could hope to find those cops and get them to tell him which FBI agents they handed off the case to. But that would require a certain amount of snooping around and asking questions. Every bit of that was risky for him.

Because the only way to save Tracy was to get her away from her handlers and help her disappear. If we were successful, someone might very well remember that Dale had been asking around about her shortly before she vanished. To put it mildly, that would be a bad thing. So he had to be *very* smooth about how he handled this. "I can help you come up with a cover story."

Dale glared at me. "Thanks. I think I can handle it." He looked away for a moment. When he met my gaze, he said, "Assuming I do find these feds, how am I supposed to talk them into letting you meet with Tracy?"

I'd been thinking about that problem for some time. I needed a story that would both persuade Tracy to talk to me *and* persuade the feds to let me talk to her. After meeting with *la familia* Gopeck, I thought I had the answer. "The truth is always the best lie. You tell the agents that I'm carrying a message from Tiffany. We're going to need Tiffany to get on board with this, because she'll need to handwrite the note and put in enough personal info so Tracy will believe it really came from her—"

Dale interrupted, his expression irritated. "A note saying what?"

I stared at him. "I get that you're on edge, but you need to calm down and listen."

Dale leaned back and folded his arms. "Go ahead."

"Tiffany's going to say that she thinks that asswipe Ronnie is molesting the younger sister, Tammy. But Tammy's afraid to come forward because she thinks no one will believe her. Tiffany needs Tracy's help. She's sure that if Tracy backs her up, Tammy will go to the cops." It seemed to me a story like that would persuade the feds to let us make contact with Tracy.

Dale didn't look convinced. "I don't know."

Now I sat back. "I'm all ears if you have a better idea."

Dale stared at his coffee, then shook his head. "Not at the moment."

I spooled out the plan. "We'll have to tell Tiffany what's really going on with Tracy, since we're asking her to help sell our lie. And who knows? Maybe with a little luck, we might be able to build a real case against Ronnie—the asshole."

"I definitely like the idea of building a *real* case against that punk." He looked me in the eye. "A lot better than whatever else you were planning to do to him."

My face was a mask of innocence. "That *was* what I was planning to do to him." Okay, so it wasn't my first choice. But it was in the mix.

Dale blew out a breath. "Of course, your plan goes down the shitter if Tracy doesn't care about getting revenge on Ronnie—or helping her little sister."

I nodded. "That's true. My plan is based on a hunch. But I think it's a good one." I did have a certain expertise in the area of molestation.

He stared out the window for a moment, then turned back to me. "Assuming this works and you do get to talk to Tracy, what then?"

I'd been thinking about that. "I'll warn her about Cabazon, tell her we want to save—"

Dale interrupted me again. "And she'll believe you because . . . ? I don't know why she'd trust you—or me. And beyond that, exactly *how* are we going to save her?"

His edginess was understandable, but it wasn't helping matters. I was nervous, too. I took a deep breath and spoke as calmly as I could. "First of all, given her background, I think she might have an easier time trusting me than you."

Dale hesitated, then gave a reluctant nod. "Maybe so. But still . . ."

"I know. And you're right. I can't make her trust me." I lifted my hands, palms up. "All I can do is hope for the best. But as for rescuing her, I do have a plan." And it'd wrap in nicely with the story we were going to sell about Ronnie abusing Tammy. I mapped out the general outlines of what I'd been thinking.

Dale pointed out some flaws and offered some tweaks. But when we'd finished, he still didn't look thrilled. "It's dicey as hell, Sam."

It was. But as far as I could tell, there was no such thing as foolproof—or risk-proof—given the parties we were dealing with. "Again, I'm happy to take suggestions if you've got something better."

Dale had a stubborn look. "I'm sure I can think of something."

"Fine. In the meantime, let me know when you get the names of those FBI agents."

THIRTY-SIX

It was after three when I headed back to the office, and I was hungry. Comfort food sounded good to me right now, so I hit the drive-through at the Taco Bell near the office and bought us a bunch of tacos and quesadillas.

As I walked through the door carrying my bounty, I said, "Who's the best lawyer in LA?"

Michy eyed the bags. "Is some of that for me?"

"Yes." I pulled one of the goodies out of the bag and handed it to her.

She gave a fist pump. "I've said it before and I'll say it again. You are the greatest lawyer in all of California." She started to unwrap it. "Is this a Taco Supreme?"

I put a hand on my hip. "What cruel monster would neglect to bring Taco Supremes?"

Michy took a bite of her taco and spoke around her mouthful. "Did I say California? I meant all of North America."

Alex came out of his office and raised an eyebrow at Michy. "It's Taco Bell, not prime rib and lobster."

Michy gave a mock gasp and covered her mouth. "Sam, tell him to stop."

I turned to Alex. "You must never put down Taco Bell. It is forbidden."

He rolled his eyes, then went over and picked up a taco. "It does smell good."

Michy gave him a superior look. "I rest my case."

I picked up a couple of tacos and told them to come eat in my office. I wanted to kick around our new information on Graham's case. When we'd all settled in, I asked Michy if Alex had given her the latest on Roan and Professor Barth.

She licked some hot sauce off her fingers. "Yeah. And now the question is, what could Roan have had on Barth that might have made Barth kill him?"

I took a sip of water. "Alex, did you get a chance to make any headway on this?"

He dabbed at his mouth with a napkin. "I bumped around on Barth's Facebook page, checked the Internet for any past lawsuits, and reviewed what I'd downloaded on Roan. So far, nothing."

I took a sip of my Coke. "And no one we spoke to mentioned anything happening between them. So whatever it was probably only involved the two of them—no witnesses." I picked up the chicken quesadilla. "Alex, did you happen to get into Barth's bank accounts?"

"Did that a while ago. I didn't see any unusual activity—no sudden balance jumps up or down. Typical professor's pay—for USC anyway. As far as other financial activity around the relevant time, I noticed that he bought a car one week before Alicia died."

I finished chewing my bite of quesadilla. "What'd he buy?"

Alex balled up his taco wrapper and tossed it into the wastebasket near my desk. It went in—all net—and he looked pleased with himself. "Nothing fancy. A seven-year-old Volkswagen Jetta."

Michy asked, "What'd he do with his old car?" She balled up her taco wrapper and made the basket as well. "Girls so rule."

Alex flicked his fingers at her. "Mine was a harder shot," he said. "As far as I could tell, he still has his old Audi. *Old* being a relative term. It's a lot newer than that Jetta."

"How much newer?" I balled up my quesadilla wrapper and made the toss—and missed. "It's the wrapper—it's bigger than yours." Michy and Alex exchanged smirks. I held up a middle finger.

Alex ignored me. "The Audi's only three years old."

And he bought a seven-year-old Jetta. That seemed weird. "Why buy an old Jetta when he's got a newer Audi? Unless he needed to downsize. But in that case, wouldn't you think he'd sell the Audi?"

Michy looked confused, too. "I sure would. And I'm sure USC pays better than most, but he's an undergrad professor. It can't be huge bucks. Besides, he's single. Why does he need two cars?"

Alex shrugged. "I think it's odd, too. But to your point, Michy, maybe he did sell the Audi and just didn't report it so he wouldn't have to claim the income."

I supposed that was a possibility—maybe even likely. But you can't develop leads by assuming anything, no matter how logical. "I think we should go check out Barth's place and see whether he still has that car."

Alex went over to the wastebasket and pointedly looked at me as he picked up my quesadilla wrapper—which had landed a solid foot to the right—and threw it in. "He lives in Mount Washington."

Mount Washington was a cool 'hood, just seven or eight miles northeast of downtown, which made it an easy commute for Barth. Lots of hills, great views, and most of the houses were custom, so the wide variety of styles gave it kind of a bohemian vibe, even though the population was solidly upper-middle class. "Then we could go tonight."

Alex looked at his watch. "It's almost seven. If we leave now, we should get there by eight or so."

I pulled on my coat and nodded toward the table with the rest of the Taco Bell feast. "Michy, feel free to take the rest of it home." Just to be on the safe side, I put my gun in my purse. I didn't expect any trouble, but why take chances?

Michy followed us out and started packing the food into the plastic bag. "Yum, tacos for breakfast."

I made a face. "That sounds awful." Alex went to his office to get his coat. I put the extra napkins into her bag. "Want to do a movie tomorrow? Or is it a Brad night?"

Michy pushed her blue Scünci back and fluffed out her hair. "Brad is dead to me. Movie night sounds great."

I was surprised. "You guys had a fight?"

She sighed. "Nothing major. It's just that he likes to drag me to all his office parties, and they have so *many* of them. And they all suck. I passed on one a couple of nights ago, and he got mad." She waved a hand in the air. "He'll just have to get over it." She peered at me. "How're you doing? You've been looking kind of tired lately. You sleeping?"

I gave her a resigned smile. "On occasion." I wished I could tell her about Tracy and her depressingly awful family. Michy didn't know the lurid details of my childhood, but she knew that I'd been in very bad shape when we moved in with Sebastian. And, of course, she knew the narcissist that was Celeste. Bottom line: she'd understand perfectly why Tracy's situation got to me. But I couldn't do it to her. Keeping all knowledge of Cabazon from her—and from Alex—was the only thing I could do to protect them. Alex came out of his office, and we headed for the door. I waved to Michy. "I'll call you tomorrow."

We took Alex's car because we needed to keep a low profile, and it would blend in where we were going. After he navigated onto the freeway, I asked, "How's it coming with the other website owner?"

He smiled. "By the way, his name is Simon Lutz. I've siphoned three thousand five hundred and sixty-eight dollars from his website.

And his nude photo got more than two thousand hits. I'm about ready to let him know he can stop the pain by taking down his website."

The double whammy of hitting his wallet and putting him in the victims' shoes was so satisfying. "Love it. Feel free to let him twist in the wind for as long as you like. The more money for the worthy causes, the better."

Alex sighed. "I agree. But that means Laurie's photos stay up, too."

"Oh, right." I'd been caught up in the thrill of revenge.

Alex said, "How about if I split the baby and let it go for another week?"

"Or you could let Laurie make the choice."

He smiled. "Even better. I'll call her tomorrow."

We found the professor's house on West Avenue, a narrow, winding street with no sidewalks. It was blue with white trim, and it was the smallest one on the block—possibly in the whole neighborhood. It overlooked a canyon and had a detached garage that was only big enough to hold one car. The garage was closed, but I noticed it had a window in the door. A Volkswagen Jetta was in the driveway. As Alex found a parking spot farther up the street, I pointed to it. "Is that his?"

"Looks like it." Alex peered at the license plate, the pulled out his iPad and hit some keys. "Yep, that's his."

"Then he must be home, so we'll have to wait."

We couldn't go snooping in his garage and risk getting caught. "I'm betting he's not the type to stay in on a Friday night."

Alex slid down in his seat. "Let's hope not anyway."

I slid down, too, and checked the car clock. It was eight. Hopefully he'd be leaving soon. "There might not be a car in that garage. Some people use the space for storage."

Alex glanced at the property. "Especially with a house that small. He probably needs all the room he can get."

The prospect of this mission turning out to be a bust was not a happy one. I needed this lead to take us somewhere. Plus, it was freezing inside the car, and Alex couldn't leave the engine running without attracting attention. By eight thirty, I was shivering. "If he doesn't come out by nine, we're pulling the plug."

Alex shook his head. "You are such a weather pussy."

A couple approached, walking a small poodle. I leaned over and put my head on his shoulder. And noticed how much thicker his coat was than mine. Pretending to say romantic nothings, I said, "Feel the difference between my coat and yours."

He put an arm around me and pinched the fabric as he pretended to whisper softly in my ear. "It's thinner. But you're still a weather wimp. You should wear a vest."

The couple glanced at us, smiled, and kept walking. I waited until I couldn't hear their footsteps, then sat up. Leaning against Alex had warmed me up a little. "Thanks for the body heat."

He slid back down in his seat. "Anytime."

I heard a door open. It was Barth. He was leaving. Finally. "We're in business."

Alex watched over the steering wheel as Barth got into his Jetta. "Give it five minutes after he pulls out."

I watched as Barth backed out and drove down the street, then counted the minutes on the car clock. At four minutes and fifty-nine seconds, I opened my door. "Ready?"

Alex nodded. "Let's go."

We got out, checked the area to make sure no one was coming, then went over to the garage. I looked through the window. "I see a black Audi. How about you?"

Alex rubbed the section of window he was looking through and took a closer look. "Yep, that's his license plate." He scanned the area behind us, then turned back to the door.

I knew what he was thinking. I pointed to a padlock on the right side. "Unless you brought bolt cutters, we're not getting through that."

Alex looked at the sturdy lock and sighed. "Wish I'd thought of that."

"Don't sweat it. It'd be too risky anyway."

He nodded, then pulled out his phone and took a picture of the car through the window. "Well, we found it. Now what?"

I had no idea.

THIRTY-SEVEN

We headed back, and I let Alex concentrate on navigating the tight, winding roads. There were almost no streetlights, and we'd spotted more than one raccoon—and a couple of skunks—while we'd waited for Barth to leave.

When he made it down the hill and onto a main thoroughfare, Alex said, "It's not necessarily any big deal that he bought an old Jetta and kept the Audi. Maybe he just wants to use the Jetta as a daily driver. Or maybe he hasn't gotten around to selling the Audi yet."

Both explanations were reasonable. "Yeah, I don't know that this is going to lead to anything—but it is interesting that he's got it padlocked in the garage. It's not like he lives in a rough neighborhood."

Alex pulled up the on-ramp to the freeway. "But he might have other stuff in there that's stealable. And even if there isn't, why take chances?"

That was true, too. Car thieves exist in nature, even up there, and a car in an unlocked garage would be such an easy mark for hot-wiring. Still, something about this car business was bugging me. "You didn't notice anything on his DMV record?"

Alex shook his head as he pulled into the fast lane. "Couple of speeding tickets before he got hired at USC, but nothing in the past couple of years."

I mulled it over, but as Alex pulled into the office garage and parked next to Beulah, I still hadn't been able to come up with any way to push this angle. "I'm fresh out of ideas."

Alex was staring out the windshield with a stubborn look. "I'll keep thinking."

I told him not to let it get in the way of his weekend, and he said he wouldn't dream of it.

But as I opened my door, I saw that he was distracted. One of the most important traits of a great investigator is tenacity, and Alex had it in spades. I patted the roof of his car, then got into Beulah. As we drove out, I knew he'd be chewing on this all weekend.

It stayed on my mind, too, but other than my ruminations, I had a fairly peaceful weekend. Movie nights with Michy are always relaxing. We catch up on the personal and mostly block out the professional.

Over dinner on Saturday night, she told me that she and Brad had already patched things up, which made me happy—and amused. "He can't live without you."

Michy nodded, matter of fact. "True." She took a sip of her wine. "What about your pitiful excuse for a love life?"

I pointed out that Niko and I were doing well. "Not a single fight."

She gave me a deadpan look. "A remarkable achievement. But since you've only had one real date in the past seven months, you'll excuse me if I don't break out the bubbly." Michy looked down at her wine, then back at me. "He really is on the road a lot, Sam. Doesn't that bother you?"

I smirked. "Niko being on the road a lot is what makes it work."

She gave me an exasperated look. "My point being, don't you think it's time for a real relationship?"

"No."

Michy rolled her eyes, but she gave up, and we moved on to more fruitful subjects—like the film we'd just seen, which pretty much sucked.

And the rest of the weekend was fairly mundane—until Dale called on Sunday night with an update on his search for the local cops who'd handled the Maldonado murder.

He sounded agitated. "I found them. They're both in Rampart division now. The problem is, I don't know either of them, so it's kind of tough to find a plausible reason to ask them questions—especially about a case I have no reason to care about. But I was just thinking, don't you have a friend in Rampart?"

There was only one cop who could possibly qualify as a friend. And Dale was right about her assignment. "Yeah, Hank transferred over there about a year ago. I can ask her to talk to them." I thought about what I could use for a cover story. "I'll give it a shot. But I don't know how long it'll take her to get to them. You sure there's no way you can access the department database without getting caught?"

There was a pause, and I heard ice clink against glass. "Believe me, I've been trying to think of a way ever since we got into this mess. But it'd take more tech smarts than I've got to cover my tracks. Alex could probably do it, but we can't use him."

No, we couldn't. It was frustrating having to do things the old-fashioned way. You don't realize how much you depend on computers until you can't use them. "Okay, Hank it is. I'll call her now."

And I did. I told her I was checking out Maldonado's lawyer, because he wanted to merge his practice with mine. "You ever hear of Diego Ferrara?"

She was silent for a moment. "No. Do you want me to run him through the system?"

I hadn't thought of that. I'd just assumed he was a scumbag. But it couldn't hurt to see how big a scumbag he was. "That'd be great. And since you're doing me one favor, I may as well pile on and ask for another one. Ferrara claims he's got a federal case—a gang-related murder. Defendant's name is Jorge Maldonado. A couple of guys in your division caught it first." I gave her their names. "You know them?"

"Yeah. You want me to ask what they think of Ferrara?"

Again, I didn't particularly care, but it'd blow my cover story if I told her not to bother. "That'd be great. Though I don't think they dealt with him much. For some reason, they had to hand it off to the FBI. What I'd really like to find out is what those FBI agents think of him."

A young male voice in the background asked what was in the fridge. Hank asked me to hold on. "I've got to deal with the idiot I call my son." She asked him if he still knew how to open the refrigerator door, then said to me, "The boy's twenty years old, and I still don't know how he finds his way home at night."

"But you've gotta admit, your house is like a museum." Her son, Naille, was a talented artist and a great kid. His artwork filled the house. I'd represented him when he got busted for painting a mural on the side of a liquor store, which the cops ungenerously characterized as graffiti. When I presented all the declarations from the neighbors as well as the owner saying they loved the mural, the prosecutor—with a little pressure from the judge—caved in and dismissed. Naille was going to Cal Arts now, and he was tearing it up. Hank was right, though. His head pretty much stayed in the clouds.

She grumbled, but she couldn't argue. "Back to the matter at hand. Do you want me to talk to the agents? Because I'd be glad to do it."

"No, that's cool. If you get me their names—and maybe put in a good word so they won't shut me down—I can take it from there." Actually, Dale was the one who was going to talk to them. But if all went as hoped, and the agents did let me meet with Tracy, I'd be dealing with them, too. It'd help in all kinds of ways if they thought they could trust me.

Hank said she'd take care of it first thing in the morning. "Or as soon as I can get a minute to talk to those cops."

I didn't like lying to Hank, but I had no doubt she'd approve if she knew the cause. "I can't tell you how much I appreciate this. You're the best."

There was a smile in her voice as she said, "You don't suck, either."

We laughed and promised to have dinner soon. Not a bad note to end the weekend on—if you didn't count the fact that it involved a plan that Tracy's life—not to mention my life and Dale's—depended on.

Monday morning, I headed into the office feeling optimistic. For no particular reason, I was sure that everything was going to work out.

Ordinarily, that kind of thinking immediately precedes disaster. Not this time. Or at least, not yet. I found Alex sitting with Michy when I got in, and they both looked excited. "Who won the lottery?"

Michy looked at Alex. "That *would* be better."

Alex gave her a mock glare. "Don't rain on my parade." He stood up and headed for my office. "I've got news."

I followed him in and sat down on the couch. "Okay, spill."

He turned a chair around to face me. "That Audi bugged me all weekend. I kept trying to figure out how to find out more about it. But I was coming up with nothing. And then, Sunday night, we went out to dinner, and we passed by the sheriff's station on Santa Monica."

I put my feet up on the coffee table. "And? If this takes much longer, I'll have to shave my legs again."

Alex ignored me. "And that's when it hit me. The police blotter. Check the police blotter." He opened his iPad and hit a key. "And I think I've got something." He read from the screen. "Just two days before Barth bought the Jetta, there was a hit-and-run. Killed an old homeless man. And the car was described as a—"

I dropped my feet to the floor. "Black Audi?"

Alex sighed. "Not quite that good. A black sedan."

"And obviously, no license plate." Alex shook his head. "Any description of the driver?"

Alex made a face. "If you can call it that. There were two witnesses: a homeless woman who lives—or rather lived, because who knows where she is now—in a nearby alley. And a bartender who happened to be emptying the garbage behind the bar at the time. The woman thought the driver was a male. The bartender didn't know."

"Any description of the homeless woman?" Alex shook his head. Not that we'd ever find her anyway. "Where did it happen?"

"You'll like this." He read from his iPad. "West Twenty-Ninth Street."

I tried to picture the area. "That's close to USC, isn't it?"

Alex nodded. "Very."

He was right. I did like it. I'd been thinking that whatever Roan had on Barth, it had to be a secret between the two of them. I remembered Diana telling us that Barth used to hang out with some of the kids in Alicia's class—Roan included. And that totally fit the theory that was forming in my mind. I spun it out so we could hear how it sounded. "Barth and Roan go on a pizza-beer-wine run, and the professor runs over that old guy." It sounded logical to me so far. "When Roan finds out about Barth and Alicia, he gets pissed and threatens to tell the cops." I nodded to myself. "In some circles, they'd call that motive."

Alex flipped his iPad closed. "And we know Barth has no alibi for the night of Roan's murder."

I'd been assuming that Alicia's and Roan's deaths were linked. But they didn't have to be. The more I thought about our new theory, the more I liked it. "We need to go talk to those witnesses." Probably not the woman, since we were unlikely to find her. But the bartender shouldn't be a problem.

Alex stood up. "The only thing is, I'm not sure what else we can get from them."

I wasn't, either. But it was worth checking, because as of now, Professor Barth Foley was either the best red herring I'd ever seen—or he really had killed Roan.

THIRTY-EIGHT

Alex and I headed to the bar. Ernie's was a small, dingy place on South Vermont. Alex parked on the street in front of the bar, and we walked around to the alley at the back of the building. I looked for streetlights. There weren't many, but the lights from the traffic and the businesses on South Vermont Boulevard would've offered some illumination. "What time did you say this happened?"

Alex consulted his iPad. "A little after midnight. And it was a Tuesday."

That late on a weeknight meant less traffic—and less light. Which probably explained why the descriptions were so vague. We were standing at the mouth of the alley. I looked toward the street where the accident had happened. "The homeless woman would've had a great view."

We walked over to the dumpsters behind the bar to get the bartender's point of view. Alex looked out at the street. "The bartender did, too."

He really did—clear and unobstructed. But I was distracted by the stench that permeated the area. It was so bad it practically burned my nose. The dumpsters looked older than me, and they were banged up and graffitied. The ground around them was littered with dried-up lemon and lime wedges and rat feces. "Let's get out of here."

I fast-walked around to the front of the bar and hoped that the interior of Ernie's would be an improvement. It was—but only marginally. The bar looked battered, and the pads on most of the bar stool seats were torn and scarred. A collection of wooden tables and chairs—every bit as battered-looking as the bar—filled the rest of the unadorned narrow space. The owner hadn't even bothered to put up the usual string of little white Christmas lights that so many neighborhood bars used to warm up the ambience. Nope, none of that for Ernie's. This was a no-frills watering hole for locals who wanted to get ripped on the cheap and be able to walk home—or fall down on a sidewalk close to home.

We found the bartender—a tall, hefty guy, who was bald on top and had a ring of black fringe. He wore jeans, a gold earring in his left ear, and a black Affliction T-shirt that strained around his considerable gut. He was standing behind the bar, arms folded, watching the television mounted on the wall. It was tuned to an episode of *Real Housewives of Atlanta*.

Alex ordered a club soda, but I decided to try and curry favor by ordering a vodka on the rocks. He made the drinks and put them on the counter in front of us. "Here you go. Want me to run a tab?"

I wondered if he did have customers who ran a tab at ten thirty in the morning. Probably. "No, thanks. Been working here long?" The police blotter didn't list any witness names, so I wanted to make sure we had the right guy.

He wiped his hands on an old towel. "Two years."

I smiled. "Are you Ernie?"

"Nah. He's the owner. I'm just the paid help. Name's Steve." He eyed my drink. "You want a slice of lime with that?"

Having seen what was strewn around the dumpsters, I decided not to. "No, thanks." I introduced Alex and myself, then asked Steve what he thought of the so-called real housewives—he thought they were bizarre but couldn't stop watching. We chatted about other reality shows, agreed they didn't resemble any reality we knew of, and eventually I nudged us into the area of interest. "You hear about the hit-and-run on West Twenty-Ninth about a month ago?"

Steve grunted. "Hear about it? I saw it." He shook his head. "It was terrible. Poor old guy was walking along, talking to himself, and *bam*! Car came out of nowhere, just mowed him down. I called in to find out whether they caught the guy, but as far as I know, the cops never did solve it."

I widened my eyes. "Wow, that's crazy. Did the driver stop and get out?"

I was surprised to see tears in his eyes. He blinked a few times. "I thought he was gonna. He backed up and idled there for a few seconds, but then"—Steve made a curving gesture with his hand—"he pulled around the old guy and peeled out." Based on that description, it didn't seem likely I'd get anything more out of him than what we'd seen in the police blotter, but I had to try. "You get the license plate?"

Steve frowned. "I was in shock, you know? I thought I saw the first three or four letters, but like I told the police, I really wasn't sure, and I didn't want to get the wrong person in trouble."

Could we possibly be getting lucky here? I glanced at Alex. He opened his iPad, where I knew he'd written down the license plate of the Audi. I asked, "Do you remember what they were?" I nodded at Alex. "My friend's a huge crime buff."

He raised an eyebrow at Alex. I wanted to tell him, *"Hey buddy, you watch* Real Housewives,*"* but I kept quiet and waited. Steve turned to the cash register and opened a drawer at the bottom. He pulled out a cocktail napkin and faced Alex as he read from it. "It was *4HI* . . . and then I thought it was either a *K* or a *Y*."

Alex studied the screen of his iPad. "Are you sure it started with a four?"

Steve stared off to the right. "No. I'm not. Sorry."

I pressed on. "But you seem pretty sure the driver was a man."

"Oh yeah, I think so." He paused, then shook his head. "Though I guess it could've been a woman with real short hair."

I asked, "Did you happen to notice whether anyone else was in the car?"

Steve frowned for a long moment. "You know, as I picture it now, I think there was someone in the passenger seat."

I hadn't seen any mention of a passenger in the police report. That might pose a credibility problem, but he seemed pretty certain. And it was great news for me. It definitely fit my theory. "Could you tell whether the passenger was male or female?"

Steve shook his head. "No. I didn't get a good-enough look to tell you that. But there definitely was someone in that right-hand seat. I'm sure of it."

Alex closed his iPad and asked, "Do you remember what kind of car it was? A Volvo? A BMW? An Audi?"

Steve waved a hand at Alex. "Coulda been any of those." He squinted at the iPad. "Probably not a Volvo, though, come to think of it. I'd rule that one out."

I asked whether he knew of any other witnesses, and he said he saw a homeless woman who used to stay in the alley talking to the police that night. "So I assumed she saw it, too. I used to give her my leftover bar snacks, but I haven't seen her around in the past few weeks."

We talked a little bit longer about how sad and awful it was, and Alex said he'd keep working on it. "I'd like to make that jerk pay for what he did."

Steve patted the bar in front of him. "I'm with you, my friend. And I'm hell on wheels about drunk drivers. Most of my customers live around here. Those who don't either have to show me their designated driver or let me call 'em a cab—or a Lyft or whatever. My motto is, if you can afford to drink, you can afford to pay for a car."

It always amazes me how many decent people there are in the world. Not necessarily in *my* world. But they were around. It was good to get a reminder. I tipped Steve with a ten spot and waved him off when he told me I didn't need to do that.

Alex and I headed back to the car. The moment we got inside, I asked, "Was he close?"

He started the car. "Not really. The number four was wrong, and Steve said the first two letters were *HI*. They were actually *AL*. I can see how they'd look similar in the dark, and on the fly. But the last letter he got completely wrong. He said it was a *K* or a *Y*. It was actually a *Z*."

I pulled on my seat belt. "I guess there's a reason it's an unsolved." I'd been hoping we'd find sloppy police work and a pot of gold at Ernie's. What a drag. "But that doesn't rule out Barth's car."

"No," Alex said. "Is it enough to make the cops take a look at him?"

I stared at the midday sun through the windshield. "I guess we'll find out. Hang on." I typed in the address for Ernie's to find the nearest cop shop. "Olympic station is closest. We're going to 1130 South Vermont."

I had no connects there, but I hoped someone at the station had heard about Dale's case. That win had earned me creds in some cop circles. We'd see if it did anything for me now.

The station was even closer than I'd thought. We got there in less than five minutes. I told the desk sergeant that we had information on the recent hit-and-run. He checked his computer for the officer in charge, took our names, and told us to have a seat.

A mere twenty-two minutes later, a short, squat man with a buzz cut, in a police uniform, came out and introduced himself in a voice so gravelly, it sounded like it came out through a meat grinder. "Officer Norton Grimes." He put out his hand. "And you are?" I introduced Alex and myself. He smiled. "I thought that was you. Amazing job on that double homicide. Come on back."

He took us to his cubicle, and we laid out our case. The phones rang nonstop the entire time. This was one busy station. I could see he was intrigued by the fact that Barth had bought an old Jetta and hadn't sold his Audi, and that Steve had remembered there was a passenger in the car. But when I told him I thought Barth had probably killed Roan to keep him from going to the police, he raised an eyebrow. "Don't you think you're reaching just a tad?"

I backed off. "Maybe so." Roan's death wasn't his business anyway. "But even if you don't believe he's got something to do with Roan's death, you've got a good reason to look into Barth for the hit-and-run."

Officer Grimes was interested but not convinced. "You've got a car that fits the general description, but the witnesses can't make the license plate. And you've got a teacher who works in the general area, but no one IDs him as the driver. Do you know of anyone who can at least say the teacher was in the area of the hit-and-run that night?"

Not at the moment. "I could give you a list of people to talk to. From what I hear, the kids in his class used to hang out at his house. Some of them could probably tell you whether he was in the area." Of course, one of them—Alicia—couldn't. And the problem was, even if other students had been hanging out with Barth and Roan the night of the hit-and-run, what were the odds that they'd remember some random night around ten days before Alicia died?

Officer Grimes looked at me with sympathy. "Tell you what. I'll get the list of students in Barth's class—"

Alex interrupted. "I can get it for you."

The officer raised an eyebrow. "Okay, please do. And I'll call around and see if anyone remembers being with them and what they did that night."

The phones were still ringing. He'd be way too busy to make this a priority. "Okay. Thank you." I stood up. "Shall I ask for you if I find anything else?"

He nodded and wrote down a number on a Post-it. "Here's my cell. But do me a favor, don't try and do my job for me, okay? It'll only mess things up."

I gave him a bright smile. "I certainly wouldn't want to do that."

We left the station and got back into the car. I said, "How much time do you need to put that list together?"

"About ten minutes." Alex gave me a sidelong glance. "We're calling them all, aren't we?"

"Most definitely. But first get us close to the school, in case anyone can meet in person."

Alex drove to Thirty-Fourth Street and McClintock Avenue, and we started calling. Every once in a while you get a lucky break, and we hit one of them. God knows we were due. Turned out it wasn't a random night. Five of the students, including Roan, had gone to see a showing of *La Dolce Vita* at the Downtown Independent Theater on Main Street that night, and some of them had gone to Barth's house afterward for beer and pizza. Within an hour and a half, we'd found two students who'd gone to Barth's house. And yes, Roan and Barth had said they'd stopped on the way to Barth's house to pick up beer and pizza. The students remembered because Barth and Roan had come back with beer but no pizza. They'd had to order from Domino's, and it'd taken forever.

It was so easy, even Officer Grimes could've done it. We marched back into the station and dropped it all into his lap, along with my working theory: Barth and Roan bought the beer first, maybe even drank some, and were on their way to get the pizza when Barth hit the homeless man.

Officer Grimes didn't like it, but we'd done him a big favor. He stared at me, then Alex. "So you went right back out and did what I asked you not to do."

I raised an eyebrow. "And probably solved your case for you. Let's not waste time. You need to get a search warrant. I'll help you write it up."

I could see the officer was torn. A little legal help with a search warrant would make his life easier. But I was a civilian—one who'd just meddled in his case. Ultimately, the allure of making his life easier won out. He went to his computer and pulled up the form. "Okay, run the facts by me again."

An hour later, he had a search warrant—signed and ready—in hand. He thanked me—finally. "I've gotta admit, you did a good job."

He reached out to shake, but I held up my hand. "I don't need the thanks. I just need you to promise you'll let me watch the interrogation when you bring in the professor."

Officer Grimes reared back as though I'd hit him. "You've got to be kidding. I can't let you do that."

"Sure you can." I told him about all the times I'd done it before. There really hadn't been that many. I'd only been able to get away with it once since I met Dale. But Officer Grimes didn't need to know that. "Besides, I'm not asking to sit in on it. I just want to watch." And probably give some suggestions if he seemed to be blowing it. I didn't see any need to mention that part right now.

He looked very skeptical. "I'll check with the captain, see what he thinks."

I nodded. "Thanks. You might want to have him call Dale Pearson. He'll vouch for me."

The officer's lips twitched in an almost-smile. "I'll do that."

I didn't think he would, but I wasn't worried. The minute we left the station, I called Dale. "Can you do me a quick favor? I need you to call the captain at Olympic."

THIRTY-NINE

By the time we got back on the road, it was the middle of rush hour, and I was starving. "There's an In-N-Out on Seventh Street."

Alex wasn't enthused. "The last time we ate in the car, I found French fries under your seat for a week."

I shot him a dagger look. "Please. You found a single fry. Consult your alien leaders. They'll tell you accidents happen." Alex still didn't look happy. "Okay, I won't order fries."

He sighed and headed toward Seventh Street. "You can't not order fries. That's blasphemy."

The line at the drive-through was, as usual, a mile long. One of the servers had come out and was taking orders from the waiting cars to speed things up. We ordered two double-meat Animal Styles and fries. I rolled down my window to inhale the smell coming from the kitchen. Heavenly. But it only made me hungrier. I rolled my window back up and thought about the search that was about to happen at Barth's place. "You think they'll find anything on the Audi?"

Alex leaned back in his seat. "I guess anything's possible. But if I was him, I'd have taken a power washer to that thing and sprayed it within an inch of its life."

That definitely would've been my move. "Yeah, they'll need to go over that car with a magnifying glass." That's why I'd asked Dale to give the captain a heads up on the best crime-scene techs. All they'd need to find was one tiny piece of evidence that matched the victim, and they'd have something to build a case on.

We got our food, and Alex pulled into the parking lot. We ate our burgers and some of the fries, then Alex headed back to the freeway. I noticed he had the radio tuned to KNX news. "You always listen to KNX?"

Alex shot me a look. "Hell no. But I wanted to hear what they did with the story we gave them on Dr. Mortimer."

I'd been checking, too. "I noticed the AP did a little blurb on it. Did KNX run with it?"

He nodded. "They gave it a couple of cycles. What about Sheri? Did she use it on *Crime Time*?"

I shook my head. "Not yet. They're waiting to see what the coroner says." It'd be much bigger news then—regardless of what the coroner concluded.

It wasn't a ton of coverage, but it might've been enough to get people to start doubting Mortimer's credibility—especially the coroner. If all he needed was a little extra nudge to reject Mortimer's call, the story about Mortimer's screwup on the dog-bite case might just do the trick.

An hour later, we were only one mile from the office when I got a call from Officer Grimes.

His voice was tight. "Captain told me to make this call, so I'm making it. Professor Foley has agreed to come in. Your father offered to let us use the RHD interrogation room so you could *observe*. But that's all you get to do. Watch. Understood?"

I was glad he couldn't see me smile. "Of course. Is he coming in now?"

Grimes exhaled loudly. "Yeah. We've got a uni who's going to follow him in and make sure he doesn't rabbit on us. Probably get to PAB within the hour."

When I ended the call, Alex gave me a wary look. "Don't tell me I have to turn around and go all the way back downtown."

I didn't blame him for hating the idea. "You don't have to—if you don't mind missing Barth's showdown with the cops."

Alex groaned, but he turned around and headed back to the freeway—which, good news, was much less backed up now.

It was almost eight o'clock when we got to the PAB. As we followed our escort to the interrogation room, I said, "Aren't you glad I made us stop and eat?"

Alex gave me a flinty look. "I'll decide when I clean my car tomorrow."

Dale met us outside the observation room. He and Alex exchanged a back-clapping bro hug. "Nice to see you," Dale said.

Alex nodded. "Likewise. They bring him in yet?"

Dale opened the door and motioned for us to go in. "They're on their way in now."

We took seats at the window / one-way mirror just as Officer Grimes ushered Barth into the room—followed by Detective Rusty Templeton. The fact that he was involved in this interrogation told me they'd taken my theory about Barth's possible involvement in Roan's death seriously. I had my issues with Rusty. He was a classic chauvinist pig, and he was lazy as hell—but he wasn't stupid. And he knew his way around an interrogation. I could tell by his expression that he was up for this one.

Barth, on the other hand, looked like the only thing he'd be up for was a double shot of Scotch and a handful of Roan's Oxy. He was stiff-legged as he moved to his chair, and he darted nervous looks around the room as he sat down. When Grimes read him his rights, he looked like he was wondering if he was dreaming and this was all just a bad nightmare. He almost choked on the words as he waived his right to remain silent.

Rusty let Grimes lead off—it was his case, after all—but interrogation is an art, and Grimes was a paint-by-the-numbers kind of guy. He tried to press Barth on his movements the night of the accident, but when Barth either dodged or denied, Grimes let it go. I could tell Rusty was getting agitated, and I had a feeling he was about to shove Grimes out of the way.

Sure enough, after ten minutes of tail chasing, Rusty stepped in. "Look, Professor, I'm going to level with you." His confident, authoritative attitude immediately changed the atmosphere in the room. Barth had grown increasingly relaxed as he'd seen how easily Grimes was pushed off. But now, I saw his body tense. Rusty continued. "The reason we kept you waiting out there was because we got a call from our crime-scene techs."

That was total bullshit. No way the techs could work that fast. But it's perfectly legal for cops to make up stories about what they've got. The problem is, only the experienced criminals know that. Barth, obviously, did not fit that bill. His face froze. He didn't even seem to be breathing.

I glanced at Dale. "You guys would be so hosed if you couldn't lie to them."

Dale gave me a smug smile. "It only works when they lie first."

Alex raised his eyebrows. "He's got a point."

I shook my head and turned back to watch. Rusty had brought a manila file folder with him. Now he flipped it open and put on his reading glasses. "They found fabric matching that poor old homeless guy's coat embedded in your grill." He took off his glasses and leaned back. "So how about you stop bullshitting us and tell the truth?"

Barth opened his mouth, but no sound came out. He closed it and stared down at the table. When he finally spoke, his voice was thin and weak. "I—I don't know how that could be."

Rusty gave a short, humorless chuckle. "Because you thought you'd scrubbed the living hell out of it, right?" Barth's eyes grew wide, and

Rusty nodded. "Yeah, we know that, too. Look, obviously you're no criminal. I imagine this has to be eating at you. I promise you, you're gonna feel a lot better once you get this off your chest. And I also promise you that we'll tell the DA how cooperative you've been. We make lousy enemies but really good friends. And you're going to need some good friends when folks find out that you killed Roan Sutton."

Barth jerked up in his seat. "What? What are you talking about? I had nothing to do with that!" He looked confused. "I thought he . . . Didn't he hang himself?"

Rusty had been studying him. "Didn't you hear? A private pathologist says Roan was murdered. The killer strung him up to make it look like a suicide. My bet is the county coroner's going to agree with him in another day or two. So how about you tell us where you were the night he died."

Barth's shoulders slumped. "I was home. Alone." He gave Rusty a beseeching look. "But I didn't kill him. I swear."

Rusty studied him for a long moment as he drummed his meaty fingers on the table. "Let's get back to the hit-and-run for a minute. I'll tell you what it looks like to me. You and Roan were supposed to be getting beer and pizza for everyone. You bought the beer, maybe drank some, and on the way to get the pizza, you ran down that old guy—and forgot all about the pizza. Roan threatened to call the cops—and you killed him."

Barth grabbed his head. "No. He never threatened me, and I never did anything to him." He dropped his face into his hands, and the room fell silent. When he looked up, there were tears on his cheeks. "But I did hit that old man." His voice shook as he wiped away the tears. "I wasn't drunk, I swear! It was an accident. But I should've called an ambulance. I can't believe I just ran like that. I've regretted it every minute of every day since that night." His choked sobs filled the air.

Rusty peered at him for a few seconds, then handed him a box of Kleenex. He glanced at Grimes. "Stay put. I'll be right back."

That was our cue. We went out and met him in the hallway. He gave me a superior smile. "You just love to watch the greats at work, don't you? Hope you learned something."

Same old obnoxious Rusty. I spoke with sarcasm. "I sure did. I learned that some things don't change."

He ignored me and spoke to Dale. "I don't think your boy's good for the Sutton kid's death."

I folded my arms. "Seriously? You're going to write him off just like that?"

Rusty glanced at me like I was an annoying gnat that wouldn't go away. "I can smell a lie at twenty paces. But I can smell the truth, too. He didn't kill that kid."

I stared at him. "Aren't you at least going to swab him and see if he matches anything in Roan's place?"

Rusty finally turned to face me, his expression irritated. "Of course we'll swab him. But they were friends. Even if we find that teacher's DNA on Roan Sutton's neck, it won't necessarily mean much."

Alex stepped in to break it up. "Thanks, Detective Templeton."

Dale asked, "You about done with the teacher?"

Rusty glanced at me, as though daring me to object. "Yeah. I may let Grimes take another run at him, but I doubt anything will come of it."

That much I agreed with. Grimes couldn't get a dog to bark. We went back to the observation room and watched as Grimes spent another ten minutes questioning Barth about his relationship with Roan and Alicia. We didn't learn anything we didn't already know.

When Rusty suggested they call it a night, Barth asked if he'd be allowed to go home. Rusty looked like he almost felt sorry for the professor. "I'm sorry, but you can't. You've confessed to a hit-and-run. We're going to have to book you now, so you'll be staying at Twin Towers tonight. You should be able to bail out tomorrow, though."

Dale walked us out. When we got to the elevators, he asked, "You still think the teacher killed Roan? Tell me the truth; I won't tell Rusty."

I glanced at the corridor behind Dale to make sure Rusty couldn't hear me. "No, not at all."

Dale shook his head. "You just couldn't resist busting his chops."

I gave him a little smile and shrugged.

Dale looked at Alex. "Must've been fun when they went at it full time on the Sonnenberg case."

Alex rolled his eyes. "It was a nonstop laugh riot."

The elevator dinged its arrival. I gave him a cold look. "I just don't suffer assholes gladly." I got in and waved to Dale. "Thanks for this."

He nodded. "Not a problem—this time. But we can't make it a habit." He held the door open and glanced down the corridor as he added, "The last thing I need is to make him an enemy."

Rusty had been around a long time, and he had a lot of friends among the brass. Dale had only recently dug his way out of the doghouse after his murder trial. And he'd just stuck his neck out to find the local cops on Tracy's case. "Message received." I gave him a little smile. "Next time I'll ask your partner."

Dale sighed and let the doors close. As we rode down to the main floor, Alex asked, "Want me to get my uncle to bail him out?"

"Definitely. But before he bails, I want to go see him." I'd felt pretty strongly that he'd been holding out on us before. "He might be more talkative now."

FORTY

It was after ten o'clock by the time I got home. As I dropped my keys on the dining table, I admitted to myself that I had way too many balls in the air. Between my normal caseload, Graham's case, and that Gila monster Cabazon, I barely had time to breathe. Something had to give, or I'd drop at least one of those balls.

I showered and turned on the TV as I got into bed. I was flipping through the channels when I saw a reporter standing in front of Twin Towers, his tie flapping in the breeze.

I turned up the volume just in time to hear him say, ". . . reported that he'd been picked up in connection with the investigation into the death of Roan Sutton, but we've now learned that aspect of Barth Foley's arrest has been dropped." I sat up. How did they get ahold of this so fast? Then I wondered why they'd mentioned Roan's death if they knew he wasn't being charged with it.

The blonde anchor, who looked like she was dressed for an S&M party, leather choker and all, said, "Thank you, Jim. For those who are just tuning in, that was a follow-up story to our other breaking news. The county coroner has just issued a statement that he has changed his preliminary finding regarding the death of Roan Sutton. The coroner has now officially stated that the manner of death is inconclusive—meaning that he cannot conclusively state whether Roan's death was a suicide or a homicide. Yet another strange development in this tragic case."

The anchor threw to footage of Audrey Sutton that'd been taped "just one hour ago." She predictably touted the new conclusion as "proof that Roan Sutton had not taken his own life."

The anchor returned with a conspiratorial look. "We'll be posting updates on this very unusual case, so be sure to tune in."

Damn it! I'd so hoped the coroner would shut down that lying scumbag Mortimer. True, it could've been worse. He could've gone along with Mortimer's claim that Roan had been killed. But it still set off a fresh wave of anxiety. Now the cops would be rechecking every piece of evidence and reinterviewing every witness to come up with just one more thing to corroborate the neighbor who claimed to have seen a man who looked similar to Graham at Roan's door that night. One more thing, that's all it would take now to justify arresting Graham.

I was a little surprised the cops hadn't asked me to bring him in voluntarily to do a DNA swab.

Not that I'd have done it. I supposed they knew that.

I paced around the apartment as I mentally replayed the interviews we'd done and tried to think of who else might be a suspect. An hour later, I had no answers, and my head ached. I looked at the clock on my coffeemaker and saw that it was almost twelve thirty. This was getting me nowhere. I popped three Advil and put myself to bed.

At six a.m. I woke up with a blinding headache. Hoping a caffeine fix would cure it, I poured as much coffee down my throat as I could stand. As I drank down my third travel mug, the pain had begun to ebb and I let myself have a tiny sliver of hope that Barth might give us something to go on. Alex had offered to pick me up and drive us downtown, and I was glad I'd agreed to let him. The caffeine had helped, but my head still hurt.

At eight fifteen sharp, Alex texted to tell me he was downstairs. It'd been cloudy and chilly when I got up, and I didn't have to be in court, so I'd chosen a turtleneck and jeans. But as I opened the door, I noticed the sun had poked through, and it looked like the clouds were about to break up. I ran back to my closet, exchanged the turtleneck for a crewneck sweater, and hurried downstairs.

Alex did a double take when I got into his car. "Nice 'do." He drew a circle in the air around my head.

I pulled down the visor and opened the mirror. Damn. My hair was standing straight up—static electricity. I sprayed some hairspray into my hand and smoothed it down. "I take it you saw the news about the coroner."

"Yeah. Could've been worse, though, right?" I'd crossed my legs, and my foot was bouncing—a nervous habit. Alex stared at it. "But I'm guessing it ratchets things up."

I stared out through the windshield. "It definitely does. Graham's their best suspect. He's got the motive to beat all time and that neighbor gives them a lead. They'll be looking hard to find a reason to arrest him."

Alex squeezed the steering wheel. "Then I guess we'd better hope Barth gives us something to work with." He glanced at me. "You think there's any possibility he killed Roan?"

I wished I did. "I hate to say it, but I agree with Rusty. I'm just not feeling it."

We made it to Twin Towers just after nine thirty. It had occurred to me that Barth might not want to see me, so I'd asked Alex to make sure his uncle, Tomas, contacted him first thing in the morning to start arranging his bail. And, of course, to make sure Tomas told Barth that we were the ones who'd sent him.

It took an hour for us to get in to see him. Alex and I took the cubicle at the end of the row. The Plexiglas that separated the lawyers from the inmates looked like it hadn't been cleaned since George Bush was in office. The first George Bush. A few minutes later, a guard led Barth to his seat. Those orange jumpsuits don't do anyone any favors, and Barth was no exception. His face looked like a deflated basketball, and his eyes were so bloodshot and swollen I wasn't sure whether he could even see us.

I picked up the phone, and he did the same. "You get any sleep at all?"

His voice was a hoarse croak. "No. But thanks for sending that bail bondsman. He said he'd have me out by the end of the day."

On the way over, I'd wondered whether anyone had told him about our part in his arrest. It didn't seem so. I supposed he figured the police stumbled on his hit-and-run while they were poking around on Roan's case. As if they'd ever be that smart. "Good. Now I need a little help from you. I know they cleared you on Roan, but do you have a theory on who might've killed him?"

He glowered at me. "You mean, other than your client? No offense, but if he's so innocent, why'd he get a lawyer before anyone even started to question whether Roan's death was a suicide?"

I gave him a flat look. "'Cause they *were* questioning it. They always do. And because he knows that getting a lawyer doesn't mean you're guilty." I looked at him pointedly. "Just like *not* having a lawyer doesn't mean you're innocent—now does it?"

Barth dropped his gaze, and his shoulders slumped. "I guess not." After a moment, he looked up. "You know, there is one thing . . . I was afraid to tell you about it before. It involves Roan."

Just as I'd thought. He'd been holding out. Most likely because, given that hit-and-run, he wanted to stay as far away from any association with Roan as he could. "Did he find out about you and Alicia?"

He frowned. "I . . . I don't really know. He might have. The last time I saw Roan was the day Alicia broke up with him."

"He told you she'd broken up with him?"

Barth nodded. "And then he said he'd found out something gnarly about her, something she didn't know. Something that'd really . . ." He made air quotes. "Mess her up."

"And he was planning to tell her . . . why? To get revenge?"

Barth nodded. "She hurt him. He wanted to hurt her back."

Alex pointed to the phone, and I handed it to him. "Did you tell Alicia about it?"

Barth rubbed his forehead. "I never got the chance."

We tried to get him to guess what Roan was referring to, but he said he had no idea. I probed a little further, tried to get him to think, even threw out a few suggestions—like maybe something to do with her father or mother—but Barth really didn't know.

He shook his head. "I have no clue. I certainly didn't know anything quote, unquote, gnarly about Alicia."

He was obviously telling the truth. I had to let it go. I thanked him and was about to say good-bye when he said, "Just one more thing. Would you consider representing me?"

Since Alex and I were the reason he was in jail, one might say that created a bit of a conflict of interest—to put it mildly. And he was bound to find out about that sooner or later. "I really can't do that, but I can recommend someone for you."

I gave him the names of a couple of really good lawyers who wouldn't gouge him. Then I wished him luck, and we left.

Alex and I tried to imagine what the "gnarly" thing was that Roan had found out about Alicia. I remembered that the people who knew him had all said he knew his way around a computer. "He must've found something on the Interweb, don't you think?"

Alex was annoyed. "If he could find it, then so could I, and I haven't found anything even close to 'gnarly' on Alicia. I think he was full of crap. He just wanted Barth to tell her what he'd said so she'd freak out."

I detected a note of professional pique in his voice, but he had a point. "Gaslighting her does sound like something that would be up

Roan's alley. But you weren't trying to find any blackmail material on Alicia. Let's give it a shot. We've got nothing to lose."

Alex didn't look enthused. "Okay. But Roan made it sound like it was a pretty big deal. If it were for real, then why would he bother to do the revenge porn?"

"Roan hardly seems like a model of restraint. From what I can tell, he's a scorched-earth kind of guy. Why wouldn't he do both?"

Alex sighed. "I guess when you put it that way . . ."

My cell buzzed with a text. It was Dale. It read, Call me from a landline. I'm at home.

I could feel the sweat break out on my chest and neck. He'd said he was going to take the day off and go see Tiffany this morning. If she wasn't willing to cooperate, we were in big—as in huge—trouble. I didn't have a backup plan, and we were running out of time.

As Alex pulled into the garage, my temples were throbbing. I tried to act calm as we headed up to the office, but the moment I walked in the door, I sped past Michy with a quick hello and raced into my office as I told her I had to make a call.

I punched in Dale's number with a shaking hand. When he picked up, I didn't even say hello. "Did you see her?"

His voice sounded heavy. "Yes."

Was he really making me ask? "And?"

He hesitated a moment, then said, "She'll do it. But now that she knows who we really are, she wants someone to find out whether Tammy actually has been getting abused. Guess your cover story hit a little too close to home."

Relief spread through me. "That's what makes it a good cover story. Hank came through for me. I got the names of the feds. Liam Fonsecker and Noah Lavergne. I got their numbers, too." I gave them to him. "When are you going to call?"

He blew out a breath. "Now, I guess. No reason to wait."

The other part of what Dale had said sank in. "How're we going to get an investigation going on Tammy?"

Unless he had some personal friends in Riverside PD, we were screwed. Dale had no jurisdiction in Riverside, and I'd already lied my way into Shelly's house. If I went to the Riverside cops, I'd have to tell them I'd lied to her—and then I'd have to explain why. The truth—that Cabazon was extorting me—obviously wouldn't fly, unless I didn't mind being dead. And at this point, I still did.

I heard Dale's vacuum cleaner start up. He said, "I don't have any connections in Riverside PD. So I guess I'll have to dig around and see if I can find someone who does. But that's going to have to wait. Right now, I need to sell our story to my new best friends, Liam and Noah."

When we ended the call, I started to pace. As I walked in circles around my office, I kept imagining Liam and Noah telling Dale to go screw himself. My office was small, so the circles were tight. After half an hour, I was dizzy. My mind turned back to Barth's new information, the "gnarly" thing Roan thought he had on Alicia. I didn't know how it would help us find another suspect for Roan's murder, but it was the only thread we had to pull—so we may as well pull it.

I went to Alex's office. He was deep in concentration on his computer. As I'd expected, he was already mired in the problem of figuring out what Roan might've had on Alicia. I had a more pedestrian way of doing that. "Why don't we just try talking to the friends and family?"

Alex looked perplexed. "If it was so secret that Alicia didn't even know, why would they?"

I'd thought of that. "Because maybe Roan told them."

He seemed skeptical. "Why would he do that? If he wanted to freak her out, wouldn't he want to be the first to tell her—and enjoy seeing her suffer?"

I shrugged. "In theory. But he might've let it slip by accident. And we should ask her parents. Maybe they knew."

Alex still didn't love the idea. "Graham and Sandy are a good idea. The others . . ."

The others were a long shot. "But it's just a few phone calls." I told him I'd take Miguel and Roan's brother, Scott. And, of course, Graham and Sandy. They needed some extra hand-holding now that the coroner had ruled the manner of Roan's death inconclusive and backed off his preliminary finding that it was a suicide. Alex said he'd take the rest.

The calls kept me busy for the rest of the afternoon—which was a good thing. But it turned out Alex was right. Neither Graham nor Sandy, nor anyone else, had heard about the so-called gnarly secret. Roan hadn't mentioned anything to anyone—other than Barth.

That made me wonder if maybe there was no secret. Roan was a control freak and a manipulator. As we'd theorized before, Roan might've been using Barth to gaslight Alicia. I could see Roan thinking that the mention of a "gnarly" secret would seem more credible if it came from Barth rather than directly from Roan. Or maybe Roan thought hearing about an ugly secret would turn Barth off.

I supposed it might've been both.

But the way Barth had described the conversation with Roan made it seem like the secret was real.

And I had no clue how to figure out what it was.

FORTY-ONE

I'd arranged to meet Hank for dinner downtown that night, and I'd planned to leave early so I could swing by the PAB and ask Dale how it'd gone with Liam and Noah.

When I'd called him in the afternoon, he'd cut me off and said, "Why don't you come by the office?" His way of telling me he was too paranoid to even talk on a landline. Jeez. This was getting so crazy.

But by the time I'd finished my phone calls, it was almost six o'clock—too late to catch Dale. I'd be lucky if I even made it to dinner on time. I put on my coat and scarf and went out to Michy's desk.

She looked at her watch, then at me. "Kind of pushing it, aren't you?"

I sighed. Time management was not my strength. "I'll call Hank from the car."

Michy rolled her eyes. "Did you get anything on that so-called gnarly secret?"

I shook my head. I was frustrated and feeling down. "Nothing. I'm starting to think it's all bullshit."

"Or maybe it's for real, but you just haven't hit the right person yet." Michy pointed to the door. "Think positive for a change." She gave me a look of exasperation. "Go. You're gonna be late."

I was, but only by about five minutes. Hank had suggested we splurge and go to Drago Centro, an elegant Italian place with great art and classic jazz playing in the background. It was nice to be able to just hang out and catch up on life.

We touched only briefly on work when she asked if the feds, Liam and Noah, were any help with Diego Ferrara. I told her that I hadn't talked to them yet. At least that much was true.

It was a pleasant evening, but when we parted company, I felt restless. Maybe it was because I hadn't been able to reach Dale—or maybe it was just that there were so many questions still unanswered. Whatever the reason, I wasn't ready to go home. I wanted to *do* something.

I drove through downtown thinking about what Roan's secret might be and found myself on Jefferson Boulevard, heading toward USC. I drove past Diana's place and had just turned onto Denker Avenue when I noticed an older man hurrying down the street. You don't see many people walking in LA at any time of day, let alone at night, so it caught my attention. As I drove past him, I looked in my rearview mirror—and almost ran a stop sign. It was Graham.

I crossed the intersection and pulled over. As I continued to watch in my rearview mirror, I saw him go to the apartment building on the corner and press the buzzer. That was Davey's place. Why on earth was he visiting Davey? And why was he walking to the building when there were parking spaces right in front? I saw him press a button near the door. I rolled down my window to try and hear who answered. But I never heard a voice. All I heard was the buzzer that unlocked the door. Graham quickly opened the door and went inside. I drove around the block to see where he'd parked. I spotted his silver Mercedes around the corner, on West Thirty-Eighth Street. Every bit of this seemed weird to me.

I drove home trying to figure out what was going on. I could well understand that Graham and Sandy might want to talk to Alicia's friends, hold on to any part of her that they could. And her time in college had been the only part of her life they hadn't been involved in.

Still . . . it was strange, this visit. I thought about it all the way home, and as I got into bed, I made a mental note to talk to the rest of Alicia's friends and find out if Graham had paid them a visit, too.

It might be no big deal. But I'd learned from hard experience that what I didn't know could—and usually did—come back to bite me. I never let a question go unanswered if I can help it.

Sheer exhaustion won out over my usual nightly horrors, and I slept until the alarm woke me at seven thirty. I wanted to stay in bed and luxuriate in the feeling of having slept like a normal person, but I had to be in court by nine thirty for a status conference on an attempted murder case.

My client, Julia Schneider, had pulled a gun on her asshole ex— who happened to be a girl. I'd been threatening the prosecutor, Sherman Flynn, that if he made me take this to trial, he ran the risk of a straight-up acquittal. The ex was a real piece of work. When Julia broke up with her, she'd tried to run Julia down in her car, then slashed Julia's bicycle tires. The gun-pulling incident happened during a fight over the split-up of property, when the ex tried to take Julia's signed Mark Ryden print.

Since this was my only court appearance for the day, I brought a pair of jeans and boots to change into later. I planned to head out to USC to talk to Alicia's friends after I got done. I made it to court with time to spare and used every minute of it to plant fear in Sherman's heart. I showed him a photo of Julia and the ex—who was twice her size. "You think the jury's going to blame her for pulling a gun? And just so's you know, I've got witnesses who'll say your star 'victim' was a bully who'd knocked her last girlfriend around."

He stared at the photo. "Who are these witnesses?"

I shook my head. "Uh-uh. No sneak previews. You'll find out when we get to trial." It was a bluff. I had no witnesses.

His knee began to bounce. "I'll give you an ADW."

I folded my arms. "Nope. Simple assault and probation. Or get ready to put twelve in the box."

Sherman swallowed hard. "I can't deal it that low. I'll get killed."

But I knew he wanted to. I said I'd give him time to sell his boss on the deal, and we put the case over for a month. Julia wasn't in custody, so she was fine with the delay.

I headed to Nomie's dorm and caught her on her way to work. I told her I'd only need a couple of minutes. She told me to meet her at Lemonade.

By the time I got there, she was already behind the counter. Fortunately, it wasn't busy. I had only one question. "Did Graham or Sandy contact you recently?" Nomie nodded. So maybe the visit to Davey wasn't so strange after all. "Do you mind telling me when, and what they wanted?"

She stirred the vat of soup. "Not at all. It was just Graham. He called last night. He said Roan had claimed to know something about Alicia, some secret. He asked me whether I knew anything about it." Some customers came in, and she lowered her voice. "I told him I'd never heard anything like that. It's so bizarre."

Amen to that. So he'd called Nomie after I'd asked him about Roan's supposed "gnarly" discovery.

I didn't like the fact that he'd done that, but I couldn't say it was suspicious. Moving on. I knew Alex had already asked Nomie if she'd heard about the secret, but I couldn't resist taking another run at it. "Do you think Roan really did have something on Alicia? Or was he just screwing around?"

She lifted her hands, palms up. "Who knows with Roan? I don't put much past him."

No argument there. "Do you know whether Graham talked to anyone else about that?"

Nomie tapped a finger to her lips. "I think Diana said he'd called her, too."

Some more customers came in, and I saw the manager dart a look our way. I had to wrap this up. I asked her whether she'd spoken to Graham at any other time. She said she hadn't.

"Do you know if he spoke to Diana last night?"

Nomie noticed the manager, too. "Yeah, he did. I'm guessing he talked to all of us."

I thanked her and stepped away to let the paying customers through. Then I went back to my car and called Graham. I caught him as he was on his way to meet one of the partners of his firm for lunch.

He said, "We're going to BOA Steakhouse, not too far from your neck of the woods. You want to join us?"

About as much as I'd like to go skinny-dipping in a swamp. Civil lawyer shoptalk is nowhere near as exciting as watching grass grow. "Thank you, but no. I just have a quick question. I hear you've been talking to Alicia's friends?"

I heard an elevator ding in the background. "Yes, I wanted to know what they thought about Roan's secret, whether he'd said anything to them about it."

It was never good to have a client play detective, but Graham was clearly not the kind of client who took direction well, so there was no point in telling him to knock it off. In any case, it was too late to do anything about it now. "Did they have any ideas?"

He coughed. "Excuse me. This cold weather. No, no one seemed to know what he could be talking about."

I wondered about his apparent interest in this. "Was this the first time you've spoken to them?"

Graham cleared his throat. "Ah, yes. Why?"

I honestly couldn't say. It just bugged me. "No reason."

The elevator dinged again. "I'd better get going. If you change your mind, the reservation's under my name."

Not even for a free—and very pricey—meal would I dream of it. I thanked him and let him go.

I couldn't reach Phil or Diana or Gayle, but I did manage to find Davey. He was on campus. His cell phone kept dropping the call, so I told him I'd meet him at a nearby restaurant, The Lab Gastropub on Figueroa.

"The Lab" was a casual, science-themed place with large computer screens mounted on the walls, group-style seating, and a bar with chrome bar stools. Davey was sitting in one of the leather chairs in the lounge area and scrolling on his cell phone when I got there. Since I wasn't interested in funding yet another free lunch, I took the seat next to him and said I just needed a minute of his time. "Did Graham talk to you recently?"

He put down his phone. "Yeah. Yesterday. He called around an hour or so after your investigator called me. He asked about the same thing your investigator did: whether I'd heard about some big secret Roan knew about Alicia."

I knew Davey had told Alex that he hadn't known anything about that secret, either. "Was that the only time you spoke to Graham?"

He frowned. "I'm pretty sure. Yeah."

At that moment, my phone rang. It was Phil, returning my call. I let it go to voice mail. "Did Graham ever visit you at your place?"

Davey looked surprised by the question. "No. Why?"

Wait. What? I'd expected him to admit it—maybe say they'd just talked a little more about Roan's secret, or Davey's memories of Alicia, or . . . whatever. But his denial caught me off guard. I needed to regroup. Something was wrong here. "No reason."

Davey said he had to get to class, and I left the restaurant, more confused than ever.

FORTY-TWO

Before I called Phil back, I needed to figure out what was going on. Either Davey was lying or Graham was visiting someone else in that building. I didn't know why Davey would lie about that. Especially since he'd admitted talking to Graham about Roan's so-called "secret."

So the question was, if Graham wasn't visiting Davey, who was he visiting? My knee-jerk answer was that it was a woman. And in that neighborhood, it was probably a young and pretty one. This wasn't necessarily a judgment of Graham per se. It was more about the fact that he was a hotshot litigator. They tended to be very . . . active.

But talk about a bizarre coincidence: a mistress in the same building as one of his daughter's friends. What were the odds?

I called Phil back and found out he was home. I decided to go see him in person, since I was just a few blocks away.

Phil was his usual hazy self, though the house didn't reek of pot quite as much as it had on previous visits. And this time, he didn't light up after he dropped down on the beanbag chair. I couldn't help but ask. "Why so straight today?"

Phil wore a mournful look. "I'm tapped out." His face brightened. "Unless you're in pocket."

He obviously didn't remember that I'd told him I didn't smoke—or that I'd refused to join him every time he'd offered. I guessed it was true what they said about pot being bad for your memory. Or maybe Phil just didn't want to give up hope. I told him I was sorry to disappoint him. "By any chance, has Graham called or come by to see you?"

Phil laced his hands together on his stomach. "He didn't come over, but he called."

"When was that?"

He looked at the ceiling. "Yesterday? Yeah, last night. I'm pretty sure it was."

And just as he had in his calls to Davey and Nomie, Graham had asked Phil if he knew anything about a secret Roan supposedly knew that involved Alicia. Phil thought the whole thing was "bullshit" and typical of Roan's mind games.

I'd thought so, too. But I had to admit I was starting to wonder. "Was that the only time Graham spoke to you?"

He stretched out his legs. "Yeah. But I know he talked to Davey before all this business came up about Roan's horseshit secret."

I frowned at Phil. "How do you know that?"

He yawned. "Because I saw him coming out of Davey's building."

And I'd just seen him going in last night. "When?"

Phil squinted at the floor. "I'm pretty sure it was a few days after Alicia died."

Alicia? That couldn't be right. "You mean after Roan died, don't you?"

He shook his head. "No, man. It was *before* that. Roan was still alive, I'm positive. I remember because at the time, everyone was talking about how the cops should arrest him for Alicia's murder."

I thought my head was about to explode. "How did you know it was Graham?"

He answered without hesitation. "I'd seen his picture in Alicia's apartment a bunch of times." He sighed. "And, of course, I saw him on the news after she died."

That identification seemed pretty solid. I took aim on the other side. "Are you sure it was Davey he'd been visiting?"

Phil frowned. "I didn't chase him down and ask him, but who else would he be seeing there?"

My knee-jerk hunch about a mistress was turning out to be better than I'd thought. I checked my phone and saw that it was almost two o'clock. If I didn't get on the road soon, I'd be stuck in traffic for an hour. I told Phil I'd be back in touch and headed to my car.

I might've been a little more skeptical about how accurate Phil's memory was of seeing Graham exit Davey's building. But (a) this time he'd been sober as a stopwatch at a swim meet, (b) he knew what Graham looked like, (c) he had no reason to expect to see Graham there, so he wasn't just assuming the person he saw was Graham, and (d) his memory of the timing was tied to conversations that had to have taken place before Roan was dead—because cops don't usually bother to arrest a dead guy.

I mulled over all this, and my theory that Graham had a mistress in Davey's building all the way back to the office. When I got in, I convened the troops and brought them up to speed. "The thing I've been wondering is whether this was the secret Roan was talking about? That Graham was seeing a girl in Davey's building."

Michy was on the fence. "That probably would rock Alicia's world if it was like, a student or something." She made a face. "In a really gross way. But don't you think it's a pretty huge coincidence that Davey and this girl live in the same building?"

Alex leaned back in the secretary's chair. "It does, but then again, it's a student neighborhood. Graham and Sandy probably helped Alicia move in, and I'm sure a lot of students must've been moving in around the same time. He might've met her then."

That was true. "And she may not be a student." Nonstudents lived in those buildings, too—not many but some. "We'd better check this out. If Graham is having an affair with a student, and this case goes to trial, reporters are going to be sniffing around." This would be a very bad surprise to get hit with. "Alex, see if you can get a list of the tenants in Davey's building. Then dig into Graham and Sandy and go deep." I thought for a second. "And while you're at it, see what you can come up with on Davey, too."

I went into my office and had just taken off my coat when my cell phone rang. Distracted, I answered without looking to see who it was.

I recognized Dale's voice from the first syllable. "I get to bust out of here a little early today. Want to meet me at Barney's?"

The words were casual, but the tone wasn't. I'd gotten so wrapped up in Graham's case, I hadn't had time to chase Dale down. He was probably going to give me the report on Liam and Noah, the FBI agents. And, of course, Tracy. Barney's Beanery was only a few miles away. "Sure. Text me when you're close."

My stomach in knots, I paced in circles as I tried to figure out what Dale was going to tell me. Were the FBI agents willing to let us see Tracy? Had Tracy been willing to help? I wouldn't blame her if she wasn't, if she'd decided to cut all ties with a family that didn't seem to give a damn about her. With zero information to go on, there was nothing I could do but angst and worry.

And this new wrinkle with Graham wasn't doing my stomach lining any favors, either. Why so many male trial lawyers can't keep their dicks in their pants is a mystery to me. And seriously? With all that was going on, he was still seeing her now? After the coroner had just concluded that Roan's death might be a homicide? Was this girl so irresistible he couldn't put their grand amour on hold—at least until the case was resolved?

Too many problems and not enough solutions. It was making me crazy. By the time I left for Barney's Beanery I was in a truly cranky mood.

I told Michy I had some errands to run. "But I'll be on my cell if you need me."

She was glued to the computer, working on our quarterly tax returns. She waved a hand at me without looking up. I called out to Alex to let me know if he found anything interesting. He called out, "Will do."

I tried to calm myself and take deep breaths on the way over. It didn't help. When I walked in, my heart was beating so hard it blurred my vision. Dale had grabbed a table by the window and was nursing a Coke. I saw that he'd tortured the straw wrapper, which was folded over a million times. My chest was tight as I sat down. I couldn't even force a little smile. "What's the story?"

Dale was every bit as tense as I was. "The agents are on board. And Tracy's willing to listen. But they said she didn't seem thrilled. I thought she might need to see Tiffany and verify it all in person, but Liam said she only wants to see you."

How odd. "Did they say why?"

Dale tilted his head. "Not exactly. But I got the impression she doesn't trust the family much. So my guess is, she wants you to tell her if you think it's for real."

Actually, that made sense. She'd want some assurance that Tammy really was being abused, that this wasn't just a guess on someone's part. And she didn't want to stick her neck out if Tammy was going to back down—or if her mother was going to shut Tammy down. Either way, it'd be a trip down Horrible Memory Lane for no good reason. "When do you want to do this?"

Dale looked at his watch. "In about half an hour. I was right; they are keeping her local."

"What?" I'd been picturing our meeting in my mind, trying to figure out what I'd say if and when the time came. But I'd expected to have more notice. I still wasn't sure how to approach her, how to win her over. "I don't know what to say. You have any ideas?"

Dale's expression was bleak. "Sorry, I don't. I've tried to think of some surefire thing to say that'd make her trust you. But I just wound up thinking that there's no magic bullet. My only advice is to listen to your gut and hope for the best."

Listening to my gut was usually a strength. But I didn't know if I could rely on it this time. Tracy had no real reason to trust me. I'd have to tell her I was there to save her from Cabazon. But why should she believe that I was there to save her—and not just setting her up to get killed? "Great. She'll probably slam the door in my face."

He said, "Actually, it wouldn't be her. The agents are manning the door, so . . ."

I stared at him, my tone sarcastic. "That's very helpful. Thanks."

He spread his hands. "Look, at the end of the day, she'll either believe we're trying to protect her or she won't."

He picked a hell of a time to go all fatalistic on me. "'Won't is probably what's going to happen. So any idea what we do after she tells me to go screw myself?"

Dale shook his head. To be fair, he didn't look any happier than I was. "Like I said, just take your best shot."

I slumped back in my chair. What I needed to do was get her to trust me, to believe that I wanted to save her even though Cabazon—the one who wanted her dead—was the one who'd "hired" me. I had no idea how I'd manage that in just an hour or so of conversation. Until now, it hadn't hit me how much of a ridiculous long shot it was to expect her to trust someone who drops in out of the blue—and with a very unwelcome message. But I had to take it. "Where is she?"

He looked at his phone. "They're keeping her in a safe house in Beverlywood."

I'd been there a few times. It was just south of Beverly Hills. A nice 'hood but definitely not the dreamland of the rich and famous. "We should probably get going, then." It'd take us at least a half hour to get there.

Dale followed me back to my place so I could leave Beulah at home and we could ride together in his car. On the way, we talked about what to tell Tracy—assuming she trusted me to rescue her. For the hundredth time, I wished I could just tell her to recant and say she was mistaken when she'd identified Maldonado as the shooter. But even if she did, the prosecutor could just impeach her with her earlier statement. And no one would believe her if she said she'd been mistaken. According to the police report, she'd been standing right there, just a few feet away. That had bugged me from the start. "What was she doing there?"

Dale shrugged. "She was probably with one of them. Since she fingered Maldonado, I'd guess she was with the victim."

In which case she'd want to see Jorge Maldonado fry. I gave Dale a sidelong glance. "You know, even if there was no big love between Tracy and the victim, she's got to be pissed about being locked up with FBI agents—and all because of Maldonado."

Dale sighed. "It is what it is, Sam. All we can do is try."

Dale parked a few houses down, at Liam's advice. We walked up to a fairly nice-looking pale-yellow Spanish-style home with a red-tiled roof. Dale used the tarnished brass knocker on the heavy wooden door. Two knocks, a pause, and then one more. I was amused. "Really? A secret knock?"

Dale gave me a deadpan look. "Really? Cabazon is moving heaven and earth to find this girl."

I was about to tell Dale that it wasn't the most sophisticated security system, but at that moment, a man answered the door. He ushered us in so quickly, I had no chance to see him until he'd closed the door behind us. He was the Hollywood version of an FBI agent. Short blond hair, a trim mustache, and blue eyes; about Dale's height, six feet tall, with a V-shaped torso that looked like one of those gym posters. Not my type—he was a little too law-and-order for me—but I imagined he blew a lot of other skirts up. He shook my hand and told me his name was Liam, and he assumed I was Samantha Brinkman.

I admitted I was. "How's she been doing?"

Liam spoke in a low voice. "Pretty well, all things considered. But the sooner they get this case to trial, the better. She's really nervous. And depressed."

I looked around the living room. It was sparsely furnished—a couple of wingback chairs, a leather ottoman, a couch, and a coffee table. But it all looked pretty new. I wondered if they'd rented it or if the FBI kept furnishings in a warehouse for just such occasions. "What happens after she testifies?"

He gestured for us to have a seat. "We give her a new identity and relocate her."

Dale sat on one of the chairs, but I declined. "I think I should talk to her privately. It's a pretty sensitive topic." I held out my arms. "Feel free to search me." I knew he would have with or without my invitation, but I preferred to act like I had a say in the matter.

Liam gave me a very thorough pat-down. He nodded toward my purse. "You can leave that out here."

I knew they'd search it, but I had nothing to hide. I handed my purse to him. "Let's go."

I followed him down a short hallway to a room at the end on the left. I noticed his partner, Noah, was on the phone in the bedroom across from us. Noah was short, hairy, and intense. Not the hottie Liam was. He looked up as I passed by. I waved, and he gave me a curt nod. All business.

Liam knocked on the door and spoke softly. "Tracy? That lawyer's here to see you."

The door opened, and a young woman stared back at me, her eyes narrow and suspicious. Her round face had thinned, and the chin-length shaggy blonde hair was now down to her shoulders, but she was definitely the girl in the photos I'd seen. She was dressed in a black-and-red-striped, shoulder-baring shirt and black skinny jeans. The smoky-look makeup was too heavy for her blue eyes, and the silver studs that crawled up her ears gave her an elfin quality. But she seemed even younger in person than she had in the photographs. I thought she was, at most, maybe nineteen years old.

I held out my hand. "Hi, Tracy. I'm Samantha Brinkman."

She looked at my hand for a moment then slowly, reluctantly gave me hers for a very brief shake. "Hey."

I braced myself. This girl did not look inclined to cut Jorge—or me—any slack whatsoever. My heart was beating like a jackhammer. I did my best to make my voice sound calm and warm. "I thought you might like to talk to me about this privately."

Tracy glanced at Liam, then nodded and stood back.

I walked into the small bedroom that had only the necessities: a bed, a dresser, a desk that was really just a table, and a cheap folding chair. The white venetian blinds that covered the window next to the bed were closed. I suspected they always were.

I turned back and nodded to Liam. "Thanks." Then I took a deep breath and closed the door.

FORTY-THREE

I'd been trying to figure out a way to frame the situation so she wouldn't turn on me. But there was no way to romance this. I'd lied to get her to talk to me. The only thing I could do was admit it and hope for the best.

Tracy sat down on the bed, and I pulled the folding chair around to face her. "I'm going to start by telling you I'm sorry. I'm apologizing because I lied to you. They're not investigating Ronnie for molesting your little sister. At least, not yet."

She folded her arms and glared at me. "Then what do you want?"

This was it. If I didn't find a way to win her trust, she'd be dead meat—and so would we. "Someone close to Jorge Maldonado has asked me to find you. He wants to get Jorge off the hook for the murder." I looked her in the eye. "And he intends to kill you in order to do that."

Tracy blanched. "B-but I don't want to testify against Jorge!" Her eyes filled with tears. "I love him."

It took me a second to wrap my head around that. This was the last thing I'd expected. "But you identified him as the killer."

Tracy leaned forward, her hands on her knees. "I was in shock, totally freaked out, and they threatened to charge me with helping him if I didn't!"

This was the opposite of everything we'd believed about the case. "Tell me what happened. And start from the very beginning. I promise everything you say is confidential."

She swiped away the tears with a rough gesture. After taking a deep breath and letting out a long exhale, she began to speak. "Like, seven months ago, I got thrown out of the room I was sharing with a couple of other girls, because I couldn't pay the rent. Victor found me sleeping in a doorway and said he'd give me a place to stay."

I had a feeling I knew where this story was going. "Victor Mendes— the guy Jorge killed?"

Tracy nodded, her gaze fixed on the floor. "I was afraid to keep staying on the street, so I said okay. He took me to his motel room and raped me. I wanted to run, but I had no money and nowhere to go. Victor made me"—she used air quotes—"'work' for him." Her voice was flat and empty. Her gaze, as she continued to stare at the floor, was dull, lifeless. It was as though she was talking about someone else. "He got a shit-hole motel room in downtown LA. I worked from noon until four a.m., seven days a week." She lifted her head, and now I saw anger in her eyes. But she still spoke in a monotone. "It wasn't the first time I'd been pimped, but it was the worst. Victor would let his friends gang up on me for free. They passed me around like a goddamn blunt."

She paused for a few seconds, then took a deep breath and continued. "After about a month, I couldn't stand it anymore. The next time he took me to Walmart—he'd take me there to get stuff like tampons and toothpaste—I stole a pair of scissors. When we got back to the motel, I went into the bathroom and slashed my wrists."

I could barely breathe. It hurt just to listen to her story. "But he caught you." She nodded. "How?"

Tracy's eyes were flat. "When he moved me into the motel room, he broke the lock on the bathroom door so he could always walk in on me. So, when I didn't come out after a while, he came in and found me. He had to take me to the emergency room because I'd passed out and he couldn't stop the bleeding." She looked up, and her face began to brighten. "That's how I met Jorge. He was with a cousin who had appendicitis. She was in the bed next to mine."

It was a miracle Tracy had survived. And apparently also that she'd met Jorge. "How did Jorge manage to talk to you with Victor around?" Pimps didn't usually let their women talk to anyone who wasn't a paying customer.

Tracy's eyes got misty. "Victor wasn't there. He had to go get money to pay the doctor. Jorge saw the bandages on my wrists and asked me why such a pretty girl would want to do this to herself." Tracy wiped away a stray tear. "He was so nice, so . . . gentle. I told him I didn't want to live anymore. And I told him why. I don't know why I trusted him not to judge me, but I did. For probably the first time in my life, I guessed right. Jorge asked if I'd come with him. Something told me he'd treat me right. Besides, how much worse could it be?"

I couldn't argue with her logic. "He took you out of the emergency room?"

Now she actually smiled. "Yeah. The minute his cousin's boyfriend got there, Jorge just picked me up and walked out of there, put me in his car. The nurse was running after him and yelling and saying he had to pay and shit like that. Jorge didn't care; he just kept on going. But Victor came back before we could take off, and he tried to pull me out of the car. They got in a big fight, and the nurse said she was calling the cops. Victor was on parole, so he had to back off. But he told Jorge he'd be coming for him."

"And you left with Jorge?" Tracy nodded. "Where'd he take you?"

She shifted to sit cross-legged on the bed. "Back to his place in Boyle Heights." Another tear rolled slowly down her cheek. "I've been staying with him ever since. And I was finally happy. Jorge was better to me than anyone in my whole life."

The memory of Shelly's careless attitude toward Tracy came back to me. "You ran away from home when you were only twelve. Why? Because of Ronnie?"

Tracy hunched over, and the light drained from her face. "No. I mean, he knocked me around because I wouldn't let him touch me. Gave me a black eye a couple of times. But the reason I finally ran was because of his fucking father. That rat-fuck, Benjamin." She gave a short, humorless laugh. "My first pimp—or rather, wannabe pimp. I ran because I heard that he'd told one of his asswipe buddies he was planning to sell my virginity." Tracy gritted her teeth. "His buddy asked how much he planned to charge, and Ben asked how much he'd be willing to pay. I didn't believe it, but I hid under the bed that night, and sure enough, Ben came to get me. I waited until he left, then packed everything I could carry and bailed out through the window."

My God. What this girl had been through. But it explained so much. "So all those prostitution busts when you were a juvie . . ."

Her voice was harsh. "Were because I had no place to go and no one who'd help me except guys who wanted to use me to make money."

That wasn't a life; that was hell. "I don't know how you've managed to survive."

Tracy sat up, her expression fierce. "I wouldn't have if it hadn't been for Jorge."

That brought us back to the topic at hand. "So I assume Victor finally caught up with him?" She nodded.

She set her jaw at the mention of Victor's name. "We'd been keeping tabs on him. When people would say they'd seen Victor around, we'd lay low. But that night, I think Victor had to have been tailing us, because we hadn't been a public place, we'd just left Jorge's cousin's house. Anyway, we were walking toward our car, and when we passed an alley, Victor jumped him."

But Jorge had a gun, so that confrontation couldn't have taken long. "How did the cops get there so fast?"

Tracy heaved a sigh that seemed to come from the bottom of her feet. "At first they were screaming and cussing each other out. Then Jorge hit him, and Victor hit him back and . . ."

Jorge shot him. Now I remembered—I'd seen that in the police report. "A neighbor called the cops while they were yelling at each other."

"Yeah," she said as she shook her head. "Never saw 'em come that fast in my whole life. They pulled up just, like, seconds after Jorge fired. I grabbed the gun from him so I could hide it, but . . ."

"They caught you before you could get rid of it." Tracy nodded, her expression glum. That explanation filled in a lot of blanks for me.

Her voice was filled with despair. "I was so scared. They said they'd charge me with murder if I didn't tell them who did it. So I told them Jorge shot him. And now I'm stuck. They say if I don't testify against him, they'll get me for being an . . . uh . . ." She gave me a questioning look. "An accessory?"

I nodded. They definitely could tag her for being an accessory after the fact. And Jorge would probably go down for second-degree murder—though there was a chance I could sell a jury on manslaughter. But Cabazon wasn't interested in taking any chances with a jury—or more importantly, with Jorge having to spend any time in prison, where others—inmates as well as cops—could get to him and squeeze him for information on Cabazon and his operations. This was one sad story. "Have you been able to talk to Jorge at all?"

Tears sprang to her eyes again. "I asked, but they won't let me." She gave me a beseeching look that wrenched my heart. "Can you help us?"

I gave her as confidant a look as I could muster. "I'm definitely going to try. Do the feds know about you and Jorge?"

She shook her head. "No. I told them I'd been living on the street and he was just a guy I met that day." Tracy had a puzzled frown. "I'm not even sure why I lied about that." She shrugged. "Just habit, I guess."

But that habit had come in handy. The less they knew, the better. I told her to make sure she didn't tell them anything about Jorge. And on the off chance she was allowed to speak to anyone else, I told her not to let anyone know she'd met with me, other than the feds who obviously already knew. "And I don't have to warn you not to tell the feds anything we talk about, do I?"

Tracy stared at me like I'd told her not to get hit by a bus. "No, duh. Of course not. Has anyone else been looking for me—I mean, besides you?"

I didn't want to tell her about Diego Ferrara, but I had to be honest. "I think so. My advice is to let these agents do their job."

I told her I'd figure this out as fast as I could and that I'd be in touch very soon. Then I went out to the living room and thanked Liam. "I'll be back to take a complete statement after I've spoken to Tammy." I delivered the lie pretty smoothly, I thought.

Dale thanked him, too, and we headed for the car. The moment we got in, he asked me, "So? How'd it go?"

"Great. She's on board." He heaved a sigh of relief, and I joined him. But when I told him Tracy's story, he looked as sad as I'd felt.

He sighed as he pulled away from the curb. "I've been hearing about the human trafficking epidemic, but jeez . . . twelve? And that monster was going to sell her virginity?"

It was hard to believe. "I'd love to find a way to nail him for it. But Tracy didn't hear him say it herself. Someone else told her about it. I didn't get a chance to ask, but I'd bet it was someone in the family, and given who they are, I have zero hope any of them would come forward."

Dale's grip tightened on the steering wheel. "We can't do anything about it right now anyway. We've got to focus on saving Tracy. But if I do find a way to nail either of those assholes . . ."

"We'll find a way." Or at least, I knew *I* would. I turned my thoughts back to our immediate problem. "Did you get Liam to tell you why they're so hot to trot to nail Jorge?"

He nodded. "Like we thought, they want to squeeze him for information on Cabazon."

"Did they offer Jorge a deal?"

Dale barked a grim laugh. "Try a complete dismissal."

I'd never heard of a deal that sweet in a murder case. "They must really think he can deliver Cabazon."

He turned right on Sunset and headed for my apartment. "And probably with good reason. The fact that Jorge hasn't taken the deal tells me he knows exactly who Cabazon is."

That sounded about right. We discussed our rescue plan again. "But I don't think we can risk telling Tracy."

Dale nodded. "No, she might let something slip."

Now that I knew the whole story, I thought I might have another angle I could work. "I'd like to talk to Jorge."

Dale gave me a look of alarm. "Don't you think that's risky? Cabazon will find out for sure, and I doubt he'll like it."

"That's why I'm going to ask his permission."

Dale pulled into the driveway of my building. "And how do you plan to get in touch with him?"

That was the easy part—unfortunately. "I don't. All I have to do is wait."

Cabazon was due to come knocking any day now.

FORTY-FOUR

It was after five o'clock when Dale dropped me off, but I'd left Alex with a lot to do on Graham's case, and I wanted to see what he'd found out.

When I got in, I blew Michy a kiss and headed straight for his office. I knocked on his door. "Your high school gym coach called. He—"

The door opened, and an annoyed Alex held up a hand. "Stop. No more. Or I won't tell you what I've got."

I hesitated. "You sure? It's a good one."

He put a hand on his hip. "I don't believe you. Quit while you're behind."

"Fine. What've you got?"

He went back to his desk, and I sat down across from him. He tapped a key on his computer. "I've got the list of tenants in Davey's building. Found six girls between the ages of nineteen and twenty-one. And I couldn't find any logical connection Graham might have to the rest of the tenants."

More than I'd expected. "So Graham really might be hooking up with someone there."

Alex shrugged. "Only one way to find out."

We'd have to go talk to them. Because there was no way Graham would admit it. He'd made it clear by now that he wasn't going to level with me. "How about tomorrow?"

Alex looked up from the monitor. "We've got a better chance of catching them tonight. It's a Wednesday night. They're probably studying for midterms."

I was tired, and driving downtown was about the last thing I felt like doing. But Alex was right. I told him he'd have to drive.

I went out to see Michy. I had a very strong feeling I'd be hearing from Cabazon soon. I didn't think his goon squad would come to the office without making sure I was there, but mistakes happen, and I didn't want Michy to be on the receiving end of theirs. I told her to pack up. "There's nothing you need to do that can't be done tomorrow."

She gave me a puzzled look. "I'm almost done. I just need to finish a couple of things. What's the rush?"

I picked up her coat and draped it over her shoulders. "You've been working too hard. Come on. Out you go."

Michy grumbled about being bossed around, but she shut down her computer and picked up her purse. She started to take a file with her, but I snatched it out of her hand and dropped it back on the desk. "I'm giving you the night off. Take it."

She huffed, "Okay, okay. I'm going."

Alex came out of his office, and we all left together.

Alex had called one of the girls before we left. She'd agreed to talk to us, and she was sure the other two girls who shared the apartment would, too. That took care of three of the six girls in that building.

On the ride over, I made calls and set us up to talk to two more of the girls. I tried calling the sixth but got no answer. I told Alex, "Hopefully she'll come home before we're done."

It was almost seven o'clock when we got there. I told Alex to park around the corner. As we got out, I asked, "What if we run into Davey? What's our story?"

Alex pursed his lips. "We're working on another case?"

I rolled my eyes. "Sure. That's totally believable." But I was too tired to think of anything better. "Let's just hope we don't see him."

We hit the party of three first. I showed them the photo of Graham that I'd uploaded on my cell phone. "Do you know this man?"

The girls passed my phone around. Each of them shook their heads. The girl with one long braid said, "But I think I've seen him around here a couple of times. Why?"

I studied the group. They were average-looking girls, and none of them seemed the type to hook up with an older married guy. But you never know. "Just wondering if he's seeing someone in the building." Knowing it was too much to hope for, I asked the girl with the long braid, "Did you happen to see who he was visiting?"

She shook her head. "I only saw him coming into the building as I was going out."

Why couldn't anything in this case come easy?

The girl wearing fingerless mittens made a face. "Kind of old, isn't he?"

The third girl, who was wearing footie pajamas, studied the photo again and said, "Wait, I'll bet he's rich." She looked at me. "I'm right, aren't I? Is he looking for someone?"

The other two yelled, "Ew! You're so gross, Marnie!"

She shrugged. "Just saying. He's not bad—for an old guy."

Alex and I thanked them for their time. Three down, three to go.

The next two roommates seemed a bit more likely. Wendy, a brown-haired, green-eyed beauty, had a sultry voice. When I showed her the photo of Graham, her eyebrows lifted. "Interesting. No, he's never visited me." She passed the phone to the other girl, named Kendra. "You know him?"

Kendra was a mixed-race beauty with long, shiny black hair. She studied the photo for a long beat, then shook her head. "Don't recognize him."

So much for girls four and five.

Alex asked about the sixth girl. "Do you happen to know Nancy Moulin?"

Wendy said, "Sure. She lives on the third floor. Why?"

"Does she have a boyfriend?" Alex asked.

Kendra's lips twitched. "If you're thinking Nancy might be seeing that guy, I can save you some time. Her girlfriend's pretty possessive."

We were zero for six.

Alex and I regrouped when we got back in the car. As I put on my seat belt, I said, "Do you think anyone was lying?"

He started the car. "Not that I could tell. But it wouldn't surprise me. After all, you're talking about a cheating situation."

Unless we wanted to put a tail on Graham—which I wouldn't mind but really couldn't afford; Alex couldn't do it, since Graham would recognize him—we wouldn't be able to bust the liar unless we wanted to take more drastic, i.e., hacking-style measures.

Though it wasn't a foolproof gauge, my gut told me these girls hadn't been lying. For now, I was going to let the mistress angle go. "If none of the girls is lying, then he must have been visiting Davey."

Alex nodded. "But why would he have gone to see Davey *before* Roan died? To talk about Alicia?"

I stared out at the sky. The wind had swept it clean, and the stars sparkled like crystals. "Probably. But why would Davey and Graham lie about seeing each other?" Both had said they'd only spoken after Roan died.

Alex shook his head as he steered onto the freeway. "Either they're just off on the timing, or they're hiding something."

Those were certainly the two options. "Have you had a chance to check out Davey yet?"

Alex moved into the left-most lane. "I'm working on it. So far, nothing new. But I did track down that paralegal. The one who filed the sexual harassment claim against Graham back in the day."

It'd be good to know what she had to say. If reporters managed to find her, I wanted to be prepared. "Wasn't that at a law firm on the east coast?"

He pulled out the notepad he kept in the center console and handed it to me. "She's out here in LA now. As I recall, she lives in Sherman Oaks."

I flipped to the last page of the notepad. She lived on Greenleaf. I knew the neighborhood. A very pretty—and redundantly leafy—slice of suburbia, lots of trees and well-tended houses, just a canyon away from my office. I read her information. "Emma Lucas, divorced, no kids, fifty-five years old, unemployed." I looked at Alex. "She lives pretty well for someone with no income."

Alex raised an eyebrow. "Who said she has no income? The ex left her with a pile of dough, and she invested it well. She doesn't need to work."

Sweet. "Let's go see her. Can you set it up for tomorrow?"

He gave me a self-satisfied grin. "Already done. I told her I'd confirm with a text tonight."

I smiled back at him. "What on earth would I do without you?"

He knitted his brow. "That's a very good question."

Traffic was light. We flew back to the office, and Alex dropped me off at my car. As I drove home, I could feel my eyelids growing heavy. I was working a lot of long days, and it was getting to me.

When I got home, I put myself straight to bed and deliberately avoided turning on the television. Whatever disaster struck tonight, it'd have to wait until tomorrow.

When I got to the office the next morning, I found Alex raring to go. He handed me a cup of coffee. "Emma's confirmed for nine thirty." He looked at his watch. "We should leave now."

Michy and I exchanged a look. When Alex was on the hunt, he had only one speed: supersonic. "Good morning, Michy. Good-bye, Michy." She laughed. "We should be back by this afternoon."

I volunteered to drive, but Alex waved me off. "We need to take the Canyon, and Beulah's got too much sway."

Benedict Canyon was a winding road, but it was a beautiful ride. The rains earlier in the month had turned the brown hills green, and the sun was shining in a deep-blue sky. I rolled my window down to inhale the clean, fresh air. Then rolled it back up again. The sun might be shining, but it was still cold as hell.

We pulled up to Emma's house—a white Tudor-style with green trim—right on time, and I noticed a fairly new black BMW 535i in the driveway. "You weren't kidding. She really is doing well."

Alex rounded the car and joined me as we walked up the brick pathway to the house. Iceland poppies of all colors lined the walk, and purple princess bushes flowered at the foot of the steps. It was a gorgeous riot of color. The door was painted the same forest-green color as the trim, and a shiny brass knocker was mounted in the center. Even from the outside, I could tell the interior would be tasteful.

Alex dropped the knocker once, and Emma answered right away. She'd aged very well. Her honey-blonde, perfectly highlighted hair was parted on the side, and it fell to her shoulders in soft waves. Her blue eyes had barely any crow's feet, and her black yoga pants and T-shirt showed a body that was still trim and fit. She invited us in and led the way to a living room. The style was modern but not austere—a big, thick oatmeal-colored area rug and low-slung beige sofa and molded matching chairs arranged around a glass-and-chrome coffee table. And there were French doors that opened onto a beautiful backyard with a swimming pool and lush trees and rosebushes.

Emma sat on one of the chairs, and we took the couch. As her eyes traveled between us, I noticed they lingered awhile on Alex. I glanced in his direction to see if he'd noticed. He had.

He took the lead and thanked her for meeting with us, compli-mented her house, and did his overall charming routine—then he zeroed in on the reason for our visit. "We wanted to talk to you about Graham."

Her face clouded. "Such a terrible thing, what happened to his daughter. I feel so badly for him. And to know that she was killed in such a horrible way, her throat cut—" She stopped abruptly and looked away for a moment. When she'd composed herself, she continued. "So I don't want to pile on. He's been through enough."

I definitely liked the sound of that. "I agree. But just in case the press tries to run with this, I thought we should find out what caused you to file the complaint against him."

Emma looked worried. "Well, no one's contacted me yet."

Alex reassured her in his usual smooth way. "And they may not. We just need to be prepared. Just know that anything you tell us will go no further. This is strictly confidential."

She still seemed a little uncertain, but she finally nodded. "This was all so long ago. Graham was a first-year associate, full of himself and loaded with testosterone—like a lot of those trial lawyers. He kept making dumb comments like, 'Can I get fries with that shake?' and, 'That skirt shows you've got a lot of talent.' Idiotic things like that."

Alex nodded, his expression disapproving. "Pretty obnoxious. Did he ever touch you?"

Emma was emphatic. "No, and honestly, he was no worse than any of the other smart-ass young turks." She sighed as she shook her head. "That kind of harassment was so common back then. All the girls were sick of it, but they were afraid to say anything. So I decided I may as well be the one. I reported on all three of them."

"Then it wasn't just Graham?" Alex asked.

She shook her head. "I'd hoped that would send a message, put a stop to it with all of them." Emma paused, her expression hardened. "But the only one who got punished was Graham. They didn't even discipline the other two guys." She gave me a sardonic smile. "I bet you can guess why."

Sadly, I could. "Because their daddies were partners."

She nodded. "So poor Graham—who, by the way, was the only one who apologized to me—got fired, and the other two got to stay. After that, the partners treated me like dirt. I hung in there for a few months. I didn't want to let them win. But I finally decided life was too short, so I quit and moved out here."

I didn't blame her a bit. "I'm sorry it turned out that way. But good for you for taking a stand, Emma. Have you had any contact with him since that time?"

"No," she said. "Not because of any ill will. Just . . . why? We weren't buddies; we were just coworkers. I didn't even know he lived out here until his daughter . . ."

Got murdered. She looked away as she said it. I liked Emma. But more importantly, I liked that she had no ax to grind. I wouldn't have to worry about any shots being fired across our bow from her corner.

FORTY-FIVE

When we got back to the car, Alex stared at the house for a moment. "That was cool, the way she took on those assholes for harassing her."

I sometimes forgot that Alex might have suffered from similar kinds of mistreatment. "Were they like that at the dealership?"

He turned and looked through the windshield. "And in high school, and at Jimmy's, the diner where I worked during high school, and at—"

I held up a hand. "I get it. What kinds of things would they do at the dealership?"

His mouth turned down. "They'd say something—or someone—was 'so gay,' or they'd imitate customers they thought were gay, wave their hands around and talk with a lisp." He looked at me. "And it went downhill from there."

I clenched my teeth. Never had I been happier about the fact that he'd ripped off that dealership for those cars—or sadder that he'd been caught. "Did you report it?"

Alex sighed. "No. I couldn't afford to lose the job. My family needed the money. But I've regretted it ever since. Me? I could take it, but I knew others there who couldn't. One of them quit. If only for him, I should've spoken up."

I could relate. "Don't beat yourself up too much about it. I had a supervisor in the public defender's office who managed to find a reason on a daily basis to pat our asses or do a boob sideswipe, and I never said a thing." Largely because I'd been through so much worse. To me, it was laughably childish and just kind of sad. But also partly because I knew that if I complained, I'd be the one who suffered.

Alex nodded. "I understand. You get so used to putting up with crap like that, you almost feel silly for calling someone out."

Which was exactly what empowered the jerks to keep on doing it. "Anyway, I'm glad to hear Graham apologized. And for what it's worth, I've never seen him act like that."

"People can change. Sometimes all it takes is for them to realize that it's not just a silly joke, that they're actually doing harm."

I said with some bitterness, "Not often enough."

"No, I agree." Alex started the car. "Anyway, I confirmed that the leads I got from Mandalay & Stokes are in pocket for most of the day. Unless you have something else that needs doing first, we should get them out of the way."

I leaned my head against the window. A nap would be so nice. "Yeah, may as well."

When the story came out about Graham's sexual harassment complaint, I'd asked Alex to check out the rest of his work history. After Graham left the law firm where he'd worked with Emma, he'd moved out to LA and joined Mandalay & Stokes. He was there for a few years before he moved to his current firm, Hocheiser, Leslie & Friedman, where he'd made partner. The prevailing sentiment at Mandalay had been that Graham was a "great guy," and Alex had said there was a fair amount of reluctance to say anything that could even remotely be called "talking smack" about him. But Alex had reminded them that we were on his side, that everything they said would *of course* be confidential, and that we were just trying to make sure we were prepared.

The upshot was that one of the female partners and one male associate independently confided that Graham did seem to be "particularly close" to three of his female clients. They'd both played down the stories as likely gossip, but Alex had taken the contact information for the women anyway—better to talk to them and find out now whether we had a problem than to assume there was nothing there and get gobsmacked by bad press that would likely hit at the worst possible time.

Since the firm offered full service to their corporate clients—which necessarily included estate planning—the women all lived locally, and they all lived well: in the "Platinum Triangle" that was comprised of Beverly Hills, Holmby Hills, and Bel Air.

We'd dressed for our foray into Boardwalk and Park Place in slacks and blazers. Alex looked particularly gorgeous in his black blazer and white button-down shirt. I was hoping that would come in handy. "Let's start with Olivia Torrinucci." She lived in the westernmost area of the three, in Bel Air. We could start there, then work our way east.

Alex typed her address into his phone and headed back to Benedict Canyon.

When I'd seen that Olivia lived in Bel Air, I'd expected to find mile-high gates and a mansion shrouded in towering trees. I wasn't even close. She lived in a medium-size ranch-style home on Somera Road. True, it was perched on a hill, so it probably had a great view of the canyon. But it definitely wasn't the spectacular grandeur that I thought of as typical Bel Air.

And she didn't have the expected uniformed maid service, either. When Alex knocked on the door, Olivia answered it herself. She was a petite brunette with a stylish bob and a warm smile—one that was particularly directed at Alex.

Honestly, I'd say this gets old—and it does—but I can't complain about something that makes my life so much easier. Olivia ushered us into a spacious sunken living room with two sliding-glass doors that did indeed offer one hell of a nice view of the canyon. We sat down on a low-slung chocolate sofa that was piled with color-coordinated fur-covered pillows.

"Can I offer you anything to drink? Coffee? Tea?" she asked.

We both thanked her but declined. She sat down on a comfy-looking quilted beige chair, and Alex reiterated what he'd told her about our mission, AKA our cover story: that we were looking for potential character witnesses in case Graham wound up in trial.

Olivia gave him a solemn nod. "Of course. It'd be my pleasure to help him in any way I can, that poor man." She shook her head. "Such a terrible thing." She looked at Alex. "He was very kind to me after my husband died. Graham was primarily focused on my husband's busi-ness. He owned a string of Jack in the Box franchises. So technically, he didn't have to take my calls after Carson died. We did have an estate-planning lawyer. But he could be a little . . . hard to find when I had questions. Graham always made time for me, and he was so gracious. He never made me feel like I was a bother." She smiled. "Though I most certainly was."

Alex beamed at her. "I'm so glad to hear it. Are you still in touch with him?"

Olivia glanced out the window for a moment. "We exchange Christmas cards, but that's about it. Once the estate got sorted out, we kind of lost touch."

I tried to assess her tone. Did that disappoint her? If so, was it because she'd lost a lover? Or just a friend?

Alex was studying her, too. "Just to get a sense of how well you knew him, did you spend any social time together? Go out to lunch or dinner?"

Olivia's smile turned nostalgic. "Both. We'd have lunch when I came in to the firm to sign papers, and whenever I was in the area around dinnertime, I'd give him a call. I'd say I got to know him fairly well."

Which only made me wonder: How well? Alex tried a version of that. "Did you ever have him over to your house for dinner?"

She colored a little. "Once. He invited me out to dinner because Sandy and Alicia were out of town—visiting Sandy's parents, I believe—and he was lonely. I thought he probably needed a homier experience, so I invited him to come here."

Alex paused—probably wondering if he should go for it—and then he did. "I don't want to upset or embarrass you, but since the other side might ask the question, I need to find out what your answer will be. Did he spend the night?"

Now, she colored a lot. "No, he did not. And he never acted inappropriately with me. He was always a complete gentleman. That's why I knew it was safe to let him come to the house."

I gave an inward sigh of relief. Whatever the truth really was, if she didn't want to admit to having had an affair, it'd be really hard to prove otherwise. We were safe. If we put her on the stand, Graham would come off smelling like a rose.

Alex kept after her just to make sure there were no cracks or fissures that might let anything ugly seep through, but Olivia seemed solid.

Half an hour later, we were back in the car and headed toward Holmby Hills and the residence of Sarah Feinstein. Driving through all these wealthy neighborhoods was a study in how the other half lives. The cars we passed were a mix of Teslas, Bentleys, and top-of-the-line Mercedes and BMWs. And when we passed the lone Toyota Corolla, I saw that the driver was a middle-aged Hispanic woman who was transporting two white toddler kids—who were scrolling on their brand-new iPads.

Alex pulled to the curb in front of a house on Delfern Drive that was partially shielded from view by a dense collection of a variety of palm trees. The wrought-iron fence that surrounded the property was low, and it wound around a third of the block. We pressed a buzzer at the gate, and a voice asked who it was. Alex identified us. The gate swung open, and we walked up the driveway through the forest of palm trees and cacti that led to the house. It was a brown two-story Spanish-style—LA is very big on Spanish-style houses—with a red-tiled roof and a heavy arched wooden door that had an iron-grilled peep window.

I rang the doorbell—a classic ding-dong bell sound—and an older Hispanic woman in an apron answered the door. She stood back to let us enter, then led the way into a room the realtors call a "great room," i.e., a very spacious room that's usually created by knocking out the wall between a living room and a family room. In contrast to the Spanish exterior, it was jarringly furnished in a style best described as seventies Palm Springs—lots of bright oranges and yellows and whites and acres of leather furniture. It even had a neon palm tree in the corner. I was desperate to put on my sunglasses.

Sarah was already seated on the long, curved white leather couch, and I noticed she was holding a highball glass that looked like it held Scotch on the rocks. Her boozy smile confirmed it. I glanced at my phone and saw it was just past noon. You've gotta love a woman who can tank it up that early—and one whose inhibitions might just be low enough to tell us the truth. She had a wild head of thick, bottle-platinum hair that fell down to the middle of her back and a pretty face that looked a lot younger than her hands, which I noticed, as I reached out to shake, were covered with age spots.

I introduced myself and, even as we shook, her gaze drifted over to Alex.

Alex made a little bow over her hand, and I thought for a moment he was going to kiss it. Thankfully—because I would've barfed—he didn't and simply gave her a smile that would've made Enrique Iglesias envious.

He ran through the same questions he'd asked Olivia. Sarah wasn't the vulnerable widow Olivia had been—her husband was very much alive, and Sarah was actively involved in "Green Machines," their lawn-mower-manufacturing company—but she'd definitely gotten some star treatment from Graham.

Sarah tossed her mane and smiled at Alex. "He was very good to me. My husband is overseas a lot because he negotiates the deals for some of our parts with a Chinese company. So a lot of the day-to-day business dealings fall to me."

Alex gave her an admiring look. "Then you turned to him for professional advice?" She nodded. "Did you ever spend time socializing? I mean as a friend?"

Her smile hinted that it was more than just friendly, but she said, "We'd have lunches—and an occasional dinner now and then. But that was all."

He raised an eyebrow. "Do you think Graham was hoping it might go further?"

She gave Alex a sly look, then, with a careless shrug, said, "I don't know, maybe." Her smile said, *Definitely.*

The problem was, I couldn't tell if this was just ego or a fair assessment of Graham's intentions. Alex asked her if she still kept in touch with Graham, but she said she hadn't spoken with him "in years." He tried a few other angles, but either she was stonewalling us or there really was nothing more.

When we got back to the car, I said, "Do you have any idea what it's like to be invisible?"

He chuckled. "You're not invisible. Just much less . . . interesting."

I punched him on the arm. "Drive. I can't wait for this day to be over." The truth? I thought Alex's success with the ladies was great—and kind of funny. And I was glad to be hearing such glowing reports on Graham.

Alex headed for our last stop: Heather Jorgenson. She lived just a short hop away on North Palm Drive. It was one of those extra-wide streets south of Sunset Boulevard that was lined with trees and perfectly manicured lawns. Here, almost all the houses looked like Sarah's—two-story Spanish-style homes. But there were no fences around any of the properties on Heather's block.

We walked right up to the front door, and I noticed a white BMW 750Li in the driveway. Nice. When I knocked, a woman in her fifties who had to be Heather Jorgenson answered the door. I introduced myself and Alex, and she confirmed that she was indeed Heather. Unlike Sarah, our hostess was pretty in a tasteful way. Her shiny brown hair was pulled back in a low ponytail, and she had the kind of high cheekbones and dark—almost black—eyes that gave her features a Native American cast.

After we all shook hands, she stood back and said, "Come on in."

If the outside of the house was similar in design to Sarah's, the inside was a study in contrasts. Heather led us into a living room that was furnished with impeccable taste. Persian rugs gave the room warmth and color, and the deep blue and burgundy chenille couch and matching wing chairs coordinated to make the high-ceilinged space feel cozy. The room faced the street, and a large picture window covered with a gauzy layer of curtains filtered the sunshine to let in a soft light.

Heather offered us something to drink, and this time I had to accept. I was thirsty as hell. "Water would be great."

Alex agreed, and Heather went to get it. I looked around the room and saw photos of a man I assumed was her husband. He was handsome in a leathery way, with a wide smile and dark-blue eyes.

Heather came back carrying a tray with two ice-filled glasses and two bottles of water. I filled my glass immediately and drank. Heather hadn't been as glued to Alex as the other two—though her smile definitely got a little wider when she looked at him—but he was on a roll, and I was happy to let him take the lead.

The questioning—and the answers—took a similar path to the others, except that Graham hadn't been Heather's—or her husband's—lawyer. One of the managing partners was representing her. And it was her business, not her husband's, that the partner worked on. Heather had owned two hotels, one in Aspen and another in Deer Valley. She seemed like the sporty type who skied and snowboarded; she had that lean, fit look.

Heather said she'd run into Graham when she first signed on with the firm. "And I believe we had lunch a few times. Sometimes I'd visit him just to chat. He was a great listener and a lot of fun."

"Did you ever do dinners or have him to the house?" Alex asked.

Heather stared out the window for a moment. "I believe we may have had a dinner or two. But no, I never entertained him here."

And no, she wasn't still in touch with him.

Alex asked, "Then if anyone asked what you thought of Graham . . . ?"

Heather smiled. "I'd say he was a great guy. And if you're wondering whether I heard about that sexual harassment claim, the answer is yes." She shook her head, her expression unfazed. "He never behaved that way when I knew him. Not that I doubt the truth of the claim, but that was a long time ago. He probably *was* thoughtless and dumb—like they all can be at that age."

From what I could tell, there was nothing to worry about with any of these women. At least as far as what they might say publicly. And that was good enough for me.

We wrapped up the interview and took off.

It was time to find out who, if anyone, had been lying.

FORTY-SIX

We headed back to the office. "Who's your pick?" I asked Alex.

He'd put spyware on Graham's phone to see if any of the women we'd interviewed called him after we left. If one of them did, it wouldn't necessarily mean she'd been lying. It might be totally innocent—just an old friend letting him know that she was on his side and that she'd told us how wonderful he was. But it might also mean he still had something going on with one of them. If so, I needed to know now, before anyone else found out.

Alex headed east on Sunset Boulevard. "Sarah's the most obvious choice."

I gave a little laugh as I pictured her boozy smile. "She really is." But then I thought about how Olivia had blushed when Alex hinted at a closer connection with Graham, whereas Heather had merely nixed it with an amused smile. Both reactions could shield a lie. "I can't choose." I glanced at Alex. "So the suspense builds."

He laughed. "I'm on pins and needles. But we'll have to wait until we get back to the office."

That was probably for the best anyway. We needed to give them time to call Graham. Thanks to crosstown traffic, it took half an hour. But the minute we got in, Alex pulled out his phone.

I gave Michy the update on our interviews and told her what Alex was doing. She looked incredulous. "I thought you didn't want to do that. You said you couldn't risk getting caught."

I had. "That was when we were talking about a long-term operation, so I could monitor what Graham was doing and stop him from screwing things up. That was too risky. This is only a temporary thing. We'll delete the spyware tomorrow."

Alex had been scrolling and tapping on his phone. Now he looked up. "I can't believe it. It worked. We actually got one."

I couldn't believe it, either. Or maybe I just didn't want to. I tried to reassure myself as I said, "It's probably totally innocent, Alex. Don't get excited."

He met my gaze. "Okay, I won't. Sure you don't want to guess?"

I shook my head. "Let's hear it."

He took another beat, just to torture me, then said, "It's Heather."

Michy looked from Alex to me. "Meaning, she called Graham after you left?" I nodded. "How long after you left?"

Alex looked at his phone. "Had to be within a minute. Want me to take down the spyware now?"

I mulled over our next move. "No. Leave it on until tomorrow, as planned. Let's see how much activity we get."

Alex held up his thumb. A single phone call to Graham to pay respects, to say, "How are you doing?" was one thing. A flurry of calls between them was another. It was worth the risk of leaving the spyware intact for another half day to find out.

I started to head into my office, then stopped. "Oh, and Alex, let's find out more about Heather, like—"

Alex cut me off. "Already on it."

I gave him a high five from across the room—the only kind of high five I don't mind giving—and went into my office. I really hoped Heather's call was just an innocent "heads up" to let Graham know he had her support.

I figured I'd find out soon enough. And then I remembered that I still hadn't gotten Alicia's autopsy report. I knew it could take as much as a month to get the official report, but I didn't want to wait that long. I wanted to see if there were any unanswered questions I could use to my advantage.

There was only one person who could help me with this. Dale. I sat down on my couch, put my feet up on the coffee table, and called him—from my landline, of course. Mr. Paranoia wouldn't even let me call him about dinner plans on his cell anymore.

His voice was wary as he answered. "What's up?"

We both got keyed up when one of us called. The Cabazon Effect. "Nothing new. Just wondered if you'd heard when Alicia's autopsy report is coming out."

He exhaled loudly, and I could hear the relief in his voice. "Alicia's report has been delayed. Something about the murder weapon being reexamined."

I sat up. The knife had been found under her body, but since it'd been in water for some time, I'd doubted they'd find anything useful on it. But maybe I was wrong. "Do you know if they've found prints?"

I heard someone call out to Dale. He spoke hurriedly. "I don't know. I didn't hear why they were looking at it. All I know is there's a holdup. Gotta go."

As I ended the call, I hoped they'd found prints on the knife that didn't match Roan. That might give me a new straw man for Roan's murder. But there was no point obsessing over a possibility that might never materialize. I wouldn't know anything until I got the print expert's report. I put it out of my mind for the moment and got busy on the rest of my caseload. By six thirty, I was so tired I was seeing double.

I'd just decided to call it a night when Michy came into my office. She snatched my coat off the couch, came over, and draped it across my shoulders. "Time to go. You're done for the day."

I was getting a dose of my own medicine, but I didn't mind. I stood up. "See how I cooperate and don't fight like a four-year-old who won't go to bed?"

Michy shot me a dagger look. "I was in the middle of . . . Never mind. Let's go get Alex."

But Alex, eyes fixed on his monitor, wouldn't budge. I stood in the doorway, my arms folded. "Enough already. The Internet won't disappear between now and tomorrow."

He didn't even look up. He just made a shooing motion with his hand. "Go, and let a man do some work around here."

"Okay, Archie Bunker," I said sarcastically. "On the serious side, any more activity between Graham and Heather?"

"Not so far." He finally looked up. "Do I still pull off the spyware at nine a.m.?"

I gave it another thought. Graham sometimes went into the office late. "Give it until ten a.m. Oh, and can you check his recent calls to see if any of the girls in Davey's building called Graham after we talked to them?" I was pretty sure those girls had been telling the truth when they denied knowing him, but it couldn't hurt to make sure. And if they were telling the truth, then I'd have to conclude that Graham *had* been visiting Davey. What to make of that—and why they'd both lied about it—would be my next question.

Alex gave me a thumbs-up. "'Kay, bye." He dropped his gaze back to the screen.

I looked at Michy. "I believe we've been dismissed."

As we headed down to our cars, we talked about planning a shopping trip for the coming weekend.

I was still thinking about the gaps in my wardrobe when I pulled into the carport at my apartment. But as I headed for the stairway, I noticed an SUV roll up the driveway.

My brain barely had a chance to make the association when two very muscled and tattooed men jumped out and ran over to me. Each one grabbed an arm and practically lifted me off the ground as they hustled me, my toes dragging along the pavement, toward what I now saw was a black Range Rover. I started to scream, but the one on my left stuffed a filthy rag into my mouth. I twisted back and forth as I struggled to break free, but they held me with a grip as strong—and almost as painful—as a bear trap.

When we reached the car, one opened the back door, and the other shoved me inside, then slammed the door. I fell onto the seat—and nearly into the lap of another beast in a black do-rag, who held a nine millimeter that was pointed at my head. I barely had time to sit up before the driver threw the car into reverse. It jumped backward with a screech of tires, and I slammed into the front seat. Before I could catch my breath—or my balance—he threw the car into drive and stomped on the gas. I got thrown backward, and my head banged against the backseat.

Dizzy, disoriented, and terrified, I started to reach for my seat belt, then thought better of it. If I got the chance to jump out of the car, I didn't want to blow it by fiddling with the buckle. I held onto the headrest of the front seat and braced my other hand against the door. The part of my brain that wasn't occupied with staying alive realized that I was about to see Cabazon. The question was whether I'd ever see anything else after that.

As we hurtled westbound on Sunset, I wondered whether he knew I'd already found Tracy. He couldn't have found out . . . could he? If so, we were all dead. The thought started a buzzing in my brain. I gripped the headrest as my heart pounded like a trip-hammer. *Don't go there*, I told myself.

I'd assumed they were taking me to his house, but as we flew past Stone Canyon, I realized that this time, we were going somewhere else. I wanted to ask where, but my mouth had gone too dry, and I was having trouble breathing. Besides, I knew these animals wouldn't tell me jack shit.

Suddenly, the driver made a hard right onto a very dark, narrow street. He slowed down only marginally as the houses gave way to thick shrubbery and massive trees, and the asphalt gave way to rocks and dirt. We were in total darkness, and there were no signs of life that I could see. It was the perfect body dump.

Two seconds later, the driver hit the brakes, and I slammed into the front seat again. The gorilla sitting next to me still had his gun pointed at my head. My breath was fast and shallow as I tried to see what the driver was doing. I heard the glove compartment open, then the unmistakable sound of a magazine being shoved into a handgun. My head began to swim as I fought to regain control and breathe. This really was it.

I pulled on the door handle, but the lock was disabled. At that moment, I heard a car door slam somewhere nearby. As I looked around to see where the sound came from, my door was flung open, and one of the tattooed guys who'd grabbed me in the driveway yanked me out of the Rover. He dug his fingers into my upper arm so hard I gave out a yelp of pain. He stuffed that same dirty rag into my mouth again.

The other tattooed asshole came over, and each one took an arm again as they dragged me over to a black Maybach and threw me into the backseat. And there, waiting for me, was Cabazon.

With a gun in his lap.

FORTY-SEVEN

Cabazon saw me look down at the gun and fixed me with a narrow-eyed glare. "My patience is at an end. Where is she?"

Relief flooded through me at hearing that question. He didn't know I'd already found Tracy. Unfortunately, it didn't resolve my other fear: that he'd kill me anyway because I hadn't. I'd already planned my answer to this question—assuming I got the chance to give one. "I have reason to believe that your nephew may know where to find her, or at least have a very good lead. Have you spoken to him?" Not that I thought he had, but I needed to make sure.

His face became a solid mass of cold anger. "He knows better than to contact me. The police are most certainly monitoring every number he calls."

I'd been counting on that. "Then you should let me visit him. If I'm right, I can get him to help me find Tracy. And if you have a message for him, I can deliver it." I paused to let that sink in, then added the final bait. "I can also find out exactly what the police are asking him—and what they've offered him."

His eyes became glittering slits of black ice. "It seems you already have information. What have they offered him?"

It took everything I had to keep my voice from shaking. "I don't already have information. But I'm a criminal lawyer. I know how the cops work. Jorge killed a worthless scumbag. There's no reason for them to care about the case. But they obviously do, because they've buried Tracy so deep, even Dale and I—with all our connections—are having a hard time finding her. That means she has to be in protective custody—a lot of trouble and expense for the murder of a gangbanger with a mile-long rap sheet. Especially since Jorge has almost no criminal history at all." Cabazon frowned. "So the cops have to be using this case to squeeze him. And the only thing Jorge's got that they'd want this badly is information that'll help them nail you."

Cabazon did not look fazed by my deduction. "If she is in protective custody, then it should be easy for Dale to find her."

I'd known that was coming. "Only if she's in state custody. But he already ruled that out. That means she's in federal custody. And Dale has to be careful about accessing official databases. He has no legitimate reason to be looking into a federal case."

He spoke in a cold, quiet voice. "Then why is Jorge still in Twin Towers?"

That remark told me that he'd already tried to get to Jorge—and I knew it wasn't to send him a Happy Thanksgiving greeting. Jorge might be a beloved nephew, but he was also a threat now, and for Cabazon, there was no such thing as a tolerable threat.

I answered him honestly. "It might just be a question of convenience. It started out as a state case. Twin Towers has maximum security, and they might be afraid to risk moving him."

Cabazon stared at me with hooded eyes for a long beat. "Go see him. But you must not let the police suspect you are working for me."

Yeah, no shit. No worries there. "I'd like to find a better way of giving you updates." I pointedly tilted my head toward the Range Rover where I'd just endured a near-death experience. "A phone number would be nice." I might be getting a little cocky now that I knew I wasn't about to die. But I really did need to end these heart-stopping encounters. My life span was probably already a few years shorter just from this last ride alone.

He didn't answer. He tapped the driver on the shoulder. "We are finished."

The driver gave the horn a fast tap, and the tattooed gorillas opened my door. They were a little more civilized this time. They let me walk to the Range Rover on my own—albeit with one on each side of me.

The driver sped through the streets almost as manically as he had on the way out. I guessed it was just his style. How he got away with it, I didn't know. If I drove like that, I'd get busted within ten seconds. The constant stream of adrenaline that'd kept my juices flowing had abruptly ebbed by the time they dropped me back at my building, and my body felt like it was weighted down with sandbags. I barely had the strength to make it up the stairs.

The moment I got inside, I poured myself three fingers of tequila and downed most of it in one gulp. The mix of tequila and waning adrenaline was not my best idea. I felt queasy, and my head started to spin. I had to lie down on the couch.

But the alcohol eventually won out, and for the first time that evening, I took a full breath. Feeling better, I got up, locked the door, threw the deadbolt, and poured myself a double shot. I took it to bed with me and turned on the television.

I found a *Friends* rerun—the visual equivalent of comfort food—sipped my drink, and tried to put my encounter with Cabazon out of my head. Ten minutes later, as Ross reminded Rachel they'd been on a break, I felt the empty glass slip from my fingers.

And that was the last thing I remember until the raucous sounds of a *Brady Bunch* rerun woke me up at seven thirty a.m. I'd slept for eight hours. I couldn't remember when I'd last managed to do that. I rolled out of bed and shuffled into the bathroom. My stomach was still a little dicey, and my brain was fuzzy, but the steamy shower helped, and the first two cups of coffee restored me to almost full consciousness. I got dressed, poured myself a third cup, and went out to the balcony to take in the city. Between that final shot of caffeine and the icy wind that was bending the palm trees almost horizontal, I woke all the way up. My gaze drifted east toward downtown and the Twin Towers, where Jorge Maldonado was being held. Cabazon really was out of patience. I'd have to make time to see Jorge today—tomorrow at the latest.

I went back inside and put on a vest, my coat, and my black wool scarf. It wasn't easy to do because my arms were killing me. The Neanderthals had really done a number on them, and my biceps sported big Technicolor splotches. I grabbed the leftover toast I'd made the day before and headed for the office.

Alex was standing next to Michy's desk when I walked in, and Michy's mouth was hanging open. I stared at her. "What? You just found out that Tom Cruise isn't gay?"

Michy said, "This is so weird."

Alex looked stoked. "You told me to check out Heather. So I decided to start by looking under her maiden name. And look what I found." He held out his iPad.

I took it and saw a birth certificate. The mother's name was Heather Moser, and the father was listed as unknown. And the baby's name was David. It took me a second to put it together. Then it hit me. "Holy shit. Davey Moser . . . Davey? She's Davey's mother?"

Alex nodded as he took back his iPad. "And get this, he was born one year after Heather signed on as a client with Graham's law firm."

One year. It was easy math—but a crazy equation. "You've got to be kidding me. Graham's the father?"

Alex spread out his hands. "I didn't believe it, either, so I accessed Graham's phone records for the past year. Heather called him the day the news hit about Alicia's murder."

And she'd called Graham right after we'd spoken to her. It seemed pretty clear, but there was only one way to know for sure. "I'm going to have to talk to Graham."

Michy looked worried. "Don't you think it'll piss him off to know that you've been checking up on him?"

"Probably. But this is something he should've told me himself. I'd like to know why he chose not to."

Not that I didn't get it. No one would love the idea of having to admit that they'd had an affair, let alone one that'd produced a child. But he knew our conversations were privileged, and this was a truly bizarre coincidence. If the reporters found out that Graham's illegitimate son had been friends with his daughter, the story would go viral. And it wouldn't do Graham any favors with the jury pool. I needed to figure out how to minimize the damage before that happened.

Alex pulled up the secretary's chair. "And FYI, not that it's any surprise now, but none of those girls in Davey's building called Graham after we met with them."

I nodded. He was right. It was no surprise . . . now.

Alex continued. "I guess now we know why Graham was visiting him."

I thought about that. "I'd say so. In which case, Davey must know that Graham's his father. And Alicia is—was—his half sister. But then why didn't Davey tell me?"

Michy leaned back and folded her arms. "Because maybe Davey doesn't know. Heather probably wouldn't want him to find out that he was the product of an affair. And the same would go for Graham—especially since he chose not to be a part of Davey's life."

Alex agreed with her. I supposed that made sense. I wanted to talk to Graham about it, but I also needed to get downtown to see Jorge today. I decided to try and squeeze Graham in this morning and go see Jorge in the afternoon, since that would take more time. "Michy, see if you can get Graham in here before noon. If not, try and set us up with a meeting tomorrow."

I went into my office, thinking I'd get some work done while I waited to find out what the plan was. But Michy called to let me know that Graham was in the neighborhood. "He'll be here in ten minutes."

Damn. That was fast. "How did he sound?"

"Kind of pissed." She shrugged. "My guess? Heather told him you were snooping around, and he wants some answers. And I think I'm edging up to a big 'I told you so.'"

I could feel my anger rising as I prepared for the fight. "I don't care. He needs to get that he's jeopardizing his own life by shutting me out."

Michy sighed. "This should be fun."

I told her to show Graham in to my office when he got there. Seven minutes later, Michy knocked on my door, and he strode in.

She'd been right. He stood in the middle of my office, red-faced with anger. "What the hell are you doing digging around in my life? I hired you to represent me, to watch my back. Not to investigate me."

I gestured to the chair in front of my desk. "Have a seat." He glared at me as he came over and sat down. "Let me explain to you how it works with a case like this. The press doesn't give a crap about mergers and acquisitions. But they care a great deal about a salacious murder case involving a high-priced lawyer." I told him what I didn't know could hurt him—badly. And that it'd come to my attention more than once that there was a lot I didn't know. "Things you *should* have told me. For instance, how long have you known that Davey was your son?"

Graham clenched his jaw. "I knew Heather had my child. But I didn't find out that child was Davey until right after Alicia . . . died."

I remembered what Alex had said about his phone records. "When Heather called you?"

A look of alarm crossed his face. "How did you know about that?"

I wasn't about to let him drag me into a defensive posture. "So you knew you'd gotten her pregnant, but you didn't know anything about the child?"

He shook his head. "No, I mean I didn't even know I'd gotten her pregnant until the child was a couple of years old. Heather had wanted to take care of everything on her own, but her business had taken a big downturn. So she asked me for financial help, but she didn't want me to be involved, and I was okay with that. I sent her monthly checks until she got back on her feet."

This much made sense. The rest, however . . . "Didn't Alicia tell you she was friends with Davey Moser?"

Graham stared over my shoulder. "No. She only told me she was friends with a boy named Davey. Heather never told me what she'd named the baby, didn't even tell me whether it was a boy or a girl. And I never got the chance to meet any of Alicia's college friends in person."

Right. Alicia'd only been at USC for a few months. I supposed if Graham had met Davey in person when Alicia had first moved in, he might've seen the resemblance between them—though I certainly hadn't noticed it. Only now, having learned that they were related, did I see the similarity in the shape of the brow, the curve of the lips. "But surely once you spoke to Heather, you found out?"

Graham nodded. "She told me when she called to extend her sympathy about Alicia. And she said that Davey told her they were friends. I asked whether Davey knew Alicia was his half sister, but Heather said no. She'd never told him about me."

I'd come back to that later. "Why did you go visit Davey?"

He sighed and looked down at my desk. "I'd just lost my daughter and found out that my son had been a good friend of hers. I guess it was a way of hanging onto some part of her." Graham met my gaze. "I'm sorry I lied to you about it, but I didn't see what it might have to do with the case."

Was he kidding? This was tabloid manna from heaven. But there was no point getting into it with him now. "Did you tell him you were his father?"

A wave of sadness washed over his features. "No. It's too late for that."

Then Michy might be right. Maybe Davey didn't know Alicia was his half sister. Still, the fact that they'd become friends struck me as too much of a coincidence. "Don't you think it's a tad bizarre that they just happened to go to the same school, and then just happened to wind up being friends?"

Graham shrugged. "I don't know. I suppose so. But then again, they share some DNA. Is it so strange that they'd make similar choices? And USC is a popular school, they both live in LA . . . I mean, it's not like Davey moved here from Atlanta."

That was fine, as far as it went. But it still didn't explain how they wound up being friends. In fairness, though, Graham couldn't be expected to know the answer to that question.

He asked me if the police had contacted me yet about bringing him in for more questioning. I told him they hadn't so far. "And I'd be surprised if they did. The lead detective knows me well enough to know that I'd tell him to take a flying leap."

Graham nodded, then asked in a tense voice, "But they don't have enough to arrest me yet, right?"

"No, not yet." I'd already told Graham that I was sure the cops and evidence analysts were going through everything with a fine-tooth comb to find just one more link to justify his arrest. I decided not to tell him that they'd held up Alicia's autopsy report. I didn't know what their questions about the murder weapon had to do with her cause of death, and it'd only drive him crazy to tell him something I couldn't explain. I just said that I'd be in touch the moment I heard anything. "In the meantime, is there anything else you haven't told me?"

He swore there wasn't. I studied his face as I searched for the lie. I didn't see enough to know either way. It was the hell of representing a trial lawyer: it meant he was one hell of a poker player.

After Graham left, I went out and told Michy and Alex what he'd said and how he'd learned about Davey and Alicia being friends. "But I don't believe in coincidences." We'd learned a lot, but I knew there was more, a lot more. I asked Alex, "What've you found out about Davey?"

He didn't look excited. "Not much. The only thing that's even mildly interesting is that Davey transferred to USC the year before Alicia entered. He started at Loyola."

I shook my head. "I disagree. That wasn't even mildly interesting." I looked at my phone. It was almost noon. "I've got to go see a client at Twin Towers."

Hopefully, that *would* prove to be interesting.

FORTY-EIGHT

As I drove downtown, I thought about how I could let Jorge Maldonado know what his *tío* Cabazon was up to without tipping off the guards who monitored jail visits. Attorney-client visits were supposed to be confidential, but I was sure Cabazon had connections everywhere. I couldn't take any chances.

I showed the guard at the reception desk my ID, and when I gave her Jorge's name, I asked whether he was still in maximum security. She typed on her computer, then peered at the screen. "Yeah. In fact, he's in solitary."

Just as I'd suspected. They weren't taking any chances. If he were in general population, he'd probably be dead before he finished his first fruit cup.

By the time I entered the attorney visiting room and sat down at a cubicle, I had a few ideas about how to clue Jorge in to what I was doing. Of necessity, my language would have to be cryptic. I'd just have to hope that Jorge was smart enough to get it. Five minutes later, a guard walked him down the row, and I sat face-to-face with Tracy's savior.

I'd expected to see a multiple-tattooed and -pierced tough guy. That was not who sat across the Plexiglas divide from me. Jorge Maldonado was tall, slender, had one small tattoo of a rose just under his left earlobe, and no piercings whatsoever. He wasn't a beauty; his eyes were a little close together, his nose was a little big for his face, and his ears stuck out at right angles from his head. But his smile was warm, and when he picked up the phone, he greeted me with a soft voice.

He gave me a curious look. "I was surprised to find I had another lawyer. Are you replacing Diego?"

If only. I spoke carefully, so that every word would sink in. "No. I've come to bring you information. Your little mother misses you terribly. She wishes there was something she could do to help you." I'd said "little" mother to clue him in that I was talking about Tracy. I looked into his eyes and tried to convey the fact that he had to read between the lines.

He stared back at me for a long moment. When he finally spoke, his eyes were shiny with tears. "I miss her, too. So you've seen her? Will you see her again?" I nodded. "Please tell her I said it's not her fault I'm in here."

I was so relieved I almost smiled. He got it. He knew we were talking about Tracy.

He asked, "How is she?"

"She's fine. People are protecting her." I waited to see if he understood I meant she was in protective custody. He nodded. Good. Now, I had to convey the threat Cabazon posed. "But there's concern that she might be getting sick. And at her age, any illness might be fatal."

Jorge gripped the telephone and stared into my eyes. "I wish there was something I could do to help."

I returned his gaze. "All she wants is for you to take care of yourself. I think you should consider finding someone you can talk to, share your feelings with." I paused to make sure he got what I meant: that he should consider rolling over on Cabazon if he could find someone safe.

Jorge stared at me intently. "But it hurts to talk about feelings. It even hurts to think about my feelings."

He was telling me he knew he was in grave danger whether he talked or not. "I understand very well. There's no rush. I'm going to see *tu familia* very soon, I think." I said it in Spanish to let him know that I meant Cabazon. "I will tell them that your mother is ill and needs good care."

Jorge nodded emphatically. "Yes, please tell them that it's important to me that she recover her health. If she doesn't, I'll be very, very upset." He paused and looked into my eyes. "And if I get that upset, I will have to talk to someone, share my feelings."

He was telling me that if Tracy were harmed, he'd tell the cops everything he knew about Cabazon.

I gave him a steady look to let him know I understood. "If all goes as planned, she'll get better soon. But if anything changes, I'll be back." I was telling him I had a plan to help her, and that he shouldn't take action until we spoke again. I waited for him to let me know he'd understood.

He gave me a slow nod, then thanked me. "Please tell my little mother I love her."

I promised I would. We hung up, and I left the jail. I'd hoped Jorge would back my play, and he had—beautifully. If Tracy got killed, Jorge would start talking. I'd give Cabazon the message when he next got in touch. Given his state of impatience, I was sure that'd be soon. I'd go over the plan with Dale one more time, just to ensure we'd done all we could to make it succeed, but basically, we were ready. A part of me was even anxious for Cabazon to make contact. The sooner he did, the sooner we could get Tracy out and put this insanity behind us.

As I headed back to my car, my thoughts refocused on Davey and Alicia. Was that the secret Roan thought would rock her world? It was certainly possible. I wasn't sure I'd call it such a "gnarly" secret, but the knowledge that her good buddy Davey was her father's bastard son from an affair he'd had years ago definitely wouldn't be pleasant news.

But how could Roan have found out? It'd taken an incredible amount of digging for us to do it. And no matter how I'd ribbed Alex, he really was ten times the Internet detective Roan could ever have hoped to be. The only other way he could've found out was if Davey told him. But according to Graham and Heather, Davey didn't know Alicia was his half sister.

I called Alex from the car. "Can you find out where Davey is? We need to have a chat with him."

Alex said he'd known that was next. "According to his class schedule, he's got a lecture until two, and then he doesn't have another class until three o'clock. Since you're already downtown, why don't I meet you there?"

We picked an address that was closest to the lecture hall. I told him to text me if he was running late, then ended the call. I didn't want to talk to Davey without Alex. It's standard operating procedure to always have someone else present when you're interviewing a witness. Especially one who might decide to "forget" what he'd said. A lawyer can't testify in his or her own case, so I needed to be able to call someone to the stand who could testify to what the witness had said during the interview.

But this time, if Alex were running late, I wouldn't wait for him. I didn't know whether this lead had anything to do with Roan's murder, and I couldn't afford to diddle around. The cops might come up with probable cause to bust Graham any minute now. I needed to either find out why this secret about Alicia was important or cut the cord and move on. And I was tired of feeling like I was being lied to. I wanted some answers, and I wanted them now.

I got to USC with time to spare and realized I was hungry. I wasn't in the mood to sit in a restaurant, so I hit the drive-through at McDonald's and ordered a Coke and large fries. About as unhealthy as it gets, but for some reason, fries and a soft drink always seem to help a hangover stomach.

I drove to the appointed meeting place and enjoyed my junk-food lunch. Alex showed up at a quarter to two. Perfect timing. We hurried to Davey's lecture hall and got there just as it'd begun to let out. I searched for Davey as the stream of students flowed past us. He was one of the last to leave. I called out to him and waved. He waved back and headed over. Was that a wary look on his face? Or was I overly suspicious?

He stopped to sling his backpack over his shoulder. "Hey, what's up?"

I pointed to a quiet spot where there were a couple of concrete benches and a concrete square that served as a table. "Want to sit? We just need a few minutes."

When we all sat down, I got right to it. "I was wondering how you met Alicia."

Davey frowned at me. "Why does that matter?"

I forced a little smile. "Just humor me."

He didn't like the question—that much was obvious. He stared at me for another beat, then said, "I ran into her and the others in the cafeteria during the first week of classes."

I pictured the scene. "Yeah, Alicia was pretty hard to miss."

Davey was dismissive. "Whatever. We just all started talking and . . . I don't know. They were nice; they had a lot of questions about what classes to go for, what profs to watch out for, things like that."

That made sense, since Davey was a junior. It was time to play my hunch. I threw out my fastball. "Tell me, did you ever hook up with Alicia?"

His eyes flew open. "What? No! Never."

The shocked reaction made me 60 percent sure my hunch about him had been right. Of course, if it wasn't, my next question was really going to ring his bell. But I believe in shock value. I hit him with it right between the eyes. "Seems to me like she dated around a bit. Why not with you? Is it maybe because you knew she was your sister?"

Davey blinked rapidly as his mouth opened, then closed. He stuttered. "I—uh . . . well." Then he took a deep breath and swallowed hard. Finally, he said, "Yes."

I was right. He had known. I was glad he'd admitted it. "When—and how—did you find out?"

Davey's cheeks were bright red. "I figured it out a few weeks after I met her, when she mentioned her father's name: Graham. I remembered seeing the checks my mother got every month when I was a kid. The name on the top was G. S. Hutchins. I checked him out on the Internet and saw that he'd been at the law firm my mom used back then. I saw the dates and the timing was right, and then I found his photo . . ."

That seemed believable to me. "Did you tell Alicia?"

He played with a thread on his jeans. "No. I was going to, but I wasn't sure how she'd take it." He looked at me, his expression pained. "I mean, her dad cheated on her mom with my mom. It's not exactly cause for celebration. I didn't want to ruin anything for her."

Fair enough. "Did you tell Roan?"

Davey's expression was a mixture of alarm and anger. "Why would I tell a loser like him? No. I didn't tell Roan—or anyone."

I sat back and let Alex take over. But after a few minutes of *I don't know*s and *I can't remember*s, he gave up.

We let Davey get on with his day. After he left, I thought about what he'd said. "The only thing that bugs me is how he met Alicia and company."

Alex squinted in the sun. "Too easy?"

Was that it? "Yeah, maybe."

I wasn't sure how—or if—this new discovery about Davey related to Roan's death. And if Graham had told me about it right up front, I might've let it go. No one's perfect, and he'd taken good care of Heather for a number of years. As they say, no victim, no crime.

But he'd tried to hide it from me, and Davey's story just didn't sit right with me. And as I thought about it, there was a pretty simple way to check it out. "Do you know where Nomie is today?"

She was the one person who'd told me the truth from the start. It'd be refreshing to talk to someone without constantly wondering what she was holding back.

FORTY-NINE

Alex scrolled through his phone. "She's got a lecture. Should be out at three."

We had time, so we strolled over to her lecture hall. But when class let out, we found no sign of Nomie. I looked around, exasperated. "Who said she could cut?"

Alex spoke with sarcasm. "Kids today."

I shot him a dagger look. "I'm not joking. We don't have time for this."

He raised an eyebrow, still sarcastic. "You'd think she'd know that."

I ignored him. "Maybe she went to work?"

But when I called Lemonade, they said she didn't work on Fridays. I searched my phone for her number but didn't find it. "Do you have her cell phone number?"

Alex pulled out his phone and scrolled. "Yep. Shall I text her?"

I didn't have the patience. "No. Just call her. I want to figure this out right now."

He called but shook his head as he left a message and asked her to call us back. "Let's give her a few minutes. I can't think of any reason for her to drop off the radar."

I couldn't, either. But that didn't mean anything in a case that kept throwing me one curveball after another. We walked around the campus for a while, but after twenty minutes, I decided to give up. We'd just turned to head for our cars when Alex's phone rang.

It was Nomie. Alex told her we needed to ask a few questions. When he ended the call, he told me she'd cut class to work on a paper. "She's at the dorm. We can go see her now, but we've got to keep it short."

"Fine by me." The quicker we resolved this issue—which could turn out to be nothing—the better.

We headed to Nomie's dorm and found her buried in what looked like several marked-up drafts of a term paper that covered the space on the desk around her laptop and her bed. Nomie looked stressed and tired. I could relate. I'd pushed every paper to the very last minute when I was in school. I nodded toward the mess. "Due on Monday?"

Nomie glanced back at the computer. "I wish. It's due today."

No wonder she'd cut class. She started to clear some room on her bed for us to sit, but I shook my head. "No need. This will only take a minute. Do you remember how you all first met Davey?"

She gave me a puzzled look, then squinted at a point over my right shoulder for a moment. "I think at the cafeteria." She nodded to herself. "Yeah, Diana brought him over and introduced us."

That was a little different than what he'd said. "How did Diana meet him?"

Nomie blew out a breath. "Hmm. I believe she said he'd bumped into her in the library, kind of came on to her."

This sounded a *lot* different than what Davey'd said. "But Diana wasn't interested?"

Nomie shook her head. "She *was* interested. *He* wasn't." She gave a brief smile. "Kind of a first for Diana."

I'll bet it was. "Thanks, Nomie." I stood up and nodded toward her cluttered desk. "Okay, carry on."

She was surprised. "That's it?"

I smiled. "Told you it'd only take a minute."

We wished her luck and left her to it. When we got outside, Alex said, "Diana?"

I thought for a moment. "Do we know where she is right now?"

Alex took out his phone and scrolled. "I don't see any classes for her today, but I think she works at The Pink Palace on Fridays. I'd assume that whatever she's doing, she'll have to go home and get ready pretty soon."

I looked at my phone. It was four o'clock. We could just go over there and hope to get lucky, but I didn't want to waste the time if she was out. "I'll call her."

She was home. But so was the whole crew: Phil, Gayle, and Davey. I decided this was doable on the phone. "I want to ask you a question, but I need you to keep it on the down low. Can you do that?"

Her voice was wary. "Uh . . . sure. Give me a sec." I heard her footsteps. After a few seconds, she said, "Okay, I'm alone."

"Do you remember how you met Davey?"

She gave a short laugh. "Ha. Yeah." She spoke in a low voice. "In the library. He came on to me big-time, acted like he was totally into me. Asked me what I was doing for lunch. When I told him I was meeting some friends, he invited himself to join us."

This fleshed out Nomie's version of events. "Who was at lunch?"

"The whole crew: Nomie, Gayle, Phil, Alicia—and maybe a couple of others, but that's all I remember."

"Did you and Davey ever hook up?"

She paused for a moment. "That was the weird part. After he made that big play for me in the library, I was sure he'd ask me out. And I think I let him know I'd be up for it. But he never did."

I thanked Diana and ended the call, then told Alex what she'd said.

He shook his head. "That's not the way Davey described it at all."

And I strongly suspected there was a reason. "Sounds to me like Davey cozied up to Diana so he could meet Alicia."

Alex nodded. "In which case, I'd think he already knew she was his sister."

But that was problematic, too. "And if that's true, then he lied when he said he hadn't figured it out until after they'd met."

Alex looked skeptical. "But maybe not. Maybe he really was interested in Diana, but after he met the group and liked them, he decided hooking up with her might make things weird."

I didn't buy it. "What guy does that? Diana's hot, and she was down with it. You really think he'd pass on a chance to get with her just because it might jeopardize a friendship?"

Alex huffed. "We're not all sex-crazed apes. Yes, I do believe a guy might think friendship is more important. Especially when it comes to someone like Diana."

I knew what he meant. "Yeah, if he was looking for more than a hookup, Diana wouldn't be his ideal candidate." She didn't give off the vibe of someone who'd be into a long-term thing. I'd sensed a wall between her heart and the rest of the world. I could relate. For the most part, that was true of me, too.

Still, as we headed back to our cars, the inconsistencies—and coincidences—seemed to be mounting.

I'd reached Beulah and pulled out my keys when I thought of a way to start resolving them. "Can you find out when Alicia applied to USC?"

Alex stared at me for a moment, then slowly nodded. "Probably. Going back to the office?"

There was no reason not to. "Yeah. How long do you think it'll take?"

Alex looked pointedly at Beulah. "I could be done by the time you get there."

I glanced at my untrusty steed. "Come on, let's show him, Beulah."

Alex laughed as he got into his car. I jumped in and gunned the engine, but, of course, he peeled out first. On the way, I tried some fancy traffic-avoidance maneuvers, but when I pulled into the parking garage below the office, I saw that Alex had beaten me.

As I walked in, I found him already at his computer. I told Michy about our contest. "The truth. How long has he been here?"

Michy glanced up from her computer. "The truth. He's been here for at least ten minutes."

Alex called out, "More like fifteen."

Michy held up her hands. "What were you dreaming? A speed contest . . . with Beulah?" She sighed. "Anyway, did you write down your time at the jail?"

Damn. I had to lie to her again. "They had a lockdown. I didn't get to see him." I launched into a description of what we'd learned about Davey, so she wouldn't ask any more questions about my jail visit.

We chatted about the possibilities for a while, and then I went to my office and got to work on my other cases.

By six o'clock, I was running on fumes. I decided it was time to pull the plug. I'd just stood up to put on my coat when Alex came in, brimming with energy. "It's good to have a daddy who's well connected— though to be fair, Alicia didn't need the help. She had a 3.8 GPA."

I sat back down. "That figures. So who does Graham know at USC?"

Alex flipped open his iPad. "The dean of Communication and Journalism used to be a client, then became a golfing buddy." He looked up. "But here's where it gets good. Alicia put in for Early Decision at the end of her junior year, which is *way* before anyone else was allowed to do it."

I'd never heard of that before. "What's Early Decision?"

Alex explained. "It's a way of finding out whether you got into your school of choice early. But it means you're obligated to go to that school if you get accepted."

The implications began to set in. "How did you find out about it?"

Alex tapped a key on his iPad and showed it to me. "From Alicia's Facebook page."

I saw the entry on her page saying she'd been accepted to "the school of my dreams."

I'd thought there was no way Davey could've known Alicia would wind up at USC before he'd transferred there. But I was wrong. The picture that was starting to take shape looked very different than it had just forty-eight hours ago.

Davey and Alicia winding up at USC together was not a coincidence.

This was why I hated coincidences—because they usually weren't.

FIFTY

Of course, that answer only led to more questions. But it was late on a Friday night, and I was really looking forward to my plan for the weekend: to sleep in. I told Alex, "Come on, let's blow this Popsicle stand. We can talk on the way to the garage."

I gathered my briefcase and purse, then went out and told Michy to pack up. She held up a hand. "You don't have to tell me twice." As she shut down her computer, she said, "I heard what Alex told you. It sounds more and more like Davey deliberately targeted Alicia before they ever met. But I don't get why didn't he tell you he knew she was his sister from the beginning."

As Alex joined us I told her I'd been wondering about that myself. "Maybe he was hoping no one would find out. It is a pretty bad time for Graham's affair to go public."

Michy pulled her coat closed as a cold draft blew up through the elevator shaft. "True. But you always tell witnesses that everything's confidential. And even if he didn't trust that, the fact that he changed schools so he could meet her seems like an awful lot of effort to go to."

I didn't necessarily blame Davey for not trusting me to keep the story quiet. No matter how much I try to reassure everyone, some just don't buy it. But transferring schools to meet Alicia—that, I had to agree, was a bit much. We all pondered that as we rode down to the garage. I wasn't sure what to make of the fact that Davey had gone to such great lengths to meet Alicia. "I get that he might want to know more about her." I'd been happy to get to know my half sister, Lisa, when she'd offered to testify on Dale's behalf during his murder case. But that wasn't a fair comparison. Neither Lisa nor I had been the product of an extramarital affair, and Dale had told me about Lisa the day he first walked into my office—even before he revealed that he was my father, too. We exited the elevator and headed for our cars.

Alex zipped up his jacket. "I don't know. Maybe we're making too much of this. The guy doesn't have much family. No siblings, no father. Doesn't it kind of figure that he'd want to get to know his sister?"

"I guess." It was a decent point . . . I supposed. And I supposed I could also understand why—given the circumstances—he'd be afraid that if he told her, it would ruin their chance at a friendship.

As we all got into our cars and headed out, I reviewed the thoughts I hadn't shared. Privately, I'd had much darker suspicions about Davey. The effort he'd made to meet Alicia, and the fact that he'd lied about it had given me enough pause to wonder whether he'd killed Alicia—and/or whether he'd been the one stalking her. What made me stop short of actually buying those theories was the fact that Davey was the only one who *had* believed she was being stalked. Beyond that, I hadn't seen even a hint of evidence that Davey had any desire to harm Alicia. I'd spent a not-insignificant amount of time with him, and I hadn't seen a shred of rancor or resentment in Davey's attitude toward Alicia. To the contrary, he seemed to genuinely care for her.

Nevertheless, where there were two lies, there were bound to be four. As I stopped at the light at Sunset and Crescent Heights, I called Alex from the car and asked him to keep digging into Davey.

I was still thinking about that when I drove up the hill to my apartment and found a black Range Rover idling at the curb. My insides clenched like a white-knuckled fist. This was it.

I left my briefcase and purse in the car as I got out. No sense tempting them to compound their usual assault with a robbery. This time, when the goon squad began to approach, I held up a hand and hurried toward them. Anything to avoid those vicious iron grips. When I got to the car, one of them opened the rear passenger door, and I climbed in.

Cabazon was in the seat next to me. This time I didn't see a gun in his lap. I hoped that was a good sign. "I went to see Jorge today."

He nodded. "I trust my name did not come up."

I glanced at the front seat to see if either of the flying monkeys had a gun trained on me. Not that I could see. "No, it did not. And Jorge isn't talking. So far." Cabazon's eyes briefly widened at the implicit threat, then narrowed with menace. I tried to keep my voice from shaking. "What is your impression of Jorge's relationship with Tracy Gopeck?"

He frowned. "Relationship? Why would he have a relationship with a *puta*?"

As I'd suspected, he didn't know about Tracy and Jorge. "You need to know that she is not a whore. She's a victim." Cabazon looked at me like I was an all-day sucker. There was no point explaining the horrors of human trafficking to someone like him. "The man Jorge shot had been beating and abusing Tracy. Jorge rescued her. And Tracy loves him. More importantly for you, Jorge loves her. I've learned that the agents told him they'd dismiss the charges against him if he tells them what he knows about you." Cabazon's eyes lit up with fury. It was a truly terrifying sight. I had to force a calm poker face as I continued. "And he said that if Tracy is harmed, he'll start talking."

Cabazon gave a snort and turned to look out his window. Anger crackled like fire in the air around him. When he turned back to me, his gaze was steely, but his voice was low. "If she testifies and he is convicted, what will his sentence be?"

I didn't like that question, but he could easily find out on his own. "Probably fifteen to life."

His eyes narrowed to icy pinpoints. "I cannot trust that he will stay quiet if he is given a life sentence. I have too many enemies."

Everything now hinged on selling my next answer. "I believe I have a way to fix this problem. And it won't require that anyone get killed."

His eyes bored into mine. I took his silence as an invitation. And began to talk.

When we'd finished, I ran up the stairs to my apartment as fast as I could, feeling a tingling in the spot on my back where I imagined a bullet would hit. I was gulping for air by the time I got into my apartment and locked the door.

Cabazon hadn't agreed to my plan, but he hadn't disagreed, either. He'd only said he would "be in touch." If I never heard those words again, I'd die happy. I called Dale to give him the news, using language almost as cryptic as I'd used with Jorge.

Dale asked, "What's your take? You think he'll go for it?"

I really couldn't tell. "I wish I knew." I said I'd get in touch with him as soon as I heard anything and ended the call.

I spent all of Saturday catching up on chores. I'd planned to go clothes shopping with Michy on Sunday but decided I really couldn't afford it. We opted for dinner instead.

I was getting ready to go out and meet her when Alex called. A pleasant surprise. "Hey, what's up?"

I heard "Freddie Freeloader" by Miles Davis playing in the background. He must be at Paul's place. Alex didn't share my love of straight-up jazz. He said, "I just wanted to let you know that I did a little extracurricular work today and hacked Davey's phone."

All this phone hacking was making me a little uneasy. "Are you sure you can't get caught? I mean, I love it, and I'm glad, but . . ." Anyone can slip up.

There was a smile in his voice as he said, "I appreciate your concern—though you should know better. There's not a chance I'll get caught. I only jumped in to see what he had in the way of photos, e-mails, stuff like that."

Good. That was the kind of thing that might at least show whether Davey had been stalking Alicia. "And?"

He sniffed. "*Nada.* Clean as a whistle. At least as far as Alicia's concerned. He's got a prof in marketing who might want to avoid dark alleys, though."

"So maybe I'm just being way too suspicious. Hard to believe, I know. But there it is."

Alex laughed. "Maybe this one time. Anyway, just thought you'd want to know."

I thanked him and headed out to meet Michy at the Tower Bar—a classic Old Hollywood lounge and restaurant on Sunset that had great views and even better drinks. It was a splurge, but we decided we could afford it, since we'd saved all that money by not going shopping. Over icy vodka martinis, I told her that Alex hadn't found anything suspicious on Davey's phone.

She was less surprised than I'd been. "I think he was just intrigued by the fact that he had a sister. And then he found out she was really cool—and had nice friends." She shrugged. "He found a little family of his own. I can see it."

That was certainly one way of looking at it.

We talked and laughed till after midnight, then we both Ubered home. All in all, it'd been a pretty nice weekend, and by the time I got into bed, I'd decided to drop the Davey and Alicia issue. It was going nowhere. Michy was probably right.

But the next morning, I had a change of heart. When I got to work, I told Alex and Michy to come to my office.

After they'd settled in, I said, "I'd been wondering whether Davey might've killed Alicia. But that didn't fit. He really seemed to care for her. What might fit is the possibility that Davey killed Roan. He did seem pretty protective of Alicia. What do you think?"

Alex wrinkled his brow. "Seriously? Are we desperate enough to throw Graham's son under the bus?" He held up a hand. "Dumb question. Of course we are. Do you want me to tail him?"

The idea didn't thrill me, but I didn't know what else to do. "Yeah, for a day or so." I drummed my fingers on my desk. "Michy, you have any ideas?"

She gave a sidelong glance at the television. An ad for Pepto-Bismol was playing. A little smile played on her lips. "What was the name of that place where Alicia and Diana used to dance? The Pink Panther?"

I'd forgotten about that pole-dancing business. "No, I wish. It was called The Pink Palace." Michy made a face. "Right? Awful name."

But that was an angle we hadn't pursued. I turned to Alex. "Give it a day. If you don't come up with anything on Davey, that's where we'll dig next."

I had some ideas already.

FIFTY-ONE

Alex hit the road—he planned to catch Davey as he left for his first class—and I spent the rest of the day clearing the decks on my other cases. If Alex came up empty-handed, I'd have to start running on Graham's case full time. And then, of course, there was Tracy. Our plan was in Dale's hands now. But it wouldn't take long for him to pull his end of it together. For possibly the thousandth time, I wondered why everything had to happen at once.

I powered through lunch and into the evening. When Michy left at six thirty, I barely looked up to say good night.

Alex called at eight o'clock to say he was sitting outside Davey's apartment. "So far, so nothing. When do you want me to pull off?"

I'd had hope but no real expectation that we'd get lucky with this last-minute surveillance. Nevertheless, it was a bummer. "Give it until midnight if you can stand it."

Because I hate to ask him to do anything I wouldn't do, I stayed in the office until past midnight. I didn't hear from Alex until I'd gone home and gotten into bed at one thirty a.m. He texted to say he'd just pulled off. Davey hadn't done a thing but go to class and go home.

I texted him back to say we'd hit the ground running tomorrow—but not until ten a.m. I wrote, "Get some sleep."

Of course, he didn't listen. When I got into the office at nine a.m., I could hear him typing furiously on his computer. This time, as I knocked on his door, I didn't even bother to make a lame joke. "What the hell are you doing here?"

He called out, "Much better."

I opened the door. "Much better?"

He paused and looked up. "Than your usual effort at clever."

I glared at him. "At no time was I attempting to be clever. I aimed to torture. And clearly, I succeeded." I nodded at his computer. "What are you working on?"

Alex glanced back at his screen. "I was just collating our reports on Alicia's buddies to see if there was something that didn't fit."

"And?"

He scrolled for a moment. "Like Michy said, the pole-dancing stalker seems like a place to go. I think it's interesting that Phil was the only one who knew about it."

I'd been running down the same path. "And the long hair and mustache—and glasses—seem like an easy disguise. If it was a disguise, then the stalker must've known Alicia." Otherwise, he wouldn't need one.

Alex gave a half nod. "Maybe. But anyway, it's a working theory."

Phil was the only one of her circle we really hadn't zeroed in on. If he was the stalker, then he might've been upset enough by Alicia's murder to kill Roan. I couldn't say I really bought that theory. Nothing about Phil's behavior squared with his being the killer. Plus, although I knew better than most that it didn't take any particular "type" to commit murder, it was pretty hard to imagine that stoner doing something that . . . active. But even if the Phil angle was a dead end, it couldn't hurt to look into it. The cops could dig up something that'd give them probable cause to bust Graham any day now. If there was evidence that'd help us point the finger at anyone other than Graham, I needed to reel it in fast. So the more stones we kicked over—regardless of the theory—the better. "Let's hit Davey up, find out whether Phil ever mentioned anything to him about the strip club."

Alex shut down his computer and stood up. As he grabbed his coat, I noticed he had a little grin.

"What?" I asked.

He shook his head, still smiling. "I was just thinking how cool it would be if Davey said he'd seen a disguise like that in Phil's room."

I rolled my eyes. "You mean like in *Columbo*?"

Alex laughed. "Probably more like *Dick Tracy*."

I gave a short laugh. "Yeah, the good old days."

When crimes could be solved that easily. There wasn't a chance in hell that we'd get that lucky. But it didn't mean I wouldn't give it a shot. Because as they say: I'd rather be lucky than good.

As we headed out to Michy's desk, Alex said Davey didn't have class until noon today, and Phil was in class until three.

I slung my purse over my shoulder. "That should work out perfectly." I told Michy what we were up to. "I'm guessing we'll be back around five."

Michy gave me a mock salute. "See ya when I see ya."

We headed out on what was probably a fool's errand, but desperate times and all that. I decided to go straight to Davey's apartment and hope that the element of surprise would shake something loose.

We made pretty good time and got there by ten o'clock. When Davey answered the buzzer and heard it was me, he didn't sound thrilled—but he did agree to talk to us. He spoke into the intercom. "I've got to go see my TA in econ, so I don't have much time."

I told him that was okay, that we wouldn't take long. As we headed for the elevator, Alex said, "He didn't exactly sound thrilled to see us."

I pressed the button for the elevator. "Can you blame him?"

Alex shrugged as the elevator arrived. "Well . . . no, actually."

Lately, all we'd been doing was confronting him with lying and accusing him of holding out on us. We'd been right, but why should he look forward to more of that?

On the way up, we agreed to double-team him and trade off on the questioning. Keeping witnesses off-balance could make them give up more information than they'd intended.

Davey let us in, and I could see he'd been hard at work. Papers and books were strewn all over the living room, and he had dark circles under his eyes. We sat down on the small, worn couch, and he pulled the chair away from his desk to face us.

I apologized for the intrusion, then went straight to the point. "Have you been to The Pink Palace?"

He frowned. "That the place in Glendale?" I nodded. "I think I've heard of it, but no. Why?"

I watched him shift in his seat. "Did you know Alicia was dancing there?"

Davey looked rattled. "What? No. I don't believe you."

Was he really shocked? Or was it an act? I couldn't tell. "It's true. But we're interested in finding out what you know about a guy with glasses, a mustache, and long hair. He used to show up whenever Alicia was dancing, and he only seemed to go when she was there."

Alex joined in. "It seems like that was a disguise."

Davey stared off for a moment. "So she *did* have a stalker." He looked back at me. "Who do you think it is?"

I again wondered whether we were just watching a good act. "Most likely someone who knew her, someone who was afraid she'd recognize him."

Davey's expression froze. "Wh-what are you saying?"

Alex took over. "Phil knew she was dancing there. It might be him. And if it was, he was a lot more into Alicia than anyone knew."

Davey looked from Alex to me. "Then you think he might've killed Roan?"

I nodded. "Do you ever remember seeing a disguise like that—a wig, a mustache, glasses—in his apartment?"

Davey took a deep breath and rubbed his hands on his knees. "I really haven't been in his room much, but no, I haven't."

I watched him closely. "Do you think you might find a reason to go to his place and look around? Let us know if you see anything like that?"

Davey had a pained expression. "You mean spy on him?"

Pretty much. "No, no. I'm not asking you to eavesdrop or snoop around. Just . . . look around, be observant."

Alex added, "Davey, if it makes you uncomfortable, don't do it. We just need to get to the bottom of this."

Time to work in a little emotional manipulation. "And I honestly don't believe Graham killed Roan, so I have to do whatever I can to solve this case. He just lost his daughter." I looked him in the eye. "And he only just met his son. After all he's been through, it'd be a tragedy if he winds up getting arrested for a crime he didn't commit."

Davey looked away, but I could see his expression was sad. "Yeah, I do feel bad for the guy."

I remembered that I'd wanted to ask him about Graham's visit. Regardless of whether Phil was right about the timing being before Roan's death, I wanted to know what Graham had said. "This must be pretty hard on you, too. You find out you have a sister, only to lose her. But it must've been good to find your father, right?"

Davey clasped his hands together on his knees. "Graham never told me he was my father. We just talked about Alicia, what she was like, whether I thought Roan had killed her."

I kept my expression neutral as I recognized what seemed to be an inconsistency. The last time I'd questioned Davey about his conversation with Graham, he'd said he only spoke to Graham once, a few days ago, when Graham had called to ask him about the "gnarly" secret

Roan claimed to know about Alicia. But the conversation Davey had just described didn't seem to have anything to do with that secret. Was Davey just remembering more of the conversation they'd had about Roan's secret? Or had he slipped up and accidentally revealed an earlier conversation with Graham—one that'd taken place before Roan's death? Davey's answer had just raised so many questions. "But you knew he was your father by then. Why didn't you say something?"

Davey shrugged. "I thought since he didn't bring it up, he probably didn't want me to know. Which is pretty much what I'd figured, since he clearly didn't want me . . . period."

There was a world of hurt in those words. I wanted to tell him, *It wasn't that he didn't want you. He never knew you.* But that would only lead into territory about his being the product of an illicit affair—more pain. And I didn't know what his mother had told him about how he was conceived. Though I doubted she'd told him as hurtful a lie as mine had—unlike Celeste, Heather Jorgenson seemed to be a normal human—it seemed wiser not to go stomping blindly through this minefield. Besides, I had a much more immediate issue to broach. "When he asked whether you thought Roan had killed Alicia, what did you say?"

He shrugged. "That I didn't know who else would do it."

Now the timing of this conversation was critical to find out whether it'd taken place before or after Roan's death. "And you guys had that talk before Roan died, right?"

Davey looked confused for a moment. "N-no. It was after."

I again tried to figure out whether this was just a good act, or an honest answer. I wasn't sure. I decided to try and shake him up a little. "That's weird, I could've sworn you said it was before."

Alex took the cue. "Yeah. Phil said he saw Graham leaving your building before Roan died. Sounds like that conversation probably happened then."

Davey frowned and shook his head. "No. He's wrong. I never spoke to Graham before Roan died. It was after. I'm sure."

I studied him. He seemed sure now, but just seconds ago he'd wavered. What was true? Certainly there was nothing in it for me to push his version of the timing. If they'd had that conversation before Roan died, it'd look like the grief-stricken father was making sure that he was planning to kill the right guy. So I wanted to believe that they'd talked only after Roan died. I needed it to be true. The problem was, Davey had wavered, and Phil had been certain they'd spoken before then. I couldn't tell what was true.

As always in this case, I felt like there was a whole other story playing out just beneath the surface.

We chatted a few minutes longer, then Davey had to leave for his appointment. As Alex and I got into his car, I pointed out Davey's stutter step when I'd asked whether he'd spoken to Graham before Roan died. "What'd you think?"

Alex lifted his hands, palms up. "He might've just been momentarily confused about it."

I pulled on my seat belt. "Yeah, I can't tell whether that means anything. But something's just . . ."

Alex finished off the cup of coffee he'd brought from the office. "I know."

I sighed with frustration. "Let's go see Phil."

FIFTY-TWO

We had a couple of hours to kill before Phil finished his classes for the day, so we decided to go have lunch on campus at The Lab Gastropub. I hadn't had a chance to eat when I'd met Davey there last time, and I wanted to check it out.

We shared the spinach artichoke dip as an appetizer. I had the Baja fish tacos for a main course. Alex had the Lab burger. Nothing inspired, but it'd stay down.

At three o'clock, we headed to Phil's place. He'd just gotten home, so the smell of pot was a whisper instead of the usual scream. He remedied that by flopping down on his usual beanbag chair and whipping out a blunt the size of two cigars. As always—ever the good host—he offered us a hit. As always, we declined.

I decided I'd best jump right in, before he slipped into the purple haze. "Did you tell anyone about Diana or Alicia pole dancing?"

Phil blew out a stream of smoke so thick it looked like there might be a chimney in his stomach. "No, definitely not. Diana obviously didn't want anyone to know. It wasn't a fun, crazy thing for her."

I was taking shallow breaths. "Like it was for Alicia." He nodded. "But you didn't tell anyone about her, either."

He shook his head. "It was a dumb thing for her to do, and I had a feeling she'd regret it. I guess I just wanted to protect her from herself."

So many people seemed to have done that for her. Phil's gaze was getting droopier by the second. "Just one more thing. Are you sure you saw Graham leaving Davey's building before Roan died?"

Phil took a long toke and squinted at me as he held it in. Smoke drifted out in little tendrils as he spoke. "I think so, yeah." He popped his jaw to make doughnut holes as he blew out the rest. "But, you know, I guess I could be wrong."

Great. Perfect. Now we weren't just getting stalled, we were actually losing information. I stood up, and Alex joined me. "Okay, thanks, Phil."

We started for the door. Then I stopped. I had an idea. "I bet you guys throw a lot of parties here."

Phil grinned. "That we do."

I grinned back. "You ever party at Davey's place?"

He shook his head. "Sometimes, not often. But it's cool. He always contributes when he parties here. Brought some gnarly Kush last time."

I somehow never pictured Davey as a smoker. But I guessed bringing it didn't necessarily mean he was smoking it. "We've been bugging you guys to death. I think we owe you a break. How about if you all get together? The booze and food is on me."

Phil squinted at me through the haze. "That's super nice. You sure?"

I gave him a thumbs-up. "Absolutely. How's tomorrow night?" It was a Wednesday, but I had a feeling that wouldn't slow down anyone in this group.

Phil gave me a hazy grin. "Works for me. I'll get back to you on the others."

I told him to give me a call in the morning to confirm, and we left him to enjoy his high.

When we got back to the car, Alex turned to me, perplexed. "So we're throwing a party? How do we afford this?"

"We don't. Graham will foot the bill." As Alex headed for the freeway, I mentally replayed my plan. Foolproof it definitely wasn't, but I didn't have time for anything more elaborate. "Something's going on, but we keep running into brick walls. We need to take out the blasting caps. I don't get any kind of vibe that Phil's hiding something. You?"

Alex shook his head. "None. He feels pretty straightforward to me. Davey, on the other hand . . ."

"Exactly." I told Alex what my plan was. When I'd finished, I said, "Please feel free to improve on that. I know it's not my proudest piece of work."

Alex shook his head. "It really isn't. I'll kick it around between now and tomorrow, but as of this moment, I've got nothing. Anything else we can do right now?"

I was all out of moves. "Unfortunately, no. Home, James." As we headed back to the office, I tried to figure out how Roan might've learned that Alicia was Davey's sister. "We put it together, but it took a lot of work. How did Roan manage it?"

We were inching along in the rush-hour traffic, and it looked like we'd be stuck in it for a while. Alex sat back and steered with one hand. "I don't know. Something had to have tipped him off to make him start digging. But what that was . . ." Alex shrugged. "Because it's not as though Alicia and Davey look alike."

I'd detected a few subtle similarities in the shape of their eyes and the angle of their jawlines, but I'd never have noticed it if I hadn't known to look for a resemblance. "And Roan never met Graham." So he wouldn't have seen the resemblance between Davey and Graham.

Alex rolled his shoulders back and leaned against the headrest. "Right. So he must've stumbled onto something else that put him on the trail. After that, it probably wasn't that hard to figure out. It's always easier to find something when you know what you're looking for."

I considered what would happen when—and it was *when*, not *if*—the press found out about Graham's love child. The only question was how bad it would be. Because an affair, a child he paid for but never met—none of it would play well.

It was almost six o'clock by the time we rolled into the office, and I was ready to call it a night. I dropped my briefcase in my office. No sense bringing it home. I wasn't going to get any more work done tonight.

I told Michy to pack up, and as we all trooped out, Alex and I gave her the latest news and told her about the party we planned to throw for Phil and company.

Michy got into her car and rolled down the window. "I don't know why you think you have to do that. But you'd better make sure Graham will pay for it, because I barely covered our electricity bill this month."

I nodded and opened my car door. "He'll pay. And we'll do it on the cheap anyway."

Michy waved me off. "Whatever."

Alex and I got into our cars, and we all headed for our respective homes.

When I got back to my apartment, I dropped my keys on the kitchen table and flopped down on the couch. I went through my mail, read the news on my laptop, and answered some e-mails. At ten thirty, I poured myself a double shot of Patrón Silver and took it to bed. I was confused and aggravated. And depressed. I honestly didn't know whether Graham had killed Roan. But I did believe there was a lot more to this case than I'd been able to find out, and the unanswered questions were like a constant low-level buzz in the background that wouldn't go away.

When the alarm woke me at six thirty a.m. the next morning, it felt like the middle of the night. For a moment, I forgot why I'd decided to get up that early. Then I remembered that I had an appearance in the San Fernando court at eight thirty. It was just a continuance. The deputy

DA was trying to get her boss to let my guy plead to a second-degree burglary for a county lid. My guy, being the experienced inmate that he was, had said he could do a year, no problem.

That was it for my court appearances for the day, so after I was done, I swung by Twin Towers to check in on Jorge and make sure he was still alive and well. He seemed fine, though understandably nervous about Tracy. I tried to reassure him that she'd be okay, but I wasn't entirely certain that was true. And when I left, I had the feeling that between my own anxiety and the vague kind of code we had to use to maintain secrecy, my effort to reassure Jorge had largely been a bust.

Since I didn't have any meetings scheduled for the rest of the day, I decided to stop at home and change into jeans. I'd just thrown on jeans and a sweater and was about to head for the office when Michy texted me to say that Phil called, and she gave me his number. I tapped it into my phone and hoped the party was still on.

He said, "Hey, man. Midterms are happening. The only day everyone can do it is Friday. That okay?"

I told him it was. "How many am I buying for?"

He counted off the names of the group, then added, "And they'll probably bring people. You'd best buy enough for fifteen."

I calculated the cheapest and easiest food to deliver—I'd only be able to sell Graham on so much for this enterprise. "Tacos and pizzas okay?"

He said that was cool, then chuckled. "Hey, this'll be something different. I've never partied with a lawyer before."

I didn't have the heart to tell him I didn't intend to hang out with them.

Or that I *had* partied with a pothead before. But I guess that was less remarkable.

FIFTY-THREE

Since I didn't have to set up a party, my day was wide open. Having just seen Jorge, I thought it might be a good idea to go check in on Tracy as well. I was just about to call Dale and ask him to clear my visit with Liam and Noah when my phone rang. I looked at the number. It was Dale. "That is so weird. I was just about to—"

He interrupted me, his voice tense. "It's on for today."

My heart began to pound. He'd warned me that—for security purposes—he wouldn't be able to give me much lead time to get ready to launch our plan, but his call still made me feel like I'd slipped on an invisible patch of ice. "What time?"

"I'll be there with the note in one hour. You need to get to Tracy by noon and make sure you're all on the road by twelve thirty. I don't want to give them any more time than necessary to check out our story."

The story being that Tammy was in the urgent care clinic in Costa Mesa, the victim of a beating by someone she wouldn't name—yet. Tiffany—in the handwritten note Dale would deliver—begged Tracy to come to the clinic and persuade her younger sister to name the perpetrator and give a statement to the police. Tiffany was sure it was

Ronnie. But without Tracy's backing, her little sister Tammy would never tell the truth.

We'd decided to have Tiffany send a note instead of just call so Liam and Noah would have something they could verify. Since Tiffany really had written the note, they'd be able to verify that it was her hand-writing—because it'd match the first note she'd sent to Tracy—and if they decided to run the note for prints, they'd find the prints matched Tiffany, too. In addition, Tiffany was standing by in case they decided to call her and confirm the story on the phone.

The note would give the name of the urgent care clinic, and when the feds called, they'd find that Tammy had indeed been checked in for treatment of severe blunt-force trauma. But that, of course, wasn't true. The girl who'd really checked in was Dale's other daughter, Lisa, who was close to Tammy's age. Dale had hooked her up with a fake ID in Tammy's name and very real-looking bruises—courtesy of a fabulous makeup artist I'd represented on a DUI case a few years ago. So every-thing would check out.

We knew Liam and Noah would insist on driving Tracy, but they'd never make it to the clinic. It was in a sparsely populated area, and the road leading up to the clinic was long, winding, and usually deserted—which was why Dale had chosen it. Dale and two of Cabazon's men would wait for them on that road, cut them off, and "kidnap" Tracy—actually, take her to one of Cabazon's secure locations, where she could hide out until Jorge's case was dismissed. And that shouldn't take long. The feds had told Dale that although they'd been trying to come up with other evidence against Jorge, they hadn't found anything, or any-one, who could help them make the case without Tracy.

One of the many tricky parts to this whole setup was that Tracy didn't know about any of it. We couldn't risk her letting something slip that might tip off the agents.

It was a dangerous plan, to say the least. But with Dale there, it was much less likely anyone would get seriously hurt. As for Tracy's safety, we were counting on Cabazon's fear of what Jorge could tell the feds to keep him honest.

But I'd hoped to have a little more than an hour to at least get myself mentally prepared for all this. The whole scheme depended on my ability to sell the agents—and Tracy—on our story.

I swallowed hard and tried not to sound nervous. "Okay. See you when you get here."

I called Michy and told her I was stuck in the San Fernando court-house because I'd agreed to stand in for another lawyer. "After that, I'm going to meet Dale for lunch, so I might not be back until late after-noon." Michy said she'd let me take the rest of the day off. I thanked her and said I might just do that.

I hung up and spent the next hour and a half rehearsing my per-formance for Tracy and the agents.

Dale showed up at a quarter after eleven, carrying a manila enve-lope. He snapped on a pair of latex gloves, opened the envelope, and pulled out a business envelope that was addressed simply to "Tracy." He handed it to me. I held up my hands and pointed to his gloves, but he shook his head. "They'll expect to find your prints."

As I took the envelope, I looked at his taut features and thought again how risky this was for him—in every possible way. I had to make this go right. There was no room for mistakes. "Want something to drink? Water?"

He shook his head and looked around the room. "Where's your phone?"

I went and got the phone from the kitchen counter and handed it to him. "You made sure they're all at the house?"

Dale nodded. I could tell he was too keyed up to talk. He called Liam and Noah and said I'd told him I had a serious issue to discuss with Tracy. Twenty seconds later, he ended the call and handed the phone back to me. "You're cleared to go see her." I nodded as I took a deep breath and exhaled. Dale gave me a long look. "You can do this."

I nodded. "Yeah. Piece of cake." As he headed for the door, I felt a sudden stab of panic. This plan could wrong in so many ways—some of them lethal. I might never see him again. And if I didn't, it'd be my fault. After all, my plan had put his life in the hands of Cabazon's maniacal minions—*safe* was not their middle name. "Hey, be careful. Okay?"

He paused and turned back. "Thanks." He gave me a grim smile, then left.

I checked out the envelope. I'd hoped to read the letter from Tiffany, but it was sealed. Outside, I heard Dale's car back out of the driveway. I had to get moving. I'd noticed it was pretty cold when Dale left, so I grabbed my fleece-lined bomber jacket, then headed down to the carport.

My hands were shaking as I started the car. I told myself to calm the hell down. If I acted scared or overly nervous, it could ruin everything. I forced myself to take deep breaths as I drove. I made it to the house at noon on the dot. This time Noah answered the door. He gave me a curt nod and watched the street over my shoulder as I stepped inside. The moment I did, he closed and locked the door.

He patted me down—and not gently—then searched through my purse and pulled out the envelope with Tiffany's letter. "What's this about? And what's the status of the investigation on her brother?"

"Stepbrother." I pointed to the envelope. "And that's what the letter is all about." I told him the story about Tammy being admitted to the urgent care clinic in Costa Mesa.

He opened the envelope, removed the letter, and read it. When he'd finished, he said, "She wants Tracy to go see her in person?" I nodded. "We can't risk that. The trial starts in one week."

One week. And Tracy would be the first witness called. If this plan didn't work, we were doomed. There'd be no time to come up with a plan B. My heart thumped so hard and fast I almost couldn't speak. I forced a deep breath. "You can verify everything in that letter." I tried to keep the pleading note out of my voice as I said, "This is critical, Noah.

If Tracy doesn't go see her, Tammy will never talk—which means this asshole will get away with it *again*. And who knows what he'll do next time? 'Cause you know there will be a next time."

He set his jaw and tapped the envelope against the side of his leg as he frowned at a point over my left shoulder. After a few moments, he said, "Stay here."

Noah left the living room and headed down the hall. I guessed he'd gone to confer with Liam. That was good. Liam was less of a tight-ass. I wanted to pace, but I didn't want to look as anxious as I felt. As I waited, I could feel beads of sweat gathering inside my bra and springing out on my scalp. My hands were wet and clammy. I wiped them on my thighs.

I craned my neck to look down the hall, then glanced at my watch. It was twelve twenty-five. Noah was taking forever. Was something wrong? Had they figured out it was a bullshit story? I couldn't help it; I started to pace. At twelve forty-five, Noah finally came back. Liam was with him. I forced a calm—yet concerned—expression. "I assume everything checked out?"

Liam nodded. "So far. We're waiting for an answer on the print run. Are you sure this is legit?"

I nodded. "Very. And I'm hoping Tracy will be willing to go talk to her, because this might be our only chance to lock the asshole up. Can I see Tracy now?"

Though Liam seemed more sympathetic, he didn't look any happier about this than Noah. "Yes. Just make sure you tell her we've got to finish verifying all this information before we decide whether she can go."

I knew the prints would come back to Tiffany, so I wasn't worried on that score. And I was fairly sure that once they got confirmation on the prints, the feds would let Tracy go. My only worry at this point was that Tracy might not want to. If she refused, I'd have no choice but to fill her in on the plan and hope she could keep it together. "I'll tell her. Can you let me show her the letter?"

Liam shook his head. "Not yet. It's being scanned for prints. Just tell her you'll show it to her when we're done."

I'd been hoping to start off by having her read it, thinking it might soften her up a little. But I had to play the hand I was dealt. "Got it." I headed down the hall and knocked on her door.

Tracy seemed happy to see me, though she was very upset about the reason I was there. "They told me Tammy got beat up. I bet it's Ronnie. That fucker!"

"That's what Tiffany thinks, too. You'll see her letter when they get done with it. But she wants you to come to the clinic and talk to Tammy, tell her she's got to tell the police who did it. And that you'll back her up. Otherwise, she doesn't think Tammy will do it."

Tracy bit her bottom lip and frowned. "I want to help, but the cops won't believe me." Her tone was sad and bitter. "They never do. No one ever cares about what I say."

"I get it, Tracy." In fact, I understood better than she could possibly know. Our housekeeper had called 9-1-1 after seeing Sebastian grope me. A lone officer had responded, and though I'd told him it was true, when Sebastian clapped him on the back and said, "Kids have great imaginations," he'd laughed and agreed. And walked away. The housekeeper got fired.

So Tracy's feeling of hopelessness was very familiar to me. But things have changed—they're not perfect, but they are better. Kids are getting more credibility nowadays. I told her that the cops would have to take her seriously if both she and Tammy said Ronnie had abused them, and I pointed out how much it'd mean to Tammy to have her support. "It'll really help her to know that you've been through it, too, and that you'll back her up. She won't feel so alone—or like it's all up to her."

We talked a little longer, and for a minute, I was worried that Tracy wouldn't go. But she finally came around and said, "Well, even if it doesn't work, it'd be nice to see Tammy. Will Tiffany be there, too?"

A stab of guilt shot through me at the sight of her wistful look. But if I didn't get her out of here, she'd never see anyone—or anything—ever again. "I think so, yeah. Let me go see what those guys have decided."

She reached out and grabbed my hand. "Wait. Will you come with me?"

That wasn't part of the plan. But I had to do whatever it took to make sure the plan worked. And if my going along for the ride helped smooth the way, so be it. I smiled. "Of course."

I'd intended to tell her about my visits with Jorge but now I thought it probably wasn't a great idea. We couldn't risk her getting excited and letting a stray comment slip. The agents were already so hyper, the smallest misstep could kill the whole operation. In fact, I was afraid they might even be listening at the door.

I found Liam and Noah in the bedroom across the hall. The letter was laid flat on what looked like a scanner. I stopped at the doorway. "Tracy's willing to go—if you'll let her."

Noah gave me one of his flinty looks. "Everything checks out, so she can go." I felt relief spread through me. "But we're going with her."

As we'd predicted. "Fine. She wants me to come, too."

Noah wasn't happy about it, but Liam interceded. "No problem. You seem to have a rapport with her."

I looked at my watch. It was almost one o'clock. Dale had said they'd be at the interception point by two. "We should get going. If they release her before we get there, she'll wind up back at home, and then no one will be able to make her talk."

Liam said we could leave right away. "Go ahead and tell Tracy."

I fetched Tracy, and as we headed to the living room, Noah moved past us and inched the heavy drapes aside to look out the front window. He spoke with his back to us. "Liam's going to clear the area. Be ready to go when I tell you."

Liam went to the front door and turned to Noah, who held up a hand. When he dropped it, Liam walked outside. Over Noah's shoulder,

I saw Liam scan the street as he walked toward a green Ford Explorer that was parked at the curb. He opened the driver's door and examined the interior of the car, then came back to the sidewalk and nodded at Noah.

Noah waved us toward the door. "Go straight to the car and get in the backseat. And don't lag. I'll be right behind you."

We walked out at a brisk pace and headed to the Explorer. I saw that Liam had now opened the back passenger-side door closest to the curb and was watching the area around us as we approached.

We made it into the car without incident. For a moment, I was amused by the fact that I was the only one who knew we weren't in danger. Not yet, anyway. That thought was less amusing.

Noah got into the front passenger seat and told us to put on our seat belts and slide down low. Liam got into the driver's seat. He pulled away, and after a few minutes, I noticed he wasn't using the car's navigation. I wondered if that were a security precaution, whether someone could trace you when you used it. I made a mental note to ask Alex about that—assuming I made it out of this alive. I saw Tracy looking out the window hungrily. It was probably the first glimpse she'd had of the outside world since she'd been taken into custody.

We rode mostly in silence as Liam navigated from one freeway to the next. Ordinarily, it would've taken an hour and a half to two hours to reach Costa Mesa. But thanks to Liam's very "special" driving maneuvers—which had me stomping an imaginary brake the whole way—we got there in just over an hour. And I'd thought Dale's driving was bad.

Liam got off the freeway and headed toward the stretch of road where I knew we were going to be "hijacked." It was a lonely, deserted area, and Joshua trees and other cacti filled the open land on either side of the road. My palms were sweating, and my pulse was racing so fast I felt like I might stroke out. Everything depended on the next few minutes. It could all go swimmingly—or it could end in a bloody sea of dead bodies.

We'd just passed a billboard advertising a casino in Murrieta Hot Springs when two black Range Rovers—Cabazon must get a fleet rate on those things—suddenly appeared on either side of us. One roared ahead and pulled in front of the Explorer, while the other pulled to the left side of us.

Liam swore and tried to swing around to the right to pass the Rover in front of us, but there wasn't enough road, and there was no room to maneuver on the shoulder because of all the cacti. In the meantime, the Rover on our left swung into the side of the Explorer. The sickening screech of metal on metal blended with Tracy's screams as Liam pulled hard to the right. Tracy and I fell forward like crash test dummies as we landed in an unnavigable patch of cacti and lurched to a full stop. The Rover in front of us immediately turned to the right and cut us off. We were trapped.

Tracy was now crying and screaming incoherently. She reached out and clutched my arm, and I could feel her whole body shaking. I grabbed her hand. "It'll be okay. I promise."

But just as the words left my mouth, four men in black ski masks, armed with AK47s, jumped out of the Rovers and swarmed our car as they cursed at the agents and yelled for them to put up their hands in Spanish and broken English.

Liam had immediately reached for the gun in his shoulder holster on seeing them, but now he stopped and slowly held up his hands. Noah did the same. Two of the men yanked open the front doors, grabbed the agents, and threw them out of the car. I heard Liam grunt as he hit the ground. The other two men pulled us out, dragged us over to one of the Range Rovers, and shoved us into the backseat. Tracy was now so terrified she'd stopped crying—and breathing. Her face was white, and her eyes were wide.

The car was running, and the second we landed inside, it took off, wheels churning up a cloud of dust as it leaped onto the roadway and sped off. As I struggled to fasten Tracy's seat belt, I listened for the sound of gunshots behind us as we drove away. I didn't hear any. Cabazon had promised the agents wouldn't be harmed, and I knew he preferred it that way because dead agents would only mean a big headache for him. Still, you never knew what his Neanderthals might do. I could only hope they were sane enough to keep Cabazon's promise.

Our driver, who was doing at least a hundred miles an hour, also wore a black ski mask. I knew that was Dale. Behind us, in the cargo area, a man wearing a Richard Nixon mask was aiming a .45-caliber at our heads.

I'd finally managed to snap my seat belt into place when Tracy finally caught her breath and started to scream. "Please don't kill us! Oh please!"

The man behind us in the Nixon mask said, "Shut up! *Cállate!*" He put the barrel of the gun to her temple. Tracy gasped, then squeezed her eyes shut as she began to sob. I took her hand and whispered, "It's okay, Tracy. You're safe. Don't worry."

But I was finding it harder and harder to believe that myself as we hurtled down the winding road at what felt like a hundred miles an hour. A few seconds later, the driver suddenly stomped on the brakes, throwing Tracy and me against the front seat. A man in a black ski mask ran up to the car and jumped into the front passenger seat. Before his door could close, the driver hit the gas, and we roared ahead.

As he weaved his way around the few vehicles on the road, Tracy and I fell from one side to another. We were going so fast that when we hit a speed bump just before an intersection we actually caught air. My head banged into the roof as the car landed and I let out a yelp of pain. Dale was driving more maniacally than I'd ever seen—no doubt to impress the company—but damn. I wished he'd take it down a notch; this was getting too crazy. Especially because now we were moving into a more populated part of town. But instead of slowing down, he sped up, maneuvering through the traffic as though it were an obstacle course.

As we approached the red light at the next intersection, he suddenly yanked the steering wheel and made a hard right turn—and cut off an approaching car. The driver in the lane behind us was forced to make a sudden stop, and I heard the brakes squeal as he leaned on his horn long and hard. It sounded like he was just inches away. Tracy screamed again. I would've screamed, too, but my heart was beating too fast to catch my breath. This time, the guy in the passenger seat turned around and said, "Shut the fuck up!"

Dale, heedless, continued to weave through traffic doing at least eighty miles per hour. I'd been holding my breath so long my lungs felt like they would burst. I was terrified that we'd wind up wrapped around a light pole.

A few seconds later, I saw that the freeway on-ramp was just ahead. I was trying to figure out whether I was glad or even more terrified that we were about to get on the freeway, when Dale suddenly jerked the steering wheel to the left and turned onto a small side street with a cul-de-sac. He zoomed to the end of the cul-de-sac, then came to a screeching stop. What the hell was going on? I opened my mouth to ask, but before I could speak, the man in the front passenger seat jumped out, opened my door, unbuckled my seat belt, and yanked me out of the car. As I flew out I banged my head on the sidewalk and landed hard, like a sack of potatoes. The man hopped back into the car, and as the Rover sped off, I heard Tracy's screams over the sound of squealing tires.

I curled up on the curb and held my throbbing head. I felt like I was on a Tilt-a-Whirl, and the spinning wouldn't stop. I had to put my head between my knees and breathe. As I fought to unscramble my brain, I tried to figure out what had happened. Either Dale had been forced to modify the plan, or something had gone very, very wrong. After a few minutes, the throbbing and spinning subsided, and I managed to push myself up to a sitting position. I started to heave, but my stomach was empty. I coughed out a thin stream of bitter saliva. I wanted to call Dale and ask him what was going on, but he was in no position to have a chat right now. I sat there for a few moments, too dazed and nauseous to think.

It occurred to me that I needed to find a way home. I supposed I'd just have to call Uber. It'd cost a fortune. I'd just begun to imagine how pissed off Michy would be when I realized I couldn't call Uber. I didn't have my purse. It'd been left behind in the Explorer when Tracy and I had been "kidnapped."

Now what? I couldn't call Michy or Alex. There was no way I could explain what I was doing here. The only thing I could think to do was find someone who might let me borrow their cell phone so I could call a cab—and leave a message for Dale. I should probably see if I could find a grocery store or a mall or . . . something, but I was still feeling too disoriented and groggy from my crash landing to stand up—let alone walk.

I folded my arms on my knees and dropped my aching head. I was so exhausted I couldn't bear the thought of having to stand up and make my legs move. But I had to find a way home somehow. I'd just begun to ponder the possibility of hitchhiking when I heard the *click-click* of doggy toenails on the pavement and felt a shadow fall over me. I looked up to see a beagle whose leash was being held by a shaggy-haired teenage boy.

He stared at me with a mix of curiosity and concern. "Are you okay?"

I considered the question. "Basically. By any chance, would you happen to have a cell phone I could borrow for a second? I left mine at home, and I need to get a ride."

He studied me for a moment, then nodded. "Sure." He fished an iPhone out of his front pants pocket and handed it to me.

As I pressed in Dale's number, the beagle gave me a good sniffing, then began to lick my hand. I scratched between his ears and waited for the call to go to his voice mail, but it didn't.

"Hello?" Dale's voice sounded strained.

It took me a moment to get over the shock of hearing him answer. "Hey, it's me. I'm borrowing someone else's phone. Are you—"

His voice was panicked as he shouted, "I've been calling you for hours! Where are you? Where's Tracy?"

What the hell . . . ? "What do you mean? You just took off with her!"

"I didn't take off with anyone! They ditched me! We were supposed to meet at noon. They never showed up."

Oh my God. His answer knocked the wind out of me as I realized what it meant. I barely croaked out, "They screwed us. They totally screwed us."

FIFTY-FOUR

Dale told me he could pick me up; he was still in the area. I asked the boy for the name of the street I was on and gave Dale the address of the nearest house. He said he was on his way.

I handed the phone back to the boy. "Thanks." His dog was still licking my hand—which I now realized wasn't as cute as I'd thought. I'd scraped my hand when I'd been thrown from the car, and he was licking off the blood.

The boy pocketed the phone. "No problem. You've got a ride?" I nodded, feeling faint. He gave me a little wave. "Okay. See ya."

I gave him a feeble wave, and the boy and his dog ambled off. I dropped my head between my knees as another wave of nausea hit me. Dale showed up a few minutes later. He was driving his personal car, the white Lexus. I got in and slumped down in the seat, my arms wrapped around my middle. "Just FYI, I might heave."

Dale turned on the air-conditioning and rolled down the window as he pulled away from the curb. "Tell me what happened."

The blast of cold air felt good. "First tell me if Liam and Noah are okay."

He said they were a little banged up but otherwise fine. I let out a sigh of relief. At least one ton of guilt was off my plate. I told Dale the whole—but actually rather brief—story. When I'd finished I said, "So they've got her. Now what do we do?"

Dale drove up the on-ramp and merged onto the freeway. "Nothing. We can't reach Cabazon, and it wouldn't matter if we could. He's done with us."

Dale was right. Cabazon had gotten what he wanted. Tracy was out of the picture, and now the feds would have to dismiss the case against Jorge. The reality of Tracy's situation hit me like a frying pan to the face. "The only thing keeping Tracy alive now is fear that Jorge will talk."

Dale glanced at me, his expression grim. "But Jorge's going to get out of jail pretty quick. And once he does . . ."

Cabazon might very well decide to punish the nephew who'd dared to threaten him. And there was only one punishment that would ensure Jorge would never be able to threaten him again. "He'll kill Jorge. And that'll be the end of Tracy."

Dale swallowed. "Let's not go there right now. He might not. After all, Jorge is family."

But Cabazon was the kind of family who ate his young. Nothing came before his own need for self-preservation. Not even a beloved nephew. I leaned back against the seat as tears sprang to my eyes. After all our efforts to save her, the only thing we'd managed to do was serve her up to her killer on a silver platter. A wave of guilt and misery washed over me.

I closed my eyes to squeeze back the tears and turned to look out the window. All I could do now was hope that Cabazon had enough love for Jorge to let him—and Tracy—live. Or that Tracy somehow managed to escape. The latter seemed highly unlikely given what I'd seen of Cabazon's operation.

We said very little during the ride home. There wasn't much to say. I could see that Dale was feeling just as upset and guilty as I was. That only made me feel worse. "Don't beat yourself up over this. It's all my fault. I know that."

Dale glanced at me out of the corner of his eye. "I didn't have to go along with it. Besides, all things considered, it wasn't a bad plan. We had no choice but to collaborate with Cabazon, and that was going to be a dicey proposition no matter what we did. So I'll give you the same advice: don't beat yourself up. We did the best we could."

But it hadn't been good enough. And if Tracy didn't make it, I'd never forgive myself.

When Dale dropped me at home, I asked him if he'd mind getting my purse from the feds tonight. "I'm not in any shape to drive right now."

Dale said he would, and I got out and slowly made my way up the stairs, feeling a hundred years old. I fished my spare key out of the planter near my door and let myself in. I knew I should call Michy and make up some excuse why I hadn't come back to the office—and given the way I was feeling right now, why I'd probably stay home tomorrow, too. But first, I needed a long, hot shower, where I could cry with no one watching.

Half an hour later, dressed in a robe, my hair wrapped in a towel, and a double shot of Patrón Silver in my hand, I'd just picked up my phone to call Michy when there was a knock at the door. Fear exploded in my chest—then I remembered that Dale had said he'd drop off my purse. I went to the door and looked through the peephole. Sure enough, it was him. I opened the door.

Dale gave me my purse, and I held up my drink. "Want one?"

He shook his head. "No, thanks. I'll wait till I get home." He frowned at me. "You okay?"

No, I wasn't. But he had enough on his plate. "Better than nothing, I guess."

Dale nodded. "I'll check in with you *mañana*."

He left. I dropped my purse on the kitchen counter and called Michy. I told her I felt like I was coming down with the flu. She volunteered to bring me drugs and chicken soup, but I told her I just needed rest.

I was about to end the call, when she stopped me and said, "Hold on. What about that party you were going to throw for Phil and the gang? Do you still think you'll be up for it?"

I'd forgotten about that. "Yeah, I should be back in commission in time to party with those animals on Friday." I asked her to have enough pizza and beer for fifteen delivered to Phil's house. "Alex and I can pick up the tacos on the way."

She sighed. "Are you sure Graham will foot the bill for this? More to the point, why the hell are you doing it?"

I decided it'd be best to give her plausible deniability and not fill in the details of what Alex and I planned to do. "Just compensating them for being so cooperative." I added with a little laugh, "I know you're dying to come."

Her voice was heavy with sarcasm. "Sure. Cheap food and booze, clouds of pot, kids puking in the flower bed and screwing in the bathroom. Count me in."

I had those same fond memories of college. "I'll put you down for the pizza and pot."

When we ended the call, I crawled into bed. I couldn't stop hearing Tracy's screams, seeing her terrified face. Filled with anxiety but helpless to do anything about it, I lay in bed and imagined the worst until sheer exhaustion won out. By ten o'clock, I was fast asleep.

I spent most of Thursday alternately icing and heating my bruises—that fall from the Range Rover had done more damage than I'd thought—and worrying myself sick about Tracy.

I devoted every waking moment to surfing the news on television and the Internet for any mention of her, knowing that if there were any mention at all, it'd likely be bad.

As of Friday morning, I'd heard nothing. I chose to take that as a good sign.

Michy peered at me when I walked into the office. "How're you feeling?"

The trick to lying is to keep it simple. "I'm better. Just tired now. I think it was a twenty-four-hour bug."

She sighed. "What a drag. Needless to say, Mr. Hyper-Prepared over there"—she tilted her head toward Alex's office—"will have whatever drug, tincture, or other remedy you might need if you start to go downhill."

I smiled. "His OCD does come in handy sometimes."

Michy rolled her eyes. "Yes, we're fully covered in case of a zombie apocalypse. What time do you want to head over to Phil's?"

I hadn't thought to ask him. "I guess around six-ish. Maybe six thirty."

She tapped a key on her computer. "Then I'll have the booze and pizza delivered at seven."

I said that sounded great, then headed into my office. I had plenty to keep me busy: a motion to admit defense expert testimony and a trial brief on an upcoming murder case that I still hoped might settle.

Alex came in around lunchtime to firm up our plans for the evening, but other than that, I worked undisturbed the entire day—other than my constant surfing for news of Tracy. Still nothing.

The next time I looked up, the little patch of sky I could see through my window was dark, and Michy was standing in my doorway. She tapped her watch. "It's after six o'clock. You should probably get going."

Right. Phil's party was set to start at seven. "Thanks, Michy."

She sighed. "I still don't get why you think you have to do this, but I'll go get Alex."

I grabbed my coat and scarf and found Alex standing near Michy's desk. I told Michy, "You can bag it for the night." And as I said that, I realized I no longer had to worry about Cabazon's beasts showing up at the office. I supposed it was an upside to the Tracy debacle, but the knowledge only filled me with pain.

Michy picked up her coat and purse. "May as well. I've got to get home anyway."

We rode down to the parking garage together, and I asked Michy why she needed to get home.

"Because I'm meeting Brad for dinner. Just the two of us for a change, no mind-numbingly boring associates or partners."

"Sounds good—but not as good as picking up munchies for a bunch of stoner kids. I know you wish you could be me right now."

Michy got into her car. "Almost as much as I wish I could grow a third nipple."

Alex drove, and we decided to go to a Taco Bell that was close to USC so the food would still be hot when we got there. I stayed glued to my cell phone and searched for news of Tracy all the way to Phil's house. Still nothing. I tried—and failed—to stop seeing images of what might've happened to her.

We found a Taco Bell just six blocks away and bought a mountain of tacos, burritos, and enchiladas. As we headed into Phil's neighborhood, I could tell the party was already in full swing because I could hear Drake's "Hotline Bling" blasting from a block away. And when we walked in with our bags of food, we found a house full of very high—and very hungry—partiers. For some reason the pizza hadn't arrived yet, but the alcohol—and, of course, the weed—had. The partiers were all pretty blasted and very hungry. They cheered when they saw us walk in with the Taco Bell offerings.

I scanned the room and saw that the gang was all there. Perfect. I waved to Davey and Nomie, and Gayle came over to give us a hug. Diana and Phil helped clear a space on the coffee table for the food.

Phil thanked us. "This is really cool, guys." He gestured to the booze at the other end of the room. "Help yourself. Time to kick it."

I told him I was sorry, but we had to beg off. "We've got an emergency meeting with another client."

Alex said, "Rain check, okay?"

Phil nodded. "You got it."

Phil bro-hugged Alex and real-hugged me—a little longer than necessary—and we left.

Alex drove us to our next destination as fast as he dared. We didn't know how much time we had before Davey came home.

FIFTY-FIVE

Luckily, we'd made some friends in the building during our interviews, and Wendy—one of the girls we'd spoken to—buzzed us in.

We headed up to Davey's apartment. I'd had Alex check his schedule to make sure he'd be available to party tonight, and I knew midterms were over, so the odds that he'd be in the mood to cut loose were with us. We knew there was a risk that he'd pass on the party and decide to just stay home, and if he did, we'd have to regroup. But fortunately, Davey behaved true to type. I figured we had at least an hour.

Alex worked on the locks while I stood guard. Twice, he had to stop and pretend to be chatting me up as I leaned against the wall and smiled and flirted. But finally, we got inside and hurried to the bedroom.

Alex went straight to the desktop computer and got to work to try and hack into Davey's e-mail accounts and see what he could find on Davey's movements or information on his interactions with Roan or Alicia.

I looked around at the room. There was nothing particularly remarkable about it. Framed photos hung on the wall: Davey with his mother, Davey with his high school football teammates, Davey with older friends, presumably from Loyola and USC—and a poster for a concert featuring the latest U2 tour. I spotted a textbook from his marketing class on the nightstand and his black backpack that'd been left on the floor near his bed. I went over and searched it. Nothing. Just notebooks and an econ textbook. I looked under the bed. Nothing but dust bunnies. I looked in his dresser drawers. Nothing but clothes. My heart was sinking. My last hope was fading fast.

My eyes fell on the closet door. Something about it seemed odd, but I wasn't sure what. I walked over and looked at it more closely. The doorknob was . . . wrong. What was it? I stared at it for a second, and then it hit me. There was a keyhole in the doorknob. It had a lock. No closet I'd ever seen had a lock on it. Someone had installed it. Davey? Or some previous tenant?

I reached out and gave the doorknob a twist. It was open. I pushed the door back, expecting to find the usual tiny space, but I saw that it was long and deep. The light switch was inside the closet, on the wall to my left. I flipped it on.

The sight that came into view stopped me in my tracks. I stood transfixed and stared. It was a shrine. To Alicia. The clothing racks on the right and left side of the closet were empty. The walls were covered with her photos, and there were dozens of them. The ones closest to me seemed to have been taken surreptitiously. They showed her walking to class, getting into her car, heading home—her expression showed she was completely oblivious to the camera.

He'd been stalking her—judging by the sheer number of photos— for quite some time. I stepped inside, and saw that farther back, there were photos of Alicia pole dancing. And I recognized the background— it was The Pink Palace. We definitely had our stalker.

Then I noticed that the back wall of the closet—which at a glance seemed to have been painted black—was actually covered with a black velvet cloth. I walked to the back and saw that it was thumbtacked to the wall. I grabbed the top corner of the cloth and pulled. As it came loose, I realized that what I'd just seen was only the tip of the iceberg.

The entire back wall was covered with Alicia's nude photos—the selfies she'd sent to Roan—and they'd been blown up to poster size. How had he managed to get them? Then I remembered how easily Alex had hacked Graham's phone. And Davey's. He'd hacked Alicia's phone.

Revulsion spread through me. The other photos had shown a creepy obsession, but this crossed way over the line into a truly sick perversion. And in that moment, it all came together: Davey's lies about when he'd discovered Alicia was his sister, the way he'd tracked her on Facebook long before they'd met—and then transferred to USC when he'd read that's where she'd enrolled—the way he'd engineered their meeting at USC and ingratiated himself into her crowd. It creeped me out even more to remember that Graham—Alicia's *father*—had visited Davey in this very apartment, just feet away from this diorama of depravity. Had the knowledge of that given Davey a secret thrill?

I took a step back, repelled by what I'd seen, and noticed that the black velvet curtain had also covered a shelf made of a wood plank atop bricks on the floor below.

Neatly lined up on that shelf were a fringed scarf, a small silver bangle, and a pink Scünci—no doubt all stolen from Alicia. At the end of the shelf was a spiral notebook, the kind I used to have in high school.

Thinking it was probably another item he'd stolen from her, I bent over and flipped it open with my fingernail, careful not to get my prints on it. But the handwriting didn't look feminine. It was heavy, masculine. And when I read the title, I saw that this wasn't Alicia's notebook. It was Davey's.

The title read:

To Alicia, My Sister, My Lover, Forever.

I skimmed through random pages. Bile rose in my throat as I saw that page after page was filled with his sexual fantasies—lurid, graphic descriptions of what he planned to do to Alicia when they were "finally together." So graphic, my seesawing stomach forced me to stop reading.

I backed away from the notebook as though it might sprout tentacles, and hurried out to tell Alex what I'd found in that closet. "You've got to see—"

Alex interrupted me. "He did it. Davey posted the revenge porn."

I hurried over to him. "What? How do you know?"

He leaned back and pointed to the screen. "Alicia's selfies." He moved the cursor and clicked on a folder. "And here's the link to the porn website where he posted them." He moved the cursor again and clicked on the Facebook icon. "And here's the alias he used to become one of Alicia's 'friends.' He did it all—sent her photos to the porn website, to her Facebook page. It wasn't Roan. It was Davey."

I told Alex what I'd found in the closet. He looked confused. "What? I don't get it. If he was so in love with her, why did he revenge porn her?" He frowned up at me. "Do you think Davey killed Alicia?"

I was about to answer when I heard the heavy thud of footsteps approaching the bedroom. Alex pushed away from the desk and jumped up just as Davey threw back the door. I screamed as he charged toward us.

Alex stepped in front of me, and Davey ran straight into him. He grabbed Alex by the throat, and they both fell to the floor, with Alex pinned under Davey.

I looked around for something to hit him with, but the closest thing to a weapon I could find was a stapler. It looked too flimsy to do much, but it was all I had. I picked it up and raised my arm to smash it into his head, but at that moment, Alex managed to push him off to the side.

I dropped the stapler and started to grab Davey's arm to pull his hand off Alex's neck, but Davey twisted away and threw a leg over Alex's hips, immobilizing him. Alex's face was turning red as Davey continued to choke him. I leaped behind Davey and kicked him in the head. He howled but didn't let go. I stomped on his elbow. This time his grip loosened. Alex broke free and punched him in the face with fast, hard blows as he pushed up from the floor. I heard something crack, then saw blood flowing from Davey's nose.

Davey reached for Alex's throat again, but Alex flipped him on his stomach, lifted his head, and slammed it into the floor, once, twice, three times. Davey's eyes rolled back, and he went limp.

I heard sirens in the distance, and as I listened, I could tell they were getting closer. Someone had called the cops. Davey was groaning and starting to come to. I told Alex to flip him over so I could see him. Alex rolled him over but kept a foot poised over his head to stomp him if he tried anything.

I waited until I saw his eyes focus, then said, "You killed Roan. Admit it." He turned his head to the side and said nothing. I tried again, but he didn't answer. I grabbed him by the chin and made him look at me. "You killed him because you were in love with her. So why the hell did you post the revenge porn?"

The blood from his nose had congealed, and he was having a hard time breathing. His voice was muffled and nasal. "I didn't."

Alex—his neck still bright red from the attack—pointed to the computer. "It's all there, asshole, so get serious. Why'd you do it?"

That question seemed to get to him. Though he was bleeding and battered, he was agitated. He finally looked at us. "Roan was . . . no good. I . . . had to . . . make her break up."

Alex glared at him. "So you humiliate her? You sick fuck!" He drew back his leg to give Davey a swift kick to the gut, but I stopped him.

"Don't do it, Alex." By now, the sirens were right outside. I put a hand on his arm. "I'm right there with you, but we need to stand down and let the cops handle this."

Alex stood over Davey, still breathing hard. "You don't think he killed Alicia?"

I stared down at the bloody face of Alicia's brother—and stalker. "I'm not saying it's impossible. The cops should definitely check out that angle. But no, I don't." It's not that I didn't think he was capable of killing her. In fact, if he'd made his move on her and she'd turned him down, I could definitely have seen him doing it.

But there was no way that could've happened. Alicia had been killed just two days after her nude selfies had been posted. No way Davey would've moved in on her that fast. Not after having spent years stalking her. He was many things, but impatient wasn't one of them. The police siren abruptly shut off, and I heard car doors slam.

I called Graham. "Listen, I want you to be prepared. Davey's about to be arrested for killing Roan."

There was a long beat of silence. "Why? What happened?"

I decided not to tell him about the shrine I'd found in his closet or the proof that he'd posted the revenge porn. Graham was already on shaky emotional ground. One shock at a time. "There was . . . evidence in his apartment. I'll explain later. But you can stop worrying. I think you're off the hook." I paused. "I'm sorry it turned out to be Davey." Graham didn't really know him, but still. Davey was his son.

Graham's voice came out in a croak. "Are you sure?"

As sure as I could be. "I'd say so."

At that moment, there was a loud knock on the door. A male voice called out, "Police! Come out with your hands up!"

Graham said, "The police! They're arresting him right now?"

I said they were, then told Graham I'd be in touch with more information later and ended the call.

The police were young unis, one male and one female, and they crouched with their guns drawn as they entered and took in the scene. With our hands in the air, we told them who we were and what we'd found.

I told them it was Rusty Templeton's case. "I can call him for you."

Alex, his hands still in the air, said, "We're not armed."

The unis relaxed a little. The male officer told us to keep our hands in the air, and as the female officer kept her gun aimed at us, he patted us down. When he finished, he looked down at Davey, who was staring at them with wide, scared eyes. He turned Davey over and handcuffed him, then stood up and told me, "Okay, run that by me one more time."

I went through it all again and ended by repeating my offer to call Rusty Templeton. The female officer, who still had her gun drawn, said, "You've got his number?" I nodded. She lowered her weapon. "Go ahead."

I called Rusty and filled him in—adding that he might want to take a look at Davey for Alicia's murder as well, just to be on the safe side—then gave the phone to the female officer. She listened, nodded, said, "Will do," then handed the phone back to me.

Rusty told me he'd ordered her to arrest Davey and asked that Alex and I come in and give our statements.

I asked, "Right now?"

He spoke sarcastically. "No, take your time. Is next week good for you? Yeah, now. And you'd better hope this guy doesn't sue you for breaking and entering and who the hell knows what else."

I said, "We'll get there when we get there."

He said he'd expect us within thirty minutes or he'd send out a patrol unit and bring us in in handcuffs. Since we could easily get to PAB within thirty minutes—and I knew he'd only love to find an excuse to drag me into the station in handcuffs—I didn't argue.

Also because he'd hung up before I got the chance.

The unis called for backup to preserve Davey's apartment as a crime scene, and Alex and I took photos of the closet and the images on the computer monitor to show Rusty. I pointed out the notebook and advised the unis to have it bagged and tagged, then we left.

As we walked to the car, Alex said, "Is all that stuff we found going to be admissible in court? We didn't have a warrant or anything."

I gave him a little smile. "Only cops need warrants. We're not an arm of the state. We're private citizens. It's all totally admissible."

He was skeptical. "But we broke in. I mean, that's . . . invasion of privacy, isn't it?"

I nodded. "For sure. And Davey can sue us—if he can find a lawyer who'll take the case. But he can't keep the evidence out."

Alex was silent for a moment. "I've been thinking . . . I get that Davey was obsessed enough—and crazy enough—to go after Roan for killing Alicia. But don't you think Graham's motive was just as strong?"

"It's certainly similar." They both wanted to avenge Alicia's murder. "The thing is, Roan got killed just days after Alicia. For all anyone knew at that point, she might've been the victim of a home invasion. Granted, that was less likely. But a rational person probably wouldn't leap to a conclusion and then act on it that way."

Alex pursed his lips, then nodded. "Yeah, rational doesn't seem to be Davey's strong suit."

Of course, that didn't mean Graham couldn't have killed Roan. But playing out all the odds, and given what we knew, it seemed less likely to me. At the very least, even if they didn't find evidence to prove Davey had killed Roan, we had the mother of all red herrings. Good luck to the prosecutor who tried to convict the grieving father when there was a twisted, semi-incestuous stalker in the mix.

When we got to the PAB, I expected a uni to take us straight up to Rusty's floor. But we sat in the reception area for almost half an hour. And then it was Rusty himself who showed up. I walked over to him. "Just so you know, Davey admitted he'd posted the revenge porn, but he wouldn't admit that he killed Roan."

His expression was dark. "Yeah, well, there might be a good reason for that. Your client just turned himself in. Graham Hutchins confessed to Roan's murder."

What. The. Fuck.

FIFTY-SIX

I demanded to see Graham immediately. "Where is he?"

Rusty jerked a thumb toward the ceiling. "In the interrogation room."

I put my hands on my hips. "You need to stop questioning him. Now."

Rusty glowered at me. "We don't need to stop anything. He waived."

I glared back at him. "You have to tell him I'm here, and I want to see him. And believe me, if you don't, I'll get his statement thrown out."

He didn't like the sound of that. His chin jutted out. "The hell you will. It was a solid waiver."

I looked straight into his eyes. "Made by a man who's completely unhinged—and who's been denied the right to see his lawyer. You willing to take the chance?" To be perfectly honest, I was overplaying my hand. Rusty was right; my client had waived. The statement probably wouldn't get thrown out. But I knew he'd be afraid to take the chance. I held his gaze.

Rusty's eyes narrowed. I could see him calculating the risks. Finally, he made a curt gesture for us to follow him and headed for the elevators.

We rode up in silence. When we reached our floor, Rusty pointed Alex to the observation room and led me to the interrogation room.

I went over to Graham and sat down. His face was pale, his expression bruised and anxious. As I'd suspected, he was a complete mess.

Across the table sat a black detective I'd never met. Rusty introduced him as his new partner, Detective Shane Brown, then introduced me.

I said, "Nice to meet you. I need to talk to my client. Alone."

Detective Brown gave me a stubborn look. "Your client already decided against that."

Rusty's tone was sullen. "We'd better let her." He glowered at me. "You've got ten minutes."

Detective Brown gave me a cold look. He gave his chair an unnecessarily harsh shove as he pushed it back into the table, then followed Rusty out of the room. I waited for the red light on the camera to go off, then faced Graham. "What have you told them?"

His eyes were bouncing around the room so fast they were practically spinning. When he spoke, his voice was shaky. "I t-told them I did it. That I killed Roan."

I stared at him. "All this time you've been insisting you had nothing to do with it. And only now, when Davey's on the hook, you decide to confess? You and I both know that's bullshit, Graham." I waited for him to make eye contact. "Look, I get it; you want to take the fall for your son. The problem is, it won't work. I'm sure they swabbed you by now, right?" Graham nodded. "I'm sure by now they've swabbed Davey, too. They're going to run both your DNA samples against the crime-scene samples, and that'll prove he did it."

Graham's mouth opened, then closed. Finally, he said, "I—uh, maybe it won't."

He must still be reeling. "You need to think about what you're doing. Tell the cops you want to invoke for now. You can always change your mind. Just take a little time to clear your head before you decide to go to prison for a crime you didn't commit. We're talking the rest of your life, Graham. You owe it to yourself—and Sandy—to at least give this a little more thought."

He stared at me for a long moment, his expression numb. "No, I . . . I know what I'm doing, and I . . . I just want to . . ." His gaze drifted as his voice trailed off.

I couldn't let him do himself any further damage. He was barely coherent. Even if he really had killed Roan—which I'd always been willing to believe was possible—he needed to think about whether he wanted to make it this easy for the cops to nail him. "Just give it forty-eight hours, okay? That's all I ask. If you won't do it for yourself, do it for Sandy."

His shoulders drooped. Finally, he sighed and said, "Okay."

I glanced up at the cameras to make sure they were still off. "Graham, you need to come clean. If you're holding out on me, you need to stop it right now. What else haven't you told me?"

He didn't say a word; he just gazed at me with vacant eyes.

I was so frustrated I wanted to shake him. I was sure there was a lot more to this story than he was telling me—regardless of whether he'd killed Roan. I considered showing him the photos of what I'd found in Davey's apartment. That might persuade him to stop covering for that pervert. But it might also push him over the edge, and I couldn't predict what he'd do if he completely fell apart. I needed him to calm down and get his feet under him before I threw another emotional grenade.

I gave up for the moment and went out to the hallway where the detectives were waiting. I said, "He's invoking."

Rusty looked disgusted. "If you don't mind, we'll just go confirm that for ourselves."

I gestured to the door behind me. "Be my guest." I went back inside, and they followed.

When Rusty asked Graham if he really wanted to stop talking to them, he paused. I stared at him, thinking, *If you cave, I'll strangle you with my bare hands.*

But he swallowed, then said with an audibly dry mouth, "Yes, I'm invoking."

Rusty called for a uni to come and take Graham to a holding cell. We waited for the uni to arrive before we left the room. Once outside in the hallway, I told Rusty, "I'd like to talk to Davey."

He gave me an unpleasant smile. "Join the club. He invoked and lawyered up."

I didn't think he knew any criminal lawyers. Heather must've sent in some civil lawyer she kept on retainer. "Who'd he get?"

Detective Brown, answered. "Public defender." He looked at his phone. "Name of Frank Levy."

I knew Frank from my days in the public defender's office. He'd never been a star, but he wasn't a dump truck, either. I got his number from Shane, then moved on to a more immediate concern. "Where're you going to put Graham?" He was older, and he was a complete cherry. Not to mention fully capable of suing everyone involved if anything went wrong while he was in custody. They had to be careful with him.

Rusty and Shane exchanged a look. Rusty said, "We've been talking about asking Beverly Hills to put him up for the short term."

The Beverly Hills jail was probably the safest place Graham could be. They didn't get many hardened criminals in that part of town. "You have my number. Let me know where you take him."

I picked up Alex, who was still in the observation room, and we left. When we got into the car, he asked, "What's happening with Davey?"

I told him Davey had invoked. "I'm calling his lawyer now." As Alex steered out of the parking lot, I pressed Frank's number. I got his voice mail and left a message telling him to call me ASAP.

And he did. Five minutes later, my phone rang. He said, "I had a feeling you'd call."

He didn't sound particularly happy about that. "Then you heard that Graham tried to take the fall for your client?"

There was a long pause. "Actually, I hadn't. I only heard he'd gone in to the station."

"I'd guess Davey's going to find out pretty quick, so you'd best tell him soon." I had no doubt that news of Graham's confession would leak within hours. Gossip travels fast in jail, because what else do they have to do? So Davey would certainly know—probably by tomorrow morning—that Graham had given a statement implicating himself.

People charged with a crime like murder—especially first-timers—are scared and suspicious of everything. If they think their lawyer is holding out on them—or worse, that their lawyer isn't on top of the case—that can put a serious kink in the relationship.

Frank sounded annoyed. "I'll try and get down to the jail tomorrow." His voice was sarcastic. "So you called to give me your professional advice?"

I sighed. No good deed, as they say. "No. I'm calling to let you know that it's a crock of shit. Graham's just covering for him."

There was another long pause. "How do you know?"

I didn't, of course. But if Frank had information I didn't have, I wanted to hear it. "Are you trying to tell me something?"

I heard a click on his end. He had another call. "No. I *am* telling you something."

He ended the call.

When I told Alex what he'd said, Alex was alarmed. "Is he saying he's got proof that Graham killed Roan?"

That was one possibility. "Or he doesn't really know, and he's just messing with my head."

Alex was disbelieving. "Seriously? Why bother? Now that they've got everybody in custody, the DNA will sort it all out, won't it?"

I leaned back and closed my eyes, brain-tired. "You'd think." But I'd learned long ago never to underestimate how many lawyers love to play stupid mind games.

We lapsed into silence until Alex pulled into the garage. "Are you going to tell Graham what we found in Davey's apartment?"

I knew I'd have to eventually. This might not leak as fast as Graham's confession—the crime-scene techs would do their best to keep it under wraps—but it'd come out soon enough, no matter what they did. Cop shops all leak like sieves. "Yeah, I just haven't decided when."

Alex parked next to Beulah and cut off the engine. "I know she's only his half sister, but still . . . that scene in the closet, posting the revenge porn, it's so sick."

I'd been trying not to think about it. Seeing that notebook, the inside of that closet, was like looking directly into the abyss of a very twisted mind. I could feel the perverted, obsessive energy behind that shrine. It was part of the reason I was so sure Davey—not Graham—was the killer. "I keep wondering how he could be that bizarre with no hint of anything in his past. I hate to say this, Alex, but is it possible you missed something?"

Alex gave me a mock glare. "No." Then he shrugged. "Sure, it's possible. Juvenile records can be a little more difficult to dox. But remember, even though Alicia kind of suspected she was being stalked, she never caught him. So maybe he'd stalked other girls in the past and just never got caught."

That was possible. Davey was in control of his instrument. He was disturbed—but he wasn't psychotic. I supposed he could fly under the radar. "I didn't see any evidence that he'd been stalking other girls, but I guess the police could come up with a whole treasure trove hidden in a storage locker somewhere."

Alex sighed. "Not that it'd make his insane obsession with Alicia any less grotesque." He made a face. "The whole thing makes my skin crawl."

I had to agree. Given my own history and what I do for a living, I didn't shock easily—but this was at the far end of sicko. His own sister.

My God. "I'm going to need to put this out of my mind for now." I got out and talked to him through the window. "You should do the same."

But as I followed him out of the garage, the images in that closet came rushing back. When I got home, I stood under a hot shower for as long as I could stand it and scrubbed my body till my skin burned. Then I put on my fuzzy pajamas, opened my bottle of Patrón Silver, and scrubbed my brain.

I lay down on the couch in the living room, turned on the television, and found a rerun of *Breaking Bad*. It was one of my favorite shows, but all it did was make me worry about Tracy. I fell asleep with the television on and didn't wake up until the morning light came pouring through the sliding-glass doors. I saw the empty glass on the coffee table—an unfortunate reminder of what I'd been drinking to forget.

As I rubbed my eyes and sat up, I heard my landline ring. No one called me on that phone. In fact, I'd been thinking about getting rid of it. I listened for the mechanical voice that would identify the caller. It said, *"Pearson, Dale."*

Still bleary-eyed and more than a little hungover, I stumbled over to the kitchen counter and picked up. "What?"

His voice was harsh. "They found a body near the LA River. I just caught it on the news."

All the blood left my head, and the room started to spin. I leaned back against the wall and sank down to the floor. "Is it . . . ?" I couldn't bear to say her name. I hung my head between my knees.

"They don't know yet. It was burned beyond recognition. The news report said that the size of what few remains they have indicate the victim was probably a female. But right now, that's it. The only things left that're identifiable are the tires."

Microwave ovened. Team Cabazon style. My eyes filled with tears even as my brain reasoned that Tracy was far from their only enemy. "So there's no way to know?"

"They're reporting that they found some hairs close by that had to have been left there recently. They don't know yet whether the hairs belong to the victim."

I was sure Tracy had left a hairbrush behind at the safe house. "Are they going to try and see if they match Tracy?"

"Yes. I called Liam, and he said they're moving fast. We should know in a couple of days."

I lay my head on my knees. "If that's her . . ."

"Stop. Don't go there. We don't know anything yet."

We agreed to get together soon. We had a lot to catch up on. But right now, I was in no mood to talk—about anything.

The next few days would bring answers to everything—and in the meantime, I'd be eating my stomach lining for breakfast, lunch, and dinner.

FIFTY-SEVEN

To say it was one of the worst weekends of my life would be like saying waterboarding was uncomfortable. I put in a call to Liam's cell phone to find out if he had any news on the DNA testing of the hair found at the scene—but got his voice mail. I left him a message asking him to call back, but I didn't think he would. I'd been the one who'd pushed for the trip to Costa Mesa to supposedly see Tammy. I was definitely not on his Christmas-card list. That thought only led to a fresh wave of anxiety over whether Dale and I had covered our tracks well enough to keep them from finding out that the story about Tammy was bogus. I didn't know how I'd survive the guilt if, on top of Tracy's death, Dale got caught for having set up Tracy's kidnapping.

And then there was Graham—and *his* DNA tests. I was a mass of nerves when I went in to the office on Monday. There was at least a possibility that we might get some results back, and I knew they might not be the answers I wanted to hear.

Michy was anxious, too. "What if that public defender was right? What if the DNA does come back to Graham?"

The more I'd thought about Frank's remark, the more it'd pissed me off. "First of all, I don't think Frank knows diddly-squat. Second of all, if it does come back to Graham . . ." I'd been suffering over that possibility all weekend, and I could think of only one recourse. "I'll have to try and get him a deal for manslaughter."

But it'd be a tough sell. Even though he had an emotionally appealing reason for killing Roan, the evidence showed that the killer had tried to make it look like a suicide—not so emotionally appealing. And even if I managed to get him a manslaughter, I didn't see any judge giving Graham probation. He'd get at least three years—and the stress of even one year in prison could kill a guy like him. Even if he survived, his life would be ruined.

Michy saw my expression. "Okay, let's live on the bright side for now. It might be good news." She forced a tight smile. "I'm sure it'll be good news."

I appreciated her effort to lift our spirits. "Right."

I went into my office, dropped my briefcase on the floor, and went to my computer. I checked for e-mails from Rusty. *Nada.* I put my cell phone on my desk so I'd be sure to see if Liam called. Then I tried to get some work done. But that was pretty much impossible because I kept checking my e-mail, staring at my cell phone, and pacing.

Alex was downtown talking to the crime-scene techs. I'd asked him to get copies of the crime-scene photos from Davey's apartment and check for any evidence that the closet door lock had been picked or forced in the past. I'd had a hunch that Roan might have found Davey's shrine to Alicia. That thing truly would qualify as a "gnarly" secret—to say the least. And if Roan had found it, I thought it was very possible he'd have told not only Alicia but also Davey, just to torture him. It was the kind of thing I could totally see Roan doing.

And that would give Davey yet another motive to kill Roan, which was my goal right now: to put together the most compelling case against Davey that I could, then pray the cops didn't make an even more compelling case against Graham.

Alex got back to the office at four thirty. I'd been pacing, arms folded against my stomach, elbows gripped in my sweaty palms. Happy to have this exciting activity interrupted, I went out to see him. "I could really use some good news."

His smile was a welcome sight. "The tool mark guy thinks there is evidence of an earlier . . . disturbance, some scratch marks that may indicate the lock was forced in the past. It's not conclusive, and obviously he couldn't say who did it or when. But he said he would testify that the lock may have been forced."

"That's good. Puts another nail in Davey's coffin." But it was far from a slam dunk.

I rolled out the secretary chair and sat down next to Michy's desk. Since I wasn't getting any work done, I figured I may as well hang out with Alex and Michy. We talked about Davey, his sick obsession with Alicia, and what the DNA testing might reveal.

At a little before five, we found out. The report came to the office e-mail address—which Michy had been checking nonstop.

She read it out loud. "A mixture that includes the profiles of Roan Sutton and David Moser was identified in the sample taken from Roan Sutton's nightstand. DNA detected in the hairs found on Roan's shirt match the profile associated with David Moser."

Alex looked at me. "How good is that for us?"

I sighed. "It's nice, but it's not a game ender. They were friends . . . sort of. Davey could've visited Roan's place before the murder, and people shed hairs constantly. Plus, hairs can cling for a while. So the prints, the hairs, both could've been left at some point before the night of the murder."

Michy had continued to scan the report as we talked. She didn't look happy. My stomach knotted. "What else?"

She read from the screen. "A mixture that includes the profiles of Roan Sutton, David Moser, and Graham Hutchins was detected on the cord around Roan Sutton's neck."

I sat forward. "Wait. What?"

Alex stared at me. "They *both* did it?"

That just couldn't be true. "Did they give a result for the swab of Roan's neck?"

Michy nodded. She read from the monitor. "Foreign alleles consistent with the profiles of both David Moser and Graham Hutchins were found in the sample taken from the neck of Roan Sutton, but there was insufficient DNA to identify a complete profile."

Alex began to rub the back of his neck. "So they can't tell whether the foreign alleles came from either Davey or Graham, or both."

Exactly. "Because they're father and son. Half their DNA is the same." This was maddening. "Did they include the final coroner's report?"

Michy tapped a key on her computer, then nodded. She read from the screen. "It's the same as what we heard, 'blah, blah, blah,' inconclusive: 'although I have determined that the cause of death is asphyxiation, as to the manner of death, neither suicide nor homicide can be ruled out. The manner of death is therefore inconclusive.'" She looked up at me. "What does all this mean? That Davey and Graham *both* did . . . something?"

Good question. Though I wouldn't have thought it possible, this insane case had just gotten even crazier. I threw up my hands and spoke with frustration. "I guess." I went over to Michy's computer and read the coroner's report over her shoulder. The pathologist had found wounds on Roan's neck that indicated there was some—albeit very low—blood pressure at the time of the hanging. But even a very low level of blood pressure meant that Roan had still been alive when he was hung. That could mean he'd committed suicide. And I didn't see any reference to defensive wounds that would indicate there'd been a struggle.

But I saw that the pathologist had also noted, "A possible abrasion is found on the chin; such a wound is typical of manual strangulation." I knew from past cases that a victim's chin can get scraped when he lowers his chin to resist and protect his neck. But the pathologist found the wound to be "mild and superficial" and so hadn't been able to say for sure it was the result of strangulation. So it was also possible that Roan had been strangled—just not quite to death—and then hung in order to make it look like he'd committed suicide. This kind of wishy-washy autopsy report was good—but not great—for me. If I wanted to keep Graham out of the courtroom and the clutches of the twelve-headed monster, AKA the jury, I needed more.

Alex sat on the edge of Michy's desk. "But the neighbor only saw one person knocking on the door that night."

That's right. I'd forgotten about that. "Which means they didn't go to Roan's place together. One of them got there first. And he's got to be the one whose DNA is on Roan's neck."

Michy tilted her head. "AKA, the one who strangled Roan, right?"

I nodded. Though the coroner couldn't come to a conclusion on the basis of medical findings, that didn't mean a conclusion couldn't be drawn based on logic. And logically speaking, now that we knew whose DNA had been found on Roan, it seemed clear that one of them had tried to—and maybe succeeded in—strangling him.

If that DNA had come back to one of Roan's friends—say Diana, for example—I'd have argued that it wasn't necessarily proof that Roan had been strangled. They were intimate, so the presence of her DNA on his neck wouldn't mean there'd been any kind of violent contact. But since the DNA either came from Davey, who was unlikely to have had a friendly interaction with Roan after Alicia's death—or Graham, who was even less likely to have made friendly close contact—simple logic dictated that one of them must've at least tried to strangle Roan.

So the coroner might not be able to say it was a homicide, but a jury sure would. "Which means that neighbor might be our best hope for Graham."

Alex stood up. "I assume we're going to see her?"

"Yep. You have photos of Davey and Graham?" Alex nodded. I was sure the cops had already shown the neighbor their photos, but it didn't matter. I needed to find out for myself what she'd say.

It was five thirty. It'd take us at least an hour to get there. But the later the better. It upped the odds that we'd find her at home. I told Michy to take off whenever she wanted. "We won't be back tonight."

She gave me a mock salute. "Just do me a favor? Call me after you talk to the neighbor. I've got to know."

I said I would.

It wound up taking us more than an hour to get to Jody Sondheim's house. By the time I knocked on her door, it was almost seven o'clock. A white woman in her sixties, with short gray hair, dressed in jeans, a sweatshirt, and sneakers answered the door.

I confirmed that she was Jody Sondheim, then introduced myself and Alex and told her why we were there.

She looked from me to Alex. "A detective came by a little bit ago and showed me some photos."

Rusty probably showed her a six-pack. "Did you identify anyone?"

Jody shook her head. "I didn't see the man's face, and the detective only had head shots."

That figured. "I have full-length photos. Do you mind if I show them to you?"

"Not at all," she said.

Alex had cut and pasted so that Davey's and Graham's photos appeared side by side. The problem was, they didn't look that different. Davey was wider—both in the hips and in the shoulders—but they were about the same height. It'd be hard to tell the difference—but it wasn't impossible.

I mentally crossed my fingers and hoped for a miracle as Alex showed her the photos. She studied them carefully, then shook her head. "I'm sorry. I can't rule out either one of them."

I was deflated, but I had one more question. "After you saw the man knocking, did you see him go inside?"

She paused for a moment and bit her lower lip. "Not exactly. I was on my way into the house at the time. But he must've gone inside, because I'd forgotten to pick up the daily rag—they keep leaving it on my doorstep even though I've asked them to stop—and when I went back out to get it, I didn't see him anywhere."

Alex asked, "And he couldn't have left?"

She shook her head. "I'd have seen him. It was just two seconds. He didn't have time to get that far away."

I thought of something else. "Then Roan let him in right away?"

She glanced in the direction of his house. "Yes, he must have."

I asked, "Did you hear any loud noises or raised voices?"

Jody said, "No. But, like I told the police a while ago, I went to do the laundry after that, and the machines are at the back of the house."

We talked to her a little while longer, just to see if we could shake out a memory she didn't realize she had, but there was nothing more to get. I thanked her, and we headed for the car.

On the way back, I thought about what Jody had said. "If the guy she saw at the door had been Graham, there's no way he would've gotten in so fast—or maybe at all."

Alex paused for a second, then nodded. "That's right. Roan was the main suspect in Alicia's murder. If her father was knocking on his door, I can't imagine Roan would've been so quick to let him in. I know I wouldn't if I was him. I'd be pretty scared of what Graham might do to me."

I played it out in my head. "That's what I think. And even if he was inclined to let Graham in, he'd talk to Graham at the door for a bit and get a feel for whether he seemed likely to get violent. So the guy she saw knocking had to be Davey."

Alex paused for a homeless man who was jaywalking across Temple Street, bent almost double under the weight of an overstuffed, battered backpack. "I know you said Davey's prints and hairs didn't do that much for us, but what if Alicia's friends say that Davey never visited Roan? It didn't sound to me like he was a big Roan fan."

Certainly possible. "That'd help, but it wouldn't rule out the possibility that Davey got into it with Roan earlier that day but left Roan alive. Davey might even say he went over there to confront Roan and find out if he killed Alicia."

Alex frowned. "But what about that shrine? You think someone that obsessed with Alicia would just confront Roan and then walk away?"

I shrugged. "If I was Davey's lawyer, I'd argue that the shrine might show he had a sick mind, but it didn't necessarily show Davey had the mind of a killer."

The homeless man made it to the sidewalk, and Alex headed for the freeway. "You know, for a softy, semirich kid, he sure is holding up well under all this. I'd have expected him to crack by now."

I'd thought about that. "Me, too. But it's not like he just killed his best friend. I'd bet he feels like a hero. That asshole Roan killed Alicia. Davey avenged her murder. I'm thinking he feels justified, maybe even proud."

Alex turned right and headed up the on-ramp. "So bottom line, we're still stuck with the fact that Graham was involved—maybe very involved."

I sighed. "Right. We don't know when Graham showed up." If it was right after Davey, he could even have helped strangle Roan. I needed to get to the bottom of this. Unless I found a tiebreaker, Graham was going to go down for Roan's murder.

I knew what I had to do.

The Beverly Hills jail, where Graham was being kept, allows attorney visits 24-7. When Alex dropped me back at my car, I asked to borrow his iPad, then headed straight over there.

Graham had the luxury of a cell all to himself. At my request, they let me visit him there. He didn't look good. The first night in custody never goes well, and this was probably the only time Graham had ever been near a jail, let alone inside one. He sat slumped on his bunk. The skin around his eyes had grown so puffy his eyes had narrowed to slits, and they had a vacant, hundred-yard stare.

I told him about the DNA results, how they showed he was involved in Roan's death. Then, I asked him to tell me what had happened that night. He turned his face to the wall and said nothing.

Time to pull out the blasting caps. "You don't want to talk. Fine. Then you can just listen. As you know, Alex and I were in Davey's apartment the night he got arrested. But you don't know why we were there, so I'm going to tell you. It's because we searched his place. And I think you should see what we found there." I pulled out Alex's iPad and waited for Graham to turn back to me. When he did, I held it up and tapped the screen to show image after image of Davey's photos of Alicia, a few of the more lurid pages from his journal, the photos of Davey's computer screen showing Alicia's nude selfies, and the link to the revenge-porn site.

At the first sight of Alicia's photos, Graham's eyes stretched in their sockets, and by the time I hit the journal pages, he'd begun to growl—low at first, then with increasing fury. By the time I'd finished, he was screaming incoherently, his face a dangerous shade of red as he pulled at his hair.

The guard came running, but I went over and told him it was okay. "I just had to share some very bad news. He'll calm down in a minute."

The guard gave me a skeptical look, but a few seconds later, Graham stopped. He hunched over and rocked back and forth, his arms around his torso. He looked twenty years older. The guard gave him one last look and moved off.

I went over and sat down next to Graham. "You're sacrificing your life for someone who tortured Alicia. Imagine how awful it was for her to see those photos posted on that hideous website, and then on her Facebook page. All that suffering was because of Davey. It's time to stop, Graham. He doesn't deserve your sacrifice. Now tell me what happened."

He stared at the floor and said nothing for so long I was afraid I'd pushed him over the edge. But finally, in a hoarse, raw voice, he began to speak. "As you know, Heather told me about Davey being my son the day after Alicia was killed. I was . . . completely thrashed. I'd just lost my daughter, and then I learned that she'd been close to the son I'd never met." He stopped for a few moments, then continued. "I wanted to find out more about him, see where he lived, so I drove to his building. As I was pulling up, I saw him come out and get into his car. I don't know why, but I decided to follow him."

He paused again. I thought I knew where this was heading, so I prompted him. "He drove to Roan's house?"

"Yes," he said. "But I didn't know that at the time. What got my attention was the fact that he parked and then walked around the corner to the house. There was no reason for him to do that; there were spaces right in front. I thought that was odd, so I parked across the street from Roan's house and waited to see what he'd do."

I pictured the scene. "Did you see Roan answer the door?"

He nodded. "Davey went inside, and I got a really bad feeling about what was going on. So I went up to the door and listened." Graham stopped and stared at the floor again. He began to breathe faster. "I heard a loud thump, then another thump. I tried the door. It was open. I went inside and found Davey standing over Roan, his hands around his neck." He paused to catch his breath. "Davey's expression was . . . crazed. That's the only word for it."

This strange story was actually making sense. "Was Roan fighting back?"

Graham swallowed. "No. His eyes were open, but his whole body was limp. He was dead."

I knew the rest, but I prompted him anyway. "What happened next?"

"I walked in and closed the door and finally, Davey saw me. He dropped Roan, and for a second I thought he was going to attack me. He had this look in his eyes . . . but I held up my hands, told him I didn't mean him any harm, and that . . . that I'd help him." Graham paused for a moment, his frown puzzled. "I don't know why I did that. Or why he believed me."

I had a feeling I did. "Maybe because Davey already knew you were his father."

Graham looked at me, confused. "How? Did Heather tell him?"

I shook my head. "I'll explain later. Go on."

He took a moment to refocus. "I started searching Roan's place, trying to think of how I could make it look like an accident or . . . something. In Roan's bedroom I found an old rope that someone had used as a dog leash, and . . ." He held up his hands, then let them drop.

I homed in on the weak spot. "And you helped Davey string him up, because you thought Roan was already dead?"

Graham stared at me blankly. "Thought? Are you saying he wasn't?"

I had to tell him at some point, and even if I didn't, he might well hear it from someone else. "You remember the coroner had said the manner of death was inconclusive? That it could've been homicide or suicide?" Graham nodded slowly. "The official report just came out. It said that Roan might have been nearly, but not actually, dead when he was hung."

He sagged even farther. "You mean I really did kill him?"

I couldn't lie to him. "It's possible. I'll need to talk to the medical examiner who did the autopsy." But—bizarre as it was—I didn't doubt Graham's story. He was in no condition to lie—not that well. Graham's skin was gray; he was going downhill fast. I thought he looked like a candidate for a heart attack. I needed to get him out of here. "Has Sandy arranged to bail you out?" The desk sergeant had said his bail was set at five hundred thousand. That shouldn't be hard for them to make.

Graham seemed to be in a near stupor. I put a hand on his shoulder and asked again, "Is Sandy arranging for your bail?"

His lips mouthed her name. "Yes. I think so." He paused and squinted at the wall. His voice was faint. "Wait. I think . . . I think . . ." He trailed off for a moment, then continued. "Uh . . . I think she needs to talk to you."

I started to ask what she wanted to talk about, but he was lost in a world of pain. Assuming Sandy had told him, I doubted he'd be able to remember. "I'll give her a call. You take it easy. I'll check in on you tomorrow. Okay?" He stared at me for a moment, then nodded. I squeezed his shoulder and called out to the guard.

FIFTY-EIGHT

I called Sandy from the car. When she answered, I told her I'd just seen Graham. "The sooner he gets out, the better. Are you having trouble getting a bail bondsman? I can put you in touch with someone who'll have him home in two hours." Tomas was that good.

There was a hitch in her voice as she said, "Thank you, but I already have someone. He says he'll have Graham home tonight." Her voice wobbled. "I—I need to show you something."

Her tone was fraught but also urgent. "Tonight?"

She exhaled. "Yes. I—I just got it a couple of days ago, and I think you should see it."

I drove to Sandy's house. She did indeed have something important to show me.

I spent the drive home and most of the night thinking about what it meant—and what to do with it.

The next morning, as I was getting ready to leave for the office, Dale called. I held my breath as I picked up the phone. This had to be about

Tracy and the DNA results on the hair found near the burn victim. "Is it . . . her?" I knew better than to say the name Tracy.

Dale paused, then exhaled sharply. "Yes."

I sank down on the couch. "Oh God." I felt sick to my stomach.

"Sam, listen to me. We did all we could."

But I couldn't hear that right now. Tears slid down my face. "If I hadn't had that dumb idea to—"

He cut me off. "No, stop it. You can't blame yourself. Look, I have to get to work right now, but I can come over tonight if you want."

I didn't know what the day would hold or when I'd get home. I had a full day ahead on Graham's case. And I wasn't sure I'd want company. "Thanks, but not tonight. Maybe tomorrow or . . . this weekend."

Dale sighed. "Okay." He said he'd call me tonight anyway, just to check in. "Oh, and I don't know if you heard, but Davey Moser fired his public defender."

It took a moment for the remark to penetrate my haze of guilt and misery. "Is he hiring someone else?" I assumed it wouldn't be a public defender or court-appointed counsel. His mother had the money to afford private counsel.

"I'd assume so. But I haven't heard any names being thrown around."

I thanked him for the intel, and we ended the call with a promise to connect in person that weekend.

I headed downtown to the county morgue to talk to Dr. Sathyagananda, AKA Dr. Sat, the pathologist who'd conducted the autopsy on Roan. He was a good two inches shorter than me and at least two feet wider, with glasses as thick as the bottom of an old Coke bottle and a comb-over that consisted of about three long strands that stretched from one ear to the other.

His tiny office was packed to the ceiling with books, notepads, papers, and diagrams. I had to clear a pile of stuff off one of the two chairs to find a seat. When I got settled, I asked, "Is it possible that Roan could appear to have been dead by the time the rope was placed around his neck?"

Dr. Sat steepled his fingers above his chest. He had the singsong voice typical among East Indians. "Most certainly. Strangulation would cause unconsciousness within twenty to forty seconds. Death can occur in as little as two minutes."

"Then if someone had been strangled for, say, a minute to a minute and a half, he would appear to be dead?"

He shrugged. "Or he might even be dead. The amount of time it takes any particular individual to succumb can vary. But certainly he would be very close to death."

I consulted the report. "You say there was still a small amount of blood pressure when Roan was hung. Is that why you concluded he might've still been alive? And could that mean it was a suicide?"

Dr. Sat pushed up his glasses to rub his eyes. "Yes, could be. The toxicology report showed that he had a very high level of OxyContin in his blood. Not enough to be lethal but certainly enough to significantly lower his blood pressure. So even though the bleeding into the tissues showed low, perimortem-level blood pressure, that did not rule out a suicide. But it could also mean someone strangled him and then hung him."

I thought about how long Davey had been alone with Roan. "But if Roan was high on Oxy, it wouldn't have taken much to strangle him, right? Wouldn't he have passed out a lot faster?"

Dr. Sat shrugged. "Maybe. It would depend on his tolerance for the drug. I don't know how long he was a user, or how much he regularly used."

I needed more. "Were there any wounds that could only have been caused by strangulation? As opposed to hanging?"

He gave a grunt of irritation. "Arguably, yes. But I don't argue, because I am not a lawyer. I'm a doctor. If my findings do not justify a firm conclusion either way, I say it is inconclusive." He waved a hand at me. "I let you people fight it out in court."

It was time for the money question. "Would Roan have survived if he had not been hung?"

Dr. Sat frowned and pursed his lips. It made him look a lot like Yoda. "Very unlikely. He was very nearly dead—might even have just expired by the time he was hung."

Graham would be relieved to hear this. But it didn't solve the core problem: I had no corroboration for his claim that he hadn't been involved in strangling Roan. All I had was Graham's word for it.

I thanked Dr. Sat for his time and went back to my car. I drummed my fingers on the steering wheel as I thought about what Sandy had given me. I called Frank Levy. This time he answered—with a very uncordial, "Yeah?"

I really ought to block my name from the caller ID. "I hear you got fired. True or false?"

He sounded irritated. "True. And no, he doesn't have anyone else on deck yet. So if you want to bug the shit out of his next lawyer, you'll have to wait."

That was a little surprising. Defendants usually don't fire a lawyer until they've got a replacement. "But he plans to?"

A horn blasted in the background. Frank spoke sarcastically. "For some reason, he didn't see fit to share his plans with me."

He ended the call. I stared at the phone and sighed. "Dude, it's not my fault he dumped you."

But this was my opening. It might be my best—and only—chance to talk to Davey. I drove to the Twin Towers jail, showed my bar card, and said I needed an attorney visit with Davey Moser. He could definitely refuse to allow it, so I added, "Please tell him I've got something to show him. Something he'll want to see."

Half an hour later, I followed a jail deputy up to the attorney room and chose the first partitioned seat in the row. It took another fifteen minutes for them to bring Davey out. As I gazed at him through the glass, I saw that his eyes, underlined by dark circles, had a haunted look. He frowned at me as he sat down. A deputy led another inmate to a cubicle farther down the row, and as they passed behind him, he jerked around in his seat and watched until they were several feet away.

I picked up the phone, and he did the same. "How're you doing, Davey?"

He glowered at me. "What do you want to show me?"

I ignored the question. First, I needed to make sure this meeting was legal. "Have you hired another lawyer yet?"

He shook his head. "But my mom's looking for someone." His expression was grim. "So what is it? What do you want to show me?"

I was in the clear. I pulled the notebook Sandy had given me out of my briefcase. It was leather-bound and embossed with Alicia's name in gold lettering. Sandy had given it to her for her fifteenth birthday, after Alicia had said she was thinking of becoming a writer. She'd been writing in it ever since. I held it up so he could see it. "Do you recognize this?" I was careful to hold it by the edges, so I wouldn't smear any prints.

A sad look crossed his face. "Yeah, I remember seeing that in Alicia's backpack. She carried it with her everywhere."

I nodded and turned to the last page. Alicia had been one of those left-handers who took pains to make her writing legible. Hers was downright pretty. I held the notebook up to the glass. "This was her last entry. Can you read it?"

Davey didn't answer. He stared at the page as though he wanted to devour it; his expression burned with a palpable intensity. I watched his face as he read the words I remembered verbatim.

My body is . . . everywhere. For all the sick, twisted freaks in the world to see. I keep imagining their eyes on me, their ugly, sweaty hands on me . . . I can't stand it.

And the stink of that asshole's breath in my face. His filthy hands on my body . . . The horrible things he said to me. And more will come. This will never end. I'm so scared.

But worse, I'm ruined now. There's nothing left of me—at least, nothing I can stand to be.

You stole my life, Roan. You destroyed me. You killed me. And if I'm lucky, if this goes right, that's what everyone's going to think.

Mom, Dad, I'm so sorry. I know this will be bad for you. But the daughter you had is gone, and she'll never be back. I hope you understand. It's better for everyone this way. I love you forever and always.

Alicia

I watched as Davey's face drained to a pale white. Sweat broke out on his forehead. I saw his lips move as he read the final words. I spoke quietly. "So you see, Davey, *you* actually killed Alicia."

He stared at me, his face wooden. He was so still, he didn't even seem to be breathing. "Then Roan didn't kill . . . she . . . she . . ."

I nodded. "She committed suicide." I gave him a direct look. "Because of *you*."

No one ever suspected that Alicia might've been the one who committed suicide. Probably because there was no information to go on. The investigation into Alicia's death had been kept under wraps. Since it was widely believed to be obvious that Roan had killed her, and—unlike in Roan's case—no one was pushing for a different conclusion, the coroner's office had been able to delay the official report. I'd wondered about that delay, why it'd been taking so long. Now I knew.

Davey's face crumpled like a Prius in a head-on collision. He began to sob. "No! It's not true!" Not my Alicia!" He raised his eyes toward the ceiling. "You couldn't—you wouldn't do that to me!" He dropped the phone and grabbed his head with both hands; then he turned and started to bang his head against the wall. His voice was muted but distinct as it came through the glass. "I did it for you! I just wanted to save you from him! You were supposed to be mine!" He dissolved into tears.

The deputy came running. I tried to catch his eye as I waited for him to get close enough to hear, then shouted into the phone so Davey would hear it. "You killed Roan, didn't you? Because you thought he killed Alicia."

But Davey wasn't listening. The phone was still swinging from its cord as he leaned his head against the wall, eyes closed, and sobbed. "Alicia, it was all for you. I paid him back . . . for you!"

I looked at the deputy to see if he'd registered what Davey had said. He met my gaze, gave me a brief nod, and pointed to the name tag on his chest. Then he tapped Davey on the shoulder. "Come on. Visit's over."

Davey had been lost in his fantasy dialogue with Alicia. Now he slowly sat up and looked around, disoriented. After a moment, tears still rolling down his face, he stood up, his shoulders slumped, head bent. There was an expression of unbearable pain on his face as the deputy led him away.

The entire room had fallen quiet. And as everyone in the room watched them go, I could still feel the damp, cloying weight of unhinged misery in the air. I had to take a few moments to regroup before heading back to my car. I reflected on the profound irony of that journal. The last thing Alicia had done before she died was mail it to Sandy and Graham. But she'd accidentally transposed two numbers of the address. It was delivered to the neighbors down the block, who'd been out of town. When they got back three days ago, they'd delivered it to Sandy.

Had Alicia addressed the envelope correctly, it would've arrived days before Roan was killed. And Alicia's plan to get him convicted for her murder would've been thwarted. But because of that mistaken address, Alicia had won. In a bigger way than she'd ever hoped.

And Graham was safe. Between Davey's confession and the coroner's statement, Graham would be off the hook for murder. He'd get tagged for being an accessory after the fact, but given the circumstances, I was sure he wouldn't do any time. So I'd won. But as I headed back to my car, I found little joy in it. Alicia was still dead—a tragic suicide—and now Graham's and Sandy's world would be filled with even more darkness and pain. And Davey's conviction would change none of that.

And then there was Tracy . . . the thought of her tore at my heart.

My next stop was the PAB, to see Rusty and turn over Alicia's journal. And, of course, to needle him about the fact that, once again, I'd solved his case for him. I wasn't so sad that I couldn't take a little satisfaction in that.

He made me wait in the reception area for more than twenty minutes. I swear he does it on purpose. He couldn't always be that busy. When he walked out of the elevator, I stood where I was and made him come to me.

He put his hands on his hips. "Now what?"

I pulled the journal—enclosed in a padded envelope—out of my briefcase and gave it to him as I told him what it was and how I'd gotten it. "How come you didn't tell me the coroner was looking at Alicia as a suicide?"

He took the envelope. "Gee, I don't know. Maybe because I don't report to you?" I glared at him. Surprisingly, he relented. "Because they didn't want to piss off your client and start a shit storm until they were a hundred percent sure. I'm guessing they'll issue the report in a week or so." He held up the envelope. "This'll probably grease the wheels."

I served him up the coup de grâce and told him I'd gotten Davey's confession. "And I've got an independent witness." I gave him the name of the deputy. I folded my arms and waited.

He gave me a hooded glare, then huffed a barely audible, "Thanks."

I nodded. "Now go talk to Davey. I've softened him up enough so even you should be able to get a statement out of him. I'd rather not have to take the stand."

A defense lawyer who testifies for the prosecution doesn't inspire a lot of confidence in the criminal community.

EPILOGUE

The case wrapped up quickly after that. Rusty took my advice and went to see Davey that afternoon. He gave a full, official confession.

I was sure it hadn't taken much persuading. Davey had his issues. But he wasn't a psychopath. The discovery that Roan hadn't killed Alicia after all, that Davey himself had killed her with his insane machinations, had sapped him of all his strength. He had nothing left to live for.

On Thursday, as expected, the prosecutor agreed to let Graham plead guilty to being an accessory after the fact to Roan's murder in exchange for straight probation. We'd have to negotiate with the state bar to keep him from being suspended, but all things considered, I liked our chances. It was about as good a resolution as could be expected.

With the distraction of the criminal case out of the way, Graham and Sandy would have to deal with the tragedy of Alicia's loss and the knowledge of who and what Davey was. But at least they wouldn't have to do it with Graham behind bars.

I went back to the office after taking the plea. The mood was upbeat, though tempered with sadness. I'd stopped to get us a six-pack of Coronas and Doritos. A post-win tradition. I'd even remembered to buy the limes.

Now, we all toasted. I raised my bottle. "To justice." We all clinked.

Michy took a long pull. "Man, this was a weird case. A suicide that looked like a murder. A murder that looked like a suicide." She shook her head. "What did the coroner's report say about Alicia?"

They'd finally issued it. As Rusty suspected, the discovery of Alicia's journal had put it on a fast track. "Remember they found the knife in the tub, under her body?" Alex and Michy nodded. "So the first thing they noticed is that they were able to find her prints on the handle but only a partial of a foreign print. Not enough to even run through the database."

Alex took a fistful of Doritos. "But the killer could've worn gloves, and since the knife was hers . . ."

"Exactly." I squeezed the lime into my mouth and took a sip of beer. "And it made sense that the killer wouldn't want to reach into the water to get it because Alicia was bleeding all over the place. The last thing he'd want to do is leave her apartment dripping bloody water. But what they didn't find were any—"

"Defensive wounds, right?" Alex asked.

I nodded. "Nice." He'd been studying up. "That was actually the first thing that bothered them." Especially with a stabbing, the victim usually resists, which causes at least a few random cuts on the victim's hands or arms. "The second thing was that the shape and angle of the wound didn't match what they should've found if the cut had been inflicted by someone standing over her."

Michy looked pained. "I get that she wanted to frame Roan, but . . . it's such a horrible way to go." She gave an involuntary shiver. "I can't even imagine being able to do that."

I had to agree. "I think she had a full-on breakdown."

Alex wiped the chip dust off his hand with a napkin. "Just the fact that she expected her parents to keep it secret so Roan would go down for her murder shows you she was pretty far gone." He stared at the floor and shook his head. "It's all so horrible. That poor girl."

I could see the sadness in his eyes. I nodded. "Alicia's suicide was such an incredible tragedy. But Roan's death is looking a lot different now, too, isn't it?"

Michy's mouth turned down and she looked like she was holding back tears. "Yeah. He was a real dick, but he didn't post Alicia's selfies, and he didn't kill her. At least he's cleared now."

I was sure that'd be cold comfort to his friends and family, but I supposed it was something.

The following day, I called Dale and invited him over for dinner. I was feeling in a more celebratory mood. "My place. How's seven thirty? Can you get off work in time for that?"

He said he could. "How about if we order in? Or I can bring something in. Your choice, whatever you want, burgers, chicken, you name it."

My culinary skills being what they were, I didn't blame him. But I told him even I couldn't screw up steak and salad. "I won't put the steaks on until you're here. You can supervise."

He relented. "In that case, okay. I'll bring the wine."

I spent all of Friday pulling the rest of my caseload up to speed. The last few days I'd neglected everything but Graham's case.

I left the office a little early so I could clean up my apartment. I'd neglected that, too. Ordinarily, I'd leave it messy just to irritate Dale, but it was so bad even I couldn't stand it.

I decided to set up our dinner in the living room, where we could enjoy the view of the city. It was a clear night, and you could see the city lights below and the stars above against a velvety black sky, all the way from Century City to downtown.

I'd just finished putting the salad together when Dale arrived, a bottle of Ancien Pinot Noir—a mutual favorite—in hand. I asked if he wanted a cocktail before dinner. "I'm having a shot of Patrón Silver on the rocks."

He said he'd have the same. "Give me the corkscrew; I'll open the bottle, let it breathe."

When we settled in the living room with our drinks, I brought him up to speed on Graham's case, then told him I'd received an interesting e-mail. "Want to see it?"

He gave me a wary look. "I don't know. Do I?"

I pulled my laptop off the side table. "I think so." I opened the computer and found the e-mail. It had come from a library. There were no words, just a link. I turned it around so Dale could see, then clicked on the link.

It revealed a photo that gave a panoramic view of a beautiful coastline, white sand, a sparkling blue ocean, and lush green hills that stretched out into the distance under a warm orange sun. It was titled, "Los Suenos, Costa Rica."

As Dale took it in, a slow smile spread across his face. He looked at me. "Then that wasn't her body. They made it after all."

I nodded. Cabazon had promised me that if it all went down the way it should, he'd send Tracy and Jorge out of the country. I'd told Jorge—in code—about that promise during our last visit and asked him to send me a signal to let me know that Cabazon had made good on it. Jorge had replied, "I hear Los Suenos is beautiful this time of year." When I'd found the e-mail with the link in my inbox, I'd taken the first deep, guilt-free breath since the day she was kidnapped.

Dale sat back in his chair and exhaled. "Such great news." He frowned. "But did you know Cabazon was going to set up that body to fake her death?"

I shook my head. "Hell no. That's why I was so freaked out when they found it." I could only hope he'd picked someone who was already dead—or at least someone who'd deserved it. Given Cabazon's crowd, the probability of both was very high.

But I had to admit, the identification of that body as Tracy's had certainly sped things up. The FBI had been forced to throw in the towel on Jorge's case almost immediately. He'd been released just two days later. And now, he and Tracy were sunning in Los Suenos.

I held up my drink. "I guess all's well that ends well."

Dale held up his drink, and we clinked. "Sort of."

I nodded and took a long sip. We hadn't seen the last of Cabazon, and I knew that as long as he was alive, we never would. To me, the solution to our Cabazon problem was clear—if incredibly difficult to pull off. But I wasn't sure I could lay all my cards on the table with Dale. As far as I knew, his sole foray into homicide had been killing that hooker after she'd threatened the life of his other daughter, Lisa. But that'd actually been an accident—an impulsive reaction to a direct threat. An accidental killing in the heat of the moment was a far cry from the premeditated assassination of a crime lord. At least for now, I'd have to go solo.

I closed my laptop and put it back on the side table. "Look on the bright side. Cabazon's in a dangerous business. Someone's bound to get the jump on him sooner or later."

Dale didn't seem cheered. "I guess."

I stood. "Shall I throw the steaks on?"

"Sure." He looked up at me. "Just one more thing. I got another call from Tiffany."

I sat back down. "Oh?"

I knew it wasn't about Tracy's "kidnapping." Tiffany never knew about that, because the FBI had withheld her name from the press in the hope it'd discourage Cabazon from killing her and buy them time to find her. But now I'd be able to tell Tiffany that although she might never see her sister again, Tracy had finally gotten the chance to live happily ever after.

Dale peered at me. "Yeah. Remember she got pissed because I didn't get back to her about Tammy fast enough?"

"Yeah, right." When Dale had failed to move on Tammy's situation immediately, Tiffany had taken matters into her own hands and talked to Tammy herself. And, predictably, learned that Ronnie had indeed been molesting Tammy. Unfortunately, and also predictably, Tammy had refused to report it to the police—for all the usual reasons: no one would believe her; Shelly, her mother, wouldn't back her; her bastard of a stepfather would take it out on her. I knew where Dale was headed—and that it was going to be bad news for me. I tried to act like I was just bummed for Tammy—not worried for any personal reasons of my own. "So I guess there's nothing you can do. What a drag."

Dale polished off his drink. "It really is—or rather *was*. But Tiffany called me yesterday to thank me. I had no idea what she was talking about, so I asked her what she was thanking me for. Seems Ronnie has a prior conviction for child molesting. And he's on the sex-offender registry. Someone in the neighborhood called the cops and asked why he was being allowed to live in the same house with a girl who was a minor. Family Services made him pack up and move out that day. Tiffany thought I'd told the neighbor to call it in. I told her I'd love to take the credit, but I never knew he had a prior conviction—or that he was on the registry. Did you?"

I put on a confused expression. "No, I had no idea."

He gazed directly into my eyes. "Funny thing is, Ronnie swears he was never convicted. Says it's totally bogus. To tell you the truth, I thought it *was* kind of weird that no one had ever noticed it before."

I gave a nonchalant shrug. "People don't check those registries as much as they should. It's a good thing someone finally did." I stood up again. "How about I get those steaks going? I'm starving."

I headed for the kitchen. Really, it was all Dale's fault for telling me that story about how some dudes with no particular skills had made money by hacking into a police database.

I hadn't needed to tell Alex the whole story about Tracy. I'd only needed to tell him I had solid evidence that a young girl was being victimized and was afraid to tell the police. I suggested that Ronnie's prior conviction for molestation should be "found," and then entered on the sexual-offender registry. I was sure "someone" would notice it and bring it to the attention of the proper authorities.

Afterward, Alex had laughed at how easy it'd been to hack into the databases.

I knew that if Ronnie fought it, they'd eventually discover that the molestation conviction was bogus. But by then, I'd have had time to figure out a more permanent solution to Tammy's problem. And Alex knew how to cover his tracks. I wasn't the least bit worried that we'd get caught for inputting that fake conviction.

Dale, however, was another matter. He knew me, he knew Alex, and he could probably get a computer expert to track it all back to us. I purposely didn't look at Dale as I seasoned the steaks. But my hands were shaking.

Dale followed me into the kitchen. "Anyway . . ."

I turned to put the steaks into the broiler as I wondered how many years we could get for hacking the database and inputting that fake conviction.

I closed the oven door and faced him. This was it. I held my breath and tried to keep the apprehension out of my voice. "Yes?"

He set his empty glass down on the counter. "I just wanted to say that it's great the way karma works sometimes."

I exhaled and smiled. "It really is." I pointed to his glass. "Freshener?"

He handed it to me. "Love one." As I poured him another shot of tequila, Dale added, "Oh, and more good news. Turns out the rapist Uncle Pete lives in LA—and close by, in Echo Park."

He raised his glass, and as we clinked, my thoughts returned to Cabazon.

Maybe I wouldn't have to go solo after all.

ACKNOWLEDGMENTS

As always, my infinite gratitude goes to Catherine LePard. Without her support, I would never have had the courage to reach for the childhood dream of writing crime novels.

Thank you, Dan Conaway, agent extraordinaire, the best there is. I'm lucky to have you.

Charlotte Herscher, it's no exaggeration to say that you are by far the best editor in the world—and quite possibly the universe. It's a delight to work with you!

And I want to give a special shout-out to former Los Angeles Deputy District Attorney Melissa Cheslock and Dr. Stephany Powell, who are champions in the fight to save the young victims of human trafficking. Though Tracy Gopeck is fictional, her plight is tragically emblematic of too many girls whose life situations make them easy targets for exploitation. Thanks to programs like Journey Out—headed by Dr. Powell, and to the Los Angeles District Attorney's diversion program, which Melissa Cheslock helped run—as well as new legislation that punishes human trafficking more severely and prohibits minors from being prosecuted for prostitution, these young girls now have a better chance of escaping a hopeless life of imprisonment on the streets.

ABOUT THE AUTHOR

Photo © 2016 Coral von Zumwalt

California native Marcia Clark is the author of *Blood Defense* and *Moral Defense*, the first two books in the Samantha Brinkman series, as well as *Guilt by Association, Guilt by Degrees, Killer Ambition,* and *The Competition*, all entries in the Rachel Knight series. A practicing criminal lawyer since 1979, she joined the Los Angeles District Attorney's office in 1981, where she served as prosecutor for the trials of Robert Bardo— convicted of killing actress Rebecca Schaeffer—and, most notably, O. J. Simpson. The bestselling *Without a Doubt*, which she cowrote, chronicles her work on the Simpson trial. Clark has been a frequent commentator on a variety of shows and networks, including *Today, Good Morning America, The Oprah Winfrey Show*, CNN, and MSNBC, as well as a legal correspondent for *Entertainment Tonight*.